MAKING
ARRANGEMENTS

··

FERRIS ROBINSON

Peachtree Press

Lookout Mountain, Ga.

Peachtree Press
P.O. Box 366
Lookout Mountain, GA 30750
www.ferrisrobinson.com

Publisher's Note: This is a work of fiction. Names, characters, places, and incidents are a product of the author's imagination. Locales and public names are sometimes used for atmospheric purposes. Any resemblance to actual people, living or dead, or to businesses, companies, events, institutions, or locales is completely coincidental.

Making Arrangements/ Ferris Robinson -- 1st ed.
ISBN 978-0-9656481-1-0

For Dan

When everything goes to hell,
the people who stand beside you without flinching –
They are your family

–Jim Butcher

ONE

....

Lang leaned on the shovel and tried to slow her breath.

She should be packing for their celebratory trip for her one-year remission, not trying to divide a wayward clump of Lenten roses. Jack could easily dig up the stubborn plant when he got home. But he'd been doing her bidding all year, and she was tired of asking.

The spot right above her left temple itched, and she snatched the brim of her white floppy hat and flung it to the ground. There was no one nearby to see her scalp, but she looked around furtively anyway, just in case. The bristle of new growth on her head had eased into something besides bald-ness—not quite hair, but not prickly, either. She rubbed her palm over her scalp, feeling the knobs and hollows she'd never known existed when she had hair. Lang heard the mailman idle his engine and made out the boxy vehicle through the magno-lia branches. She shoved the hat back on her head.

Lang pictured the love letters she'd written Jack after the cancer had returned, stacked and tied with the pink grosgrain ribbon. Just when she'd made it to the five-year mark and was finally beginning to take full breaths of air again, not reading something into every single cramp and itch, it had come back. The doctors hadn't even given her twelve months.

Yet here she was, one full year later. Lang didn't want to tempt fate, but she couldn't help but feel smug knowing that the letters she'd written to ease him through that first year without her were tucked away, unopened.

She knew them all by heart, their occasions labeled neatly

on the envelope: *Christmas. Your birthday. My death.*

> *Dear Jack,*
>
> *I shouldn't feel glad at all after the news.*
>
> *But I do. I'm grateful for the warning. That it wasn't sudden. That I have a chance to prepare you.*
>
> *I hate to miss the next part, the one that was supposed to be so golden. Eggs Benedict late on a Tuesday morning. Napping after lunch like cats in the afternoon sun.*
>
> *No regrets, except I wish I'd eaten béarnaise sauce on everything. Condensed milk, too. Not worried about the size of my hips.*
>
> *I sit here, reeling from the doctor's words. Only four more seasons on earth, at best?*
>
> *You have that long as well, to get used to the idea.*
>
> *Love,*
>
> *Lang*

She'd debated the line about her hips in the first letter, the one she'd written after getting the bad news. But she left it in, almost defiantly. He worried enough about her hips for both of them.

A scarlet cardinal skimmed across the yard and perched on the feeder, dapper and energetic. She scanned the garden for his mate and found the drab-feathered female scuttling in the dry, brown magnolia leaves, searching for food. *Lang and Jack Eldridge if they were birds.* The long, curled leaves rattled sporadically, and Lang looked at the thick, twisted trunk of the tree, its lower branches spread out and covering the ground like a skirt.

Lang placed the shiny tip of the shovel against the thick

creamy stalks of the Lenten rose and lifted up the dense foliage with her tennis shoe. Two mourning doves startled her when they suddenly flew out from under the magnolia branches, beating their wings frantically to hoist their heavy bodies into the air.

She waited for her breath to slow, then put all her weight on the shovel, balancing carefully as the earth gave way and the metal easily slid in the damp November ground. She hadn't smelled the earth in over a year. She closed her eyes and breathed in the rich, damp scent of dirt.

She held on to the shovel for support and tried to remember if she'd washed her nightgown as she gazed up at the house. Her great-grandfather had built it before the Civil War, and it had housed both Confederate and Union troops during various points of the war. He had rebuilt it after it had burned in a drunken brawl during the Union occupation, and although it was over 150 years old, Fancy, her grandmother, had always called it "the new house," so she did as well.

She had promised Jack she would be packed by the time he came home from tennis—he would kill her if she still had laundry to do. She tried to deepen her breath as she squinted at the siding—chipping already. Two years ago, Jack had hired Teddy, their son, to paint it the same pale butter color her great-grandmother had chosen.

Teddy-to-the-Rescue was the name of that business the two of them had started—one of many. Jack had assured her that they were fine, that none of the businesses required much capital, and that they needed the tax write-offs. Not one of the businesses had panned out, especially Teddy's Tennis Tots, which had basically been a practice net set up in the driveway. She'd told them it made her think of "tater tots," and they had both laughed and rolled their eyes. "Of course, she would think of food," they had said in unison.

They had been sued over that one—apparently Teddy stole the idea from another tennis pro. She was glad Jack managed their finances—keeping up with all the paperwork seemed overwhelming to her.

She carefully angled the shovel straight down so she wouldn't shear the roots, and then rested her foot on the blade, leaning onto it heavily for a minute. She should have clipped greenery instead of digging. This was too much.

Lang pulled the shovel up from the ground and felt a snag in her belly, like the long seam holding her together might split. She lifted her shirt to see if the barely knitted edges of skin had ripped apart.

She shouldn't have. Her belly looked like some bloated sea creature, pale and damaged, and she looked around again to make sure no one had seen.

She staggered over to the primitive wooden bench Jack had built for her garden, leaving the shovel stabbed in the ground.

TWO

....

L ang was mortified to suddenly see Hank Campbell's face looming over her, so close he probably could smell her breath.

She'd fallen asleep again. Had she been drooling? Was her mouth agape like some ancient person's in a coma? Oh my god, where was her hat?

She turned her head and checked the corners of her mouth for sludge, then ran her fingers over her fledgling hairs before asking Jack's tennis partner if everything was okay. He looked pale, shaken even, and she offered him a glass of iced tea. He declined. Then accepted. She walked slowly up the steps to the house, aware of the swish of her thighs. Bottom heavy, Lang looked like a thin person until she stood up and her rear end loomed out of proportion to her torso. Her shoulders were narrow, giving her a frail appearance, and there was no meat on her chest. She wished she'd made Hank go in front of her, or even better, stayed seated.

"Was there lightning?" she asked as she stirred the sediment in the pitcher of tea. "I told him not to play today. Storm warnings are everywhere, but not a drop of rain. Crazy weather." She turned around to face him, catching her breath for a moment as she leaned against the rail. "He forgot his shoes?" Jack rode his bike to the courts, routinely sending Hank by to collect things he'd forgotten: PowerAde, cell phone, racket.

"Lang, something's happened. They took Jack in an ambulance. I came to get you," Hank said, blurting out the words.

"Is it his knee again? Was he wearing his brace? I reminded

him!" she said. "You think he'd remember to wear it after the last time it dislocated." She stuck a gel pack in the freezer and told Hank it should be cold by the time they got back. Remains of carrots, apples, and celery lay in nameless heaps in the sink, and she was embarrassed Hank saw them.

But when she got in Hank's car, she noticed a petrified orange in the drink holder of Hank's car, puckered and browning. She wanted to hold it, feel its weightlessness, as they careened down the interstate, weaving recklessly through traffic.

Hank threw the car in park squarely in front of a sign that said "Ambulance Parking Only."

"I don't think you can park here," she said.

Already out of the car, he led her by the elbow through the heavy glass doors. She looked back at his blinking hazard lights, a steady pulse of warning.

She heard the doctor say the words *massive* and *artery* and *aneurysm.* None of them made sense.

"I think we're parked illegally," she told the doctor when he told her Jack was dead. "We should probably move the car."

Her husband the bodybuilder ran six miles a day and didn't eat anything that had ever breathed air.

Lang wasn't even supposed to be alive, starting last week.

"Give me the keys," she said to Hank, holding out her hand. She looked down at the dark rinds of dirt under her nails, then quickly hid her fingertips in her fists.

"Is he okay? Is Jack okay?" a woman said behind her. She turned to see A. J. Cole stylishly dressed in a tiny brown-and-pale-blue knit tennis dress and a matching jacket. An actual diamond tennis bracelet flashed on her wrist, and her knuckles were stacked with jewels. On top of everything else, she now had to deal with the grammar butcher of Barrington.

"I was on the next court. There weren't no courts open at the club. So," A. J. said, choosing this time to explain why she was playing tennis on the public courts.

"They say he's dead," Lang said as if it were a rumor.

"Oh no, honey, I'm so sorry," A. J. said quietly.

The doctor interrupted them, asking Lang to come back in the room with Jack.

"Just let me move the car," she said.

"Here, hon. Let me. Gimme the keys. I'll move it and come right back. Be glad to," A. J. said.

Hank wrapped his fist around the car keys and said he would move it and that A. J. should stay with her.

Why would it be better for Lang to be with a woman she barely knew and disliked for the most part at the most terrible moment of her life? She watched Hank, pale and shaky, back away from them as he spoke.

"Do you need a minute?" A. J. asked her.

"A minute?" Lang asked, as though all she needed was a few seconds to touch up her lipstick and powder her nose and she would be ready to see the lifeless body of the man she'd loved for nearly forty-two years.

A. J. opened her purse, brown with pale blue stitching, and handed Lang a piece of peppermint gum. "Here, pop that in your mouth," she said, and snapped the purse shut.

Lang knew her breath must be atrocious.

The man on the table was not Jack.

The five o'clock stubble on that pale, waxy face was not her husband's.

Lang turned away from his body and pictured Jack scraping his empty ice-cream bowl with the large soupspoon, over and over in a deliberate circle, hoping for one last taste, his whiskers dark against his rosy face.

Lang imagined Hank was relieved that A. J. drove her home from the hospital. She stared at the glowing red orb above each intersection as A. J. began inane sentences without finishing them. Her words were slow and twangy. Lang wondered how she had found her way into Barrington; most of the residents were three generations deep.

"They say things happen for a reason, if that could be any constellation . . ."

Lang thought about telling her the word she wanted was *consolation*. But there was no consolation for Lang in that correction. She wondered if Hank's car had been towed or if she'd been rude to him.

"Do you want me to call Teddy? Is he here? In town, I mean?" A. J. asked. "I will."

She put two syllables in her last word. *Weeee-uuul.*

Lang imagined Teddy's reaction if A. J. called to tell him his father was dead. He would surely think it was a prank call. *Day-uuuud.*

"What? What's funny?" A. J. asked, narrowing her eyes at Lang.

"Nothing. I was just thinking of something," Lang said, thinking how funny Jack would have thought her story about Teddy's reaction to A. J. was.

THREE

....

J arred out of what must have been sleep, Lang lay still on her side of the bed, listening for the sound of him. She waited for the slow, soft whoosh of his breath, his sudden intake of air. There was a thickness in the room, like a covering of unexpected snow.

She willed the stillness to be the residue of another unspeakable dream, like so many she'd had before: Katie D. drowning in a shallow swimming pool, her face smiling up at her, three inches under the shimmering blue water. Jack clinging to her shoulders as they plummeted through the sky to their certain deaths. Lang herself having sex against the sacristy wall with the new priest, reassuring him she did this with all the clergy.

After every one of these terrible dreams, Lang would lie stunned, her breath unable to keep up with her clattering heart. She would ease out of bed and feel her way to the bathroom in the dark to change out of her sweat-soaked nightgown. She would fumble for the edge of the antique pie safe to get her bearing and then feel for the round spools on the fourposter bed and finally the nubby coverlet across the foot, careful not to wake Jack. Her husband would be asleep next to her, and her world still intact. Overcome with relief and gratitude that her granddaughter was safe, she would ease silently back into bed, away from the dampness on her sheet and listen to the irregular rasp of her husband's breath.

Now, she stared at the panes of glass on the window as the pale band of morning eased up into the gray sky.

She reached her hand over to Jack's still-made side of the

bed and spread her fingers over the brown-and-cream toile pillow sham sitting formally over his memory foam pillow.

Lang finally got up, pulled the bedspread up over her side of the bed and walked into her kitchen. A. J. sat at her kitchen table, drinking coffee out of the old mug that was covered in thin lines and curves that, upon inspection, were actually cows engaging in different variations of coitus. Teddy had given them to her when he was in college, however briefly, and they'd turned out to be extremely durable. She wondered if A. J. was aware of the unorthodox bovine positions in her hands.

"I stayed over," A. J. said. "You don't need to be alone for now. You want sweetener in your coffee? What all?"

"Black, I guess," Lang said, suddenly as unsure of that as she was of everything else. The planet seemed unfamiliar.

"Listen, I finally got Teddy, and he's on the way. Or I got Sarah actually. I just called her at the tennis center. Are they married? Sorry. Not neither here nor there," A. J. said, waving her hand as if dismissing the idea. "Anyways, I'll stay until he gets here."

If she had been able to articulate, Lang would have told her to go home. But she couldn't arrange the words to both thank A. J. and release her from her self-imposed duty.

"Th-th-th," Lang stuttered. She stopped speaking, unwilling to focus on forming the word.

"Should I put the phone back on?" A. J. asked. Her expression had changed from pity to curiosity.

Unresponsive, Lang sat down at the table. It had been so long since she had stuttered she'd almost forgotten the exercises. She pressed her tongue hard against the roof of her mouth but didn't try to speak.

She wondered if Sarah and Teddy were ever going to get married. The so-called engagement was going on six years now, and she gathered it was more off than on. She never knew why Sarah had changed her mind about the marriage in the first place or why Teddy hadn't put his foot down and insisted upon it.

"You want you a English muffin?" A. J. asked.

Lang took one off the plate and looked at the round, spongy bread. "They've been sitting out all morning. Prob-leee reeaaall crunchy. Here, let me toast a fresh one."

"I know everything I need to do. I wrote it all down for Jack last winter," Lang began slowly, relieved the words flowed unhindered from her mouth. "Back when the doctors said I had a year at best. We were both prepared for death. Just not his. God, he wasn't ready at all. He didn't even have a minute to collect himself." Lang put the muffin back and walked to the kitchen sink. She felt the old pine boards give slightly as A. J. eased over beside her.

"Is there anything special you need me to do?" A. J. asked. "Can I call anyone? Emmeline Harrison? Or anyone else from the board? I know they'd want to know. I think we'll need more coffee, and I'm putting the phone back on the hook. I'll get it," A. J. said quickly, looking at Lang.

"Y-y-y-you don't need to," Lang said as the phone rang.

"Oh, Emmeline, yes. I know, it's terrible," A. J. said into the receiver. She mouthed the words "It's her" and arched her eyebrows.

"Very sudden. Oh, that would be so lovely," A. J. said, obviously pandering to the president of the Barrington Women's Club. She raised her index finger to indicate she'd be with Lang in a minute and turned her back to her. "Of course, anything would be appreciated, but please don't trouble yourself. You are so kind to think of her. No, Cole. *C-o-l-e*. Wife of Dr. Cole over on Summertown Road. On the brow side. Yes, of course. I will."

A. J.'s tone of voice had changed completely and *will* had

only one crisp syllable, as opposed to her usual two, or even three.

"That was Emmeline. She's bringing a tomato pie. Oh, Lord, I bet I look a mess," she said, looking at her reflection in the glass-front cabinet and fluffing her hair.

"There's a bathroom down the hall," Lang said as A. J. brushed past her. "I'll be in the shower," she said out loud to no one as A. J. clicked the latch on the bathroom door.

Suddenly the front door flew open, and Lang's granddaughter, Katie D., came barreling toward her, clutching a dingy blue bunny in the crook of her elbow. She wrapped her arms around Lang's knees, and Lang buried her face in the child's hair, breathing her in. Baby powder. Play-Doh. Nutmeg.

"Alligator food," Katie D. whispered in her ear.

"Alligator food, too," Lang said to her. Without sound, the shape of these words and "I love you" look exactly the same on the lips, and it was their private message.

"Great's gone?" Katie D. asked.

"H-h-h-he loved you so much," Lang said.

Sarah, tall and willowy, stood in the doorway, watching them. She wrapped her arms around herself and leaned to one side, like a tree being blown by the wind. Her blonde hair seemed to float around her shoulders, light and weightless.

"Come on in, honey," A. J. said to Sarah, Katie D.'s mother. Lang looked at Sarah but said nothing. She didn't have it in her to coax Sarah the way she usually did. It was all she could do to remain upright and hold on to her grandchild.

FOUR

....

W*hat do you wear the day after your husband dies?*
Lang wondered, damp from the shower. She put
on her old sweatpants and Jack's practically disintegrated Auburn sweatshirt because they were
so soft. She wanted to feel something easy on her skin. She
pressed the frayed ribbed collar to her nose and breathed in
the sharp smell of aftershave and bacon grease. Jack's smell.

Teddy sat hunched over the kitchen counter with Sarah and
Katie D. on either side of him. Sarah leaned into him, her
cloud of pale hair floating out over the back of Teddy's brown
sweater, hovering with static electricity. Lang watched the
three of them for a moment from the doorway. She could hear
murmurs of their sentences: Katie D.'s singsong voice, Teddy's
hoarse rumble, apologizing for something, and Sarah speaking
so tenderly her voice didn't sound human.

Lang closed her eyes, holding on to the doorjamb for balance, and felt Sarah's words like they were something physical,
covering her softly. Gently.

"Mom!" Teddy said, scraping the chair away from the counter. She jerked to attention.

He looked like he hadn't slept in days; the collar of his but-
ton-down shirt was uncharacteristically wrinkled, and his azure
eyes were flat.

"Oh! I didn't hear you!" A. J. said, appearing suddenly from
the hall bathroom. She looked Lang up and down, grimacing.

"You still got that rubber band around your wrist." Lang pulled the frayed cuff down to her knuckles, holding the soft fabric in her fists.

A. J. looked like a different person except for her crumpled tennis clothes. Her hair was styled and her eyes were bright and her skin was dewy. She looked like she'd found a day spa in the hall bathroom. Lang sniffed the air, detecting vanilla and deodorant.

"I smell something," Katie D. said.

"Halston," A. J. said, flapping her hands in circles about her neck in an effort to spread the heavy perfume around the room. Katie D. crinkled up her nose.

Lang ran her fingers under her own eyes, trying to remember the last time she'd looked in a mirror. She should have put on some makeup after her shower. Concealer under her eyes at least. She reached her hands out toward her son, then curled them into useless fists as she shook her head slowly.

Teddy wrapped his arms around her, and she felt her boy sink into her, collapsing for a second. His breath caught, and his chest shuddered against her shoulder.

"Shhh," she said. "Don't cry." She felt him stiffen before he stepped away.

"How you holding up?" Teddy asked brusquely. "Who would have thought, huh? Sorry, bad joke. Dad would have laughed, though."

Lang squeezed the edges of her mouth up into a semblance of a smile. No one would have ever thought Jack would be dead instead of her. *Hilarious.*

"I'm going to head out," A. J. said. "I was going to wait around for Emmeline Harrison so I could officially introduce myself, but will you tell her I was here?"

"What?" Lang asked.

"No, you can't be bothered right now, I know. But I know

your club, *the* club, is taking new members after that Mrs. Vandergriff died last year. And somebody else. So."

"Oh," Lang said, realizing A. J. was auditioning for a spot in the historic club. She would never get in; it would be easier to reinstate Mrs. Vandergriff's dead body than this backwoods doctor's wife.

"Anyways, my cell number is on the counter if you need anything. I laid out an outfit for you. On the bed."

Lang felt relief that A. J. would finally take her leave. And take whatever hideous perfume she wore with her.

She'd never understood the intimacies of unrelated people acting like family. She didn't really know A. J. well, although they'd played tennis together every Monday for over thirty years. It was clear that the rest of their foursome—A. J., Camilla, and Peggy—were "close." That term perplexed Lang. How did unrelated people become so familiar with each other? Walking right in each other's houses without knocking, knowing exactly where the spices were kept or the spoons. So intimate.

They always asked Lang to join them for a club salad after tennis, but she rarely accepted. If it weren't for her love of tennis, she wouldn't socialize with anyone. Not that her foursome was ideal. A. J. cheated. She called the ball out if it was anywhere close to the line, but worse than that, she acted like an expert on everything from plastic surgery to raising children. Actually, she *was* an expert on plastic surgery; she was probably in the *Guinness World Records* for most elective operations. But her son lived somewhere in Europe, and Lang gathered they were estranged. So she should keep her child-rearing advice to herself. Lang snapped the rubber band around her wrist for being judgmental; she was trying to be less so.

Anyway, it was a moot point now. She had quit the game last fall, preferring to spend her remaining time with Jack and

Katie D., and her garden.

"Wait!" Teddy said to A. J. "Are you coming back?"

"Well, I can. Sure. I'm glad to. So," A. J. said. She said *kin* for *can.*

"No, you've done enough. Thank you," Lang said, forcing cordiality into her words.

"It's just that people are going to be coming over here, and I don't have any idea how this works. I don't even know where to start," Teddy said, plastering his dazzling smile on his face and not bothering to lower his voice.

"Well, Emmeline is on her way, and I know you don't want her to see your house like this. Not that you don't have a good excuse. Not that it's an excuse," A. J. said.

A. J. and Teddy looked around the little house, and Lang followed their glances.

The dining room table looked beautiful, heaped with glossy eggplants and creamy white pumpkins and all manner of colorful peppers and unusual squash. Extravagantly set for Thanksgiving dinner, the table looked like a magazine cover (if she said so herself).

"The centerpiece don't look that bad, all things considered," A. J. said. "It's just vegetables and stuff. Not real flowers, but do you know how many phytochemicals are on that table? Just one of them carrots has a gazillion. You'd think being on the board you'd of used something more fancy, but I like it. So."

Teddy focused on the living room. Haphazard stacks of books stood everywhere, and several strays lay opened and plopped page-down on various side tables and chairs. Katie D. walked over to the table and picked up Jack's place card. The word "GREAT" was scrawled over the construction paper in uneven capital letters.

"I'll keep it for him," Katie D. whispered as she stuck the card in her pocket, apparently aware of the forces at work in

22

the dining room.

"Books don't bother me. They make you look smart. Plus, I love to see what other people are reading," A. J. said, turning her head so she could read the spine of *Atlas Shrugged*.

"Jack is reading that," Lang whispered, but only Katie D. heard her.

"Tell you what. What we'll do is go get Cokes and ice and more coffee for now. And we'll find all the serving pieces, so don't worry about it. We need to sweep the front steps and sidewalk right now, though. Before anyone from women's club comes," A. J. said to Sarah, thrusting a broom toward her.

Lang had almost forgotten Sarah was there. She seemed to appear out of nowhere, conveniently for A. J.

"I'll go," Sarah said.

"That'll be better, in case Mrs. Harrison comes by. Emmeline, rather. She hasn't called, has she?"

"Check the answering machine. All those old bluebloods sound alike to me," Teddy said. "Nobody pronounces their Rs."

By the time Sarah returned with four twelve-packs of Cokes and two gallons of iced tea, A. J. had laid a fire in the fireplace, picked up sticks out of the front yard, taken out the garbage, and swept the rock steps leading from the front yard down to the road. She proceeded to organize the silver platters with scraps of paper that said things like "Vegs" and "Shrimps," still in her tennis clothes from yesterday. Lang was exhausted just watching her.

A. J. organized a social gala at her house, while Sarah looked around furtively for an exit. You'd think they'd balance each other out, that between the two of them they'd be one average helper. But they each made Lang equally uncomfortable.

Even though there was no official visitation, people began

to trundle up her sidewalk the day after Jack died, bringing refrigerated salads and casseroles and pound cakes.

Teddy's old tennis coach, Katie D.'s kindergarten teacher, Mary from the church (Lang couldn't think of her last name), and Mrs. Eubanks from down the street were the first to arrive.

She remembered these first people clearly. The coach held her hands, his face winced up tight. Mary told her if there was *anything, anything she could do*, while Lang desperately tried to think of her last name. Mrs. Eubanks stood askew in the dining room, watching her quietly.

For two days, the well-intentioned kept coming and coming. Lang vacillated between making mundane conversation about the generalities of unexpected death and the division of hosta, and feeling like she was free-falling down some bottomless black *Alice in Wonderland* vortex. It was hard to be gracious.

Lang slipped into the laundry room to be still for a moment. She leaned against the dryer, smelling Clorox and mildewed kitchen rags, and concentrated on getting oxygen into her lungs, then back out again. She tilted her head back and looked at the dusty jars stacked pyramid-style on top of the cabinets. Mason jars. Jelly jars. Old milk bottles. There must be hundreds of them. Her grandmother's collection of old lanterns hung above them on nails, and as far as she knew, they'd done nothing but gather dust for decades. Jack had hounded her to get rid of them—he'd wanted the space for his sports equipment. It occurred to her she should clean them out now, and she snorted at the irony.

She heard Teddy and Hank right outside the door, one of them rattling ice cubes in an empty plastic cup.

"You tell me. You're the lawyer and the banker—what are her options?" Teddy asked.

"It was already late," Hank said. "He missed the one before, and I covered for him, but it's out of my hands now. I could lose my job."

"She'll have to sell. How long before the bank takes it? Let me have a couple of days, and I'll get back to you," Teddy said.

Lang wondered what new mess Teddy was in and what Sarah could possibly have to sell.

"Excuse me, Teddy. I can't find your mother nowhere. Her mother is here," A. J. said. "Your grandmother, actually. So."

"Teddy! You are so handsome! You put Paul Newman to shame!" Lillian crooned. "I'll tell you right now, you boys are going to have to speak up."

Lang clenched her teeth at the sound of her mother's voice. It hadn't occurred to her to track her down and relay the bad news.

"Oh, well, what can I say?" Teddy said. Lang pictured the practiced smile on her son's face.

"I'm Lillian. Elizabeth's mother. Is that a Cohiba?"

"Who?" Teddy asked. Lang wished Lillian hadn't asked about the cigar, and been forced to explain why she called her daughter Elizabeth.

"It is," Hank said. "Sorry. A cigar is certainly not appropriate. I forgot I had it."

"That is my favorite," Lillian said. "Of all the cigars, the Cohiba Robusto Cameroon is the best."

"Oh. Please, take it. I insist," Hank said.

Lang knew Lillian wouldn't protest. Of course, smoking cigars at Jack's wake would be a perfect way for her to get even more attention.

"Is it going to be a good-size funeral?" Lillian asked. "It should be with his age. People come in droves for everybody under sixty. Depending on the weather. Weather changes everything."

"I'm sure there will be plenty of people," A. J. said. "You need to smoke that outside. Lang was president of the club for two shifts. Everybody who is anybody will turn out."

"Terms. Two terms. Her grandmother founded the presumptuous thing, so of course she was," Lillian said. "And it's not the only club in town."

"The Barrington Women's Club?" A. J. said. "That's Lang's grandmother?"

"Her grandmother's name is Katherine Langford Barrington Deakins to be exact. You'd think she founded the entire country, not just Barrington," Lillian said.

"That club is all over the country!"

Lang strained to hear them, wondering if they'd tiptoed away from the door. "I take it you're not in it?" Lillian finally said.

"Why? How do you know I'm not in it?"

"I can just tell. I was never asked, either," Lillian said. "But that's neither here nor there. At least not anymore. Now I'm going to need some face soap. And fresh towels."

"I put hand towels out in the powder room already. So," A. J. said.

"I can't dry myself off with a hand towel!" Lillian snapped. "Bring them to my bathroom, please." Her mother hadn't changed. She obviously still considered herself the center of the universe.

"She thinks I look like Paul Newman?" Teddy asked Hank after Lillian and A. J. left. "Isn't he, like, dead?"

"Are you kidding? Are you just completely clueless about everything?" Hank said. "Sorry. I'm wrapped pretty tight about this loan."

Lang stayed in the laundry room until all she could hear was distant tinkling of silver on china and the indistinct sound of chatter in the living room. No one noticed her open the laundry room door and slip into her room.

Making Arrangements

The days between Jack's death and his funeral were excruciatingly long. The sun seemed to hang in one place in the sky, and the moon clung like a lustrous ornament on a vast dark backdrop. Both celestial bodies forgotten. Neither one moving.

Lang wanted to curl up somewhere dark and examine the extent of her wound, like an injured cat holed up in the crawl space under the house. But the doorbell rang incessantly.

Hank and Buddy and Charlie, the remains of Jack's tennis foursome, came by together at some point. Lang didn't remember the day or the time, only that it was so odd to see them all. They were so lifelike; their faces had such good color. She blocked the image of Jack's lifeless body and pictured him clipping his toenails carefully over two double pages of newspaper as he read the horrid headlines out loud. Littering the small type under "Man Murders Family in Triple Suicide" in pale slivers of nail.

"W-w-we just wanted to come back by, Lang," Hank stammered. "See if there's anything else we can do. We are just so sorry."

Buddy and Charlie stood by awkwardly, murmuring in agreement and nodding their heads. Lang wondered if they had all designated Hank to be the speaker, and if so, how he had practiced for this. In the mirror? With his wife?

"Either you go out, or I go," she had told Jack a year ago, realizing ruefully she was going to be going soon either way, whether Jack did what she wanted or not.

"Don't," he'd said, stricken. "Don't joke."

"I mean it. You call Hank and Bud and whoever, and you go out with them. Weekly. This is hard enough, Jack," she had said, turning away from him.

Jack had insisted they play on the public courts, which contributed to his knee problems. Lang didn't understand why he had refused to play at the tennis club where the clay courts were soft and easier on the joints.

A. J. brought her several black outfits from a boutique to wear to the funeral.

"Pick which one you want, and I'll take the others back," A. J. said, shaking the hangers with their stylish plastic covers at her.

"I have something. It's a brown dress," Lang began.

"I'm awares. Just try them on."

A. J. manned Lang's home for days, venturing out periodically for supplies and returning with jumbo rolls of toilet paper and bags of ice, and toward the last few hours of the unofficial wake, a big bottle of Scotch.

Clutching a fifth of Dewar's, she looked at Lang sheepishly and said, "You do drink, don't you?"

They sat on the old camelback sofa that needed recovering and poured the Scotch. Lang wrapped herself in the worn wedding ring quilt that Fancy had stitched by hand as a girl.

Lang had patched the frayed squares of gingham and kettle cloth where the tufting was visible, matching the fabric as best as she could. The quilt was too fragile to be used anymore, but she kept it folded over the back of the couch for decoration. She needed it now for comfort.

She didn't remember where Teddy and Katie D. were or what had happened when yet another visitor had come to the door with a Bundt cake. She only knew that three days after Jack had left her, she and another woman, a stranger really, sat in her living room with the late afternoon sun pouring through the windows, illuminating dust particles in the air and neatly stacked columns of books.

A. J. raised her glass and said simply, "To Jack Eldridge." Lang lifted her glass and, for the millionth time since Wednesday, slowly shook her head in disbelief and whispered, "Jack."

FIVE

....

The morning of Jack's funeral, Lang was dismayed to see a little dog cowered on the edge of her front porch by the steps, not daring to venture twelve more feet up to the door. Its snout was short, smashed almost, as if it had run into a wall at top speed, and his dark eyes protruded, goggle like. His fur was matted down, a dark uneven color. He crouched low, and his jaw practically touched the ground as his tail beat the wooden floor like it was a percussion instrument.

"Poof. Disappear," Lang said quietly, using the same words Fancy had said anytime something irritated her, be it a mosquito or a persistent doorbell.

The little dog scurried down the wide stone steps, then sat in front of the dried-up Lenten rose she'd tried to dig up the morning Jack died. The foliage lay limp on the ground, the edges brown and withered, and the ashen, exposed roots curled into themselves. She tossed the plant on the compost heap, wishing she'd never disturbed it.

The black dress A. J. had chosen for her felt like sandpaper on her skin. The zipper grated against the back of her neck, cold and jagged. Worse, the fabric gripped snugly on her hips, riding up and emphasizing her bottom half.

After arriving at the church, Lang moved slowly down the pew to her seat, aware her rear end took up two places. She shifted closer to Katie, hoping that would conceal her girth.

She knew the congregation was overflowing without ever looking out at the church—the concentration of whispers and covered coughs and body heat in the sanctuary felt as endless as the sky. Lang sat quietly in the front pew of the church, concentrating on the rod-shaped buttons on her itchy black dress. They were pale and irregular, with dark etchings scattered randomly on them. She tapped her fingernail on the button holding her cuffs together and wondered if it was made of bone.

The priest stared at her, saying her name loudly as he talked about Jack. Lang scratched her shoulder.

"It was clear when you saw them walking down the road, always together, that there was a deep abiding love between them," the minister boomed. She tried to remember the last time she'd walked down the road with Jack. She wasn't much for exercise.

Lang bit the inside of her lip and critiqued the horrendous flowers on the altar as the priest eulogized her husband. She squinted at the pale peach gladiolas and willed herself not to think of Jack. Not here. The flowers unfurled evenly, gigantic fans, not a sprig of variegated ivy to soften the arrangement, make it bearable.

Lillian reached across Katie D.'s lap and squeezed Lang's hand. The skin on her mother's fingers looked firm beneath the stack of diamond rings, and Lang wondered if she'd had her hands done, if that was an option surgically. She made a note to ask A. J.

Lang twisted her hand out of her mother's grasp and draped her arm behind Katie D.'s shoulders. She looked at her granddaughter's little hands clasped together, encircling the limp blue bunny. Each fingertip pressed hard into the spaces between her knuckles. Her fingernails were the size of mini Chiclets, all freshly painted bubble gum pink. Jack would have loved that—Katie D. painting her nails a garish color in his honor.

The organ moaned out a somber hymn, and a man in a dark suit stood at the end of her aisle for a minute before Lang realized it was time for them to leave. It was over. Lillian took

Teddy's arm, the arm Lang was supposed to take, and Lang followed them alone down the same aisle she and Jack had walked down together over four decades ago.

In front of her, Lillian spied people in the crowd from another lifetime and slowly moved her outstretched arm its full range of motion. She was barely five feet tall, but always seemed larger than life with her high heels and expensive suits. And loud raspy voice. Lang watched her mother walk down the aisle of the church like it was a runway, waving like she was the newly crowned Miss America.

Later, Lang stood numbly in her own living room, fighting the urge to put her hands over her ears and scream at everyone to just leave. The dull roar of a cocktail party, just minutes after they buried her husband, was too much. Lillian and Martin Vandergriff were practically embracing by the mantel, and people she barely knew laughed loudly as they devoured meatballs and smoked salmon and whatever else A. J. had ordered. The partygoers put on solemn faces and lowered their voices when they expressed their acute sorrow to her, then ran back to the bar for another drink as soon as Lang was out of earshot.

Lang wanted to get in her bed and surround herself with pillows. Close her eyes. But instead she nodded and murmured her appreciation and looked at the hands on the black Jefferson clock that seemed to have stopped moving. Surely it was later than four o'clock.

Lang felt a tug on her hand and looked down at Katie D. offering up a plate of jumbo green olives and some chicken kebabs.

"I got the stuck chicken for you," Katie D. said.

"Thank you, sweet girl," Lang said, squinting at the beige chunk of undercooked chicken on the stick. "I'm not too hungry just now."

"My mommy says you need to eat. Even if you don't want to," Katie D. said. "That's how we be healthy. She says we must be healthy and care for our bodies." Katie D. nibbled at a thin elongated baby carrot, dropping the frail limp stem on Lang's plate.

"Yes. She's right," Lang said, overcome with gratitude that Sarah had taught her granddaughter to nourish her body with phytochemicals, hopefully keeping her safe from cancer.

SIX

....

Was it Sunday? Tuesday? Lang wasn't sure. Every time she opened her eyes and realized Jack was no longer in the world, she squeezed her face up under his pillow and breathed slowly, inhaling his scent until she was with him again.

She memorized the light. The otherworldly glow of a weak moon askew in the galaxy. The merciless shine of the sun at noon. The first hint of daybreak, so subtle she had to check the clock.

People were no longer regaling in her living room, and she was relieved not to find any remnants of the party. Her kitchen counters were wiped spotless, and the dishwasher was empty. The zip lock bags of molded cheese and the open tin can of tomatoes from before Thanksgiving were missing from the refrigerator.

There was a note on the counter that said, "I owe you new Tupperware—most of what was in the fridge I tossed out without opening. Biohazard." She studied A. J.'s handwriting; each *I* was looped and dotted with a large circle. The handwriting of a sorority girl.

The dining room table had been cleared completely. Her arrangement was gone, and there was no sign of leakage where the vegetables had been; she was relieved they hadn't rotted. She hoped A. J. had made ratatouille with the eggplant and roasted the pumpkins with brown sugar and curry and made compote out of the fruit. But based on the fact that even the cheese ball had been catered, she didn't think A. J. could cook.

33

Lang opened the pantry and eyed a can of condensed milk. She imagined the thick sweetness on her tongue and reached for the can. It was heavy in her hand, rich and decadent and comforting. She remembered taking up two places in the church and put the can back on the shelf. She poured herself a bowl of Special K instead and tried not to think of the thick creamy sweetness as she chewed the dry, tasteless flakes.

She slowly walked outside to collect the newspapers. That would be a clue as to what day it was. The dog hunkered down with his head almost touching the floor of the porch, its tail still beating an SOS on the wooden boards. She couldn't see any ribs because of his dingy malamute-like fur, but the animal seemed smaller, more diminished to her. She tried to count back the days to when she had first seen the animal. Had it been here four days?

"You picked the wrong place, buddy," she muttered as she walked up the steps with three newspapers. But she did not smack the porch rail with the paper like Jack would have done. Once he dinged a feral cat with a BB gun. *I didn't mean to hit it. I just wanted to scare it off.*

She set her half-eaten bowl of cereal down on the floor, unwilling to have a dog carcass to deal with on top of every-thing else. She had enough on her plate. She would tell A. J. to find it a home. That woman seemed to thrive on tending to other people's business so much that it made Lang wonder about the state of her own affairs.

The dog gulped down the cereal and licked the empty bowl, frantically polishing the sides. She thought of Jack repeatedly scraping his spoon over the curve of the ice-cream bowl.

Lang went inside and crawled back in her unmade bed. She burrowed deep under Jack's pillow and waited for sleep to give her relief from this pain that was both hollow and reverberat-ing.

Making Arrangements

She just reached the edge of sleep—she was riding on the handlebars of Jack's bike, laughing as the little dog from the front porch did somersaults beside them—when she heard a sharp, stern voice in her ear. *What a shame*, Lang thought as the new, heavy sadness covered her like a cold lead apron.

"Mom! You have got to get up! Get yourself dressed and get on with it," Teddy said. "Come on now. It's the middle of the day."

Lang blinked her eyes and apologized.

"Come on. I'll run you a tubby," he said in a softer voice. Lang thought of all the times she'd said those same words to her son. Lavender bath salts and a milk bubble bath historically equaled comfort in their family.

Lang didn't soak long. The porcelain bathtub felt hard under her body, and the white, weightless mounds of froth unnerved her. She wrapped herself in the old white bathrobe that needed washing and padded into the kitchen.

"Much worse than I thought. She's been in the bed . . . No . . . I'm not sure what to do. Obviously it can't go on like this. No, we'll have to find her a place," Teddy said into his cell phone.

Lang wondered whom he was talking to, wondering if everyone thought she was coping poorly. As if she should have scheduled a tennis game immediately after the funeral and invited people over for drinks. Actually she *had* invited people over for drinks. Immediately after the funeral.

What place was Teddy talking about? A smaller place? Jack had talked about it forever, trying to persuade her to sell the property and buy something else. He had even suggested the two of them move into the old stone carriage house down by the road and sell off the rest of the property. He'd acted like he was joking about renovating the tiny rock building, but only after she had reached out to the wall to steady herself.

The very idea of dividing the property made her feel unsteady. He knew she would never leave the little cottage and the grounds that had been in her family for over a century; it was not up for discussion.

The first time she'd gotten sick, five years ago, the year before Katie D. was born, she'd put the seven acres surrounding the house in a trust, guaranteeing the property would never be touched. That it would remain unchanged, even after her death. She'd rather donate it as a park than have it mutilated. Jack had protested so much she'd wondered if he'd already had the land surveyed, poised to butcher it up into tiny lots as soon as she died.

They used every inch of space in the old summer cottage. Teddy's old bedroom was now Katie D.'s; they really didn't need a guest room. They counted the deep front porch as a room except during the dead of winter. Lang had recovered the cushions on the heavy brown wicker furniture with a mocha chintz that didn't show dirt and painted the wrought iron table chocolate brown as well. But besides those updates, Fancy's front porch was the same as it had been when Lang was a little girl. The old oak porch swing still served as a daybed for summer afternoons, just like it had when she'd spent the summer afternoons curled up on it alone, watching the road for a car that might be her mother's. Imagining her mother straining against her seat belt to get to her. Or escaping from whomever had captured her and taken her away.

She had three postcards from her mother. That's all. Fancy's housekeeper had given them to her and told her to keep them in a safe place so they wouldn't get lost. Lang kept them in the green decoupage box, along with her birth certificate with both of her parents' names typed cleanly. Officially. Mother: Lillian Matthews. Father: Adam Deakins.

Darling Elizabeth,

I am still in France. I know your day will be wonderful!
Please know I love you dearly!

Love,

Your mother

P.S. The weather here is absolutely balmy! And to think
it's March?

But she hadn't come home for her birthday.

Elizabeth,

We are having a fabulous time in Sardinia! You would
love it here with your blonde hair! The Italians are outra-
geous!! Any more bread and I will have to buy a new ward-
robe (maybe I will anyway!!). I know you are doing
splendidly!!

Have fun!!

Your mother

Elizabeth,

Saw the Sphinx today! You would have been amazed! I
don't like the food here, though.

Hope you are enjoying yourself!

Your mother

The three missives were all almost the same, breezy sentences exclaiming over Lillian's view of the world. Still, Lang
had searched them, looking for clues. Did her sentence "You
would love it here" mean her mother intended for Lang to join
her in Italy? Who did *we* refer to? Did "Please know I love you
dearly!" mean her mother was coming for her?

Lang had pored over the three postcards, wearing their foreign stamps thin with her thumb. What had she done to make
her mother leave?

Lang plumped up the couch cushions awkwardly, trying to
announce to Teddy she was in the room.

"Okay, gotta go," Teddy said into his cell phone, flashing a smile at Lang.

"Can I fix you something? Tea?" Lang asked.

"That was quick. Did you even get in the bathtub?" he asked. Lang shrugged, unable to explain to him that things that used to comfort her now only accentuated her pain.

"Your mother called. Left a bunch of messages. Have you not talked to her?"

"I talked to her," Lang said, remembering how she had forced herself to be civil to the well-dressed woman who had breezed in and schmoozed the crowd.

"Did she tell you she was going to Africa on a safari?"

"She did," Lang said evenly.

"She asked me if she should go, like she really would rather stay here."

"It's a little late for that. Besides, I highly doubt she'd pass up a trip on my account. She never has before," Lang muttered.

"Okay. Whatever. We need to talk about things. How this is all going to work. I'm assuming Dad went over everything with you?" Teddy said.

Lang shrugged again, glancing surreptitiously back at the unmade bed behind her. She needed to close her eyes for just another minute.

"Mother!" he said sharply. "You have got to pull yourself together long enough to get this figured out. I mean, you are almost seventy years old, for god's sake. Surely this didn't catch you off guard!"

Lang felt the quick smack of his words.

"I'm so sorry," Teddy said, covering his face in his hands as he shook his head. "I don't know why I said that."

His voice cracked, and she remembered the year his voice had changed. He had been the last of his class to go through puberty, and he had intentionally lowered his voice a few octaves. And then when it finally had changed, he had been so thrilled he wasn't going to speak like a little girl the rest of his life that he hadn't even minded the abrupt jolts in his words.

Teddy wiped at his nose with the back of his hand and sniffed hard. His eyes were moist with tears, which made the blue so intense they looked electrified.

"Here," Lang said, offering him a tissue.

"No, I don't need it," Teddy said.

She wound the tissue around her finger, smoothing it against her knuckle.

"I know you miss him. It's okay to miss him," she said.

He turned away from her and punched at his phone. He sniffed and wiped at his eyes as the numbers pinged shrilly.

"I'm sending you back with casseroles," Lang said as she slowly stood up. "Sarah won't have to cook for a month." She would give him a minute to collect himself. She couldn't bear to watch him struggle not to cry, and she wondered when that had changed. When exactly it was that he no longer felt safe crying in front of her.

She was surprised to see her freezer organized. All the packages of frozen vegetables were neatly stacked instead of being wedged between zip lock bags of unidentified marinated meat. Tinfoil pans were clearly labeled on the sides: "Chicken Divan," "Pork Chop Casserole," "Turkey and Dressing." A heart dotted each *i*. She pulled out a stack and put it in a paper sack.

"We just need to go over everything," Teddy said from the doorway. "Make sure it's all straight. Do you know about his life insurance policy? I can't find it anywhere."

"Probably with all his stuff in the desk. We just went over all that stuff this year. Hank made me sign papers," Lang said.

Teddy's face was splotchy, but his voice was level. "What papers?" Teddy asked. "What did you sign?"

"Honey, I don't know. Hank took care of all that. Just routine updates, he said. Tax stuff, I think. Look in his desk," Lang said.

"I'm really sorry, Mom," Teddy said, rooting through the drawers. "About what I said. I'm just worried about you. You know, with Dad not here to go over everything."

Lang knew that he meant the cancer. He was right. Jack had taken care of her when she had been so, so sick. He'd split cherry Popsicles in half and eaten them with her when her throat was too scorched from radiation to swallow. He curled up in bed with her and endured *Legally Blonde* without complaint, massaging her bald head with warm almond oil. He had nursed her through the worst part of her life. Or at least she had thought it was the worst part.

Teddy left abruptly, forgetting the sack of casseroles. His face looked blanched, and she berated herself for not being able to comfort him. Lang headed straight to her bedroom and was almost to her bed when she heard Katie D.'s familiar tap at the door. The child couldn't reach the door knocker, so she tapped on the sidelight that ran the full length of the door. Sarah stood beside Katie D., shifting nervously from side to side as she checked her cell phone.

"Hey, is Teddy still here?" Sarah asked. Lang wanted to push Sarah's hair back out of her eyes. Pin it back so it would stay.

"He just left. I'm sending you home with casseroles. He forgot to take them. I think he's having a hard time. With his dad and all. With him being gone, I mean." She couldn't say *dead*.

"Oh," Sarah said. "Well. Yes." She turned away, then called out for Katie D. who had run over to the side gardens.

"There's a baby dog!" Katie D. squealed.

"Careful!" Sarah shouted. She ran toward Katie D., wrapping her arms around her and lifting her off the ground, which Lang found a little excessive.

"He showed up a few days ago. The day of the funeral, actually," Lang said. "I need to find a home for him. He's certainly not dangerous!" Lang looked at the miniscule dog wagging its tail and looking hopefully up at Sarah.

"Oh, Mommy! Please? Can we? I want a puppy so bad! He won't die. He doesn't look like he will," Katie D. said as she inspected the dog for signs of poor health.

"No, sweetie. We can't have pets in our apartment. You know that," Sarah said, still holding her. Sarah turned away from the dog, presumably so that if it lunged up at them, Katie D. was out of reach.

"It's not fair! I hate the apartment! I want a door to the grass. Not a room for a prisoner!" Katie D. shouted.

"Katie D., that is no way to talk," Sarah said.

"I am *not* a fairy-tale princess. I just want a real house like Grandie has!" Katie D. said.

Sarah shrugged her shoulders and looked at Lang apologetically. "We make-believe we're Rapunzel. There're bars on the windows, but we've never had any trouble," she said quickly.

"Except for danger," Katie D. said.

"What danger?" Lang asked.

"Nothing. Someone was robbed, but that could happen anywhere," Sarah said. "Katie D., stop reaching for that dog. We don't know anything about him."

"She's nice. She's a nice animal, and nothing bad is going to happen to her! You think everything's going to die just because one baby did," Katie D. shouted.

"Sorry," Sarah said to Lang. "She's exhausted. We'll come back another time."

"What is she talking about? What baby?" Lang said.

Sarah just shook her head quickly, indicating it was not up for discussion. She turned around quickly and carried Katie D. down the stone steps to her car. Her hair seemed weightless, floating behind her, pale and beautiful against her dark coat.

Lang looked at the little dog. Its eyes seemed to plead with her as it sat perfectly still, moving only its tail back and forth. It seemed a little fatter, thanks to the dog food she'd broken down and given it. Regularly. She reached down and scratched its ears as it wriggled around, rolling over so she could reach its tummy.

Lang smiled as she walked inside and called the vet to see if anyone was missing a dog. It obviously belonged to someone.

"No, but I know all about her. Mrs. Cole checks with me every day to see if anyone's turned up—either to adopt or claim. Bring her up to the office and I'll make sure she's up to date on everything," Dr. LePeyre said.

"It's a male I'm pretty sure," Lang said, suddenly aware she had alluded to male genitalia to the warm, friendly voice on the telephone.

SEVEN

....

B etty's Burritos was the last place Lang would have chosen for lunch. And if it wasn't Katie D.'s sixth birthday, she would never have gone out five days after she buried her husband. But the child had been planning this outing for months. For some reason, she loved the little hole-in-the-wall diner with wobbly tables and mismatched chairs shoved so tight you couldn't sit down without asking someone to slide their chair up.

Lang, Sarah, Teddy, and Katie D. walked down the assembly line of condiments and ordered beans and guacamole and pico de gallo on their burritos as surly faced twenty-year-olds folded them neatly without making eye contact. They handled the food with their bare hands, sliding soft tortillas along the counter littered with unnamed liquids and discolored lettuce shards.

Acid rock, or what she supposed was acid rock, blasted through the ceiling so loudly Lang had to ask the servers to repeat themselves. Which did not improve their dispositions.

"Sarah, will you order for me? I've got to take this call," Teddy said, speaking loudly as he stood behind them. Lang wanted to tell him to go outside, but she didn't want to irritate him.

Sarah said the names of toppings—*pico de gallo, Texas caviar, pineapple tidbits*—in a voice so melodious Lang thought she would never grow tired of listening to it. She ordered Teddy's burrito without double-checking a single item with him, and this fact, this intimacy, made Lang feel happy for some reason.

They may not be married, but they were a committed couple, she thought.

"He cashed it out! The whole policy?" Teddy shouted on the phone. "Sorry. It's okay," he said to her quietly.

Lang realized he was talking about Jack. That there was no insurance money. She didn't know why Teddy was so upset; Jack had invested the money Fancy had left her wisely, assuring her he'd made every possible arrangement for her future.

Teddy pulled a chair away from the table, but Lang didn't know it was for her until Teddy told her to sit down. He was seating her, being a gentleman the way his father had been.

"Who was that?" she asked, touched that he was trying to comfort her in his own way.

"It's okay. You don't need to worry about it. We'll talk about it later," he said.

"I'm not worried," Lang said.

"Hang on, babe, let me grab that other chair," Teddy said to Sarah.

Teddy spoke to a four-top table of three women before pulling their extra chair to the end of the table.

"Thanks," Sarah said. "They were out of fresh jalapeños so I doubled up on the spicy salsa."

"Good call," Teddy said. He gathered Sarah's hair in both his hands and smoothed it down her back. "It's like yellow cotton candy. Spun gold."

"Teddy, please," Sarah said, jerking her head away from Lang.

"Mom, tell her to let me make an honest woman of her," Teddy said.

"Teddy," Sarah said sharply. "Please."

"Well, it would solve most of our problems. Define things anyway," Teddy said.

Lang was about to say what a wonderful idea that was, but

something about the look on Sarah's face stopped her. Her cheeks flushed a tight pink, but she didn't look embarrassed as much as she looked mortified, like she was ashamed of the very idea.

Lang slid her index finger under her scarf and scratched the spot just above her temple. Her hairs stood alertly, a little rug of friction.

"They give you chips, Grandie. You want some? They're free," Katie D. said, shoving a greasy basket onto their crowded table.

Lang took a few oily chips and tried to chew the stale unpleasantness in her mouth.

"This is a good party," Katie D. said. "I wish Gracie could come. She babysits me some. She said she couldn't, though."

"What babysitter?" Lang asked. "I want to be your one and only babysitter."

Teddy immediately coughed into his napkin, and Sarah asked for more chips in a strained voice.

"She has a red heart on her tummy. With lightning through it," Katie D. said, zigzagging her finger through the air.

"I'm getting more salsa. Anyone need anything?" Teddy asked, scraping his chair abruptly against the chair behind him. "Sorry. You eat, Katie D."

Lang knew better than to ask about the babysitter. Instead, she asked Sarah about her job at the tennis center and the potted basil she'd given her, trying to engage her in conversation. But Sarah looked at Lang like she was trying to remember exactly how she knew her, until Teddy set the little plastic cup of salsa on the sticky table and clapped his hands.

Lang watched the woman from the four-top approach them, wondering for a second if she wanted the chair back. She prepared herself to accept the woman's condolences for Jack even though she was almost sure she'd never seen her before. She racked her brain for clues about who she was and how she knew her. Things like this seemed to be happening more and more, like her brain had completely run out of storage so it just disposed of new information, letting it flutter off into the recesses of her mind, unnoted.

Maybe the woman knew only Jack. *Had known* Jack.

"Excuse me. Teddy Eldridge? I'm sorry to interrupt, but my son plays tennis on the junior circuit. Would you mind signing this?" the woman asked.

Instantly revived, Teddy stood and shook her hand, practically preening as he looked around the restaurant to see if anyone else recognized him. He introduced the woman to his family, a special bonus.

The woman stared unabashedly at Katie D., and Lang could see why. Her granddaughter was exquisite. Her eyes were like dark melted chocolate, and her curly halo of hair had a golden sheen.

"She's absolutely enchanting! Where did she get those beautiful eyes?" the woman asked.

"They're her grandfather's," Teddy said, giving her his practiced movie star smile. He kept his teeth bleached an abnormal shade of white, and his eyes were a piercing shade of blue.

Sarah leaned over the table and began cutting Katie D.'s burrito into chunks. "Chew each bite. You don't want to choke," she said.

"Twenty times?" Katie D. asked.

"Twenty times," Sarah answered.

"I'm not," Katie D. said. "I'm choking." Katie D. made a gagging noise and clutched her throat.

"Stop it," Sarah said. "That's not funny."

Lang looked away from the table so neither one of them could see her smile.

Making Arrangements

After lunch, Lang stepped into Jack's rubber clogs and moved her toes freely around in his roomy, boxlike shoes. Her feet slid with every step, and she imagined him chiding her, warning her she'd fall.

She eased her way through the yard, making lists of what needed to be done: clip monkey grass, mulch azaleas, prune rhododendron. Surely she would be up to it in a few weeks; she didn't want her chores to get ahead of her and become insurmountable.

The pain was sudden, an electric current deep in her stomach. She felt as if she'd run into a live wire. She staggered over to the bench Jack had built and pressed the number two on her cell phone. Speed dial for Jack's number. The cancer was back.

She called him automatically, realizing her mistake the second his answering machine came on and she heard the familiar intake of breath before he said his name.

Suddenly she was furious at him. She was livid that he had left her so abruptly, with not so much as a hint of his departure. Not even a single high blood pressure reading or bad cholesterol report that she could have tried to correct. She should have had the chance to feed him more vegetables and make him do yoga. Take baby aspirin.

Had he had chest pains before and not told her?

She heard the phone ring inside but didn't reach it in time. Katie D.'s voice came on the answering machine, announcing her tummy hurt and her mommy was throwing up but told her to call and see if Lang was feeling sick at all.

Lang headed straight to the bathroom and held the broken toilet lid up as she crumpled over the bowl, grateful to be violently ill.

EIGHT

....

Lang didn't realize she hadn't taken her pills the next day until the phone rang at noon, the exact time Jack had called her every day from work to remind her. "Time for Tammy," he had said during her chemo.

She was done with the tamoxifen but now took the slew of vitamins Jack had researched instead. She clutched the plastic bottle in her fist, feeling the ridges of the cap inside her index finger.

"Mom?" Teddy said. "Are you okay? Sarah said you were sick. Do you think it's food poisoning?"

"She just now told you?" Lang asked, immediately realizing she was being self-centered; Sarah and Katie D. had both been just as ill.

"No. Yes." Teddy paused. "I stayed out of the apartment. In case it was a bug."

"Well, I'm better. Are they okay? I'm glad you didn't get it." Lang wanted to tell him that taking care of your family when they were sick was part of being a family. The main part. But she just asked him what he'd ordered on his burrito.

"They're fine now. But I need to talk to you about something. Have you talked to Hank?"

"Hank? Yes, they all came by before. I think it was hard for them," Lang said.

"No. I mean today. Has he called?"

The doorbell rang just before she could ask Teddy why.

"Hank!" she said, touched he was being so thoughtful and checking in on her. She appreciated it but didn't feel like trying to sound chipper, or worse, reminiscing.

"Lang, I'm sorry to barge in like this. I need to talk to you," Hank said. He looked terrible. Much worse than she did, and that was saying a lot. Bruised skin hung in pouches under his eyes, and his cheekbones were pronounced. She imagined what bumps and hollows were hidden by his hair.

He took her hands in his, then let them go. He seemed to be fascinated by the dozens of hideous floral arrangements in the house as he avoided eye contact with her.

"Please, take some. I insist actually," she said. She moved a vase of red carnations toward him.

"Lang, I'm not sure how to say this," he began.

"I know. It's hard to fathom," she said. She scooted a pastel ceramic boot of calla lilies next to the carnations. "Those, too."

"We have a problem. There's a problem. And I feel so terrible about bringing it up now. It's terrible. The timing," he said. He laid a thick stack of papers on the coffee table between them.

"What's wrong?" She squinted at the pages, wondering where she'd put her glasses.

"It's the house. Jack had borrowed money against it. He didn't want to bother you about it with you being so sick."

"It's in my n-n-n-name!" she stuttered. She hadn't stuttered in years. Decades. And now she seemed to stutter all the time. She focused on the corner cabinet and tried her best to relax. "Smile!" she heard her speech therapist say—a trick to stretch her mouth. "That's impossible," she said robotically to Hank, grinning wildly. "He'd never do that, and he couldn't do it. Legally."

"I did it. He thought . . . He didn't think you'd be . . ."

"He thought I'd be dead? That it wouldn't matter?"

"Lang, I'll lose my job. He was already late with the October payment, so it's red flagged. It's going to be out of my hands."

Lang picked up the ceramic boot and noticed a little beaded spur on the heel. She should have put the house in the trust as well.

"Why would he need money? Why didn't he talk to me? This is not Jack!"

"It was another business he was starting. With Teddy really. He just didn't want to worry you."

"So I'm *she*, not Sarah," Lang said, remembering the conversation she had heard outside the laundry room.

"What?"

"Never mind." She handed him the boot and went to the kitchen.

She stood at the sink and wondered what would happen if she took the little medley of vitamins with Scotch. She remembered how furious Jack had been when she put the land in the trust, how she'd placated him by leaving the house out of it.

She swallowed her insurance against a recurrence of cancer, wincing as the whiskey burned her throat.

NINE

·····································

L ang outlined the red stamped letters with her black pen again. "PAST DUE!"

She looked at the official papers Hank had left her a couple of weeks ago, all now doodled with psychedelic tulips and owls, the only two things she knew how to draw. She filled in the *D* with black ink, carefully staying within the lines.

She needed $1,325. By Monday. She drew a neat row of dollar signs followed by exclamation points.

She walked through every room in the house, appraising the contents. She knew the wormy chestnut breakfront in the dining room was valuable. It stood ten feet tall and still had the original wavy glass in the doors. She pulled a drawer open and ran her finger over the dovetail corners, squeezing the cast-iron hardware. It felt cold and heavy against her fingertips.

Her great-grandfather had built the piece by hand and ferried it across the Tennessee River as a wedding present for her great-grandmother. Supposedly they'd built the house around it, and she wasn't sure how she'd get it out if it sold.

Still, she wrote $800 on a sticker, spreading her fingers out over the uneven glass as she pressed the price tag onto the piece.

She made a sign that said "Antique Furniture Inside" and pulled everything she could lift out onto the porch—which wasn't much. She still felt her stitches tug every time she moved.

She carried the Haviland china plates with their pale violets two at a time, remembering the cucumber sandwiches Fancy had served her on them. One hundred dollars. Surely Fancy would want her to save the house over her wedding china. And the spool beds. And the hope chest and the monogrammed linen bread cloths.

It was too cold for a yard sale. The sky was heavy and gray, seeping a dampness you could feel and almost see. Lang felt a cold panic creep up her spine as she warmed up her coffee. No one was coming. She wouldn't get the money. She wrapped her hands around the mug, feeling warmth in her fingers. She draped Fancy's old quilt over her shoulders, careful not to tug it too hard and rip it, and tried to think of how she could keep the house. She breathed in the musty smell of the quilt, cedar and lavender, and felt her face relax a tiny bit.

After an hour, two women, one young, one old, walked up the rock steps from the road, not meeting her eye. They looked at the dishes without interest, keeping faces slack and neutral.

"There's more inside. Furniture," Lang said. "Couldn't move it all out," she said nervously. She didn't want them in her house, but she needed them to see the higher priced pieces.

"That's an old wedding ring pattern," one of them said of the quilt around her shoulders.

"Look at the stitching on it!" the other said. "And the colors are lovely."

"How much?" the first woman said, rubbing her thumb over the wedges of fabric.

"Oh, this quilt? I'm sorry. It's not for sale. It's mine. My grandmother made it when she was a child," Lang said, stepping away from their inquisitive fingers.

"Five hundred dollars," the woman announced. It was not a question.

"I'm sorry. I can't sell it," Lang said, wondering if she was an idiot. That was a lot of money.

Clearly irritated, the two women stalked into the house and spoke between themselves, but she could hear snatches of their conversation. "Finish is French paste," "Less in Atlanta," and "Those chairs." She wondered what they were saying about the old willow back chairs, and was impressed they knew about the finish on the chest. At least they appreciated what she had. She tried to comfort herself with that fact as she carefully laid the quilt on the dining room table and began to fold it.

An older woman came up the steps, dragging a well-dressed child by the hand.

"Come in," Lang said.

"Holy Toledo, Megan. Pay dirt," the woman said, ignoring Lang as she opened the little leather trunk filled with dolls.

"Oh!" Lang said. She hadn't even opened it she'd been so busy getting everything priced. The dolls were stacked in the trunk like sardines, but upright so you could see only the tops of their heads. Fancy had collected them from all over the world. A doll from every country she'd visited. The little girl pulled out the flamingo dancer. The doll's dark hair was pulled back and her eyes slanted in concentration as she stood in her yellow dress with one hip jutted forward and her arms arched gracefully above her head. She held real cymbals in her hands. The child waved the doll from Holland, with a lace cap and dimples and wooden shoes, over her head.

"Will you take forty?" the woman asked, handing the Portuguese doll to the little girl.

"I didn't know those dolls were in there. I'd f-f-forgotten," Lang stammered apologetically. "Forty is fine for the trunk."

"I want that little dog, too," the child said, walking toward the hedge where the animal sat.

"Here's fifty, then," the woman said, closing the lid and handing her a bill.

"No, I'm sorry, I can't sell the dolls. And the dog belongs to a neighbor," Lang said weakly. She needed to find a good home for the dog but didn't think these people were candidates.

"Does this piece come apart?" one of the women yelled from the dining room.

"Which piece? I'll sell the quilt," Lang called out.

"George!" the woman beside her bellowed toward the road. "We need you!"

A. J. pranced up the steps dressed in what Lang doubted was yard-sale-perusal wear—yellow leather flats, black stretch pants that made her legs look six feet long, and a yellow swing coat that Lang assumed was waterproof from its sheen. A. J. struck a pose in the yard as George walked up the sidewalk and the two women came out on the porch yelling more questions, and yet another customer walked up and unwrapped the silver sugar tongs Lang had played tea party with as a child.

"I'm taking it. All of it," A. J. said, snatching the sugar tongs and grabbing the doll from the child. "Five thousand for all of it."

"What the hell?" George said. "I just wanted to see the house. And the magnolia. I saw the documentary. But it doesn't look like anything historical to me."

"It was the first house built in Barrington. She's a real Barrington!" A. J. said, presenting Lang to them like this fact was important. "And everything's sold. As of now."

"Looks like you got a leak in the roof," George said.

Lang squinted at the ceiling, hoping it was an old stain.

"Oh, I'm sure she bought the contents of the house. Little Miss Modern hasn't even seen anything. Does the breakfront come apart? How do we move it?" the woman called from the dining room.

A. J. waved a stack of bills in the air like she was fanning the heap of items, then handed the money to Lang.

"Okay, she accepted my money. Sold them to me, so. Excuse me please," she said to George, who stared lustfully at her. She scooped up the little dog and clutched it under her arm like it was an accessory to her outfit. Lang wanted to tell her it clashed.

The shoppers finally left, but not without a day's worth of drama. The little girl wouldn't let go of the doll she'd already named Mimi. The women in the house said that was no way to operate a yard sale and told Lang she should never expect to have a customer ever again, and George asked A. J. if she wanted to get a drink with him.

When A. J. finally shooed everyone away, the moisture that had been thick in the air all day turned to large, heavy drops. Lang and A. J. looked at each other and then suddenly, like they had been old friends who read each other's minds without speaking, ran in opposite directions around the yard, grabbing everything that wasn't waterproof. Or at least A. J. did. Lang tugged at the chest full of dolls the woman had left outside until A. J. picked it up and carried it up to the porch. The rain stopped as suddenly as it had started, leaving so little moisture Lang questioned if it had actually rained.

"I don't lift weights for nothing," A. J. said as Lang collapsed on the wicker chair.

"What are you doing? I know you don't just walk around with that much cash," Lang said.

"You don't know that. You have so many beautiful antiques, and they're all from your family. It's a crime to sell them at a yard sale. And I don't approve of crime," A. J. said. "Where's Teddy? He can move all this stuff back for you."

"Oh, it's fine. I hate to bother him about it," Lang said.

"Why?" A. J. asked. "It would take him about a minute, and I can tell it hurts you to stand up straight."

"Oh, no. What's that smell?" Lang asked, changing the subject. Dog mess oozed up around the edge of Jack's rubber shoe.

A. J. held her nose as she slipped it off Lang's foot gingerly.

"Where's the hose? I'll spray it outside," A. J. said.

"No, don't bother. How did you get so wet? It barely rained! Come in, and we need to talk about this money," Lang said, digging the thick wad of bills out of her back pocket. She was relieved that the breakfront still loomed over her dining room table, albeit empty of the pale bone china. But that A. J. had her nerve, busting in and taking over, assuming Lang would sell everything for $5,000. Lang rounded off everything in her head, realizing she was $2,500 ahead.

"You paid me too much," Lang said.

"Don't worry. This ain't my first rodeo. Actually, I didn't pay you near enough for what you have. I watch *Antiques Roadshow*, just so you know."

"Are you sure you have a place for all this? Some of the pieces are really big. Did you measure your rooms?" Lang knew she should shut up before A. J. had buyer's remorse and came to her senses, but she felt very uncomfortable about the whole transaction.

"I did not. Look, I don't really want this stuff. Not stuff, sorry. Your things. Antiques. I was hoping to make a deal, sort of," A. J. said.

"I'm listening," Lang said. She reminded herself of some movie character but couldn't think of which one. Clint Eastwood?

"I want to be in the women's club. You're a past president and on the board. I've tried everything I know to do. Donations. Volunteering. I've been sucking up to that Emmeline Harrison for years and nothing."

"You want to *buy* a spot in the women's club?" Lang asked.

"No. It doesn't work that way, or I already would have. And not just *a* women's club. The Katherine Barrington Women's Club of America. It's the only club in the south listed in Women's Society of America. So."

Lang just stared at her, trying to understand the significance of this statement.

"Do you do volunteer work? Or garden? I'll be glad to divide some of my plants with you if you want."

"I garden!" A. J. snapped.

"Well, the meetings are all about tutoring and volunteer programs," Lang said. "Mainly the Children's Inner-City Ministry this year. Some flowers. Not much."

A. J. heaved herself down at the head of the dining room table and collapsed her head over her folded arms. Her breath came in deep pants. Lang looked at the Jefferson clock, then stood behind A. J., hovering her arm just behind the chair.

"I don't know nothing about plants," A. J. said, sitting up straight. "Or children. Mine included, when you get right down to it. The only thing I do is give parties. And I don't even cook for them. I just arrange them," A. J. said.

"Parties are impossible. You're in charge of the fund-raiser at the museum every year, aren't you? I don't know how you do it. Or why," Lang said.

"Anybody can do that. The museum would let anybody stupid enough to volunteer organize that. It's not like the women's club, where you have to have credentials."

"Oh, for Pete's sake. You shouldn't give that club a second thought."

"I think about it all the time, if you want to know the truth. I just want to be in it."

"Why?" Lang asked.

"Why? Only someone in it would ask that question," A. J. said. "You don't get it. You were born here. In Barrington. You've always had a place. You belong."

"That's silly. You live in the biggest house on the brow of the mountain, with a view to die for. Everyone in that club wishes they could live in your house."

"Don't matter. They won't never let me in. Just because my mother ran a beauty shop out of our *fo-yay* and my daddy worked third shift. When he worked at all," A. J. said.

"Where was the beauty shop?" Lang asked.

"Fo-yay. The front hall. Not that it was anything like yours size-wise. The point is, even with the fix you're in, I doubt you'd install a sink and a swivel chair by the front door. Not that my mother could afford an actual swivel chair," A. J. said.

"Well, sounds like she was resourceful," Lang said.

"She was that. Same old story. She sacrificed to send me to community college—I followed Walker to Chapel Hill and lived in a boarding house—and I guess I thought that was the end-all. Marrying somebody like him. Doctor and all. Orthopedic even." A. J. raised her eyebrows when she noted the type of doctor he was.

Noted, Lang thought.

"Sorry, I'm just not sure I understand the significance of the women's club in all this," Lang said.

"You wouldn't get it. That is so iconic. You don't even see the forest for the trees," A. J. said.

"Ironic?"

"Ironic then. Fine. That's another thing. I know all of you make fun of me. I know I should probably just not even speak in front of any of you because my vocabulary is not all that. Just forget it. I never should have brought it up," A. J. said. She walked to the door and peered out the sidelight by the front door.

"No, wait. I wasn't making fun of you. I just wondered about the word *iconic*. Which would actually be a perfect description for the women's club, or at least the way you see it." A. J. scowled at the edge of the quilt.

"Here's what I see. You're perfectly gorgeous. Your figure is to die for. You are absolutely beautiful, and you dress like you just popped out of a fashion magazine. We're a bunch of over-the-hill bags who are too jealous to have you in our midst. Now, I'm getting you something dry to put on although it will swallow you whole. Here, let me just put this quilt around you. Easy now, it's old," Lang said as she wrapped the quilt around her. "I guess technically it's yours now anyway."

"Technically. That little dog out there looks soaked," A. J. said.

"He's been there for days now. I should probably call animal control, but I don't trust them to find him a home. I know not to feed him. But I've been giving him leftovers, so I know he won't leave on his own now," Lang said. "Are you cold?"

"He's a cute dog," A. J. said, staring out the window. "If a wet dog can be cute. Is this you?" A. J. picked up the photograph of Lang from the wormy chestnut chest of drawers in the front hall. Lang looked lost on the top step, scabs on both her knees, her new front teeth oversize for her face. The shutter had clicked just before Lang's face had collapsed in a sob.

"There was a dog, and it leaped out of my arms just when my grandmother took the picture," Lang said. "I remember it like it was yesterday."

"Well, it's cute, but if I was you, I'd put out a better picture. Maybe one from elementary school? Took by a professional? They don't print 'em if you don't look good. So."

"I'll do that," Lang said knowing she didn't have any other childhood pictures of herself. Maybe she would put Katie D.'s picture out.

"Oh, my gosh, look at your arrangements!" A. J. said.

Lang looked at the unidentifiable remains of the funeral flowers. A few stems of statice still stood upright, holding their lavender color.

"I can pull the live ones out, make a little bouquet if you'd like it? You'd be doing me a favor. Obviously," Lang said as she plucked the remaining live flowers from the vases and quickly arranged them in an old birch-bark planter. She'd carved a big heart with her and Jack's initials on the side: "L. E. + J. E."

"I want that, but with my own initials. And Walker's. That's about the cutest thing I ever seen," A. J. said. "You have a way!"

A. J. pointed at the white, embossed pitcher on the kitchen table filled with pumpkin-colored bittersweet and maple leaves. Then she walked over to the counter and reached for the glossy green leaves of the laurel that splayed out over the silver bud vase. She'd arranged them both the week before Jack died.

"Your bouquets. They're beautiful and so natural looking. You should sell them," A. J. said.

"Oh, anybody could do those. They're just out of the yard. Shrubs. Some are weeds even," Lang said. "The laurel blooms in spring, though. I'll root you some if you want."

"I wouldn't know what to do with it. Walker has everything landscaped, so the yard's done. So."

Lang knew her yard would never be done. She would never want it to be. She would never tire of layering the low branches of hydrangea and azalea with rocks and planting the new little plants that formed.

"A.J? I couldn't have let those strangers take my things. I— I—I—I . . . Thank you," she said finally.

"You'll have to keep them for me. All my new things. My new old stuff. But I'm not paying you to store them," she said, wagging her finger at Lang as if Lang had asked for a storage fee. "But I'll take this. I like the way it looks. I don't care if it is weeds," A. J. said, picking up the loving cup filled with box-wood. "Fabulous! In an old trophy!"

Lang quickly took the boxwood out of the trophy and put it in a jelly jar. She tied a rattan ribbon around it and handed it to A. J.

"Sorry," she said. "I couldn't even price them. They're Teddy's trophies."

"Well, cute! I like this just fine, so." A. J. turned the arrangement around as she held it up. "You should sell these at the tennis club. I bet you they'd go like hotcakes. People pay out the wazoo for flower arrangements. If you can make 'em look this good in the dead of winter, I can't wait to see what you do with real flowers."

"Anyone could make these," Lang said.

"Maybe, but they don't. I'm telling you, you might be looking at the answer to your money woes right here. You might be looking at the trees dead on."

"The trees?" Lang asked.

"From the forest. Try to see them, Miss I'm-So-Smart-I-Can't-See-the-Forest. For the trees!"

A. J. finally left, theatrically walking down the sidewalk with the bouquet clasped to her stomach like she was somebody's bride. She turned around at the top of the steps and rubbed her thumb back and forth across all four fingertips, like she was feeling money.

TEN

....

Lang squeezed herself down in Jack's leather chair, wedging her hips against the sides, and pressed the power button on the remote control. The screen did not react. She punched official-looking buttons on all three remotes, futilely trying to turn on the television.

She called the number of the cable company, and waited fifteen minutes before she was advised to call back later due to an unusually high volume of calls.

Click. She was disconnected.

This was Jack's job. He was the one in charge of movies and shows and recordings, not her. She'd never watched this new television without him. Lang smacked the phone hard on the side table, then hurled it at the TV that was flashing useless bits of information. The phone clattered onto the wooden floor, and Lang went to bed without picking it up.

The next morning, she did not get out of bed. She could not carry this heaviness another day. Her grief seemed to have been absorbed in her cells. Every microscopic molecule of her being seemed to weigh a thousand times more than it had before Jack had died. She could barely hold a toothbrush, much less move her hands to pick the phone up off the floor.

Lang wasn't sure she could go on in this world without Jack. Wasn't sure she wanted to. She burrowed her head under his pillow that still smelled faintly of medicated shampoo and sun-drenched straw, and drifted back and forth between unconsciousness and hopelessness.

The discomfort of her swollen bladder finally forced her

out of bed. She walked out the back door in her pajamas, hoping the cold air would act as an anesthetic. Deaden her pain.

She scanned the yard for the little dog and was surprised she felt disappointed not to see him. "It's for the best. He deserves better," she said out loud, pressing the cheese cube she'd brought for his treat between her fingers.

She began clipping, almost unconsciously cutting the tips of boxwood from thick, gnarled branches and boughs of hemlock with miniature pinecones still attached. She didn't notice the little dog until he purred. The throaty whir he made sounded like a placated cat, not a cold, lost dog. She tossed the cheese cube toward the dog, and he wriggled his appreciation before gulping it down.

She carried the armful of greenery to the kitchen and stood in front of the sink, exhausted. She sat down in the old, torn armchair in the kitchen just as the weak afternoon sun eased through the clouds. She tilted her face up to the light and closed her eyes, like she was sunbathing.

Everything she did took so long because she couldn't complete one thing without resting in the middle of it. At least once.

Lang made her way back to the sink and breathed in the sharp, acrid smell of cut greenery. She felt some of the heaviness ease off her as she snipped stems of glossy mountain laurel on the diagonal and scraped lower leaves of pyracantha. She clipped a bough of white pine, littering the tassels on the counter. She added nandina, their clusters of red berries hanging like bunches of miniature grapes; bittersweet, the pumpkin-colored seeds bursting out of their pods; and hydrangea blossoms, faded rose and pale green, but still springy to the touch. She wove liriope through the stems that were underwater, a thin, green eel holding them together.

When she realized it was too dark to see the color of the

berries, she flipped on the lights and studied the way the flowers cascaded gracefully and how all of the berries complemented the deep plethora of reds and purples in the hydrangeas. She walked around the stunning arrangement, adjusting strays and clipping here and there, then sat down in the old club chair and looked at her creation for a few minutes. It was absolutely beautiful.

She walked around it one more time before snatching her perfectly cut clippings out of the arrangement and hurling everything onto the compost heap, saving herself the trouble of dealing with it when it all died.

ELEVEN

L ang heard the heavy thud of the cast bronze door-knocker and saw A. J. peeping through the side light. Had she forgotten something?

A. J. clattered her perfectly manicured fingernails on the glass as Lang glanced around the living room, scanning the furniture for lost eyeglasses or a designer pocketbook.

"Hey, hon. I just wanted to check on you. See how you're doing. Check on my antiques. Maybe even have a glass of wine?" A. J. said hopefully, taking off her white rabbit fur trooper hat and tousling her thick blonde hair. It fell to her shoulders and looked like she had just left the salon. "I brought a little something."

"Oh," Lang said, stepping back from the door. A. J. apparently understood that to mean uncork the wine and serve the appetizers.

"You don't have any of that caramel cake left over from the funeral? Oh, sorry. That came out wrong. Never mind, I don't need it," she said as she quickly emptied a bag of baby carrots onto one of Lang's Haviland plates.

A. J. pulled up two chairs around the new granite bar that Jack had put in a few years ago. They remodeled the whole wing because a limb from the ancient magnolia had crashed through the little kitchen during a storm. The kitchen used to be sequestered away from the rest of the house by a narrow hall and swinging wooden doors. She'd protested about changing the house in any way, and this had enraged Jack all over again about the land trust. It was easier just to let him take down a wall.

Jack had hired an architect to design the new kitchen on the sly, and she had made it "open" to the rest of the house. Now there was an enormous island where the wall used to be, and a bank of windows where the pantry and little utility room had been. The old metal cabinets that creaked when they opened were removed, as were the faded red linoleum countertops that gave under her elbows. Shiny brown granite was everywhere, and light cherry cabinets disguised the refrigerator so that unless you knew where it was, you had to open cabinet doors until one released cold air.

Now when Lang stood in her kitchen she felt exposed. She had to be decent to go into her own kitchen because anyone at the front door had a clear shot of the whole house.

She missed the little closed-off kitchen where she could reach the stove and the sink and the obvious fridge without taking more than one step, and she missed being able to take the last few bites of whatever dish she was cleaning up without Jack noticing.

And the smell was gone. The smell of her grandmother's kitchen. Spray starch. Coffee grounds. Vanilla. This kitchen smelled faintly of formaldehyde and nail polish remover, and the countertops were so hard and cold they made her recoil whenever she inadvertently rested her forearms on them.

The only thing she liked about the new kitchen was the picture window in the breakfast nook. She could see the bird feeder while she ate and didn't have to walk all the way over to the kitchen sink to watch the birds.

"I need you to keep this piece dusted," A. J. said, rubbing her finger along the edge of the gigantic breakfront and cocking her head. Lang noticed the thin layer of dust hiding the sheen of the wood. How long had it been since she'd cleaned anything in the house?

Making Arrangements

"So all these trophies were Teddy's?" A. J. asked as she eyed the row of loving cups and plate-size medals lining the shelving just under the crown molding.

"Are. He's still collecting them. Playing again and doing great. This one's new," Lang said, holding the silver-plated disk out. "You know he was in the semifinals in the US Open and the French Open the same year."

"I knew he was in all those magazines, so."

"*Sports Illustrated, Tennis Magazine,* and the cover of *Tennis World.* All before he was fourteen. He had an endorsement contract with BMW and a sports car before he even had his learner's permit," Lang said. "That was a headline in one of them."

A. J. peered at the framed magazine articles in the hall. "What happened really? I mean, I read everything about his temper, but was that why he quit?"

Lang looked up at her, remembering Teddy's first city tournament. He was in the finals against a boy a head taller than him and about to lose the match in a third set tiebreaker.

Lang saw the ball skim off the service line and sat numbly as Teddy called the ball out.

The tall opponent hurled his racket with such force it ricocheted off the court and clattered a few times before settling on the court next to them. Immediately a middle-aged woman with her hair pulled back into an unflattering bun hurried down the bleachers and walked right onto the court.

The boy followed her to the tournament official, and then shook Teddy's hand before walking off the court.

It took Lang a minute to realize the woman had made her son forfeit. The boy was one point away from winning the city tournament, and his mother had let him know in no uncertain terms that his unsportsmanlike behavior was unacceptable. Period. She didn't care what he had just forfeited.

Teddy had blinked a few times in disbelief, then raised his arms up over his head in victory. Lang remembered that as a milestone win. Not because it was the first city tournament Teddy had won, but because she realized she would allow him to win, no matter what the cost.

"His knee. He blew it out right before Wimbledon," Lang said. "Those stories about his temper weren't even true."

"He quit?" A. J. asked.

"No, he did not quit," Lang snapped. "Sorry. He was hugely successful and extremely talented. He's working his way back into tennis now. Shouldn't have any problem."

A. J. arranged the carrots in a circle on the plate. They looked like chunky sunrays.

"That little dog is still out there," A. J. said. She pulled at her pearl necklace, and Lang noticed how stunning it looked against her sage-green cashmere sweater. She made being beautiful look effortless. "You should check back with the vet."

"No, he has my number," Lang said, aware of the series of unwashed stains on Jack's old sweatshirt that was her uniform now.

"He has your number, does he?" A. J. said, cocking her head and raising her eyebrows. "Okay, I got you something." She dug through her oversize leather pocketbook and handed Lang a fistful of pink sparkles. It took Lang a second to realize it was a monogrammed dog leash and collar.

"A. J., I'm not keeping that dog. I'm sorry. These are so, so sparkly, but I can't keep him! He needs a home. I need to find him a home. I can't stand seeing him out there," Lang said. "You monogrammed his collar with my phone number? Why don't you take him yourself?"

"Oh, I can't. Walker's allergic. Asthma. I can't even open the windows in the house. We've got some regulating air device, but that's not neither here nor there. I'll find a good home for him. We'll put this on him and make him more photogenic. Now, by no means am I a dog breeder, but I think we need to clean him up first. I coogled it already, and Dawn dishwashing liquid kills fleas. So," A. J. said.

"Coogled?" Lang asked.

"Looked it up on the computer. I'll take his picture and send out an e-mail after the bath," A. J. said. "Do you have any plastic gloves? Those dishwashing kind? And Dawn? He's filthy!"

A. J. put pot holders on her hands and held the little dog straight out in front of her, away from her elegant sweater like she was holding a baby with a dirty diaper. She hadn't even asked if she could bring the dog inside.

TWELVE

....

Lang wanted to leave the official-looking letter from the bank in the mailbox. Not claim it.

She knew what it said without opening it.

She stuffed it in her jacket pocket, unopened, and walked to the compost pile to survey the remains of her arrangement. The little dog followed her, keeping a respectful distance.

She'd gotten a few calls from people who'd seen the posters plastered on telephone poles and in shop windows, but none of them were right. One wanted to breed "her" (she didn't explain the pink collar) and one wanted a watchdog in a warehouse. The least she could do was find the dog a decent home.

There was something blooming year-round on her property, and even when the ground was frozen and the trees were barren, the garden Fancy had planted offered a lush retreat. The camellias formed a glossy green wall behind Jack's bench and were covered in blooms in the middle of winter. Lang squinted at the fuchsia petals of the Julia Drayton camellia. They weren't tightly coiled like the others, but almost flat, splayed out wide, like the blossom had been shoved into a wall. She looked at the dog's pug nose. He jerked his head up at her quickly in acknowledgment. "We'll find you a good home," she said, then looked around her vast garden to make sure no one was within earshot.

Yellow tassels of witch hazel splayed out behind the camellias, and the japonica had already erupted in a riot of pink ruffles. Snowdrops burst out of the ground with their delicate teacup blossoms, lime green etched on their edges like a china pattern, and for a minute, Lang wished she had her clippers. But then she knew she'd only waste anything she cut; fresh flowers seemed to mock her pain.

She sat on the bench and wondered what the hell she was going to do. A. J. was kind to loan her money, but that almost added to her problems. It would be easier to pay off Jack's loan than it would be to get A. J. into the women's club. In the meantime, she didn't want to be indebted. The amount she owed was staggering.

The last time she'd sat on this bench was the day Jack had died, and she'd fallen asleep. At least now she was awake. Tired but not unconscious. She tried to cling to that one positive thought as she made her way over to the compost pile. It was past time to turn it.

Her clippings, still green and colorful, lay on top of the pile, making the mound look like it was alive. Which it was, technically. The whole heap of compost was teeming with organisms, transforming itself from grapefruit peels and apple cores into dark, rich dirt. Black gold.

She gingerly pushed the shovel into the bottom of the pile and waggled it back and forth a couple of times before deciding that was enough for today. Her stitches pulled a little but not like last month. Still, what would she do if something happened?

Lang took a deep breath and scraped up a shovelful of rotting fruit and coffee grounds and clumsily scattered it over the remains of her arrangement. The dog sniffed at an eggshell before scarfing it up, then rooted around in the compost for another one.

"No! Stop it!" Lang commanded before realizing the dog's digging would turn the compost and do what she wasn't strong enough to do herself. "Fine. Go ahead. Dig. Dig!" she ordered the bewildered little animal.

He scooted his nose under a rose-colored hydrangea blossom and rooted so deep into the pile his pale fur was almost hidden by pumpkin-colored bittersweet and scarlet clusters of nandina berries. She stared at the greenery she'd clipped yesterday for a minute, then gathered it up, shook if off, and took it right back to the kitchen sink.

Lang carefully collected some of the jars from the laundry room and lined them up on the countertop. The slick modern surface looked better covered with mason jars. Mustard jars. Pickle jars. She told herself it was time for them to be used and that this is what Fancy had saved them for.

She filled the jars half-full with barely warm water and began arranging the twigs and berries and faded blossoms in them, knotting twine around the threaded lips of the jars. She quickly called the tennis center before she changed her mind.

"Sarah?" she said. "Can I bring some little arrangements down to the tennis center to sell? They won't live long, and I should have given you notice, but I didn't plan to make them."

"No, it's fine. Bring them down," Sarah said haltingly. Lang wondered if she was imposing.

"I know. It's silly. Who's going to want a bunch of weeds from the yard in a jelly jar," Lang said, wishing she'd never called. Clearly, Sarah didn't want to fool with this.

"No," Sarah said. "Bring them."

"What are these?" a woman in a pink spandex warm-up asked as Lang unloaded the first of her arrangements, slowly carrying two jars at a time. "Are they for a party? Is there a party here I didn't know about?"

"They're for sale," Sarah said quickly. "Nineteen dollars ninety-nine cents each. I'll get the rest of them, Lang. You sit."

"Oh, no," Lang interrupted, embarrassed both at the exorbitant price and the fact she desperately needed to sit down.

"I'll take four. I've got houseguests this weekend. Just charge my account and I'll get them after my game," the woman said.

By the time Sarah unloaded the last of the flowers, every arrangement was sold and Sarah handed her $400.

"Well, what's your percent? I never would have sold a single one without you, so half?" Lang asked.

"No, no," Sarah said. "You take it all. It's great for the club. A service for the members and no trouble at all. Glad to do it. I guess bring double the amount for tomorrow?"

Lang carried the empty boxes to the car and wondered why Sarah wouldn't take her cut.

THIRTEEN

....

Lang assumed she would spend Christmas day with her family the way she always had; it never occurred to her to ask them to put it on their calendars. But apparently Teddy had an out of town tournament, one Lang had never heard of, and Sarah and Katie D. had other plans. Lillian called again this year to see if they could spend Christmas together, but Lang thought spending Christmas with her mother would be worse than spending it alone. Teddy still asked her why they didn't spend the holidays with her as a family, but Lang had no problem keeping Lillian at arm's length. Lillian made her bed years ago as far as Lang was concerned.

"What plans?" Lang asked Sarah. Teddy had said Sarah didn't have any extended family; she was an only child, her mother lived somewhere in Europe, and her father was dead.

Sarah hemmed and hawed so awkwardly Lang finally had mercy on her and let her off the hook. Lang sometimes wondered if Sarah had a mild form of Asperger's, just enough to make her inept in human relationships. But she seemed to do fine with Katie D. So far.

Teddy, Sarah, and Katie D. came by to exchange presents a few days before Christmas, and Lang served the last chicken divan she ever intended to eat.

Lang had bought their gifts just over a year ago, last November. A sea-blue cashmere sweater for Teddy, a cornflower-blue scarf for Sarah, and an operable crane for Katie D. She'd taken care of all the upcoming year's holidays and birthdays the week she'd been diagnosed this second time, storing her beautifully wrapped presents in shopping bags in the basement.

"Can I feed that little dog out there? He's watching me," Katie D. said. Lang looked over at Sarah, but she'd characteristically disappeared. Again.

"No, sweetie, he's a stray, and remember, your mommy didn't want you around him?" Lang said, distracting her with the stack of presents. She remembered Katie D saying something about the dog not dying. "Did a little baby die?" Lang asked.

"My baby did. My baby boy, poor thing," Katie D. said. Lang wondered about the effects of realistic role-playing; she didn't think it was healthy for Katie D. to pretend her dolls died. But there she went again, being judgmental. She flicked the rubber band, rubbing the sore spot on the inside of her wrist.

"Well, that's too bad. Where is she?" Lang asked, holding the oblong box with real miniature pinecones attached to the ribbon. "Where's your mama?"

"That makes you good?" Katie D. asked, pointing at the thick rubber band.

"Reminds me to try to be better," Lang said, rubbing noses with Katie D.

"Sarah! Come hither," Teddy called, ripping his package open like a child. Sarah slipped into the room and curled up behind Katie D. He held the sweater up to his face and batted his eyes at her before he slipped it over his head.

"Perfect. Makes those gorgeous eyes pop," Lang said. Even when he was a little boy, Lang had never bought him any color except a shade of the sky on a crisp October day. His eyes were mesmerizing, a fact that hadn't hurt his movie star status as a tennis player.

"That's beautiful!" Sarah said.

"Oh, please," Teddy said, gently pulling Sarah toward him. "You flatter me."

Sarah blushed as Teddy slopped kisses on her cheek and Katie D. squealed with delight.

"Daddy is the Kiss Monster. He kills us with kisses. Do Grandie, Daddy!" Katie D. shouted.

Teddy turned to Lang and engulfed her with both arms, squeezing her into him as he made guttural noises and kissed the top of her head. The new sweater smelled like the department store during holiday season. Cinnamon and burned popcorn oil and wool. Lang closed her eyes and felt her son's chest against the side of her face, strong and grown-up. She heard his daughter laughing and knew Sarah was smiling at them and thought how glad she was she'd lived this long. She wouldn't trade this moment for anything.

"Okay, you're next, Sarah," Lang finally said as she handed Sarah her gift. "No saving it for a rainy day."

Sarah wrapped the scarf around her neck, then pulled her hair out from under it. Her deep blue eyes seemed more intense against the scarf, and her hair flowed over it like corn silk.

"Mommy! You look like a movie star!" Katie D. said. Sarah quickly took the scarf off and packed it neatly in the box, folding the tissue paper over the top.

"It's lovely. Thank you," Sarah said.

"Babe, you should wear it," Teddy said.

"Here, give your mother her gift," Sarah said, shoving a package at him.

Teddy handed Lang a particularly lovely vase. The tall silver cone had a filigreed pattern and was discolored a little. Lang thought it might be real silver.

"This is gorgeous! Where did you get this?"

Teddy looked pleased. "World's Longest Yard sale. Seven

states and almost 700 miles. Remember? You turned me onto it when I was like six," he said, grinning. "This one lady had three tables full of junk, but I knew it was worth stopping. Could tell by the wooden spool chairs and the suit of armor that she had good stuff."

"Of course I remember." Lang turned to Sarah. "I gave him a five-dollar bill, and we came home with a zip lock bag of battered matchbox cars. He could recite the make and model of every single one."

Lang was touched he'd put so much thought into her gift, then realized she hadn't been the only one planning ahead.

Sarah excused herself as soon as Katie D. presented her with a small box, beautifully wrapped with brown paper and a sprig of boxwood tucked in the red velvet ribbon.

"Where are you going? You need to watch me open my gifts!" Lang said.

"No, go ahead. I'll be right back. I insist," Sarah said, going who knows where for who knows what.

Lang carefully unwrapped the coffee mug and stared at the picture of Jack and Katie D. on the cup, each squinting in the sun. Lang remembered Teddy taking the photograph when he'd come to pick up Katie D. from the lake last summer. Jack and Katie D. were at the end of the dock, their faces squeezed together like Siamese twins joined at their temples. Katie D. had lost her front tooth, and there was a dark gap in the middle of her perfect row of baby teeth.

"And my mommy wrapped it real nice. See? The wrapper is a grocery bag inside out, and she saved the ribbon from last Christmas," Katie D. said.

"Mom? Are you okay? I thought we should wait, find you something else this year, but Katie D. insisted," Teddy said.

"I planned it. Me and Daddy," Katie D. said.

Lang gazed at Jack and Katie D., their dark almond-shaped

eyes mirroring each other. She rested the tip of her finger on the mug, tracing the side of Jack's face.

"I love it," she said, wondering how she'd never noticed how much they looked alike.

FOURTEEN

....

O h my gosh, don't even think of baking a cake," A. J. told her when Lang said she was surprising Sarah and Katie D. with a homemade cake for Christmas. "They have the best caramel cake in the world at Café on the Corner. Oh, I'm quenching one just thinking about it. So. You could never make anything that good yourself. No offense. Not just you. No one—" A. J. stammered. "I had to throw out my good Le Creuset pan when I tried to make caramel icing. Turned to cement, and I'm not kidding. The whole thing was like a concrete piling. So."

"You have to keep stirring. Constantly. Don't worry about me. I can bake one with my eyes closed," Lang said. "What about you? What are you doing for Christmas?"

"Oh, entertaining to the hilt. Walker's family. Which means all the fine china and real silver and gold-rimmed glasses that don't go in the dishwasher. And I think Brandon's even coming home this year. Our son hasn't been home in years. I've ordered most of the food, but I'm making the turkey myself. I just took a cooking class on game birds," A. J. said proudly.

"Well, it sounds lovely! I'm sure they'll enjoy it."

"They won't. Bunch of snots. Sometimes I just wish they'd come right out and say it, that they think Walker married down. But they're way too well bred for that. So they just cut their eyes across the table at each other when I speak, like I'm too stupid to notice," A. J. said, resting her index finger on her own nose. "Anyway, I ordered the cake already, and you should, too. So."

Lang abhorred the thought of a store-bought cake. She hated it when people tried to pass supermarket pies and deli food off as homemade. Whenever her family came to her house for a holiday, Lang insisted they bring "absolutely nothing," and then she cooked herself into frenzy.

The holidays were all about cooking and decorating and preparing, and now she was at a loss without anything to do. Lang had always done the cooking herself, preferring to make everything from scratch. Two days before the holiday, she diced celery, baked corn bread, and sautéed onions for the dressing. The boiled custard took an entire afternoon of stirring over the stove, but she couldn't imagine the holiday without it. She mashed the boiled sweet potatoes with butter, eggs, and brown sugar and topped them with mini marshmallows, running them under the broiler at the last minute. Actually, that was Katie D.'s job, and she took it very seriously, making sure all the little marshmallows were standing upright on their ends and toasted to the perfect light brown, so swollen they looked like they would burst.

She would bake for Christmas, even if she didn't host. That would right her. Give her a familiar purpose.

She opened up her recipe box to Fancy's caramel cake and jotted down butter, brown sugar, vanilla, and eggs, then crumpled up the grocery list and called the café. The whole thing was overwhelming—driving across town to the supermarket, lugging groceries into the house, pulling out the mixer, and boiling the icing. But mainly the thought of running into people she knew in the store seemed too much. She would have to pretend she was managing when they swarmed her and act like the world was still a world without Jack in it. The holiday felt hard enough already. She decided to order the cake.

Lang Eldridge had never bought a cake in her life. She rarely bought a loaf of store-bought bread, preferring to use Fancy's recipe for French bread or whip up some with the sourdough starter she kept in the refrigerator. She wondered what would be next, if she'd be eating Chef Boyardee out of the can by February.

She drove south on I-75 on Christmas morning, a gigantic white box riding shotgun. If Sarah and Katie D. wouldn't come to her, she'd just go to them. She fretted about the caramel cake she'd bought at the restaurant. Of all times for her to buy a store-bought cake. She wasn't even invited! Surely they would want her there. She was family, for god's sake.

Suddenly there was the loud, deep blast of a horn that seemed to come from her backseat. She looked in the rearview mirror and saw the hood of an 18-wheeler so close she couldn't see his front bumper.

She was horrified that she'd been poking, then realized she was going seventy-two miles per hour in the slow lane. He blasted the horn again. And again. Each time the noise was more jolting and crueler. Lang put on her blinker and took the first exit. She pulled off on the shoulder, then pressed down hard on her horn with both hands.

"*What do you want me to do?*" she screamed inside her compact station wagon. "*I'm doing the best I can!*"

The veins in her flexed hands sprawled like thick, exposed earthworms, and she rubbed them to see if they still had feeling.

FIFTEEN

....

T he gigantic oak tree looked out of place on the block of tenement buildings. Its stark branches reached over the apartments like creepy animated fingers, and Lang tried to remember the movie where trees came alive but couldn't. She couldn't seem to recall anything anymore.

Lang checked the address again. She had to be lost. Surely this wasn't where Katie D. lived. Cursive graffiti exploded in vivid colors over the concrete block walls, and thick metal bars covered every window. All the streetlights were out, and she was afraid to get out of the car.

Lang grasped her keys like they were brass knuckles, a jagged edge of metal protruding between every finger. As if she had the strength to throw a punch.

This place is barely even inhabitable, Lang thought as she wound her way around the dark corridor inside. There were mirrors in every corner, and Lang checked them carefully to be sure no sinister thug was lurking where she couldn't see him. She passed some kind of bodily substance splattered at knee level, and she veered toward the other side, where cigarette butts had been ground out on the chair rail.

"Merry Christmas in there!" Lang called at the door as she rapped quickly and looked over her shoulder.

Lang felt the floor vibrate as Katie D. jumped up and down behind the closed door. She doubted it was Sarah leaping with such enthusiasm.

"Sweetie, don't jump so hard," Lang called out anxiously as

she heard lock after lock jangle open. She was afraid the whole building might collapse.

Katie D. wrapped her arms around Lang's legs, and Lang handed Sarah the large white cake box. It was freezing in the apartment, and Lang shoved her hands deep in her pockets. No one offered to take her coat.

"What did you bring us?" Katie asked. "Look! A present!"

Suddenly Lang was glad she could present the smooth white box tied with the shiny red ribbon and plastered with a sticker that said "Put Some South in Your Mouth." She doubted Katie D. would have been as excited over a homemade cake wrapped in foil.

An old woman sat on the couch, her back curved over in a semicircle. Teddy had said Sarah didn't have a single relative!

"This is Billie Crangle, our neighbor across the hall," Sarah said. She shifted the cake box from one hand to the other uneasily. "What a nice surprise."

Lang reached out to grasp Billie's hand, but the old woman stroked the cornflower-blue scarf that seemed to float around her shoulders. *Surely not.* "This is my present. Angora," Billie said. "I got to open it early because my son is coming to get me in a little while. For Christmas."

"Well, it's lovely," Lang said. She tried to spare Sarah the embarrassment of her obvious regifting by admiring the apartment, taking the focus off the elegant cloud of blue she'd painstakingly selected for Sarah.

She shouldn't have come. Sarah was in even more of a twit than usual, self-conscious and apologetic about the apartment. It wasn't as bad on the inside as Lang had expected, judging from the outside. Bless her heart, Sarah had painted the walls a pale gray and the trim a satin white. It was spotlessly clean. Sparse but inviting. An enormous rubber plant stood in the corner by a window, and a colorful, abstract painting hung over the couch.

"That reminds me of Katie D.," Lang said, making out the pale yellow ringlets and deep coal eyes of her granddaughter in the painting. "Where did you get it?"

"Oh, gosh, I did that. It's nothing, really," Sarah said. But she looked pleased. And Lang thought how much prettier she looked when she smiled.

"I love it!" Lang said. "I love it more than any piece of art I've ever seen."

Lang was impressed Sarah had gone to the trouble to arrange baby's breath, pink miniature carnations, and tropical lilies on the dining room table. But the heavy, sweet smell of rot from the lilies was so overpowering Lang could hardly enjoy her turkey. Not that she could have enjoyed the overly processed meal from the Piggly Wiggly. She should have insisted they come to her house.

They managed to talk about how delicious the dry turkey was and how tasty the industrial stuffing was and how it was hard to buy a good homemade roll. Lang thought that was an oxymoron, buying a "homemade" roll, but she didn't say it out loud. Or at least she hoped she didn't. She could barely remember anything anymore.

Lang didn't fault Sarah for not baking homemade bread, but a turkey from the supermarket? Anyone could stick a turkey in the oven and let it bake for a morning. Lang reached her index finger under the cuff of her sweater and flicked the rubber band.

"Did you get enough to eat, Billie?" Sarah asked.

Billie had made a mess of the food on her plate. Gummed turkey dribbled out of the sides of her mouth, and she methodically mashed the canned cranberry sauce into red pools that oozed through the pale conglomerate of turkey.

"I love you," Billie said softly. Sarah reached over and

squeezed her hand.

She seems to relate perfectly normally to Billie, Lang thought.

"What have you heard from Teddy? Has he had any practice matches?" Lang asked.

Sarah looked at her like she'd spoken in tongues. Or told the truth about the turkey.

"He's good," Sarah said feebly.

"He's at a tournament, right?" Lang asked, suddenly wondering if she'd misunderstood.

"Yes, yes. He's getting ready. Getting used to the courts. He's doing great," Sarah said with obvious relief as she began to clear the table.

Clearly, Teddy was not at any tournament.

"I'll serve the cake," Lang said as she assigned herself a station in the narrow little kitchen.

"Can we have those little nuts? Since it's Christmas? They're in the oven, Grandie," Katie D. called.

"No!" Sarah said sharply. "I'll get them."

Lang opened the oven door, expecting perfectly crisped pecans. But two boxes of cereal, a bag of rice, two cans of tomatoes, a can of tuna, and a package of crackers were lined up neatly on the racks.

"It's broken," Sarah said. Her face flushed a hot bright pink. "The landlord promised to fix it. He will."

"Oh. Well. Goodness. You know you can use my oven any time," Lang said. "I have no room to talk. I didn't even bake this cake. I bought it, and I even have an oven that works."

"Oh, thanks. I'm an expert with the microwave," Sarah said, quickly closing the oven door and spilling the jar of nuts all over the counter.

"Grandie, can you stay? You can sleep with me in my bed. Please?"

The idea of curling up on Christmas night with her granddaughter and drifting into a deep, contented sleep sounded wonderful. She could sleep in her clothes if she had to; she couldn't sleep any worse than she did at home. And she didn't want to be alone tonight, on Christmas.

"Oh, honey, Grandie can't spend the night! She doesn't have her things," Sarah said quickly.

"No, sweetie, I need to get home," Lang said, relieved she hadn't already burst out with a grateful acceptance. "Maybe another time. I could have a rain check?"

"We have to wait till it rains?" Katie D. asked. "We can't spend the night with you till it rains?"

"No, but we'll have to invite Grandie another night. When she can pack her overnight things," Sarah said.

"But if it rains, we'll all spend the night together," Lang forced herself to chirp.

"My son will be here any minute," Billie said. Lang wondered how many years the poor old woman had been saying that. White cake crumbs littered the October blue scarf she had chosen so carefully for Sarah, and Lang watched the icing drip in soft tan rivulets onto its folds.

SIXTEEN

···

L ang sailed down the interstate in the dark. For a split second, there were no headlights on the other side of the freeway. Only darkness. It was eerie, and she had a sudden uneasy feeling that she was the last person on earth.

A second later, cars were coming south, and she wondered about them. Why were they on the interstate on Christmas night? Why weren't they safe at home with their families? Was there an emergency? Did they have a fight and storm out of the family gathering? Were they driving because they didn't have a place to be?

She flashed her bright lights at a car in some kind of greeting, but there was no flicker of response.

She worried about the little dog—not that he was cold or afraid, but that he was scratching frantically at the thick Dutch door that Jack had repainted last summer or digging up the jonquils she and Jack had planted before Thanksgiving. Or that Jack had planted rather. Exhausted after a few minutes of bending over and placing the bulbs in the holes he'd dug, Lang had sat on the bench and instructed him on how many bulbs to put in each hole.

"Not in a row," she'd warned him in the same tone Fancy had chastised her for once planting twelve bulbs in a perfect line. Evenly spaced.

Every year they planted hundreds on the hill leading down to the road. Fancy had begun this decades ago, showing Lang how to dig the hole and set a cluster of bulbs in it, tip up, then dig the next hole close by, making them look like they were naturally propagated. They planted each year's batch in clumps, so that the gigantic, bright yellow King Edwards were all together, the small, white narcissus were together, and the coral bright eyes were in their own section. In the early spring, the entire hill burst with yellows and whites and oranges and salmons—the only color against the dark somber tree trunks, not a sprig of green in sight yet.

Her yard looked like an advertisement for Holland. Many times over the years, Lang had found handwritten notes in the mailbox, thanking her for "making my spring" and "creating a masterpiece" and "putting a bright, happy spot in the world." Lang saved those notes, wishing her grandmother could have read them.

If that dog dug up the last jonquils Jack had ever planted, she'd kill him.

Lang rolled her window down for a jolt of cold air. Had the temperature dropped that fast? She looked at the temp on the dashboard. Twenty-three degrees. Lang wondered how cold it had to be before the newscasters advised people not to leave their animals outside. Not that she officially owned an animal. Still, there was something appealing about the little dog, the way he bowed his head to her and wriggled all over like he couldn't contain himself in her presence. Even if she couldn't keep him, she certainly didn't want him freezing to death.

Lang pulled in her driveway and looked for signs of destruction: chewed bits of newspaper confetti or mounds of freshly dug earth. But everything seemed untouched. She wondered if maybe the dog had wandered off. Maybe he finally found someone who would let him be part of their family.

Then she spotted the familiar little shape at the edge of her porch, pale against the dark stone steps, waiting for her to come home.

SEVENTEEN

·······································

L ang let the dog follow her inside. Desperate for some sign of activity, she turned on every light in her tiny house, even in the linen closet and the powder room. But the contrast of a warm, glowing house only highlighted her loneliness, and she quickly switched off all the superfluous lights.

"Ha," Lang said out loud. The joke was on her. She'd made sure poor Jack would get through this first Christmas alone. There was a vat of conch chowder in the freezer and a letter from her. But here *she* sat, the most lonesome miracle ever.

It was dark outside, but too early for bed. Lang quickly opened the can of condensed milk and ran her finger over the tin lid. The sweet richness of one finger's worth wasn't enough, and she dipped a tablespoon into the can and ate spoonful after spoonful. She didn't think about the size of her rear end until she felt sick.

She picked up *Atlas Shrugged* and tried to read, but couldn't make sense of a single sentence. She suddenly realized the dog was missing, and she called for him generically. "Here, boy! Come!"

She worried he was chewing up something valuable or peeing on her oriental rugs. She walked through the house calling for the animal. Nothing. She walked back through again, checking in closets. When she opened the linen closet door, he pranced out like they had rehearsed this whole scenario and performed it perfectly. She stared at him, puzzling over why he would sit in the dark closet, mute. But he just nodded his head up at her quickly, in triumph.

Lang wadded up some newspapers and put them in the fireplace. She piled the logs from Jack's woodbin over the paper. The wood was so dry it was practically weightless. Jack had managed the firewood, splitting it every summer, and then carefully stacking it in certain sections according to how green it was. By the time he carried it into the house, it would practically ignite if a stray cigarette ash were nearby.

When did he assume I would be dead by Christmas—at the latest?

Lang lit a crumpled edge of newspaper, and it erupted into a frenzied burst of flames. Black charred remnants floated out into the room, and she thought about calling the fire department. At least that would be a diversion from sitting all alone on Christmas night. But the fire settled down to an easy burn after the paper had vaporized, and she sat down on the couch with the letter she'd written for Jack to open the first Christmas after she died.

> *Dear Jack,*
>
> *I'm not sure how long you've been without me now, but I hope about eight months because I wanted to have my funeral in the spring.*
>
> *Not just because of the flowers, although blazing yellow forsythia and royal purple iris would have been gorgeous in the church. No, I think spring would have been a good time for you to begin without me. The whole world starting anew along with you.*
>
> *I get ahead of myself. I always do in the dead of winter. I start forcing the branches as soon as they swell the slightest bit and watch them until our whole house erupts in blossoms. So hopeful and optimistic.*
>
> *Anyway, I'm sorry to be gone at Christmas.*
>
> *Now, in the bottom of the freezer there is a red Tupperware bowl. Put it in the sink first thing in the morning and let*

it sit all day in cool water. Dump it in a saucepan (in the drawer by the stove—ha-ha), cover it with a lid, and turn the eye on low. Stir every fifteen minutes or so. It is the conch chowder from the South Beach Grill in St. Augustine. Remember the first time Teddy saw the beach? I know we've been asking for the recipe for years, but I played my cancer card. Told the chef it was for your first Christmas without me in forty-two years.

I hope you live a long, long time and enjoy every minute you have left. Do that for me. Please.

Love,

Lang

What had she been thinking, assuming he would even read her letter on Christmas morning? She wondered if he'd already made plans without her for Christmas.

"What are you doing? No! Down!" she yelled at the dog. She hadn't noticed him crawl up on the back of the couch, just behind her shoulder, and she was startled to feel his dry, raspy tongue, quick on the side of her cheek.

She put her hands to her face and felt a wetness on her palms. She looked at her fingers, dripping like they'd been submerged in water.

How could Jack have deceived her? She couldn't even grieve him properly, switching from desolation to fury.

She wadded up the letter into a tight, airless ball and tossed it into the flames.

EIGHTEEN

....

L ang squinted at the caller ID when the phone rang. Where were her reading glasses? She did not want to talk to anyone, especially the bank. They called incessantly, even over the holiday. She answered when she finally made out Teddy's name.

"Hey, Mom," Teddy said. "How's it going?"

"You're back!" she said. She didn't know how uneasy she'd been about him being gone until she heard his voice on the phone.

"I'mmmm baaaack," he said, dragging out the words like a movie Lang knew she was supposed to remember but couldn't.

"How was the tournament?" she asked. "Teddy?"

"Fabulous! All the way around. Great tournament. Everything's looking good on that end. Great fans. So loyal!"

"I spent Christmas with Sarah and Katie D.," Lang said. "We missed you."

"Oh. I missed all of you. Lonely little Christmas for me," Teddy said.

"Teddy, I don't know about playing in tournaments over the holidays, especially over Christmas. Katie D. is so young still, and these things, memories of her father particularly, are so important," Lang said. Her words tumbled out in a rush.

"Teddy? Are you there? Hello?"

"Okay, Mom," he said. "Well, anyway, I'm on my way over to enjoy one of your frozen casseroles."

"You need to take them! Can we do it next week instead? I'm not sure I'm really up for it at the moment," she said.

Making Arrangements

Lang hated to miss his visit, but the idea of food, especially a conglomerate of cream of mushroom soup and poultry bits, made her nauseous. She'd been heating the depressingly small foil pans up according to their directions, then choking down a few bites before scraping the leftovers into the cracked cereal bowl for the little dog.

Lang didn't realize it was dark until she heard the knock at the door. Had she been sleeping again?

Teddy walked in carrying bulging cellophane bags, and she was engulfed with the rich aroma of hickory-smoked barbecue. He popped the plastic lids off Styrofoam containers of coleslaw and potato salad and set them all on the little breakfast table.

"Carolina sweet sauce," he said, setting the little cup of thick sauce down with a flourish. "Your personal favorite."

Lang served a tiny amount of barbecue on her plate, trying to be dainty in front of Teddy. But she added another helping before she even tasted it. The smell of smoked pork made her salivate. The pulled pork was succulent and moist and practically melted in her mouth. It didn't need sauce, but she added a tiny bit since Teddy had remembered she liked it.

"Um-hum," Lang said, wiping at her full mouth with the back of her hand. She didn't want to stain the linen napkin. "Delicious. I didn't know I wanted this." She plopped spoonful after spoonful of succulent pork and sweet-and-sour slaw and creamy potato salad with bits of celery on her plate. She didn't remember food ever tasting so good. She hoped he would leave the leftovers.

"Hard to beat southern barbecue," Teddy said. "So, I was going to go on and pick up everything you have here on Dad's estate. All the financial statements. Dad's will. Any other insurance policies you know about. I don't want you to have to worry about any of it. I'm going to let you sign me over as your power of attorney, and I'll handle everything." He stacked five sections of papers on the counter, each clipped with a black metal hinge. The hinges were staggered, so they lined up in a perfect row. Lang reached for one of the clips like a raccoon reaching for a shiny object.

"Mom!" he said sharply. "Don't mix those up."

She released the tension on the clip and thought about relinquishing all the worry about making the mortgage payments. Or the second mortgage payment, or whatever it was. She felt her shoulders lighten at the idea of someone taking care of everything. Getting everything squared away with the bank. Taking care of her.

"I'll get everything all together for you, but I hate to make you worry about it," Lang said.

"It's time, Mom. I talked to Hank, and it looks like Dad made a few bad calls investment wise, but it's going to work out. You just need to revoke the trust the land is in, and we can develop this property easily. You don't need the upkeep anymore. Dad already had the plan in the works, apparently. We'll keep part of the house intact, the fireplace and mantel for sure, maybe even the staircase, and build a clubhouse around it. People will flock to see it because it's historical. I'll put in tennis courts on the back side and build a few little cottages in front. Maybe a spa down in the woods with a path. It will be a world-class tennis retreat, but with charm," Teddy said.

"What do you mean, part of the house intact?" Lang asked. She pictured the magnolia tree chopped down to make room for a tennis court and the hill bulldozed out to make room for a swimming pool and felt a sudden hardness in her stomach, like icicles were piercing her bowels. She stood up quickly, then collapsed on the kitchen floor.

"Mommy, Mommy," Teddy said. He held her head in the crook of his arm, gently bouncing it like you would a fretting baby, which made her feel even more nauseous. She rolled to her side and clutched at her stomach.

"It's okay. Too much rich food," she managed to say as she slowly stood up. "I ate too much."

"You ate a lot, but that's nothing new. Sorry. I didn't mean it like that. I ate much more than you. I just mean—I don't know. Should you call the oncologist? Isn't that what happened before? The fainting?" Teddy held both of her hands and patted them nervously.

"No, it's fine. I'm just sensitive to food now or something," she said, wishing she hadn't eaten in front of him.

"You don't think it's back, do you? What about that trial they wanted to put you in? They said you have to have someone, a support person living with you, right?"

Lang was afraid if she burped she'd vomit. She sat quietly, breathing like she'd learned to do during the chemo treatments, releasing the nausea with her breath.

"I just ate too fast," Lang said.

"I could do it. I could move in. Take care of you during the trial," Teddy said.

"Oh, Teddy. My sweet boy." She clasped his hand in both of hers. "You'd do that for me?"

"Of course I would!" Teddy said. "Of course I would."

Teddy steadied her as they slowly walked to the sofa. He propped up her legs with the pillows and covered her with the afghan before gently folding Fancy's quilt into a rectangle and placing it under her head.

"There. We can find you a place to live. Somewhere easy. No maintenance," he said.

Lang felt her stomach roil.

"Are you okay?" he asked.

"No. I'm so sorry," Lang said, clutching her throat. She felt the bitter surge of bile explode in her throat, and she gagged, vomiting all over the afghan.

"Oh no! No! Wait! Mom! You need to get to the bathroom. Hold on!" he shouted, practically dragging her down the hall as she franticly cupped her hands over her mouth.

"I'm so sorry," she whispered.

"It's okay," he said tersely. "I'm going to step out. I'm sorry. Do you want me to clean that up?"

"No, I'll do it later. You go. Go on. I'm sorry," she said.

"Okay. Sorry. I just need to get some air, Mom. I don't feel good all of a sudden. I'll call you later," he said.

Lang managed to get herself in the shower before collapsing into bed.

The next morning she found a note in the kitchen from Teddy. *I cleaned everything up. I think I'm sick. Can you bring me chicken soup when you get up? Hope you're better.*

There were traces of vomit on the heart pine floors, and the soiled afghan lay in a heap on top of the washing machine. So much for Teddy taking care of her.

NINETEEN

....

L ang centered her hips square against the edge of the bed and slowly pulled the sheets, careful not to twist or jerk her arms or otherwise hurt her incision or strain her back. It was time to change them. Past time.

She held Jack's pillowcase to her face and inhaled. How could he have assumed she was going to die? Banked on it, actually.

She left the pile of linens in a heap on the bed and looked through the refrigerator for the condensed milk. She scraped up the few remaining spoonfuls and let the sweetness dissolve over her tongue.

He was a good man. He loved me. He just didn't want to worry me.

She threw the empty can in the trash, then stuffed his pillow back into his unwashed pillowcase. She needed the smell of him to sleep.

"Mom? Are you okay? I'm fine, so don't worry about bringing soup. Can I bring Katie D. over, though? I've got a big meeting, and Sarah's at work. We'll be there within the hour. And I've got a surveyor coming next week. They need to verify the property lines just in case you decide to sell. Don't worry. You don't need to be there or anything," Teddy said on the phone.

Lang sat down at the kitchen table and waited for her granddaughter. She flipped through the dog-eared pages of *Monster Dirt Movers.* There was a gardening magazine on the counter, but she didn't have the energy to hoist herself up and walk across the room. She thought about the vitamins Jack had researched and wondered if he'd googled "herbs to kill a wife." *Stop it.*

Teddy honked just in time; she was going crazy. She needed to pull herself together and stop imagining things.

Katie D. yelled, "Here, Victoria!" to the little dog, who sat demurely at the child's feet. The dog looked at Lang, then bounded straight up to Katie D. as if there was a spring mechanism embedded in his hind parts.

"Victoria?" Lang asked.

"That's her name. She already knows it. See," Katie D. said as Victoria tossed his head up at Lang.

Lang did not have the heart to mention to Katie D. that not only was the dog a male, but he was not staying.

"Ooooh, she's so nice and fluffy. I am Blue Bunny. How do you do?" Katie D. said in a high-pitched English accent, holding her bunny's stubby leg toward the dog. The little dog stood up on his hind legs and seemed to grin at Katie D.

Lang *did* think he looked more appealing after the bath A. J. had given him. The dog's pale champagne fur felt like soft down now, like a fluffy baby chick. It should be easy enough to find a home for him.

"Good girl!" Katie D. said, popping a Red Hot into the dog's mouth.

"No! Katie D., dogs don't eat candy. Especially cinnamon candy," Lang said. "It'll make him sick."

The little dog swallowed the Red Hot and balanced on his hind legs, staring expectantly at Katie D.

"Sorry, girl," Katie D. said, looking crestfallen. "Can we take her on a walk?"

"You, madam, need a nap, and afterward we'll talk about a walk," Lang said, although she could barely make it to the mailbox without resting.

"Where's the pretty collar? The pink sparkly one?" Katie D. asked.

"I know where it is. Nap first. Pink collar later," Lang said.

"Come on, girl. Let's get in the bed," Katie D. said to the dog.

"No. No dogs in the house," Lang said, bodily barring the doorway.

Suddenly and uncharacteristically, Katie D. sat down in a heap on the floor, still wearing her fuchsia backpack, and began to sob. Lang noticed the mottled purple smudges under Katie D.'s eyes and realized the child was exhausted.

"What time did you go to bed last night?" Lang asked her.

"Daddy let me stay up late because Mommy had to work. I watched movies in my room. Not the elephant movie. He had company," Katie D. said.

Lang sat still, wondering what company Katie D. was talking about.

"What elephant movie?" Lang asked. *What company? What was it Katie D. said about the tattooed babysitter who worked at the burrito place?*

"About the mommy who was a lady and the baby elephant who thought she was his own mommy. We went on Christmas. Mommy and me."

"This Christmas?" Lang said.

"We wore our coats buttoned all up and watched all the window cartoons in the night," Katie D. said. "And then we had chili and ginormous marshmallows. Mommy says they're magic."

"What are window cartoons?" Lang asked, trying to figure out what they had done on Christmas after she'd left. Surely not. Had they spent Christmas day wandering around downtown, peeping in the illuminated storefront windows at little animated holiday scenes? And how had Sarah made chili? She had no stove. Suddenly she knew: they'd eaten chili from a can and watched marshmallows quadruple in size in the microwave.

"Well, I guess the little dog can sleep with you today. Just this one time," Lang said.

Upstairs, she stroked Katie D.'s hair until the child's breathing slowed and her face slackened and sleep shuddered over her. The dog watched Lang warily from his chokehold in Katie D.'s arms. Lang reached down to pick up the dog and put it outside, but Katie D. moaned and tightened her grip.

While Katie D. and the dog slept, Lang ironed. It was the only part of tending house she liked at all. Jack loved that about her. He tended to be neat and well kept, always checking himself in the mirror before and after eating. He was the type to immediately squirt Spray 'n Wash on a spot of spaghetti sauce and pour salt on a red wine stain.

They were different in this way. Lang had an affinity for Jack's too-stained-to-wear-cast-off-T-shirts, and she was so dismayed whenever she checked herself in the mirror, she simply avoided her reflection.

But ironing relaxed her somehow. She ironed in the basement, where the laundry had been done since the 1920s. She kept the ironing board near the high basement windows over the deep mop sink. There was no view out of the window, but the light streamed in during the afternoon, bathing her in sunlight. In winter, she craved this spot like a tonic.

Lang ironed her dead husband's clothes. She knew it was unbalanced. She knew at some point she would be giving them away. But it comforted her to spread his blue oxford-cloth shirt out on the ironing board and spray it with just the right amount of starch, and press the cloth methodically with the hissing steam iron.

Jack knew how much she loved this house. He promised he

would never sell it, ever. Even if she died . . .

She sniffed in the scorched smell of cotton and saw the dark shape of the iron burned on his sleeve. She rubbed her fingers over his raised initials on the cuff—JKE. They were still warm.

Lang rubbed the frayed cuff of Jack's sweatshirt to her cheek, then folded it neatly and stacked it with the clean laundry. She quietly opened the drawers in her room so she wouldn't wake up Katie D., then lay down on Jack's side of the bed.

Singing woke her, and at first, Lang thought Katie was in the room with her.

"There is a color we all know. Color of a hen and color of his pen? B-r-o-w-n."

Lang tiptoed into Katie D's bedroom. Her granddaughter was still curled up nose to nose with the dog, singing a little nursery song to him. The sheets under their mouths were stained a watery pink, and a few stray Red Hots littered the white pillowcase.

It wasn't until Lang pulled Katie D.'s sheets off the mattress the next day that she noticed the blue rabbit lying forgotten at the foot of the bed.

TWENTY

....

L ang was startled out of sleep by A. J. walking into her bedroom with the little dog. Had she even knocked?

"Hey, Lang," A. J. said. "Sorry to barge in, but the door was open. I saw Emmeline Harrison at the grocery store, and she didn't even call me by name. 'So good to see you,' she said like she says to everyone in that fake voice. Have you mentioned me to her yet?"

"Hello," Lang said. She knew her breath must be horrendous and pulled the sheet over her mouth. "About the women's club?"

"No. About the CIA position. Yes, about the women's club!"

"No. I haven't seen her," Lang said. The club was the last thing on her mind.

"We have a deal, you know," A. J. said. "The furniture I bought?"

"I know." The furniture A. J. bought, or at least the money she bought it with, was actually the first thing on her mind. It was almost gone, and she had a payment due in a week. The little flower arrangements were selling, strangely enough, but they weren't nearly enough. And she worried if something were to happen to the greenery in her yard. A drought? A freeze? A tornado?

Clutching the little dog under her arm, A. J. leaned down and carefully took off her scarlet leather high heels, placing them neatly side-by-side. The mattress didn't even give as A. J. sat on it.

She must weigh nothing, Lang thought as A. J. lay back on the pillow sham in a fitted black wool pencil skirt with a slight flare at the hem.

"I'm sorry. Can I get you anything? Is this a bad time for me to drop by? I'm a little abstracted. You probably noticed. Walker had to go out of town again, and I need to get in touch with him about which cocktail party he wants to accept, and the RSVP deadline is today, and he's nowhere to be found," she said.

Then she got out of the bed to Lang's infinite relief. Lang wondered if she should have told her the word she wanted was *distracted.*

"Anyhoooo," A. J. said, now clutching the little dog. "I just need to close my eyes for a minute. I've got painters all over my house. And that's another thing. I really want Walker to see the color before they go on. By no means am I an interial decorator, but it looks a little too pinky to me."

A. J. swaddled the dog against her scarlet angora sweater and climbed in the bed

again. The animal tossed his head up at Lang in a quick nod of acknowledgment.

"Wassup," A. J. said the second time he did it, tossing her own head back in response.

"I'm just going to lay here for one minute. So," A. J. said, lying down on top of the covers.

Lie! Lang pondered the woman she didn't know well at all, stretched out on her former side of the bed. Was this normal behavior? She wondered if the rest of their foursome did this after their club salads.

"I don't want the dog inside," Lang said. "Much less in the bed."

"Shhhh," A. J. said, her eyes already closed. "I've got him tucked in my sweater. He's not touching anything."

The dog's spine curled against A. J.'s chest, and he watched

Lang warily.

"Down!" Lang said sharply, and the dog immediately leaped off the bed.

"Lang! He's not doing anything! I don't know why he chose you in the first place, the way you act."

"A. J., you find that dog a home! Katie D. is getting way too attached, and that's the least of it. She named him already. Victoria."

"Victoria?" A. J. burst out laughing when Lang nodded her head. "That's too funny. I hope you never tell her that little dog is not no female."

The dog sat primly on the worn Oriental rug, gazing at the linen dust ruffle, until A. J. sat up and patted her side of the bed. "Come! I'll tuck him inside my sweater. He won't feel of a thing."

Lang didn't think the dog could jump that high, or she would have protested immediately. The box spring was extra tall so the bed would be in proportion with the ten-foot ceiling.

The animal took a small step, then sprang straight up in the air like a gymnast leaping up for the parallel bars. But just as his hind feet touched the bed he recoiled with a shrill yelp. That was the first sound she'd ever heard him make. The dog curled into a ball in the corner and licked at his hind foot. She could tell the skin was not broken, but she worried that his leg was. She glared at A. J.

"Oh, good luck finding him a home now!" Lang said.

A. J. picked him up carefully and set him at the foot of the bed. He curled up into himself, but stretched his face toward Lang and nuzzled the air as she peered down at him.

A. J. reached over to check his hurt foot, but he jerked it away quickly. "You need to take him to the vet. I'll pay. I think he's hurt real bad." She looked at Lang with a slightly shocked look on her face. "You know the vet's a widow. Widower. His wife got killed in a car wreck. He's pretty cute."

Who is this woman?

"No. I'm not taking him to the damned vet. If I take him anywhere it's to the pound. You said you'd find a home for him, so you need to take him!" Lang said, desperately trying to motivate A. J. to find a good home for the dog. Katie D. wasn't the only one getting attached.

"Well, for your information, I already found him a home. I was just giving you one more chance because you can't see the forest for the trees. In any area apparently. This dog is the best thing for you! But I'll have his new owner pick him up from the vet. There we go," A. J. said gently as she scooped him up. "So."

"I would keep him if I could, but I'm in no position," Lang said softly.

"What?" A. J. asked.

"Nothing."

It wasn't until A. J. left in a huff with the dog that Lang noticed a tightness in her hands. She held them up—two tight balls. When she spread her fingers she could see indentions in her palms. Four sets of tiny parentheses.

TWENTY-ONE

....

She'd been thinking about today for weeks. Jack's sixty-fifth birthday. She'd thought he would have been here alone, trying to fill his long, sad day. But she was the one here alone, even more lonely without the little dog.

Had he made plans on his own, assuming—maybe not despondently—that I'd be dead?

She turned on the computer to check his e-mail for clues, but forgot about it as soon as she read Sarah's e-mail.

> *The museum called and wants to talk to you about doing the flowers for the March gala. Board decided at the last minute to support local, and they've heard good things! HUGE job. I told them you would contact them directly. 267-2334.*
> *Congratulations!*

Lang wondered why Sarah hadn't just picked up the phone and called her. Was she that difficult to talk to?

Lang called Sarah's cell. Twice. She felt irritation, again, that they didn't have a landline and immediately flicked her rubber band. She left a voice mail the second time, thanking Sarah profusely but declining the order. "That's way out of my league. I've seen pictures in the paper, and it's a world-class event. I think they have the flowers shipped in from South America! And I've never even ordered flowers locally!"

She wondered what Jack would have thought about her little flower business.

He would have thought it was silly, *a drop in the bucket,* and dismissed it as a hobby the way he had the cake baking business she had considered when they were first married.

Was Jack in cahoots with Hank even before I got sick this second time? Was it convenient for him when I was diagnosed?

She quickly turned the computer off and tried to turn off her crazy, racing brain. She held his birthday letter in her hand and thought about Jack making breakfast in bed for her birthday. French toast with powdered sugar sprinkled on top. Maple syrup in the little white pitcher. For forty-two years she'd never told him she didn't like eating slumped up on pillows in her nightgown while he watched every bite she took—and probably judged how much she ate.

> *Dear Jack,*
>
> *Happy Birthday!!! I was blessed to be able to celebrate forty-two of them with you. I LOVED your birthday! Baking the cake, beating the egg whites, and boiling sugar and butter.*
>
> *I loved choosing a shirt or tie or jacket for you. I never allowed you to wear any color except that certain shade of red, and you are not allowed to start wearing tan or gray just because I am gone. It should be illegal for someone with eyes the color of melted dark chocolate to wear anything except deep carmine, the red of rare rubies. Or a ripe persimmon, but not too orange.*
>
> *Your present is in my closet. Top shelf by the stack of baskets. Wear it. Don't save it.*
>
> *Then look in the freezer in the basement. Right side. Very back. Aluminum foil. You are not surprised I know. If you had to celebrate your birthday without me, the least I could do was leave you a cake. It's caramel. Five layer. Your favorite.*
>
> *I love you.*

Lang took Jack's birthday cake out of the freezer and put it on the crystal cake stand. The icing was spread smooth, evenly lapped around the sides. She admired the cake and thought of

Jack clapping his hands like a child every time she presented him with her homemade caramel cake.

She held the cake over the trashcan and pushed the side of the cake with her hand. It didn't move, and she shoved it again. She didn't know if she'd gotten that weak or if the cake had hardened to the cake stand. She looked at her sticky palm. Flecks of the sugary crust sparkled on the inside of her hand like shattered glass.

"I have a caramel cake. Homemade," she said to A. J. on the phone less than a minute later.

"Don't cut it till I get there," A. J. said.

Lang had just sliced two large wedges when she heard the doorknocker. She saw Sarah standing at the door and motioned her in.

"Come on in! It's open!" she called. Sarah opened the door a crack but didn't cross the threshold.

"I'm so sorry to bother you, but Katie D.'s bunny? She can't sleep without it. Is it okay if I just grab it?"

"It's in my room on the bed. Go on in there," Lang said, but Sarah stood still, as if suddenly cast in concrete. Even her jaw seemed frozen.

"Well, well! Perfect timing! How did you know there was cake?" A. J. called out enthusiastically from the steps behind Sarah, shooing her inside.

"Come on, you must. I make the best caramel icing in the world," Lang said. "I can't believe I just said that. You all probably won't like it at all, and that would serve me right." She held Sarah by the elbow and steered her into the kitchen. "I just wish I didn't have to sample a vat of it every time I made it."

Sarah stood at the kitchen table until A. J. commanded her to sit, then drew her fork slowly down the cut edge of the cake, watching the thick icing curl over the tines. She held the bite in her mouth, not speaking. "I've never tasted anything so good," she said.

"Oh, it is! You should make these cakes and sell them," A. J. said. She pushed her untouched plate of cake away, but scraped her finger over the cake stand, eating her collected remnants furtively.

Lang laughed, thinking of how amused Jack would be at the very idea.

"What's funny? You should. Bou-Cakes. Cakes and flowers," Sarah said.

"Cake Power," A. J. said. They both looked at her.

"Like Flower-Power but with cakes."

"Oh," Sarah said. "Right."

"I like Bou-Cakes," A. J. said. "Make me one for the silent auction at the museum. Thick icing and go on and make a little name card. A business card with a picture on it. Of a cake. Dripping with thick caramel icing." A. J. ran her finger around the edge of the cake stand and pressed the icing into her mouth like she was forcing herself to eat it.

"No! I'm not even thinking of it! I can't design a card, and I don't know what I'd do if someone actually ordered!" Lang said.

"I'll do it. The card," Sarah said, doodling on a pad.

"All you have to do is bake the cake. Stick a bunch of them in your freezer. So."

"Fine. I'll bake one cake, and no one will buy it, but next Christmas you and Katie D. are coming here," Lang said to Sarah, wagging her dessert fork at her. "I want family all in the same place for the holidays. Family is too much of a blessing not to be together."

"So," A. J. said, looking expectantly at Sarah.

Sarah's face softened as she smiled, and she tucked her head down before stating that she and Katie D. had fond memories of being cold and alone on the streets downtown.

"That didn't come out right," Sarah said, blushing.

"No, I want you both here next year. All three of you," Lang said. "This cake was in the freezer for Jack's birthday. It's today. But usually I bake them fresh."

Sarah scooted her chair back from the table abruptly and stood just as the phone began to ring. "I'm sorry. I need to go. If I could just get the bunny? Thank you."

"Do you need to get that?" A. J. asked on the telephone's fifth ring.

Before Lang got to the phone, a man's voice boomed out over the answering machine.

"This is the third message we've left about the payment. If you don't make a payment by the thirteenth, we will begin foreclosure proceedings."

Sarah stood still in the foyer, and A. J. looked up from the kitchen table. Lang stood frozen by the phone, not picking it up. She didn't want to speak to the man, and she was mortified they had heard the message. She looked at the two women in her house and shrugged her shoulders. "Don't worry," she said weakly. "The Barrington Women's Club has a standing order. One centerpiece every month."

"That's not enough! Have they decided on me yet? Have you heard anything?" A. J. asked.

"What about the museum's flower order? They pay a ton for those arrangements. They know your work," Sarah said.

"For the gala? You haven't called them back yet?" A. J. asked.

"How do you know they even asked me?" Lang asked A. J.

"I'm on the board! I practically run the entire museum! I'm not good enough for the women's club, but the museum thinks I'm all that. But everybody loves your flowers. The way you do them," A. J. said.

Making Arrangements

"You can still do it," Sarah said quickly. "I haven't called them back yet."

"You don't understand. That is entirely too much for me. I can do little bouquets from the garden, but the museum wants drop-dead, over-the-top arrangements that are spectacular. And huge. There's no way I can do that by myself," Lang said.

"Call them now!" A. J. said. "I'll help. Sarah? Sarah?"

"Sure," Sarah said.

"No, those arrangements are like things out of magazines. Professional," Lang said.

"Okay, then start the foreclosure proceedings," A. J. said, throwing up her hands.

"I've got my checkup that week," Lang said weakly, suddenly feeling overwhelmed between the cancer and the foreclosure.

"Well, can you make your appointment later? The week after the gala?" A. J. asked.

Lang took a deep breath in and sent them each home with a hefty slice of cake. She rescheduled her appointment for the week after the gala and made a payment plan to buy back her furniture from A. J.

Lang wiped up the crumbs with the side of her hand and picked up Sarah's quick drawing. An apron-clad angel with dreadlocks and a roman nose and a white apron held an elaborate three-layer cake scalloped with squiggles of icing and adorned with candles. *Bou-Cakes—Flowers and Cakes for Any Occasion* was printed carefully underneath.

Lang felt nauseous and light-headed, but for once didn't think it had anything to do with cancer.

TWENTY-TWO

....

The week before the gala, Lang cleared every surface in the house, from the coffee table to the toilet seat. She lined up every antique dining room chair in a row, making a low table against the living room wall. The chairs were as cumbersome as they were heavy, but she did it. Something she couldn't have dreamed of doing six months ago.

All together, she had about sixty lineal feet of workspace. She emptied her wastebaskets, filled them with lukewarm water, and set them in opened drawers in the island. She checked the weather, relieved it was supposed to be thirty-five degrees with 90 percent humidity—perfect for flowers. The weather was unusual for the season, but that seemed par for the course lately.

The freeze came out of nowhere. The morning of the big event, on the day they were to arrange the flowers, there was a frozen swath across her yard from the wind whipping up from the valley. The lawns on either side of her were brown and textured, but Lang's looked like the frozen wake of some animated ice monster that had flown up over the brow and landed on her porch. Ordinarily she liked being the only one in the neighborhood to feel the crunch of frozen grass under her shoes and have the evergreens weighted down with a light coating of ice that glistened magically in the morning sun, but not today. She had flowers to be delivered and didn't want the deliveryman to slip on the icy sidewalk or refuse to walk over it at all.

She filled the Crock-Pot with bars of paraffin and surveyed the hodgepodge rendition of a florist. What the hell was she thinking?

"You don't need to ring the bell," she said to Sarah as she opened the door.

"Watch me put Edward Scissorhands to shame," A. J. called from the porch, timing her arrival on cue. "Have you got the cake? They're already bidding just based on Sarah's card."

"Yes. It's ready. I don't know about this," Lang said doubtfully.

Sarah and A. J. gasped at the same time. The cake stood in graduated layers, and thick ribbons of icing scalloped each tier. "It's beautiful!" they said in unison.

"It'll have to do. The flowers are late. Bad sign. I'm going to call to check on them," Lang said.

Her face was drained when she finally got off the phone. "They delivered them to the wrong address. Some florist across town. They're bringing them up. This was a bad idea. Flowers are so delicate, and being carted around in the cold is terrible for them."

"Not so fast," A. J. said to the deliveryman when he turned to leave after finally bringing the flowers. "Lang? Come make sure they're okay."

Lang opened the lid and gasped. Peonies hung heavy-headed in bunches, their blossoms littering the water. It was a dark melted slime of a mess.

"I can't use them!" Lang croaked. "What am I going to do? It's too late for the museum to get anyone else to do the flowers!"

The deliveryman looked irritated, then wrote "NO CHARGE" on the ticket and asked Lang to sign. "Sorry 'bout that," he said glibly, and wheeled the containers down the sidewalk.

"Do you know any florists? Maybe if every florist in the city each did a few arrangements using the same flowers they would look enough alike to work," Lang said to the delivery-man's back.

He didn't even turn around.

"What about your yard?" Sarah said.

Lang stared at her. "There aren't any peonies blooming right now! And even if there were, I wouldn't have enough for all the tables!"

"No, I mean like the arrangements you sell at the tennis club. All the greenery and berries. That's what they've seen anyway," Sarah said. "They actually take five of your bouquets each week. They send one of the docents to pick them up."

"She's right. We're not going through all this for seventeen florists to make a little money, and you lose your house after all. C'mon. Tell me what all to clip," A. J. said as she snapped the clippers close to Lang's left ear. "A problem shared is a problem halved. That's a famous quote, and it makes sense to me."

"The freeze. I'm sure everything is ruined," Lang said.

Lang tucked her fists in her sweater sleeves and walked around the yard. The rhododendrons were shriveled against the cold, but the January jasmine was in full bloom on the bank above the road—a shimmery cloud of yellow. She wondered if the deep red camellias would hold their blooms overnight and if the pink japonica would clash or complement. She held a Lenten rose blossom up to them and realized the deep magen-ta smattering of violet in the chartreuse Lenten rose would tie it all together.

She pulled her turtleneck over her nose and inhaled, feeling the warm moisture against her face as she exhaled.

"Okay. We'll need seventy-five or so long branches of this

japonica. Cut it like this," she said, clipping cleanly on the diagonal. "Right above the next set of leaves." Lang glanced over at the bed of Lenten roses, half expecting to see the little dog. She hoped A. J. had vetted the new owner thoroughly. "Does Victoria like his new home?"

"He will. He's not there yet. He's still at the vet's. New owner's out of town or something but should be back soon," A. J. said.

"Who is it?" Lang asked.

"Friend of a friend. I don't believe I've never met them myself, but know the name," A. J. said.

"What leaves?" A. J. asked.

"Here. The little nubs," Lang said. "Try not to snip them. And lots of magnolia."

"Nublets," A. J. said. "Look! Who's this?" A. J. traced her manicured fingernail over the initials carved in the trunk of the ancient magnolia tree. "L. M. + A. D."

"I think those are my parents. From a long time ago."

Fancy had told Lang they were tacky and threatened to cut down the tree. She would have, too, if it hadn't anchored the whole garden and been legendary in the town. Lang squinted up at the branches, making out the initials the troops had made during the Civil War—she'd climbed up to them as a girl, imagining B. K. pining away for D. R. and wondering if they'd married after the war.

"Here, strip the bottom ten inches, then put them immediately in the water. We'll have to take them inside every half hour because we can't have the water getting too cold," Lang said as she wrapped her hand around a branch and slid it forcefully down the length. She'd spent hours tracing the dark burled edges of her parents' initials as a child, imagining her father carving them into the sapling.

They watched her mutely until Lang handed Sarah a pair of

clippers and said they had a time frame.

"Ouch! It stuck me!" A. J. shrieked when she reached down to the base of the japonica.

"Wear your gloves! That's what they're for!" Lang snapped. She hated to sound so irritated, but they got her into this mess, and it was going to be disastrous enough even if they met the deadline.

"Now I'm going to have to glad-hand everyone tonight with this scratch across my fingers!" A. J. said.

"You're going to the gala?" Sarah asked.

"Honey, I'm *running* the damn gala. I'm chairwoman! I've been choosing art for the auction all year long. Of course, I have a committee. I'm no artist by no means. But yes, I'm going," A. J. said. "So."

"Sarah paints. You should look at her work for next year," Lang said.

"Oh, no. I have no real training," Sarah said.

"Honey, I don't know a Picasso from a Leonardo. But the things I pick sell. More than the ones the official art committee picks. Everybody knows it. So let me see your work. If your paintings are anything like that little doodle you did for Bou-Cakes, you're going to be rich. Ouch! I did it a again! Look!" A. J. squealed and held up her hand. Tiny beads of blood made a long red mark her knuckles.

"Come on. Let me get you something for that. I have to turn the heat off, or they'll wilt. So zip up," Lang said when they finally brought the last of the white plastic buckets inside. Mounds of blossoms cascaded over the edges and splayed out over the sides. She turned the temperature down another notch—it wouldn't take anything for them to wilt.

Lang showed them how to glue hot wax to cardboard cake rounds, then carefully disguise it with a thick carpet of moss.

"That looks like what I just threw out of my refrigerator," A.

J. said. "Green mold an inch thick."

"At least you have a refrigerator," Sarah said under her breath. If Lang didn't strain to hear every word Sarah said, she would have missed it.

Lang gathered up lanterns from Fancy's lifetime collection, some wrought iron, some copper, and they filled them in with Lenten roses and pale waxy camellia blossoms and witch hazel in stages, so that it wasn't until the twenty-fifth one was finished that they had the full effect. They were breathtaking. The shapes and colors of the blossoms contrasted with the spires of japonica, and the clusters of berries Lang had tucked strategically made each one pop.

The three women stared at the lush ambush of flowers and didn't speak for a minute.

"They are so beautiful!" Sarah said.

"Better than store-bought," A. J. said. "So."

"Well, you all go warm up. I'm sorry I have to keep it so cold, but they'll wilt if they get warm."

"Good god, it's freezing! It really makes a difference staying busy. It's cold as a witch's tit in here," A. J. said, stomping her feet. "You go spend the night with Sarah. You can't stay here. You'll come down with hypothermia or get frostbit or something. You're welcome to come home with me, but Walker's coming home tonight. He's been out of town for a week, so."

Lang assumed A. J. meant they'd be having unbridled sex in every room, so she politely declined.

"Well, you can't stay here," A. J., said, looking pointedly at Sarah. "You are not going to spend the night freezing your tail off while you're trying to keep your white count up. You're just asking to catch a cold, and that's the last thing you need."

"You're welcome to stay with me, of course," Sarah said stiffly.

Even A. J. stopped and narrowed her eyes at Sarah.

"No, I've got an electric blanket, and I want to sleep in my own bed," Lang said.

Sarah's apartment was practically a walk-in cooler. They could have done the flowers there without adjusting the temperature.

TWENTY-THREE

·······································

Lang gazed out of the breakfast room window, absorbing the warmth from the coffee cup into her palms. The sky was dark and low in the sky, heavy with rain, and the trees were barren. The gala had been a success. A. J. said she'd been given a standing ovation when they announced she'd done the flowers, but Lang doubted this was true. It was true that the cake had sold for an obscene amount of money. But she was exhausted, feeling as empty as the landscape.

Five chickadees, perky and energetic, swooped back and forth from the feeder while a pair of doves sat placidly on a branch. Their heavy, rounded bottom halves were out of proportion with their tiny necks and heads. Lang watched them for a minute. Doves always seemed to be sitting or slowly poking about. Never swooping. Or doing anything of interest.

The doorbell chimed out shrilly, and she wondered why A. J. would be ringing it now. She never had before.

She was surprised to see a strange man at the door, holding the little dog.

"I'm sorry? Can I help you?"

"Leland LePeyre. Just like the fruit but spelled differently. Pear? Or a couple. Pair. They sound the same," he said. He reminded her of some elderly cartoon character with his small balding head and enormous girth. *Popeye's friend Wimpy? Or the butler on some old sitcom?*

"I'm the vet," he said, wiggling four of his fingers under the dog as if she would clasp them in a handshake. "Veterinarian."

"W-w-w-what's wrong? Sorry, I'm Lang. Eldridge," she said, smiling more broadly than warranted as she pressed her tongue to the roof of her mouth.

"Oh, yes. I know you. My son played tennis with Teddy. When they were younger. I'm so sorry about your husband. So sudden," he said, shaking his head.

"Well," Lang said, at a loss as to whether ask about his son, who she didn't remember at all or acknowledge his condolence. He wasn't attractive at all, and she wondered about A. J.'s taste in men.

"Well, nothing's wrong with him. He's fine. He did great. It's just that no one came to pick him up!"

"No, A. J. Cole found him an owner. She was coming to get him. The new owner. I thought a couple of days ago," Lang said.

"The so-called new owner called. It's not going to work out it sounds like. Probably for the best if she can't even manage to pick him up!" he said. He massaged the dog's neck, right under his ears.

"Didn't pick him up?" Lang reached out to pet Victoria and jumped back when she accidentally rubbed Dr. LePeyre's fingers.

"I can't get in touch with A. J. Do you want me to keep him at the office? We don't have a standard procedure. Usually whoever brings the dog in for surgery picks him up afterward," he said. He didn't sound sarcastic at all, just bewildered.

"Okay, here. Just put him down gently. Is he okay? I'll call A. J. and let her know the woman no-showed, and she can get back on it. She's trying to find him a good home."

"What's the matter, Tuff Stuff?" Dr. LePeyre said directly to Victoria.

The vet finally looked up at Lang expectantly, and she was relieved he hadn't waited any longer for 'Tuff Stuff' to answer.

"Was his leg broken? When he jumped up on the bed he knocked something," she said.

"Or maybe he stubbed his toe?" Dr. LePeyre asked.

"You're kidding, right?" Lang said. Did she sound testy?

"This type of dog—the Chihuahua part—tends to knock their toenails in. It's painful, isn't it, buddy?" he said to Victoria, rubbing his ears. "Kind of like stubbing their toes. Bet he knocked it on the bed rail when he jumped."

"So, it's a Chihuahua? Don't people like those?" she asked. She found herself smiling at the dog. The animal strained to reach her, wagging his tail and imploring her to take him with his eyes. She scratched his chin, careful to keep her hands away from his ears, where Dr. LePeyre was massaging.

"Yes, Chihuahuas are very popular. Thanks to the movie stars. Where did you get him? The shelter?" he asked.

"No," she said. "He's not mine. He never was mine. He just showed up. I'm trying to find him a home. I would keep him if I could. He's a good little fellow." For some reason, she didn't want him to think she'd committed to a dog, then bailed on it.

"Um-hum," Dr. LePeyre said, checking Victoria's teeth and probing around his stomach and head. "What's his name?"

"Well, my granddaughter named him Victoria. Don't ask. But I really can't keep him, so if you know anyone who might be interested—"

"He needs to be neutered. As soon as possible. I won't charge you," he said, scratching Victoria's belly. Lang pulled her hands away and put them safely in her pockets. "I never charge to neuter a stray." Victoria looked back over his shoulder at Dr. LePeyre, bending his paws up coquettishly by his face.

"Well, I can make payments," Lang said. "You shouldn't have to do it for free." She barely had enough money for groceries, much less a stray dog's hospital bill, but she wanted to do right by the little dog.

"I do it all the time. It's just something I do. Isn't that right?" he said to the dog. "Victoria is an appropriate name for this little guy. Looks to have gender identification issues," Dr. LePeyre said. "I believe he's part basenji, too. African hunting dog. Dates back five thousand years. They call them barkless, if there is such a thing in a canine. They pounce on their prey with no warning and chase them up trees. Really they're more like cats as far as agility, but not as far as affection. I'm not all about the felines, but don't spread that information. Professional veterinarian and all."

Lang deduced he was a nut. Were any veterinarians *not* considered professional?

"All righty then, can Victoria come in next Monday? I'll perform 'the operation,'" he said, putting quotation marks in the air with his peace fingers.

Dr. LePeyre ran his hand down the full length of Victoria's back and said, "Really, he's a good little dog."

"Yes, he is," Lang said. "He's wonderful with my granddaughter and has a sweet little way about him. I think it will be easy enough to find him a home."

"He's perfectly housebroken. Actually I've never seen anything like it. He was about to burst because the girl forgot to take him out to relieve himself. But he held it. He wasn't about to have an accident." He looked up at her, and the morning light coming in through the window lit the side of his face. She reflexively pulled her mouth into a smile before speaking, but realized she was already smiling.

"It's not that," Lang said. She didn't want to go into the fact she was terrified that the cancer was back, and that she was worried that she would soon be too sick to feed herself or shop for food or even make it to the bathroom in time. "I'm the one we need to worry about, not the dog," she wanted to say. She smiled at her little joke, pleased she could make one at a time like this. Jack would have laughed and been so proud of her for keeping her chin up.

Or would he have? She wasn't sure anymore.

Had he been completely disgusted with me the whole time he took care of me? Had my bald head, shiny and slightly misshapen, revolted him? Had he psyched himself up before rubbing it with that almond oil?

Leland looked at her expectantly. What had he said?

"I'm sorry?" she asked.

"No, I just want to be sure it's okay. If you want me to take him, I can. It is an animal hospital after all. I think I can bend the rules for once."

"Oh, it's fine. I'm sorry if I was rude. I guess I'm old and set in my ways. It's harder to roll with the punches. I mean go with the flow." She corrected herself. She tried not to complain about her punches. "He can stay here until we find him a home."

"All right. Well, feel free to call if you get worried. I'm sure he'll be fine," he said quickly.

She couldn't put her finger on it. His words were perfectly friendly. But she felt like he was disappointed in her.

TWENTY-FOUR

....

L ang checked her phone messages as she waited in the plastic molded chairs at the hospital. Three people wanted caramel cakes—two for a birthday and one woman just wanted a cake for herself. Lang never would have admitted that herself and decided the woman must be skinny.

She was making enough money to keep the bank at bay, so her heart didn't drop out through her feet every time the phone rang. Which it did constantly. If it wasn't someone gushing about the arrangements at the gala, it was someone ordering something. Both better than someone demanding money.

She checked the minute hand on the large, plain-numbered clock, nervously waiting to advance to the little exam room down the hall where she would wait even more nervously for Dr. Shuck to arrive.

Her doctor looked perturbed as she scowled at her clipboard. Lang stared at the glistening pink creases in her forehead, wondering if they'd been there before and she just hadn't noticed. Even with her mouth pursed in a hard, clenched circle, Dr. Shuck looked like the epitome of youth. Her skin was full and smooth, and as soon as she looked up at Lang, her forehead smoothed itself, leaving no evidence of ever having been furrowed. For some reason, this was a relief to Lang. Maybe nothing in her report was worth worrying over and wrinkling her doctor's skin.

Dr. Shuck clasped her hands in front of her face dramatically, set her elbows on her desk with a hollow thud, and said, "Lang, it's not what we hoped for." So much for not creasing Dr. Shuck's forehead.

"It's back?" Lang asked.

"It is," Dr. Shuck said.

Lang listened to her explanation of the trial, of what was involved and the details of the various procedures and the percentages. Or she tried to. Dr. Shuck's mascara dribbled in dark watery pools under her lower lashes, and it was hard to take her seriously. Lang wondered if she cried every time she gave a troubling diagnosis.

"What about a support system? I'm so sorry to be blunt. But before you had your husband, so it wasn't an issue. What about your son? Could he commit?"

Lang snorted as she pictured Teddy recoiling in horror as she threw up all over everything.

"What? Lang?"

"Sorry." Lang tried to steady her breath and pull herself together. Nothing about this was funny.

"Teddy's a cross between Nurse Ratched and that woman on *Gone with the Wind*, the one who knew nothing about birthing babies." Lang grinned, waiting expectantly for Dr. Shuck to smile.

She didn't.

"Lang, I need you to listen. To get you accepted into the trial, you have to have a, hang on, let me read it verbatim." She skimmed the computer screen. "A support person on call twenty-four hours who has attended the two-hour prep class."

"A support person," Lang repeated.

Dr. Shuck peered up at Lang. "Is that a problem? Can we count on him? His job is flexible, right?"

"It's not a problem. Yes. He can do it."

The swollen ridges that lined Dr. Shuck's forehead

smoothed, and she beamed at Lang.

"Prissy," Dr. Shuck said.

Lang cocked her head, wondering if she'd missed something. She didn't remember discussing any sort of primping, but she wasn't exactly focused as of late.

"The character," Dr. Shuck said. "Scarlett's maid. In *Gone with the Wind.*"

"Oh. Of course!" Lang said, nodding her head. "It was on the tip of my tongue."

A. J.'s silver-gray BMW convertible was parked in Lang's driveway when Lang pulled in from the doctor. A. J. hopped out of her car effortlessly, gripping a large wicker basket with both hands. She wore a wide-brimmed hat and skinny white jeans that made her legs look endless, and a red-and-white-checked top that flounced out over her hips, the ruffle bringing attention to how narrow they were. Lang couldn't imagine wearing something like that herself. She would look like an oversize picnic table.

"How'd it go? What'd the doctor say?" A. J. called out.

"Everything's fine," Lang said. What could she say? She suspected there was a picnic lunch in that basket, and Lang wanted to enjoy it.

"I called your mom and Sarah to come. They wanted to be with you either way, but that's so good!" A. J. said. "I knew you'd get good news!"

"I doubt those two will show up," Lang said. "What did you bring?"

A. J. set four large white boxes tied with red-and-white-checkered ribbons on the table and uncorked a bottle of white wine.

A few minutes later, Lillian walked into the house in her stocking feet after dropping the heavy bronze doorknocker with more force than necessary.

"Hello," she called out, holding Victoria in her arms possessively. "Did you miss me?"

"You need to be careful with him! He just had stitches!" Lang said.

"What? I need you to speak up!" Lillian said.

"Come on in!" A. J. welcomed her. "I want to hear all about the trip. A cruise, right? You are amazing, zipping all over the world at your age."

"Excuse me?" Lillian said coldly.

"It's a compliment. You sure don't look your age. Not that I don't know your age," A. J. mumbled.

"H-h-h-hey there," Lang stammered. She took a deep breath of air and tried to relax her face.

"What a little fur delight! He reminds me of the little dog we had when you were a baby. It was a little Chihuahua with that long hair. Meanest little snippet you ever did see, not like this little precious" Lillian said. Victoria lay back against the crook of Lillian's elbow like a newborn baby, his paws tucked up under his chin, and gazed lovingly at Lang's mother as she rocked him. "Do you remember it? I can't remember its name."

"No, I don't remember any dog. I never had a dog. I would keep this one if I could. He's a stray that showed up, and I'm trying to find him a home," Lang said as she reached out to scratch the dog's ears. Victoria made a sound that was between a purr and someone rolling the letter r off their tongue. "He's a good little dog if you want to take him home."

"Oh no, I travel way too much," Lillian cooed in baby talk, holding a lace-edged linen napkin under the dog's chin. "But I'm thinking of settling down. I don't need any place too big. That little carriage house in the back would be perfect."

"What?" Lang asked, realizing Lillian wanted to move into the little stone building at the edge of her property. "There's not any heat."

"Well, I certainly wasn't serious," Lillian said quickly.

"I'm going to serve everything up. Sarah should be here anytime I would think, so," A. J. said. She quickly set the table and filled glasses with ice then ladled a thick bean soup into bowls. She was almost magical in her efficiency. "This is what we made in my last cooking class. The Mean Bean. We did three soups, but this was the best one. Walker can't eat beans. Gives him gas. So."

A. J. plopped two ham biscuits on each plate except for one and announced lunch was served.

Lang swallowed the saliva that suddenly gushed into her mouth and wondered who wasn't getting biscuits.

"Carbs," A. J. said, putting her hands on her tight slab of a belly. "I can't. So."

Lang looked covetously at the fitted blouse proclaiming the thinness of A. J.'s waist and took one of the biscuits off her own plate.

Lillian shifted the dog to her left arm and reached out to greet Sarah who was silently peeping through the sidelight. She'd come after all.

"I can't stay. I just wanted to drop this by," Sarah said, holding out a large brown paper shopping bag.

Lang pulled out the painting of Katie D. from Sarah's apartment.

"Oh, Sarah, this is so beautiful! I can't take it!" Lang said.

"No. I want you to have it," Sarah said miserably. "I'm glad you got good results. A. J. called me."

"That looks like Gauguin," Lillian said. "The colors and how alive she looks."

"I think it looks more like Katie D.," A. J. said. "Just like her."

"You're covered in fur!" Lang said quickly, before her mother had a chance to humiliate A. J. She was, in fact, dismayed at the abstract nest of white fluff on her mother's navy suit. "Thank you, Sarah!" She reached out to hug her, but Sarah immediately stepped back.

"He shouldn't be shedding this time of year," Lillian said, swiping at the hair with her hands. "What do you feed him?"

"He eats a mixture the vet recommends," Lang said.

"The vet? Since when do you talk with the vet?" A. J. asked, arching her eyebrows a few times.

"Oh, please. Here, you all sit down," Lang said quickly.

"No, I need to head out," Sarah said, backing toward the door.

"Sit! I worked my ass off for this lunch to celebrate Lang's news, so get in that goddamned chair," A. J. said sharply. "Now!"

"The garden is lovely," Sarah said meekly as she sat.

"Not too much to see this time of year," Lillian said. "You should see this place in the spring. Summer even. Lang has the greenest thumb in the county. She could make a dead man grow. Sorry. That was inconsiderate, all things considered. I just meant she's a gifted gardener. I wish you could see it all blooming."

Lang looked out the window at the stand of birch trees. Their pale bark curled loosely along their trunks, and they looked almost like sculptures against the magnolia behind them.

"Oh, I don't know," Sarah said. "I'm partial to a winter garden. My gardening books say that's the sign of a truly gifted gardener, making the garden beautiful in the winter. Good grief, look at your Lenten roses! They're thriving in the dead of winter, a bright green heap of life out there!"

Lang sat in a stunned silence. That's the most she'd ever heard Sarah say. Even when they worked together, arranging flowers for big jobs for hours, Sarah barely spoke. Lang looked out at the bank of Lenten roses beyond the bird feeder.

"Are those things evasive?" A. J. asked.

"Eeee-vasive?" Lillian asked, enunciating the first syllable before Lang could answer. "You mean are they hard to keep track of? Do they hide? Run off?"

"I know what you mean, A. J. They're a tough little plant. But not a nuisance at all," Lang said. "They don't take over anything. And they certainly don't run off. Unlike others." Lang looked at Lillian to see if she'd noticed her barb.

"They'll come up through asphalt. Almost invasive," Lillian said, enunciating the *in* and ignoring Lang's insult. "You can't stop them from growing."

"They *are* easy to grow," Lang said, realizing it was rude to resist the ham biscuits. "She's exactly right. Do you have any?" The biscuit melted in her mouth, and she closed her eyes to relish it.

She immediately regretted her insinuation that she was willing to share her plants. She was very particular about dividing them with people, and although she'd already offered to share with A. J., it was quite clear the woman had absolutely no interest in gardening. Lang imagined she would let any plant die as she petitioned for club votes. Lang felt anxiety over A. J.'s request again. She was going to have to give Emmeline Harrison an ultimatum—throw her weight around for once. Lang smirked as she imagined herself sitting on top of Emmeline, trapping her under her large behind until she let A. J. into the club.

"Lang can grow them from seed," Lillian said.

"How do you know?" Lang asked curtly.

"Lettin' roses? Like lettin' 'em bloom or what?" A. J. asked.

"Lenten. Before Easter. They got their name when a little country girl visited the baby Jesus in Bethlehem. She was crying because she hadn't brought a gift, so an angel touched down his wings on the snowy ground, and the Helleborus orientalis—our Lenten rose—popped up in full bloom. A gift in the dead of winter, out of the barren earth." Lillian had her nerve, acting like she knew the first thing about her.

Lillian tapped the tines of her fork on the table, and her diamond bracelet clattered lightly on the wood. "They're highly poisonous. Right up there with hemlock," she said. "But I must say, Elizabeth has quite a way. Not many people can make a flower arrangement from their yard in the middle of winter."

"Well, it's nothing really," Lang said. Lang squinted at the chartreuse blooms speckled with burgundy spilling out over the vase. She'd wired baby limes in bunches and tucked clusters of viburnum berries in, keeping it low so that people could see each other. Not that she had reason to worry about that; she ate alone every night.

"This table still needs to be refinished. Has for thirty years," Lillian said. Lang noticed she spoke as if she had been monitoring the tabletop, day in, day out, instead of gallivanting about the world with her lover. *Lovers.*

"No, I love the character," Sarah said slowly. "I bet there is a story about every little dent. Every ding." She rubbed her index finger over a crescent shape embedded in the heart pine.

"Let me have it refinished for you. That will be my gift to you," Lillian said. "I want to. Martin's granddaughter has a little furniture shop that she runs out of their garage. She reminds me of you actually. Beautiful and stronger than she looks."

"That's from a hammer," Lang said, touching the indentation in the table. Her mother's words embarrassed her; she was certainly not beautiful, and she didn't want that fact pointed out. "I did it when I was thirteen. I didn't know better than to use a hammer to open an oyster, much less on an antique table."

"Oh, golly! I bet you were in a fit to be tied!" A. J. said to Lillian. "That table is an antique!"

"I wouldn't have allowed it," Lillian said simply.

Lang traced her eyebrow with her pinkie finger, pressing into the bony ridge above her eye, not speaking. Her head seemed like it was going to explode.

"A certain Mr. Vandergriff's getting serious," Lillian said, changing the subject. "His daughter is already demanding a prenup, but I don't know if I want to take care of him. He's younger than me, but still. He says you know his daughter."

"Emmeline Harrison, yes," Lang said.

"That's his daughter? The president of the Barrington Women's Club?" A. J. asked.

"That's the one," Lang said, hoping A. J. would begin to work on her mother for her nomination and ease up on her.

"Don't look at me. Emmeline is trying to sabotage our blooming romance any way she can. She already told him I was of ill repute, quote unquote."

Lang had to look away. She needed to talk to Jack, to hear him guffaw at all things Lillian and right her. Being with her mother threw her balance off.

"Ever since we hooked up he's been pushing to tie the knot," Lillian said.

"Don't call it that. Become reacquainted is what you mean," Lang said.

"How do you know?" Lillian said.

"I've got ice cream, if anyone wants dessert," Lang blurted out, scraping her chair away from the table.

"None for me. Not only fattening, but it makes me cold," Lillian said, pulling her sweater around her.

"Here, I'll turn the heat up," Lang said.

"This house always was freezing," Lillian said.

"When were you ever here long enough to adjust to the

temperature?" Lang asked.

"Sorry," Lillian said. "It's no reflection on you. They're just old windows. Single pane."

"You should put your shoes back on. You lose a lot of body heat through the feet," A. J. said. "Heat through the feet," she repeated.

"Through the head. Not feet. Hence hats. I stepped in a doggie pie in the yard. Don't tell Elizabeth Langford. I don't want to get somebody in trouble, do I? She doesn't know it, but she needs this dog," Lillian said, jiggling the dog's chin.

"You know that's not my name. My name is Katherine," Lang said.

Lillian stopped talking suddenly and stared out toward the living room. Her face, usually almost taut, had gone limp, and her cheeks sagged down, pouching above her jaw. Lang wondered if she was having a stroke. What were the signs? Laugh!

"Can you laugh?" Lang snapped her fingers in front of Lillian's face.

"What?" Lillian asked. She looked pale. Confused. "What do you mean, your name is Katherine? I named you Elizabeth. For Elizabeth Taylor."

"My name is Katherine Langford Deakins Eldridge," Lang said.

"No. I named you Elizabeth Langford Deakins. We made a deal," Lillian said miserably. "I got Elizabeth, and he got Langford for the royal ancestors." She looked at Lang accusingly, as if Lang was to blame and could right it. "And nobody told me. That's probably why they called you Lang and not Katherine. Or Elizabeth. Not that I could have done anything."

Lillian suddenly stood up and walked purposely toward the door, stopping at the chest in the hall. She picked up the photograph of Lang and put her finger on the picture, touching her daughter's cheek.

"She's going to get a better picture," A. J. said. "I like those old school pictures with the professional camera and good lighting."

"You look so little," Lillian whispered. She turned to Lang, shocked, as if she hadn't known the age of her child when she'd left her.

"I like the frame, though," A. J. said.

"Look at you," Lillian said, holding the picture up to the window. "You were a baby!"

"Katie D. has your same mouth," Sarah said. "I never noticed it before."

"Your little knees are all scraped up," Lillian said with a sadness in her voice that Lang had never heard before.

Lillian pressed her hand on the piano suddenly, as if for balance.

"Are you okay?" Lang asked, holding her elbow tentatively.

"It's so strange, how young you look in that picture," she said. "I didn't realize. I should have . . ." Lillian began, her shoulders suddenly stooped. She turned and moved slowly into the kitchen, barely picking up her feet.

TWENTY FIVE

··

L ang balked at the idea of getting dressed up and making small talk at Grandparents' Day, but she was the only grandparent Katie D. had now. Lang peered at herself in the mirror. Her skin hung loose on her face; whatever had been making it cling to her skull had given out completely. She put her fingertips on her temples and gently tugged her face back into place. She considered taking two of Teddy's sturdy black paper clips and folding a thick wad of her scalp in them, and then hiding the whole mess with a scarf.

Her eyes seemed to have lost their color. She squinted at her reflection in the mirror. Could that happen? She heard it could with hair, that an extreme shock could turn a vibrant head of hair white overnight.

Her eyes used to carry her on days she hadn't slept the night before or when she'd gained a few pounds, or all of last year, when her hair was shorn to her scalp. A mixture of celadon green and turquoise, they were the color of the ocean. And changed color like it, too. Teal or sage or sometimes deep emerald green, depending on her clothing or her mood. She had found the perfect shade of blue-green eyeliner and wore it religiously; she needed all the help she could get to detract from her hips.

Now it looked like she was wearing opaque gray contact lenses. Shark's eyes.

She put on the brown knit dress she wore year-round, stood back from the mirror, and looked at herself. Her blonde hair had been ridiculously thick, and she felt like a freak now with this short, prickly growth that felt abrasive against her hand. She didn't have the features to carry it. Her lips seemed to shatter into tiny cracks running out over the edges, and her cheekbones were hidden by her fallen, fleshy face.

She'd wanted short hair when she was younger. She had imagined jumping out of the shower, towel drying her cropped hair, and sprinting out of the door. But Fancy had told her that her hair was the prettiest thing about her, and that it was worth the trouble it took.

Lang stared at her reflection and remembered her mother brushing her hair. It was her only memory of her parents together. Her father was behind them on the bed.

But Fancy had told her that was impossible, that her father had died when she was born, and her mother had abandoned her the next day.

As Lang walked into Katie D.'s school, she wished she'd worn her silk scarf over her head. The teal one that brought out the color of her eyes. Or what was left of it.

She prepared herself to be gracious, to simply thank the people when they offered condolences. But no one mentioned it.

It was old news. Over. They'd all spun on to the next thing, be it a party or a program or another death. Lang felt the floor shift under her feet. The world going right on lickety-split without Jack, as if he'd never existed, made her lurch.

"Eldridge," Lang said, and the woman at the registration table handed her two nametags printed in elegant calligraphy.

Lang Eldridge ~ Katie D. Eldridge. And another one that said *Jack Eldridge ~ Katie D. Eldridge.*

She stared at Jack's nametag until the woman at the table said, "Is that not correct?"

"Oh, yes, sorry," Lang said, slipping his nametag in her pocketbook. He wouldn't have missed this.

Making Arrangements

Lang waved to Katie D, who raced toward her.

"Save this seat for Mommy. She's a helper but will sit here. And this one for my daddy," Katie D. said, placing both her little hands on each seat emphatically. Lang moved down two seats and put her purse on the middle spot for Teddy.

Lang looked back over her shoulder, scanning the crowd for Teddy and Sarah. She finally spotted Sarah in the back and waved, then pointed at the empty chair next to her. Sarah shook her head, indicating she couldn't take the seat, which was par for the course. Just when Lang thought she was making headway, Sarah pulled back.

She thought the man sliding in next to her was Teddy, and she actually began a sentence before realizing it was the vet. Dr. Le something. Pair.

"Is this seat taken?" he whispered.

"Yes. No. It's fine. I'll save this other one for my son," Lang said, placing her pocketbook on Teddy's seat.

"How's Victoria?" he asked.

"Oh, Victoria? He's fine. Quiet as a little mouse, and I think he's smart. You were right about the jumping." She realized she was probably overwhelming him but was unable to stop talking. "He can really jump!"

He smiled at her. His eyes were hazel and crinkled at the outside corners.

"I told you!" he said, nodding. "Do you have someone in the show, or are you just hard up for entertainment?"

"No. Yes. My granddaughter," Lang said. "You?"

"Same. Two of them. I'll show you. Are you busy after the performance? Want to grab a cup of coffee or a sweet roll?"

"Oh, that is so nice. But no, I promised Katie D. we'd go out to lunch with her parents. But thank you anyway," Lang said, feeling the heat rise in her cheeks. She did wonder what kind of sweet rolls he was talking about.

The program was something to be endured. After a ridiculously long and off-key version of "My Favorite Things," every child stood up one at a time and told the standing-room-only audience what their favorite things were. A little boy lisped about his Xbox 360, and Dr. LePeyre jabbed his elbow into her ribs as a little girl said loudly, "My new baby sister."

"That's one of them," he said.

"She's precious," Lang said, noticing his granddaughter had his dimples.

When it was Katie D.'s turn, Lang was rapt with attention.

"My favorite thing is cooking with my grandmother. Grandie," Katie D. said plainly, looking straight at Lang and silently mouthing, *Alligator food.* "She is good."

Lang mouthed the phrase back and felt a sharp sting deep in her nasal cavity, as if the bridge of her nose was collapsing in on itself. She opened her eyes so wide she could feel air on her corneas and studied the little potted palm trees on either side of the stage. They looked bare. Almost desolate.

She made a beeline for Sarah after the program, leaving Leland in the aisle.

"Hey," Sarah said. "Sorry, I needed to be near the back to watch the refreshment table. Thank you for coming. It means the world to Katie D."

"Oh, it's fine. I thought the program was wonderful. Where's Teddy?"

"You look great. Your hair looks beautiful. So chic and elegant," Sarah said.

Lang rubbed her palm over the stiff hackle on the back of her head. It felt nothing like hair.

"Leland LePeyre," Leland said, holding his hand out to Sarah.

"He has grandchildren in the program," Lang explained. Her cheeks burned, and she wondered if they were a scorched bright red.

"Well, it was just lovely seeing you again. And your grand-children are adorable. We'd better head off to lunch if we want to beat the crowd," Lang said. Leland shifted his weight to the balls of his feet then back to his heels, swaying. He looked right at her, his dimples making him look merry.

No one moved, and Lang finally took Sarah's arm and said firmly, "We need to go find Katie D."

TWENTY-SIX

....

Teddy lay sprawled out on her couch wearing Jack's old Auburn sweatshirt. His face was splotchy, and Victoria was curled up in a ball on his chest. She watched him for a minute, thinking of how lost he must be without Jack. They had been such pals.

"Hey, Mom," he said, clicking off the television set and sauntering into the kitchen. A slew of condiment jars and cellophane wrappers littered the sleek granite surface. "Dad's sweatshirt was in the laundry room, and I was freezing. Is it okay if I wear it? Where were you?"

"Grandparents' Day. For Katie D.," she said. It was strange to see him in Jack's clothes. She knew Teddy missed his father and must want the smell of him the same way she did. She imagined the soft, worn fabric comforted Teddy the same way it comforted her. She wiped at the pale dog hairs clustered around the cracked orange letters on the sweatshirt, remembering the two of them dressing in orange and blue for every game day.

"Oh. I had something come up. Business. I was actually on my way to the program, as a matter of fact, but then this," Teddy said, holding out his hands like he was Jesus. It was clear to Lang that Teddy never had any intention of attending.

"Well, she'll have plenty more programs," Lang said, giving him an out as always.

"Do you not want me to wear this or something?" He pulled the hem of the sweatshirt down.

"No. I mean, I do. It's fine. You can have it."

"Really? Thanks! Look what I made you," Teddy said, pointing at a thick sandwich on the counter and looking pleased with himself. "Your favorite."

Lang considered asking him to teach her how to operate the remote controls but decided not to bother him about it. She didn't want to ruin his good mood.

"Oh, honey, I wish I hadn't already eaten. I'll save it for tonight," Lang said, screwing the lid on the black olives and mustard and sealing up the cheese. "It looks divine!"

Lang's lunch had been awkward. Katie D. and Sarah had obviously made plans for lunch, but she had to admit Sarah handled it graciously when Lang invited herself. She couldn't figure out why her should-be daughter-in-law disliked her so much. Lang knew Sarah had liked her the first time Teddy had brought her home. For the first hour, anyway, they had had a connection.

He'd hinted for months that there was someone special, someone with *substance*, that he was involved with. And Sarah was easily the most interesting woman he'd ever brought home. They got engaged, and Lang had given him Fancy's wedding ring.

Lang had handled the introduction beautifully, considering she didn't lay eyes on Sarah until Teddy brought her home with her newborn granddaughter. Sarah had stopped abruptly in the foyer, tilting her head up, then down, as she'd surveyed Lang's little house. "Wow!" she'd said, before they were even introduced. "There's so much past here. You can almost hear the stories before they're told."

She'd handed over the tiny infant shyly, and Lang had stared at the baby swathed in a pink cotton blanket, her eyes still squeezed shut.

Sarah had appreciated the wide-plank, heart pine floors; the ceilings that soared; and the wide, detailed crown moldings.

She had run her hand along the curved, oak braces under the mantel and bent down to peer at the raised imprints of a stag on the bottle-green squares of tile on the fireplace surround.

"You act like you've never seen the inside of a house before," Teddy had said. "What's for dinner?"

Sarah had been embarrassed, stammering an apology, but Lang had taken her on a tour of the house, pointing out her great-grandparent's initials carved under the banister and the porch swing her grandfather had made from old tobacco poles.

Sarah had given Lang a beautifully wrapped bottle of French hand cream as a hostess gift, something not one of Teddy's slew of glamorous girlfriends had ever done—no matter how long they'd stayed or how famous they were.

"It's supposed to soothe thorn pricks," Sarah had said.

"Oh, do you garden?" Lang had asked, spreading the rose-scented lotion on the backs of her hands and breathing in the smell. Sarah had laughed, as if the very idea was ridiculous.

"No, I live in an apartment downtown. I've always wanted to, though. I read a lot of gardening books. I'm trying to grow basil. But it's pathetic," Sarah had said.

"Open the window! Get some daylight on them," Lang had told her.

"Bars on the windows," Teddy had said. "Won't open."

Lang had been aghast, wondering what kind of slum Sarah lived in.

"It's not as bad as it sounds," Sarah had said, shrugging her shoulders as she gently leaned over Lang's arms and eased the pacifier into the baby's mouth. Her pale hair had swept over Lang's forearm, a swath of corn silk.

Sarah had picked up the photograph of Lang and asked her whole name.

"Katherine Langford Deakins," Lang had said, leaning over Sarah's shoulder to see the picture of herself with her scraped knee.

"Oh, what a beautiful name," Sarah had said. "Do you mind if we name her that? Katherine Deakins? I want a family name."

Lang hadn't been able to speak. Her tongue had felt disconnected from her mouth, and she'd felt the tip of her nose compress. She'd opened her eyes wide and blinked back tears, overwhelmed by the tiny creature in her arms.

She'd heard Jack's footsteps behind her and whispered to the baby that her grandfather was here. "Here's our girl," she'd said, handing the tiny bundle to him.

Sarah had suddenly frozen up. Lang had known something was different before she'd looked up from the baby at Sarah's face.

She knew she should have acknowledged the honor of having the child named after her, but she couldn't speak clearly. She would have stuttered and made the special moment awkward for all of them.

Sarah had quickly excused herself, and Lang had berated herself for not telling them how much it meant, stutter or no stutter. Lang had handed Jack his granddaughter. He didn't even look down at the new baby in his arms.

"Mom, I need you to sign this paperwork to get the ball rolling. It's to list the property for sale, so here, here, and here," Teddy said, flipping through the pages. "We agree to list it with them for three months, then we can renegotiate if need be. But I'm sure need won't be. This baby will sell in days," he said.

"Lang had a vision of the cartoon roadrunner, licking his chops over his easy prey.

"Okay, I'll look it over this weekend," Lang said. She pressed the silver hinge on the black clip, imagining it hidden up in her scarf, magically pulling her face into place.

"No, don't do that. Don't get them out of order," he said,

taking the clip out of her hand. "Mom, there's no need to look it over. I've checked it out. It's just a standard agreement. Nothing to worry about." He tapped his pen at the first highlighted yellow line she was supposed to sign.

"All these?"

"I know you don't want to sell it. I don't blame you. But I'm not sure there are any other options. Not really. Maybe if Dad hadn't taken out the mortgage or cashed out his life insurance. Sorry. I don't mean to sound like I'm blaming him. I just had no idea. I thought everything was fine financially," Teddy said. "I wish he hadn't invested so much with me. I never should have asked him. He always acted like it was no big deal."

Lang stared at the papers. "No. Don't say that," she said. There was no use crying over spilt milk now, but she couldn't help being upset over it. *If he had just discussed it with me first.* "Would you like something to drink? A beer?" She'd bought beer last week in case Teddy dropped by. "It's that imported Tiger stuff you like."

"Sure. I'll get it," he said. "Are there any chilled mugs?"

It hadn't occurred to Lang to put a glass in the freezer. Jack always did that. He unloaded the top rack of the dishwasher and stuck the tall pilsner glass right next to the frozen peas. She should tell Teddy there still was one in there. Jack's last beer glass.

"No. I need to chill some," she said.

"Mom? I'm sorry about all the investments. The businesses that we started. Dad and me. Maybe if we hadn't, if he hadn't put the money up, you wouldn't be in this mess," Teddy said.

"No, don't say that. He wanted to. We wanted to," she said. If anyone was to blame it was her. She should have kept up with her money. Not handed it over to Jack and trusted him completely.

Teddy slammed the green bottle down on the wooden table. She wondered if there was a mark now, another imprinted rind.

"Oh, sorry. I didn't mean to do that," he said. "We're in a mess, Mom. Every which way."

"No, I'm making payments to the bank. Believe it or not, people are actually buying my flower arrangements. And cakes, too. For more than you would think," Lang said.

"That's great, but there's a balloon coming up at some point. Do you know what that is?" he asked.

She thought about saying a piece of latex filled with air, but she couldn't bring herself to joke.

"Yes," she said.

"Mom. I don't see any other option. I think you have to sell. Revoke that trust and sell it all. The bank is going to take the house if you don't. Is that what you want?"

"Teddy, I need to go over it is all. Look over the papers. I'm sorry," she said. "This shouldn't be your problem."

"Okay, but if the bank takes it, you get nothing. If you sell it, you can make some money. I'm working on a deal to develop it. I've got interest already. We'll have a little tennis compound right in the middle of the most elite neighborhood in the southeast. Like that place you and Dad used to go—that fancy resort?"

Lang couldn't remember the name of the resort in North Carolina where the players had to wear all white on the courts. Not even an emblem was permitted on their hats or socks. Lang had felt as ill at ease as Jack had felt entitled, and she spent most of her vacation reading on her balcony while Jack made hordes of new acquaintances.

"No. I hate that place. So pompous," she said. "I was always intimidated there."

"Mom, you don't have to vacation here. You won't even have to step foot on the grounds again. You'll have enough money to buy a house wherever you want. Or move to Shepherd's Arms," Teddy said.

"The nursing home?"

"Why not? It's really nice, and you have lots of friends there. It's safe, and they have around the clock care if you need it, and tons of trips and activities."

"I can stay here. I'm making the payments," she said.

"Are you kidding me? How long do you think that's going to last, people buying little vases of weeds out of pity?"

"Oh," she said, realizing he was probably right.

"I'm sorry. I didn't mean that. I'm glad you have a hobby and proud of you for being industrious. But, Mom, you can't hold off the bank when that big payment is due! Not by making flower arrangements. And if you wait too long, they'll take it. I need to get it in the works. You don't want to lose the house," he said. "It's the only thing you've got!"

"I don't. You're right," she said, thinking of Katie D. She had Katie D. "But I don't want a pretentious snob farm, either."

"*Farm* is the wrong word. Snob *club* is more like it. And it will be very exclusive."

"Teddy," she began, forcing a small laugh at his joke. She gathered up the sections of pages and tapped them on the table, shaking them together into a neat, even stack. The black clips lined up in a row, perfectly spaced.

"Mom, I don't think I can stay here if you don't sell this property. In Barrington. I'll have to move. Find a job. If we developed this, your family property, I'd run the project. Help with the planning and the building. And then when it was finished, I'd run it."

"I'll look it over," she said.

"Fine. You look it over. I'll be back to pick them up. But just so you know, there's a club in Oregon that's offered me a job. Head pro. Sweet package. I don't want to take it. I don't. Mom, this is a win-win. When you sell this property, you'll have the money you need for that assisted living, and if you have the assistance, you'll qualify for the cancer trial. If you need to, in case it comes back. You won't have to worry with the land and the upkeep and this old house. And I'll have a project. I'll be able to stay here. I won't have to move Katie D. out to the other side of the country," he said.

Lang stopped breathing. She hadn't thought about losing Katie D. She'd never even considered it.

TWENTY-SEVEN

Lang watched the pale yellow top of her mother's car lurch toward her rock wall. Lillian had no business operating a moving vehicle. She couldn't see over the steering wheel, so she peered under it, squinting to peep out between the finger grooves under the steering wheel and the hood of the car. Lillian careened down the roads, leaning forward in the driver's seat and clutching the wheel at ten and two, a cigar smoldering between two fingers.

Lang listened for sounds of impact, wishing her mother would plow right into the eight-foot retaining wall. Render the yellow Buick undriveable. The car was a tank, and her mother would wear a seat belt in the movie theater if she could. Plus, she was terrified of losing her license, so she never drove over twenty miles per hour. She wouldn't be scratched if she totaled the car.

Lillian's driving was getting worse every time she turned the keys in the ignition. Lang needed to have a talk with her mother and take her car away. It was on her list.

Last week Lang had gotten a call from Emmeline Harrison. Apparently Lillian had rammed into a white Land Cruiser parked behind her. The bigger problem was that she had simply shifted her gear into drive and sallied forth on her way, never even stopping.

"It wasn't right behind her," Emmeline had said. "There were five car lengths between her. Maybe six. She definitely had time to stop, but she obviously didn't see it or didn't even look before backing out. You know I hate to be the one to tell you, but what if it was a person? A child even."

"No, I appreciate you telling me. I'll speak to her this week," Lang had said weakly.

"Lang, she practically bulldozed the whole front end! And those Land Cruisers aren't flimsy cars! It's beyond merely speaking to her. Something needs to be done! I don't want to report it to the police, but really, what if it was a child?"

"Now, Emmeline. I know for a fact it was a fender bender because I've already talked to the insurance people. Not that she should be driving," Lang had said.

"She shouldn't be doing most of what she's doing," Emmeline had said. "You know she's after my father."

"That's not how I understand it," Lang had said icily, unaccustomed to defending her mother.

"Well, I don't approve of it. And I'm sure you don't, either," Emmeline had said. "You need to do something!"

Now, outside of Lang's house, the trunk of her mother's banged up car bobbled as the front tire ran up on the sidewalk. Lang waited for her to reverse and park the car correctly. Cigar smoke wafted up from the road.

The car didn't move, and Lang could see the top of Lillian's perfectly coiffed hair. Lillian finally appeared at the top of the stairs, dressed to the nines in a fitted navy suit with white piping along the sleeves and collar. Lang was relieved to see the smoldering cigar between her fingers. Usually Lillian rolled the lit cigar up in her car window, using it as a holder, and Lang had to go down the steps to the road, extinguish the cigar, and make her way all the way back up the steps.

"Hello!" Lillian called to her.

"I need you to put that out, please. I don't want smoke around me," Lang said. *What is she doing here anyway?*

"Just thought I'd pop in for a quick minute," Lillian said, as if she were reading Lang's mind.

"Mom? What's going on? Is everything okay?" Teddy asked. He must have come in from the back drive by the carriage house. There was so much commotion it was hard to keep track.

"Great! More guinea pigs! This is a new recipe. It's got fresh jalapeños, so," A. J. called from the porch.

"No, I'm not here for lunch. I just need to pick up some papers. Mom? Are they ready? Did you sign them?" he asked. She'd had a reprieve for a few days, but now it was apparently over.

"Not just yet, sweetie. I haven't had a chance to go over them. I'm so sorry," Lang said.

"Lunch first, papers later," A. J. said, herding them into the kitchen.

"No offense, but I need to go over a little family business, and then I'll leave you two gals alone," Teddy said, flashing his practiced smile.

"Well, your mother hasn't gone over them yet, so. Here. Sit," A. J. said, ladling a thick conglomerate of chili into a few bowls.

"Oh, my!" Lang said when she tasted it.

The chili was so spicy Lang started drinking beer just to soothe her scorched mouth. It made her feel better and more relaxed. The problem was, she needed a few swallows of beer for every bite of chili.

"Martin's granddaughter can't have children, either. She's tried it all. Lost one at five months. They've done all the test tube business, and now she wants to adopt. But it's so hard to get an American baby. They're all foreign. It's different now," Lillian said.

"What?" Teddy asked. "Who else is trying to adopt?"

"Oh. No one. Never mind that," Lillian said. "I didn't know you all were . . . nothing."

A. J. excused herself and went into the kitchen. Lang took a long sip of beer.

"It's nothing to be ashamed of," Lillian said.

"What?" Teddy asked.

"Adoption. I think it should be out in the open. Not a secret," Lillian said.

"If they want it to be a secret, maybe you shouldn't be telling everyone," Teddy said.

"No, not that. I just meant in general. Never mind," Lillian said.

The rest of the lunch was stiff, and by the time Teddy and Lillian left, Lang was in no shape to clean up the kitchen. She even dropped a full bottle of beer on the floor. She just released her fingers, and the bottle plummeted three feet and exploded on the wooden floor. A. J. told her to go on and rest, and that she'd finish up. Lang splayed out limp on the couch and was snoring before A. J. finished picking glass splinters off every kitchen surface.

A. J. busied herself, deep cleaning the counters between hovering around Lang, but she showed no sign of waking up. Finally, A. J. covered Lang with an old quilt that was halfway disintegrated and left.

A. J. stopped back by late that afternoon, but Lang didn't go to the door. She saw A. J.'s shape tiptoeing on the porch and then press close up to the glass.

Lang sat in the dark, staring straight ahead. Fancy's quilt lay lightly across her shoulders.

"Honey? The door was open, but I knocked anyways," A. J. said, turning on a lamp. Lang's face was blotchy, swollen, and squeezed tight. "Oh, honey, what's the matter?" Lang waved A. J. away.

"You . . . left . . . me," Lang said. The words exploded out of her, like they'd been contained under pressure.

"I left you?" A. J. repeated, sitting on the edge of the chair. "Actually, you passed out drunk on the couch while you were entertaining guests. Not that I'm no Ann Landers, but if anyone made a faux pas, I don't think it was me. So."

"You just left me. You didn't tell me good-bye," Lang said. She did not sound like herself. She clenched the arms of the Queen Anne sofa so hard the tips of her knuckles turned a pale shade of green.

"Well, I'm so sorry. I didn't know—"

"You didn't even care enough to tell me you were leaving!" Lang screamed, banging her fists on the chair. "You didn't even love me enough to tell me good-bye!"

Lang's cheeks glistened. She stared at A. J., not speaking as her face turned a deep angry red. She gasped for breath.

"Lang? Lang?" Suddenly A. J. shot across the room and grabbed Lang from behind and clasped her fists across Lang's sternum. She pulled up repeatedly, trying to dislodge whatever was obviously stuck in Lang's throat.

Suddenly Lang made a long, low sound that seemed to come from deep within her. It didn't sound human. A. J. let go.

When Lang's keening finally eased up, she was on the floor, balled up with her head on her knees. A. J. sat down on the floor, and they sat still, back-to-back, like a modern sculpture conveying the sharing of grief.

"Who abandoned you, Lang?" A. J. asked.

"Everyone. Jack. You," she said. The sharp edges of A. J.'s shoulder blades pressed against her back.

"Who else? Who, Lang?" A. J. asked again.

Finally Lang's shoulders and head slumped with sleep, and A. J. gently lowered her to the floor. She put a throw pillow under Lang's head and covered her with the old quilt, letting her rest on the worn Oriental rug.

Making Arrangements

On the back of the chair, the quilt had looked like a random pattern of tattered curves, but when A. J. spread it over her, she could see circle after circle, all joined together.

A. J. stayed all night, watching over Lang from the wing chair.

TWENTY-EIGHT

....

Now was not the time to go through the old hat-boxes in the attic, but Lang wanted to change the photograph of her with the skinned knees. She wanted a picture of Jack instead.

She emptied the slew of photographs onto the kitchen table and sorted through gray blurs of faces and formal portraits. She stared at a picture of Jack as an infant, dressed in an elaborate white gown the same length as her curtains. It trailed over his mother's arms and pooled on the floor at her feet.

She worked methodically, trying to stay on task. She did not let herself indulge in memories of him or imagine her husband as a baby or a little boy.

He loved me. He'd made one mistake. A single oversight. And it was a minor one, not like an affair or anything really life changing.

If he were alive, they would have argued about this. She would have confronted him about the loan. They would have dealt with it the same way they'd dealt with Lang planting the row of weeping cherries on the property line. He'd been so angry, screaming at her that the roots would entangle themselves like crazy spaghetti in the sewer line and render it inoperable. She'd laughed at the idea. Pasta gone mad.

But they'd worked it out. She dug every single one up and donated them to the new public garden. She hoped none of its visitors would ever have to use the bathroom.

If he were here, they would resolve his betrayal. She could tell him how hurt she felt. How he knew this house, this land, was the most important thing to her. The most important *ma-*

terial thing. She would have screamed at him, and he would have apologized and been contrite. And they would have made up.

The morning he had died, his last morning on earth, he had run his hand through her cropped hair, pretending not to be able to grab onto it. She had always laughed when he grabbed her thick hair, acting like he was a caveman grabbing her for sex. It had been funny back when she had had hair, but the warmth of his palm on her shorn scalp had made her ashamed.

It had made sense to put him off that last morning—they were supposed to be on vacation in two days, and she'd said they should wait. Draw it out. Make it more special. It wasn't like sex was a given anymore. Plus, she had wanted a wig.

She pressed the picture of Jack standing beside a collie on-to the heavy white page. Then she glued on the next photograph, the one of Jack at age six, Katie D.'s age. He was grinning at the camera with a gap in his teeth, obviously thrilled he'd lost his first tooth. His eyes were almond-shaped and sloped up at the outer corners, exactly like Katie D.'s. Lang thought she would frame this picture in a double frame, Jack on one side, Katie D. on the other, both the same age, missing the same tooth.

By the time she realized her bladder was full, she didn't quite make it to the commode and had to change her under-wear. And her pants.

In the laundry room, she put the clothes in the wash, added water to the various jars of hydrangea cuttings, rolled the newspapers into a thick curve, and stuck them in a cardboard box to recycle.

She never heard a sound. Of course, what really would there have been to hear? The dog never barked or whined or whimpered.

The picture of Jack lay in wet, dark clumps on the rug.

Chewed up and spit out. The only picture of her husband she had with his front tooth missing, the one she was going to frame, lay in remnants on the floor.

Lang picked up the dog and stomped out to her car. She felt like her skin was shrinking in against her skull, suffocating her. She put the animal in the back of her station wagon and drove to the animal shelter.

She shouldn't have to do this. A. J. had promised to find him a home, and should have checked out the person better, not promised the little dog to someone so flighty. Lang had been nice enough to keep the little dog for months. She should have done this at the very beginning, the first day she saw him sitting in the garden.

He destroyed the picture of Jack!

She heard the cacophony of dogs as soon as she got out of her car. Yipping and yowling and barking. She carried the dog into the building and set him down on the front desk.

"I need to turn this dog in. He showed up at my house. I can't keep him," Lang said. She turned to leave, and the dog leaped off the counter and followed her.

"Wait!" the woman called. "Let me get ahold of him."

Lang turned and hurried to her car, not looking back. They would find him a good home. This would be the first place people would check to get a dog.

If Lang hadn't lost her glasses and could have read the incoming number on her cell phone, she wouldn't have answered it.

"Hello?"

"Hey, this is Sue, from the animal shelter? Are you the lady who just dropped off a little white dog? This number was on his collar."

"Yes. Is there a problem?" Lang didn't mean to be curt, but she was ready to be done with this. "Is he okay?"

"Yes, he's fine. It's just that he's already neutered." The woman paused, and Lang knew that was supposed to mean something to her, but she had no idea what. "We usually don't euthanize animals that have been neutered. Unless they're aggressive or something. You need to fill out paperwork so we can get him in the system. And we're pretty backed up. We can't keep him as long as we'd like to," she said.

"Euthanize?"

"Put to sleep."

"I know what the word means," Lang snapped. "I'm sorry. I just thought you all found homes for them."

The woman exhaled quickly and made a little snort that was meant to be a laugh. "In a perfect world, maybe. We have to put down fifteen animals a day. And we're still overcrowded. We can't take care of them all. Come look through the kennels for yourself. They are made for three dogs, tops, and we've got them stacked fifteen to a cage. We start with the problems first, ones that are vicious or sick. But still, it's criminal how many healthy dogs we kill. Sorry to be blunt."

"Fine, I'll come fill out the paperwork." Lang was in no position to take care of a dog. What would happen to it when she got sick? Or died? Sarah and Teddy couldn't have dogs in their apartment, and A. J.'s husband was allergic.

When she walked up the sidewalk, she thought the dogs sounded different. More desperate. She tried not to think of them wedged in concrete stalls, peeing where they had to sleep.

The woman was on the phone. She held up a finger, indicating she'd be a minute.

"Is it moving at all? Can you hear him barking?" The receptionist turned her head away from the receiver and whispered to Lang, "Dog stuck in a drainage pipe."

Lang wandered around the area that served as some kind of

a makeshift lobby. The sounds these dogs were making were unnerving. High-pitched and pleading and so constant. She didn't know how Sue stood it, working right in the thick of it every day.

She looked down the hall. There were wire cages stacked up on top of each other, and there was a little dog in each one. They seemed to be screaming. Some kind of miniature dachshund mix howled, a dirty Maltese type with dark black goo under its eyes barked incessantly, and a tiny tan puppy with an enormous tummy whined.

And then she saw him. Victoria's fur, the color of good champagne, looked clean and soft. He stood on his hind legs with his nose between the bars, wagging his tail so hard his whole spine shook. He stared up at her, pleading with topaz-colored eyes, not making a sound.

"Sorry about that," Sue said. "Just need your John Henry right here, and you're good to go."

Lang waved away the clipboard. "I'll just take him. I'll find him a home. I can find someone to take him," she said. "I'm not leaving him."

"Well, hallelujah," Sue said, opening the cage. "It's your lucky day, boy."

The dog gave Sue a quick lick on her chin, then leaped straight into Lang's arms.

TWENTY-NINE

. . . .

A. J. didn't give Lang an option; she just appeared and insisted Lang pack the essentials for a weekend at her mountain house in Highlands, N.C. They rode in A. J.'s BMW convertible along the Hiwassee River. A. J. wore oversize sunglasses and a pink silk paisley scarf tied over her hair. She looked like an iconic movie star, while Lang futilely tried to keep her hair from lashing at her face. She cupped her hands against her forehead to shield her eyes from the sun.

A. J. insisted on bringing Victoria along, and the dog stationed his hind legs in Lang's lap and stretched his face into the wind.

The road pressed against the riverbank, following it bend by bend so closely Lang felt she was almost in the water herself. She imagined herself shooting upstream against the churning white force of water, so powerful it looked solid.

They pulled over to watch two kayakers, their neon boats bright against the turbulent white river. The rafters moved fluidly down the rapids, their almond-shaped boats flowing with the water like they were part of the current.

"I'm being considered for a cancer trial," Lang said, surprising herself. She hadn't planned on talking about it, especially to A. J., but the words just rushed out.

"What do you mean? I thought you were done with that. That you were in recovery."

"It's called remission and I'm not in it. But there's a new trial I'm hoping to qualify for. Of course the real hope was that I wouldn't be in the running because the cancer would be in remission, but it looks like I'm eligible. So." Lang realized she had just ended her sentence with *so* and wondered if she'd soon be saying *coogle* and using incorrect grammar.

"Well, what does that mean? What do you have to do?" A. J. asked.

Suddenly Lang didn't want to talk about it. The thought of living in a nursing home while her ancient magnolias were being slaughtered and the medicine making her so nauseous she couldn't even eat was more depressing than the cancer.

"Oh, I don't know. I just wanted you to know. This is your house?"

A. J.'s house looked like something out of a storybook with its ancient wide logs and long shed dormer with a bank of windows.

The cabin was surprisingly light inside. Whitewashed boards lined the interior walls, and a long heart pine countertop sat between two enormous reclaimed posts, the rough jagged bark still on one side. Worn oriental rugs accented the gleaming heart pine floors, and a heavy hand-forged iron chandelier hung over an enormous primitive pine table. French doors opened up to a view of mountains, staggered one right after another as far as she could see.

"Oh. The check for the maid. I guess she didn't come? Walker was up here with his golf buddies last weekend, so I can imagine the state of the bedrooms. I'm going to go change the sheets real quick. I'll wait and kill him when I get back. Sit. Open a bottle of wine, then I'll show you where your room's at," A. J. said.

"I can help change the sheets," Lang said as she followed her upstairs to two perfectly made beds.

"Well, his golf buddies have more home training than most," A. J. said. "You can't even tell they slept in these beds!"

Making Arrangements

"These bedrooms are adorable! They look like they came out of a decorating magazine," Lang said.

"Oh my gosh," A. J. said, stopping in the doorway of the master bedroom. "I need to make up my own bed! Walker is the one who needs home training!"

"It will only take us a second," Lang said, whipping back the wadded-up bedspread.

A flounce of crimson lace fell soundlessly on the stark white sheet. They stared at the frilly thong, not speaking.

A. J. eased down on the edge of the bed, lowering herself with her arms. Her face seemed to have fallen in spite of itself, and she suddenly looked twice her age. Defeated. Her spine curved like an old woman's, and she rested her head on her knees. Her diamond ring flashed shears of light across the room.

Lang searched for words. *You don't deserve this. I'm so sorry.* She moved her mouth soundlessly, wondering what to say. She tried to imagine a sentence she could tolerate herself if she were A. J.

Lang sat silently on the bed beside her, finally putting her arm around A. J.'s shoulders. She would just listen to her. That was best. Let her talk it out. Lang bolstered herself for what was coming. Readied herself to hear A. J.'s pain.

"My maid is such a slut," A. J. said tentatively, pushing herself up. "She brings her boyfriend up here when she cleans. This isn't the first time. I've warned her." Her voice was gaining strength as she spoke. Gathering momentum. "I'm going to let her go. This is it."

A. J. dialed a number and walked back to her bathroom, and Lang walked around the house awkwardly. How could A. J. stick her head so far down in the sand?

She picked up a photograph of A. J. and Walker dressed in ski clothes. A. J. wore a luxurious fur headband and had a skin-

161

tight black cat suit on that Lang assumed must be warm. They both smiled at the camera, A. J. with brilliant white teeth, Walker with teeth that were not so white. A. J. was so gorgeous. A movie star. Why would she put up with this?

At least Jack had never cheated on her. He never would have. Never.

Had he cheated on me, too?

"Okay, that's taken care of. She apologized, but I told her it was too late. You just have to put your foot down at some point," A. J. said.

THIRTY

....

Thank goodness for Valentine's Day, Lang thought as she finished the last dozen birch-bark flower orders. Her arrangements with the couple's initials etched into the bark containers mimicked old-fashioned romantic initials carved into a tree trunk and overflowed with camellias from the garden. Her arrangements were so popular that she finally had to start refusing orders.

> Dear Jack,
>
> I am sorry you have to go through Valentine's Day without me. If I died close to Thanksgiving, I made it one full year. I had some bonus time here. Gravy, as you like to say. Anyway, best-case scenario is that I've been gone almost three months, and that is plenty of time for "proper" grieving. Anything longer than that will get on people's nerves. People can take only so much thumb-sucking.
>
> You were always a good valentine. Remember that year you gave me "All Things Chocolate"? A big brown paper grocery bag filled with Tootsie Rolls and Rolos and Hershey's bars with almonds and Dove chocolates and M&M's. What else? Swiss cake rolls. I had to put most of it in the freezer, and it lasted all year! (That's my story, anyway.)
>
> Then the year you made dinner all by yourself? You grilled a rack of lamb and roasted new potatoes and sautéed the first asparagus of spring, and I said I couldn't eat lamb without mint jelly. You deserve some kind of badge for that one. The I-didn't-kill-my-wife-when-any-other-man-would-have award. Sorry. Bad joke. Anyway, I've always regretted

being such a little brat that year. When I told you I was so, so sorry and would carry my regret to my grave, I meant it. So now you know.

Anyway, you always made February 14 special. Dinner by candlelight and a bag of bulbs to plant (I would have been livid if you'd spent money on cut roses) and always something chocolate. An entire Coca-Cola cake from "Crackle" Barrel. (Remember when Teddy called it that at seventeen? He had no idea it was "Cracker.") A huge red satin heart-shaped box of cardboard-tasting candies.

Jack Eldridge, I loved being your valentine. You could not have made me feel more treasured, on that day or any other. Open your eyes now. And your heart. Be open to another chance.

It would break my heart to think of you being lonely and pathetic—a little wizzled-up old man. You are not a spring chicken! I don't care how many pushups you do or how many balls you run down on the tennis court.

Please, as my last wish, LIVE the rest of your life with joy.

Happy V-D.

Lang wished she hadn't read the letter. It was hard enough to keep Jack out of her head without remembering his damn Valentine's Day gifts.

She thought about the Coca-Cola cake, the thick fudge icing still warm, and tried to the block Jack forging her name from her mind. Not that it was really a forgery. Jack just hadn't worried her about it. He didn't want to bother her with his business problems or their money situation or anything that would bog her down and distract her from healing. It wasn't an actual forgery.

What else had he lied about?

Lang studied the two pale green bowls on the counter, each brimming with homemade frosting. They reminded her of early woodland flowers, pale pink and deep rose against barely green foliage. She moved them in front of the cyclamens spilling their fluttery magenta blossoms over the planter, eyed them, and then moved them away.

Would it have suited him just fine if I hadn't lasted the year? Had he been twiddling his thumbs for months, waiting on me to drop dead?

While the sugar cookie dough chilled in the fridge, Lang filled a Styrofoam egg carton with Red Hots, chocolate chips and baby M&M's. She looked through the cabinets for the remnants of sprinkles and those tiny silver pellets. She distinctly remembered buying them for the Forth of July a few years ago.

Had the stress of me living longer than expected, and his fear of my discovery of the lie, killed him? Caused his heart attack?

She found a tin of cinnamon and wondered how it would look dusted on the pale pink frosting. Would it bleed? Stain it a watery orange? She pried the plastic lid open and sniffed inside. She smelled something familiar, but it wasn't cinnamon. She put the tin back on the top shelf.

She knew she was overthinking the aesthetics of cookie-decorating preparation. She found herself managing small sections of her house this way lately, styling certain areas when she should be organizing floral orders or cleaning the toilet. It was so nice to see something perfectly arranged—if not in her life, at least on the back of the toilet.

She routinely folded ribbed, white towels in tight, perfect rectangles and plunked an oversize bar of thyme soap on top of them. She moved the large glass jar of lavender bath salts close to a decanter of milky white bubble bath and plopped a large natural sea sponge (unused) on the silver-handled tray at the end of the bathtub. She hid her cracked sliver of pale green soap under the rim of the tub. The thyme soap and loofah were not for her.

Would everyone be better off if I had just died a year ago?

She was glad when the doorbell finally rang. She needed to get busy and stop her crazy, clicking brain. No more letters.

"Hello?" Sarah called after Katie D., who barreled toward Lang in sparkly high heels that clattered on the wooden floor. Victoria leaped straight up in the air, head-height with Katie D., like a diver testing the bounce on the board.

Lang breathed in the scent of Katie D.'s hair. It smelled like sun-warmed hay. And freesia. She felt herself right a little. Balance. She inhaled once more, burying her face in her granddaughter's hair.

"We've got Valentine's Day cookies to bake! Sarah, you're in charge of the sprinkles and the chocolate chips," Lang said.

"Oh, no. I can't stay. I've got to get back to work. Teddy will pick her up, but I've got my cell if you need me," Sarah said.

"Well, they won't be as pretty, but don't worry. I'll call Teddy if we need anything."

Lang watched Sarah walk halfway down the sidewalk, then turn around. She seemed to be looking at the jonquils in the woods. There were thousands now.

"Pick some! Take a big bunch with you!" Lang called out.

Sarah looked startled, like she'd been caught doing something wrong.

Katie D. had the same look on her face when Lang went back to the kitchen.

"What's wrong?" Lang asked.

"I stole the candies," Katie D. said, pointing to three empty eggcups.

"*Stole,*" Lang said. "And you didn't steal. You just borrowed them, right? To save for a rainy day?"

"No. To eat when I get home. I stole them because they're not mine, and I didn't ask. Teacher says it's stealing. She learned us about stealing," Katie D. said.

"Well, stealing is a harsh word," Lang said, realizing suddenly she was teaching Katie D. to live by her own rules the same way she had let Teddy believe rules didn't apply to him. And look where that ended up. He couldn't keep a job and didn't really think he needed to work.

"It's bad," Katie D. said.

"You know what? You're right. Don't take things that don't belong to you. Without asking. You can have what you took. That's fine. Just don't eat them all at once because you'll get sick and your mommy will have to call the doctor," Lang said.

"I can't get sick. I promised Mommy. She cries sometimes about it," Katie D. said.

"Cries about you getting sick?" Lang asked, wondering if Sarah was a hypochondriac.

"'Sometimes she does. I want to call you. I learned my number, and I want to know yours," Katie D. said. "And Victoria's." Katie D. pointed to the numbers on the dog's pink collar.

"Eight-seven-seven-four-two-oh-two," Lang crooned in a singsong voice until Katie D. sang it by herself.

"Do you and Victoria have the same phone number?" Katie D. asked as she studied the dog's collar.

"I guess we do. For now anyway," Lang said.

Katie D. dipped her moist pinkie into the candy sprinkles in the egg carton. Lang realized she should have put the chocolate chips next to the M&M's and used a white egg carton instead of a yellow one. Then she told herself to stop. Didn't they make medicine for this new disorder of hers?

Jack just hadn't wanted to worry me.

She let Katie D. roll out the cookie dough. It would have been easier to have them already baked and cooling, but Lang wanted to teach her how to turn on the oven, grease and flour the cookie sheet, and trust the barely browning edges of the cookie more than the timer. She wanted Katie D. to know how

to let the cookies cool completely before icing them and how
to oh-so-carefully slide the spatula underneath and scoop each
one up without cracking it. She wanted to teach her everything.

She showed her granddaughter how to spread the icing in a
wide, smooth swoop and then sprinkle the candy decorations
immediately before the icing made a hard film that the sprinkles would bounce off. They stacked the cookies, each one gar-
ishly adorned with at least five different decorations, between
waxed paper in a large Tupperware container. Katie D. set a
candy heart, stamped with words like *Be mine* or *Love you,* in the
center of each one, carefully deciding which child would get
which message.

"Just so everyone gets one. Teacher, too," Katie D. said,
counting them all one more time. "And Miss Yates, Para Pro,"
she said, licking her fingers.

"That's good, Katie D., making sure there's one for every
person in the class," Lang said.

"Yes, Grandie. We don't want to leave anyone out. Hurt
someone's feelings!" Katie D. said, widening her eyes in alarm
as if Lang had suggested ostracizing someone outright, perhaps the Para Pro.

"No, we don't," Lang said, hovering behind Katie D. and
spreading her hand over the crown of her head. It felt like
warm silk under her fingers.

Lang remembered Valentine's Day in her first-grade class.
By then every sentence took her so long to stammer out she'd
practically stopped speaking in public. She'd decorated her
shoe box with red tissue-paper flowers and pink crepe paper
and lacy hearts cut from doilies. Lang remembered opening
her shoebox like it was yesterday. Empty. Not a single valentine.

She'd closed the lid quickly and twisted the crepe-paper

rosebuds on her shoe box into tight spear tips, while the rest of the class had giggled and murmured over their lovely missives of admiration.

Lang waited another hour before she called Sarah. Teddy was three hours late, and Katie D. had fallen asleep on the couch. Lang had left Teddy six messages but hadn't heard a word from him.

"I think maybe his cell died?" Sarah said when she arrived.

"Well, it's not like him to forget Katie D. Cookie?" Lang offered. "Have you had dinner? Katie D. had some soup before she fell asleep, and I've got the makings for an omelet in the fridge." She held out the platter of perfectly arranged cookies. Sarah didn't immediately refuse the way she usually did, and Lang extended the platter farther.

"They're so beautiful. I hate to eat one," Sarah said as she took a large cookie heaped with both icings. She held up the cookie and smiled. "This is so special for her."

"And me, too! I wouldn't take anything for this time with her. Baking together," Lang said. "Do you like asparagus? And I've got yellow peppers, too. You'll have to bear with me. Jack was the official omelet maker in the family, so I don't have much practice."

Sarah turned away abruptly and walked quickly toward Katie D. and scooped her up. Lang wondered if she'd said something offensive and tried to remember her exact words. Maybe she was just picky about her omelets.

Lang waited for them by the door. Katie D.'s little body draped across Sarah's left shoulder, and she was still sound asleep.

"Let me help you," Lang said, tugging at Sarah's heavy purse. "I don't want you to fall, and the steps aren't lit."

"No, really, I've got it all balanced. It's fine. Just the door, if you don't mind."

Katie D. lifted her head and turned to Lang. "No chains. See, Mommy?"

"What sweetie?" Lang asked. "Chains?"

"Thank you so much. This was great," Sarah said. "Your phone's ringing."

Lang watched their top-heavy shadowy shape move slowly away from her in the dark. She stood at the sidelight and waited until their headlights came on and the red glow of brake lights vanished. Then she locked the front door and walked toward the ringing telephone.

She realized what chain Katie was talking about. Lang didn't have a heavy, industrial chain on her door to keep her safe. She didn't need one.

THIRTY-ONE

....

O h my god, I thought you were out," A. J. said into the
receiver. "What are you doing? Never mind. Come for
dinner? You won't believe what I've made, and Walker
just got called into emergency surgery."

"No, I'm in the middle of dinner actually." Lang looked at
the carton of eggs on the counter. Twelve perfect white ovals,
all exactly the same shape.

"I don't hear any chewing," A. J. said. Lang smacked her lips.
"Listen, I've got jumbo shrimp marinated in fresh rosemary
and olive oil and some kind of French spice, and you know
how fancy the French are about food, and I roasted real beets
for the salad and crumpled up Maytag blue cheese. And I
grilled this herb-crusted beef tenderloin with a champagne
béarnaise that I'm about to scrape down the disposal. I've
worked too hard. I want someone to enjoy it."

Lang looked at the two mixing bowls soaking in the sink
and the flour still heaped in little piles on the counter. The
cookie sheets lay cold and soiled on the stove, twenty-four perfect circles outlined in crumbs.

"Fine," Lang said. "Do you need a yellow pepper?"

There was a card table set up in A. J.'s living room, right in
front of a roaring fire. Two full place settings of silver, from
the fish fork to the demitasse spoon, lay rigidly on lace white
napkins. Five assorted glasses, from champagne flutes to bran-
dy snifters, stood in graduating order by the tip of the knives.
And white tea lights were scattered all over the table, glowing

softly.

"A. J., this is exquisite! I'm sorry it took me so long, but I stepped in dog mess. Again. You shouldn't waste this on me! When will Walker be done? You should wait on him to come home."

"He won't be home until the morning," A. J. said. Her chin trembled. "I've been planning this Valentine's Day dinner for weeks now, ever since I caught him dying his pubic hair 'Midnight Sable.'"

Lang was caught off guard. Was this something people actually did? "What?"

"I came home early from tennis because Peggy twisted her ankle, and there he was, up on a stool in front of the bathroom mirror, naked except for black socks. He was checking out his newly vibrant pubic hair. I didn't say nothing, just tiptoed back to the kitchen. I thought it was for me. I do all this crap to myself for him, so I thought he was going to surprise me."

"So—" Lang paused, not knowing what to say. She didn't want to know the rest of the story.

"So, he never showed me. That's the only time I saw it. Wine?"

"Oh, how lovely! Anything's fine. I don't know much at all about what's good, so just give me something cheap," Lang said, relieved they were on a new subject. "Have you tried that wine in a box? I read it's very high quality, and that pretty soon all wines will be coming in a box. Back in the day that—"

"I did my boobs for him. I thought that was the problem. Of course, we didn't used to have a problem, but after the baby, he changed. I breast-fed, and I was great at it." A. J. leaned forward toward Lang. Her face was smooth and still, but her eyes were all lit up and shining. "You hear about all these people who don't have milk—well, not me. Mine came in by the half gallon. As soon as Brandon emptied one, it filled right back up. They felt like they were about to pop. You could see these pale blue veins squiggling across. And they leaked. I just stayed at home and wore Walker's old shirts. They were always stiff at the chest from where I'd dripped all day, and I always smelled like sour milk. Walker never should have seen me that way. It changed him."

"I was one of those who couldn't nurse. I always regretted it. I still wonder sometimes if I should have stuck it out longer, but I swear my baby was starving. The doctors were alarmed he'd lost weight, and they gave him a bottle right there in the office, just to make sure he could eat."

"That could have been it right there. Seeing me like that. A slob. Smelly. And so fat. I ate like a pig the whole time I was nursing him. Walker was just not interested after that. I marked down the days on the calendar to that six-week mark, when they say it's okay to have sex. But he wouldn't have no part of it. Nope, not even thinking about it. My breasts were the only part that had changed after I lost the baby weight. Even my stomach was flat again. I did enough donkey kicks to make my butt sit up high on its own. No implants needed there! But the breasts pooled down to empty flaps on my chest. I got to where I couldn't look at myself naked—couldn't admire my tummy or arms without cringing at my what-used-to-be breasts. So thirteen months later, I did it. Plumped them up to perfect centerfold tits," A. J. said. "Or the surgeon did."

"Well, your figure is incredible, and I can't imagine any man not being gaga over you. I'd do anything to look like you," Lang said. She tried to hold her stomach in, but it wouldn't go.

Lang didn't know what else to say. She remembered Jack marking slashes on the calendar after Teddy was born, counting down the days to the square labeled "SEX." Of course, that was a very long time ago.

"When Walker didn't flinch at the price of the surgery, I

knew he'd needed large, full breasts all along. That he couldn't care less about the butt and thighs. I was optimistic as I scheduled the augmentation, imagining him wanting me again. He was interested in the two new breasts as soon as the incisions healed. He cupped them in his hands and pressed down with his fingers. 'Are they supposed to be this hard?' That's what he said. Like he was feeling of a green cantaloupe. So," A. J. said, and finally stopped talking.

Lang wanted to say the right thing. She wanted to make A. J. feel validated, but she couldn't imagine how she felt. Jack had always wanted sex, no matter how fat she was or how bald she was.

"Well, I don't know. The media has made it so high pressure. You can't even turn on the TV without a deluge of middle-aged couples grinning because they just scored some Viagra."

A. J. had a look on her face that did not look validated.

"Hindsight, I should have just started Brandon off with a plastic bottle. It would have saved me a lot of trouble. He couldn't not care less about either one of us now. He lives as far away as he possibly can. If they start building condos on the moon, he'll be the first to buy. Once I did the boobs, I did my eyes. They were already sagging. And then my forehead looked like it belonged on an old woman's head. My boobs looked so perfect, I wanted the rest of my body to catch up. I spent most of his childhood looking like my head had dropped off Niagara Falls in a barrel. Eyelids. Forehead. Neck. Lips. It's kind of like getting a new piece of furniture. Or redoing a room. You do one thing, and it makes you realize what else needs doing. Once you start, you really can't never stop," A. J. said.

"Or there's so much to do you don't even know where to begin," Lang said. She waggled the skin on her neck, then plumped up her lips in a pout. A. J. looked away.

"I love him, Lang. I don't know who I'd be without him. I don't care about the sex. But I want to be with him."

"Well, I don't know him at all, but I know you!" Lang said. "And you are funny and delightful and loveable, so that's who you are without him."

"That's not what he thinks," A. J. said, pouring herself another glass of wine.

"Well, maybe you should surprise Walker when he comes home with this dinner. You've knocked yourself out, A. J., and he should at least know it."

"I've tried that. The surprise. You wouldn't believe the stuff I've done for him." A. J.'s face looked puffy, and her eyes were so swollen they looked like they were pulled taut toward her temples. "You'd think I'd learn after the Saran Wrap fiasco. That was a while back even. Twenty years at least. It was in *Cosmo*. The magazine? I wrapped myself in the stuff. Started at my heels. I let my feet alone so I could walk," she explained, as if Lang was considering the idea. "Went all the way up with it. I did my hair and makeup first. Heavy eyeliner, diamond earrings, a thin black silk ribbon in a bow around my throat. All that."

"Can I do anything to start dinner?" Lang asked. She wondered how much A. J. had been drinking. Her words weren't all that slurred, but they were inappropriate. She pulled the rubber band on her wrist taut and snapped it.

"I think it's been longer. It was back in the seventies. Do you remember that? All that about making dinner naked? Who was that woman? She said the secret to life was pleasing your man. I leaned forward and wrapped my boobs. That was before. It had to be 1976." She hinged forward from her hips and placed her hands on her breasts. "They looked great. I'm not kidding. No! It was before I had my eyes done the first time.

Oh my god, how old was I?"

A. J. looked away, and Lang was relieved this awkward conversation, or monologue rather, was over.

"You would never have guessed I'd need that augmentation. They were like those in girlie magazines. So I wrapped them up tight, right?"

"Yes. Got that," Lang said.

"I wrapped it real tight around my middle, like a cellophane corset, and then tried to squeeze my butt up a little higher. Everybody can use that. Even teenagers. I wrapped my thighs together, going just below my knees, then put on black stiletto heels and minced off to the kitchen, like Ariel the Little Mermaid if she had gone with porn instead of Disney."

Lang washed the yellow pepper, running the faucet at full throttle.

"I can tell you I didn't look my age. Nowhere near it."

"A. J., what could you have been? Were you even thirty?"

Lang wondered how many rolls of Saran Wrap it would take to conceal the flesh around her rear.

"I waited in front of the open refrigerator door, willing myself not to sweat. I'd already made the pitcher of martinis. Foresight," A. J. said.

"Then these big, angry, raised splotches crept out over the plastic wrap on my skin. Worse than a heat rash, but I didn't scratch at them. Finally, I heard the pea gravel crunch under Walker's tires, and I inched to the front door. I went real slow. I had this martini glass filled to the brim and extra olives on a little silver tray. Walker opened the door and looked me up and down. But not in a good way.

"'Is it vodka?' That's what he said.

"He took the drink and clunked his car keys on my tray. They got wet because I'd sloshed the drink on the way to the door. I followed him back to the den. I thought he needed a minute. He always took a little time to warm up. Videos, or I'd put on these outfits for him. To get him going. Storybook characters mainly. Gretel. That contrary Mary. None of them wore panties."

"A. J.," Lang began. She diced the yellow pepper into pieces small enough to go through a colander.

"So I'm inching on these stiletto heels. I linger around the corner, you know, real tempting like. I slither myself around the door, and he says he's ready for a refill. He doesn't even look up at me."

Lang looked down at the yellow puree on the cutting board.

"I found the receipt for Viagra in his pants pocket last week. I should have known it wasn't for me. But I just thought with Valentine's coming up and all. I just thought maybe he was planning on . . . I had a bikini wax."

A. J. looked down at her hands, not meeting Lang's eyes.

"So, long story short. No. I'm not going to surprise him," she said softly.

"Well," Lang began. She was at a loss. What do you say when something is so obvious? She felt bad for her but knew A. J. needed to snap out of it. Get on with her life. "That's bad news for Walker, but what a windfall for me. This dinner looks incredible!" Lang scooted closer to A. J. and wrapped her arm around her shoulders. "You did a good job. An incredible job."

"Oh, Lang. I've made a mess of my life," A. J. said. She draped herself over Lang's shoulder and began to sob. "And now I'm too old to start anything." Lang braced her hips against the kitchen counter and tried to keep her balance. She was still so weak, but she was determined to support A. J. Literally.

"It's okay," Lang said. "Everything happens for a reason." She muttered as A. J. cried, remembering A. J. saying the same generic phrases when Jack had died.

"You practically own the whole organization, and you can't seem to get me in. Am I a total joke?" A. J. said suddenly. She lifted her head from Lang's shoulders and looked at her. A. J.'s mascara ran in dark puddles down her face, and clear mucus ran down her nose. "Is that why they won't let me in the women's club?"

"No, of course not," Lang said. She tried to scoot back from A. J., but the counter pressed into her hips.

"I do all this stuff to look good. To try to look good. Classy, like you all. Like that makes any difference in the long run. I know people think I'm silly," A. J. said.

"Listen to me," Lang said, leaning toward A. J. "You are a decent, kind person. And you have made a difference to me. You have. Not just with the loan. With your friendship. And I don't make friends easily. And I'm going to get you in that stupid club if it kills me."

"Really?" A. J. said. "I mean not if it kills you."

"Yes. Really," Lang said. "But you need to wipe your nose. I can't eat and look at that."

"Lang?" A. J. said softly. "I don't want anything to kill you."

"Thank you. That's the nicest thing I've heard all week," Lang said, lifting her glass.

They toasted the first course with sauvignon Blanc, then the salads with chardonnay, and then finally clinked chilled champagne flutes after drinking cabernet and Riesling. Firelight from the fiery embers played across their faces.

"You missed a spot. Right there," A. J.said, pointing at her own left nostril.

Lang laughed as she wiped her nose, and her eyes flashed a vivid turquoise. Her skin gathered in soft, loose bunches on her throat and crinkled around her eyes and mouth.

"What?" Lang asked. A. J. stared at her, obviously drunk.

"No, I was just watching you, and I was just going to say

you could get that done around your eyes so easy. It would make you look ten years younger. And then you laughed, and, Lang, I'm telling you, you are the most beautiful woman I've ever seen."

"Oh, A. J. That's ridiculous."

"It's so beautiful, your face. The way it changes when you laugh or frown. Or look surprised. It's so interesting. When you smile, your whole face smiles. Not just your mouth. I've been just watching you. Your skin glows. And moves. It's so nice the way your face shows your feelings."

"Well, th-th-that's so kind," Lang said. And she decided A. J. hadn't had too much to drink after all.

THIRTY-TWO

B right and early the next morning A. J. vigorously marched in place at the door and insisted Lang join her outside. She wore black tights and a fitted pink top that had some kind of sheen to it. Her headband was the exact shade of pink as her top and edged in black. She looked like someone on a fitness infomercial.

"It's too pretty out here to be holed up in there," A. J. said.

"You act like I never go outside," Lang said.

"Well, you would spare yourself some trouble if you walked the dog," A. J. said. "You know if you walk him around the neighborhood he'll go to the bathroom there, instead of in your yard." She took a deep breath of air in and swooped both arms up toward the sky, swan diving forward until her head hung between her knees. None of the skin on her face moved at all. "So."

"Teddy wants to put me in a nursing home," Lang said when A. J. finally rolled herself to an upright position.

"A nursing home?" A. J. asked. She windmilled her arms around fluidly.

Lang raised her shoulders toward her ears, then let them fall back down. "He's worried something will happen. That I'll get sick again. With no one to take care of me. He has a name for the place—something not as bad as nursing home."

"Resisted living?" A. J. said. Lang studied A. J.'s face to see if she was kidding and realized she wasn't. "He sounds like Peter Peter Pumpkin Eater who put his mother in a pumpkin pie shell and kept her in there very well."

"That was his wife. Not his mother," Lang said. She tried not to think about A. J. dressing up like Peter's pantyless wife. "I don't know. I know he's worried about me being alone now. I'm forgetting things. He doesn't even know that, though."

"Do you want to move?" A. J. asked. "Good girl! See how she goes to the bathroom when she gets to moving around?" A. J. pumped her knees high as the dog sniffed the Lenten roses and finally squatted beside the perfect one.

"It's a *he*. Not that it matters," Lang said, tying her tennis shoes.

"I thought you loved this house. It's been in your family since Moses marched through the Red Sea."

"Are you making fun of me? Just because this house has been in my family for over a century?"

"No, I'm jealous if anything. You're actually from here. You belong. I've lived here over twenty-nine years, but I'll never be *from* here. Anyone with fewer than three generations in Barrington is an outsider," A. J. said.

"Well, my great grandfather built this house himself, A. J.! You're just as mercenary as Teddy. You'd probably raze it, too."

"Raise it? I thought you said it was in good shape, built solid and all," A. J. said. "Is there problems with the foundation?"

"Tear it down. He wants to tear down the house and build some kind of snooty resort here," Lang said. "He wants to wedge twenty houses in here. Plus a tennis court. Good boy!"

A. J. pumped her arms quickly over her head to burn extra calories as the dog investigated various innocuous-seeming patches of monkey grass. The bright blue weights on A. J.'s ankles made soft swooshing noises as they rubbed across each other, and as she marched, her knees actually made contact with her breasts, which loomed out from her chest. Lang tried to catch her breath after the effort of walking along with her.

"Well, what are you thinking?" A. J. asked. "You'd make a

killing. This is the biggest piece of property left, and we all know it's in the thick of Snootyville, USA."

"Sorry. I need to slow down a little," Lang said. She tugged her jacket down, trying to disguise her rear end somewhat. Her lungs felt like they were about to burst.

"Oh, okay. I meant about the nursing home," A. J. said. "It's very social, actually."

"I don't want to go, but he has a point," Lang said. "I had a terrible pain in my gut, which turned out to be nothing more than a bad avocado, but it scared me. I defied the odds the first time around. And now I'm dealing with the second time, second occurrence, and well, you know how that story ends."

A. J. whipped around and squared off against Lang, pressing her face five inches from Lang's. "I'll tell you how that story ends. It ends with you being strong and alive and well and old. Look at me!" A. J. grabbed Lang's chin and squeezed it. "You are going to be fine. They discover something earthquaking every day, and you are going to be here, on this earth, in Snootytown, a long, long time." A. J. let go of Lang's chin and dabbed at her eyes, then wiped her nose with her sleeve. "I cry all the time all of a sudden."

"More like Snottytown," Lang said, and A. J. nodded.

"Maybe I should go out for Snottytown Women's Club," A. J. said.

"You could get me in," Lang said, handing her a tissue. "Especially today."

They walked up the hill, and Lang was grateful every time Victoria stopped to pee. Her lungs seemed to be too full to hold any more air. She leaned against a stone wall and tried to catch her breath.

"If it comes back full force, I'll be in trouble. I'll need care, probably full time. Anyway, I told Teddy I'd go look at one. Shepherd's Arms is the one he's picked," Lang said.

Making Arrangements

"Shepherd's Arms! That's where my mother is! I'll go, too. I know where all the little activity rooms are—where you'll be making picture frames out of Popsicle sticks and weaving macramé wall hangings. So!" A. J. said, cackling.

THIRTY-THREE

....

S hepherd's Arms sat up on the side of a hill over-looking the river. Lang noticed dark stains of oint-ment on the shorn limbs of the enormous oaks that shaded the sloping front yard. The ancient trees had been taken care of properly, and Lang thought that might be a good sign.

"Look, Mom. The japonica's blooming," Teddy said.

"The what? Are you speaking Latin or something?" A. J. asked.

"That's not Latin," Teddy said, laughing. "It's just the name of the plant. I know all of them. Well, most. *Acer rubrum. Cornus florida.* I learned those before I learned the ABCs."

"Do you have to know the Latin names to be in the women's club?"

"Oh, A. J. I wish you would forget about the stupid club. None of them know the names of any flower, much less the Latin names. I'll teach you if you want to know," Lang said.

"They said no, didn't they?" A. J. asked.

"A. J., I told you I'm going to get you in, so it doesn't matter what they say," Lang said.

"I could be in the club if they cared about the Latin names. I know all that shit," Teddy said. A. J. narrowed her eyes at Teddy.

"Teddy used to play with the flowers while I worked in the garden," Lang said.

"You mean play in the dirt?" A. J. asked. "With little trucks and stuff?"

"Nope. I gave him a box of toothpicks, and he made dolls out of the blossoms. A bachelor-button head. A lady's-slipper chapeau. A daylily skirt. What else, Teddy?"

"Mom, god. That was a long time ago," Teddy said. His face flushed a scorched pink. "You make me sound like some little nancy boy."

Lang laughed. "Queen Anne's lace. That was for the wedding. He made a veil and gown and little crown out of white hydrangea blooms and Queen Anne's lace."

"Wedding! That reminds me—the museum curator's daughter is getting married, and they want you to do the flowers. They saw those bouquets of pink and green bird tulips wrapped with that preppy plaid ribbon you made for a bridesmaid luncheon, and the sky's the limit on their budget. I told them you make cakes, too," A. J. said.

"I've never made a wedding cake!"

"Sure you have. Make that white cake with raspberry filling and that airy meringue drizzle business over it. But make three of them and stack them," Teddy said.

"You know about cakes? And flowers both?" A. J. said.

"I guess I am a bit of a nancy boy," Teddy said. "At least Dad said so."

Lang stared at him, shocked he'd sensed Jack's disapproval. She remembered the long afternoons in the garden, digging as the shade from the old magnolia tree slowly spread over the flowerbeds. Teddy played so easily by himself, assigning roles to his flower people. A mother. A babysitter. A construction worker. She remembered smiling as she listened to him act out weddings, content with the smell of the earth and her little boy by her side.

Jack had put a stop to this effeminate behavior. He signed Teddy up for tennis camp at age five, forbidding Teddy to do anything in the garden but play with his metal pickup trucks.

Lang never told Jack the beds of those little trucks were lined with royal ladies in hollyhock skirts and poppy capes.

"Oh, Teddy. I loved those afternoons. Seems like just the other day you were making southern belles out of peonies and camellias. And now you probably can't even fathom that."

"What panties?" A. J. asked.

"*Peonies*. It's a flower that smells like pure heaven," Teddy said. "*Paeonia*. And the Julia Drayton camellia was my favorite flower. Of all the southern belles."

Lang stood for a moment and looked out over the expanse of yard spreading in front of Shepherd's Arms. There was no sign of perennials, and she wondered if they'd let her claim a spot of earth, if she could dig and plant and divide in a little plot of ground. It would make a difference. She tried to picture herself here, with someone to take care of her if she needed it. All her meals cooked and ready. Teddy squeezed her arm as they walked through the double doors.

The smell of ammonia and industrial meat engulfed her when she entered the lobby. Lang couldn't tell if it was chicken or beef, and suddenly her stomach recoiled at the idea of eating a meal here. Patients sat around the lobby in wheelchairs, waiting. Some turned and stared, and one woman rolled her wheelchair toward them, moving it forward by shuffling her white Keds.

"It's not a good time, really. You can't come in," the elderly woman in the wheelchair said.

"Hello!" a woman said brightly. She wore a large boxy jacket that did nothing to conceal her stump of a torso and large square glasses that overwhelmed her face. "I'm Julia, and you must be the Eldridge family?"

"Yes, I'm Teddy. Teddy Eldridge." He paused, waiting for the recognition he was accustomed to. "And this is my mother, Lang Eldridge, and our friend, A. J. Cole."

Julia inspected Lang through her thick lenses, and Lang hoped she didn't have a crust on the edges of her nostrils.

"My mother is here actually. So," A. J. said.

Julia looked at her blankly, and A. J. said, "Mrs. Ball. We'll just go visit her for now. Then go from there."

"It's not a good time. Really now. Come back another day!" the woman in the wheelchair said again, this time adamantly.

"Mrs. Webster. I'm going to put you back on your hall if you can't be more cordial," Julia chided, then rolled her back by the cafeteria doors. "It's fish today. Your favorite. So let's get you to your table." Mrs. Webster's feet couldn't keep up with the briskly rolling chair, and the tops of her shoes dragged on the floor like useless flippers.

"She's been with us awhile," Julia told them as if this explained anything. "Certainly you can visit your mother. I apologize for not recognizing you, Mrs. Cole. I'll take Teddy and Mrs. Eldridge to the apartments, and then we'll pop in the assisted living. That's correct? Assisted living?" Julia looked at Teddy for confirmation, not her.

"That's right," Teddy answered as if Lang wasn't here. "And then once they're in that part, they can be moved if necessary?"

"Oh, yes. We have three levels of care here," Julia said.

"For them, right?" Lang said, irritated they were referring to her in the third person.

"I'm sorry," Julia said. "It's just that I've been talking to your son about all this."

"I didn't want to bother you with all the details," Teddy said, shrugging his shoulders. Lang thought about Jack not bothering her with the details.

"My mother is in three-oh-four. So," A. J. said.

"I'll go with you," Lang said. Teddy and Julia looked at each other helplessly, then followed A. J. and Lang to the elevator.

The third floor smelled like a stronger version of the first floor.

"Someone put me to bed," a woman chanted, catching Lang's eye. Lang looked at Julia who shook her head and scowled.

"It's two," Julia told the woman briskly. "You know when bedtime is."

The woman called after them as they went down the hall. *Jesus.*

"Hello, Mother!" A. J. said when they walked in room 304. Mrs. Ball sat up in her bed, and her roommate, a sullen Indian woman with straight black hair, lay in the bed beside her, staring straight up at the ceiling. "You've met Miss Julia."

"No. I don't believe I never have," Mrs. Ball said.

"Mrs. Ball, of course we've met. Hello, Mrs. Gibson," Julia said to the Indian woman, but the woman did not respond.

"She never says a word," Mrs. Ball said to Lang. "It's not you. At least I don't have to worry about someone yapping my ear off like that last one I had in here. Angela Jeanette, who are your friends?"

"Let me introduce you," A. J. began.

"Are you coming to stay with me?" Mrs. Ball asked Teddy, interrupting. "You sure are easy on the eyes. You can have her bed. They could put her anywhere, and she wouldn't know the difference. Put her in a drawer for all she knows."

Lang looked over at Mrs. Gibson, horrified, but Mrs. Gibson remained expressionless. Julia forced a tight smile at Mrs. Ball, then patted her blanketed feet.

"Well, lookie here! A party!" a pregnant black nurse exclaimed, waddling into the tiny crowded room. She looked Teddy up and down and said, "Ummmmm-hummm," which he obviously took as a compliment. He beamed at her and reached out his hand as he introduced himself.

The nurse's stomach pressed so firmly against her pastel-patterned smock that her belly button bulged out. "Time for your meds, Mrs. Ball. That's right. Good girl," she said when A. J.'s mother swallowed her pills.

"Isn't it so exciting? A baby on the way!" Julia said. She clapped her hands together.

"Yes, not much longer," the nurse said, pressing her hands into the small of her back as she left the room. "You'll be the first to see the baby, Mrs. Ball. I swear it," she called back over her shoulder, but she was looking at Teddy. So was Mrs. Ball.

"You know what? Just leave her in the bed. I'll scootchy my bootchy over, and you can just set right here. Lay with me," Mrs. Ball said. She pulled the covers back and patted the bed with surprising force.

Teddy turned away, and Lang left the room without telling Mrs. Ball good-bye. She doubled over as she hobbled out of the room, squeezing her legs together to hold the stream of urine her giggles were forcing out of her bladder.

In the hall, Lang's laughter gurgled up like effervescent bubbles. She had forgotten what uncontrollable laughter felt like. She didn't want to stop.

A. J. rushed out of the room, her face flushed an angry red. Her embarrassment made Lang laugh more. A. J. squeezed her mouth tight but began to laugh. They stood in the hall of Shepherd's Arms and let it gurgle over them, showering them like a long-awaited summer storm.

THIRTY-FOUR

....

A few days later the sun actually came up while Lang sat at the breakfast table, illuminating the dark branches in the woods. For weeks the sunrise had been shrouded in mist and fog, hinting of rain. But despite the distant rumble of thunder, they hadn't had a drop of rain.

Victoria stood at the window with his paws on the sill. They both watched the pair of mourning doves sitting placidly on top of the wire feeder like they were too stuffed to eat another bite. But the birds both still picked at the food. Lang knew the feeling.

"We are taking a walk today," Lang said out loud to Victoria. "After breakfast," she added, halfway wondering if Victoria could understand English because he moved from the window and sat expectantly at the door.

Lang bundled up, attached the rhinestone leash to Victoria's collar, and apologized out loud about its tackiness.

They started out uphill, and Lang gasped at the cold air. She stopped after three mailboxes and put her hands on her knees, struggling for a normal breath. Her lungs seemed to be solid, frozen, and unyielding. Victoria sat at her feet, watching her patiently.

"Quit watching me. You're supposed to be going to the bathroom," she said as she trudged slowly toward the next mailbox. Victoria trotted along beside her, never straining or balking at the leash.

Lang wondered if Victoria had been someone's pet. Obviously, he was used to people. He knew to sit and wait for his commands, and now he heeled without being told more than once. She wondered what kind of person could change their minds about their own pet. Just decide they didn't want it anymore and drop it off, cutting all ties.

She would find him a good home. A safe home where his master would be strong and healthy and take good care of him. He deserved that.

Mrs. Eubanks, her neighbor, stopped and waited for Lang and Victoria to pass. She nodded at Lang and smiled, but didn't speak. Every morning, she walked down Lang's street, her back bent sideways with arthritis, and her gait slow and uneven. Mrs. Eubanks would stop often and stand with her hands clasped behind her back, balancing herself against unruly dogs, bicyclists, cars, and any moving object that could distract her from putting her feet down, one in front of the other. She walked deliberately, carefully, as if the rush of wind from a passing car could make her lose her balance. She was definitely the only person Lang could pass.

Lang was breathing too hard to speak as she finally topped the hill. Her scalp dripped with sweat under her wool toboggan. Three tall young women, all wearing black tights and pushing strollers, laughed as Victoria tossed his head up at them. They all nodded at Lang, not stopping their conversation, and Lang remembered A. J. saying, "Wassup?" when Victoria tossed his head up before.

She turned around and started down the hill. Laura Jean Edwards and Emmeline Harrison were walking uphill toward her at a fast clip, trying to restrain their dogs. Lang thought about continuing uphill to avoid them, but she knew the exchange was inevitable. They'd pass her within seconds. She stood still and waited, trying to catch her breath before she had to speak. Their large dogs surrounded Victoria, sniffing at him rudely, but Victoria just sat submissively. Lang took as big a breath of air as her poor lungs would allow and braced herself.

"Lang! I've been thinking about you so much," Laura Jean said. Her face was long and sympathetic. "I know it's been so hard."

"I nominated someone for garden club a while ago," Lang blurted out. "But I haven't heard back. Is there something else I'm supposed to do?"

"Yes, I know. Actually I don't think that person is in the club's best interests, but it's the board's decision," Emmeline said.

"Why not?" Lang asked. "She's lived here for forty years, volunteers at the museum, and God bless her, actually *wants* to be a member. If you can imagine."

"I know you have been through so much and have a very full plate with everything going on in your life, but I truly believe if you thought about it, you'd understand. A. J. Cole is not exactly Barrington Women's Club material," Emmeline said.

"I've been meaning to check on you," Laura Jean said nervously, shifting her weight from one foot to the other. "We walk by your house every day and have been meaning to stop by. Maybe next year would be better for A. J. Maybe she'll have a better chance."

"Because another member will be dead, freeing up a spot? Maybe she can have my spot," Lang said.

"Lang, no! That's not what I meant at all!" Laura Jean said.

"None of you will nominate her. I want her in the damn club this year. I don't want to make an issue of it any more than I have already. I'm sure you understand. And I think it's probably in the club's best interest to invite her to join. I'd hate to bother the national office about something so silly."

Suddenly Victoria jumped and skittered sideways as the

other dogs growled. "That is the cutest little dog! What is he?" Laura Jean said enthusiastically as she bent down and patted Victoria's head. "Look at him, Emmeline!"

"I'm not sure. He just showed up at my house. Part Chihuahua I think," Lang said.

Laura Jean bolted straight up and looked at Emmeline with a shocked expression on her face.

"Are you serious? Emmeline lost her little Precious last month. I think your dog is part shih tzu. Look at his eyes. Does he not remind you of Precious?"

"He does a little," Emmeline said. "But Precious was full-blooded."

Laura Jean scooped up the dog, and he tucked his paws under his chin and stared up at her. "Will you be a good baby?" she asked the dog.

"He's really no trouble at all. He doesn't bark for anything. He could be locked in a closet, and he'd never make a peep," Lang said.

"Is he house-trained?" Emmeline asked. "I just replaced my carpets."

"He is," Lang said, petting the dog's head.

"Are you sure about this?" Laura Jean asked, handing the dog to Emmeline.

"Yes, I am. He needs a good home, and I really can't take him on right now. He'll be a wonderful little companion for you," Lang said. "Just keep an eye on him. He's very quiet. Silent really and never barks." She kissed Victoria quickly on the head and handed Emmeline the pink leash. Then she trudged down the hill to her house, alone.

The nursing home didn't take pets. Her only chance was the cancer trial. It was her life or the dog.

She repeated these three sentences like a mantra as she slowly dragged herself toward home.

THIRTY-FIVE

....

Lang froze in the kitchen, sure she heard the tags on Victoria's collar jingling. Amputees felt pain in their missing limbs, and she wondered how long it took for them to feel whole after that loss. She checked the time on the Jefferson clock.

Lang squinted and tilted her head back, scanning the kitchen for her glasses. She seemed to lose them constantly now. She backtracked to the bedside table, wondering if she'd put them down while making the bed. She searched the entire car, although she hadn't driven in days, and then unmade the bed to see if they'd gotten lost in the sheets. She just had them this morning while she was working the crossword puzzle in the paper. It was supposed to be good for the brain, but she attempted only Mondays, the easiest day. Tuesday's puzzle was discouraging, and Friday's was downright depressing.

She wondered if she was losing her mind. Last week she had picked up the phone to call Teddy, but then couldn't remember his number. Yesterday she had called A. J., then immediately forgotten what she'd called about. The other day she had stopped clipping boxwood and gone inside for something but couldn't remember what it was. She had just wandered around from room to room, hoping something would trigger her memory and remind her of what the hell she was doing.

She did not want Teddy to find out about any of these lapses. He was hell-bent on moving her to the nursing home, and today wasn't the first time Lang had wondered if he had the right idea. Sometimes Lang wondered if Teddy knew something she didn't. Maybe Lang's doctor had confided in him about Lang having Alzheimer's on top of the cancer and advised him to get Lang settled somewhere before the wearing-sweaters-as-pants full-fledged dementia set in. Not that there was a sweater big enough for her enormous behind.

She didn't know how long the dog had been sitting at the front door. Lang didn't notice him until after lunch when she finally went outside.

Victoria sat stationed outside on the porch, silently waiting for her. He wriggled his whole body vigorously when she opened the door but never jumped on her.

"What are you doing? You are a bad boy!" she said. But she sat down on the top step and held him in her lap. "You're living in la-la land. You're going to have to get with the program and face reality. Believe me, you deserve better than me."

He stared up at her with soulful topaz eyes, and she swore he was smiling.

She held the dog in her lap and stroked his pale downy fur. The sun felt warm on the back of her head, and the weight of him on her legs was comforting. She imagined keeping him, having him officially as hers. Then she thought about giving him away when she moved to Shepherd's Arms. Or got sick. Or both.

"Emmeline, he showed up here this morning, but I'm on my way to bring him back to you," Lang said on the phone.

"Oh! I was wondering where he got off to last night. Lang, you won't believe this, but my sweet husband came home with a brand-new shih tzu pup! He surprised me! I would keep them both if I could, but really two dogs are too much for me," Emmeline said.

"He's been missing since last night?" Lang asked. The dog looked up at her. How could Emmeline be so cavalier about a missing dog? Unlike Lang, Emmeline had actually claimed the dog.

"I meant to call earlier. Oh, and before I forget, I need to cancel the flower order for the club. We won't be needing you."

"For this month?" Lang asked, wondering how she was going to make up the difference.

"At all," Emmeline said breezily. "We're going with something more appropriate for our needs."

"You're firing me?" Lang asked.

"Lang. Don't take it personally. As head of the decorating committee, I'm simply considering going with something more refined. Surely you can understand that, as a professional," Emmeline said. "It hasn't come before the board, but I expect they'll support my recommendation."

Lang held the phone in her lap, stunned by this unexpected news. She didn't realize she hadn't disconnected the call until she heard a dull, repetitive beep from the device.

Victoria suddenly leaped off Lang's lap, staggered toward the front door, crouched, and then heaved convulsively before throwing up on the heart pine floor.

She picked Victoria up and raced outside, but not before the little dog squirted diarrhea all over Lang's shirt. She set him down and began to unbutton her cuffs when Victoria's little body began heaving again.

Lang wrapped Victoria in her sweatshirt and drove straight to the vet. On the way, Victoria lay on Lang's lap, shuddering with sickness, but gazed up at Lang with soft eyes that seemed both mortified and apologetic.

"My little dog is so sick!" Lang told the receptionist.

"Oh, that's disgusting!" the woman said, obviously aghast at the soiled towel and the convulsing dog. "Go right back. In here!" she said, cupping her hand over her nose as she opened an examining room for Lang.

Making Arrangements

"What's wrong with Victoria?" Dr. LePeyre asked before he was completely in the room. His face erupted in a smile when he saw her, but he frowned at the little dog as he bent over him.

"He just started this suddenly. Violently. We came right in. I think he's really sick. I don't know," Lang said.

"Let's rule out parvo first off," he said, sticking a swab up Victoria's rear end, then sniffing it. Lang remembered his term "professional veterinarian" and didn't think this was professional at all.

"I'll send it to the lab, but I don't think it's parvo. That's good news. We need to get him on an IV. He's lost a lot of fluids and doesn't have a lot of body weight. Little dogs get dehydrated easily. Has he eaten anything unusual?" he asked her.

"Maybe. He was with someone else for a little while, so I don't know." She suddenly felt protective toward the little animal she'd been trying to get rid of for months. "We were just sitting down for a minute. He was in my lap. Then he jumped up and just got so sick. Over and over," Lang said.

Victoria lay limp on the table, and Dr. LePeyre said, "This is going to sting, buddy."

The dog didn't even flinch as two inches of a hefty needle went into his leg. Victoria was suddenly motionless. Lang leaned her head down to see if he was breathing.

"Is he okay?" she asked.

"Come on, boy, stay with me," Dr. LePeyre said. The dog's eyes glazed over and went blank before he finished the sentence.

"Victoria?" Lang shouted. "Is he okay?"

Dr. LePeyre didn't answer. He just injected something else into Victoria's leg and looked worried when the dog didn't react. It occurred to Lang that Victoria might die.

Dr. LePeyre adjusted the IV line and stroked Victoria's head. "He's alive. We'll keep him overnight. Let the IV fluids get a chance to get in him."

"I need you to help him," Lang said, feeling an unfamiliar tightening in the bridge of her nose. She turned away from him and said, "I need him to be okay."

She leaned over the little dog, stroked his head, and whispered, "Good boy, Victoria. That's a good little boy." He slowly moved his tail. "We'll work it out, I promise."

Lang got in her bed that night and felt the heavy loneliness that had eased a little since Victoria had started sleeping with her. Every night the little dog started out at the foot of the bed, curled in a ball, his eyes fixed on her until she fell asleep. He moved during the night, sometimes stretching out behind her and pressing his spine against hers. Once he had had his head on the pillow and his body under the covers, his mouth curved in a smile. When she would wake up in the night, she would close her eyes and adjust her breath to the dog's slow, raspy snores that came and went in an easy rhythm, bringing sleep to her.

Now she finally gave up on sleep and walked through the dark house. She sat at the breakfast table, watching the sliver of moon pinned to the vast night sky. She moved to the porch swing and listened to the chain's slow squeak, the same cadence she'd rested to as a child. Later, she lay down in Katie D.'s bed. Then she walked back to her room and out again.

Lang finally dozed off in the living room, *Atlas Shrugged* open on her chest. When the phone rang, it was still dark outside, and Lang knew this was not good news. No one called at six forty-five in the morning unless the news was bad. She walked slowly to the kitchen phone.

"Hello?" Lang said.

"Lang? Leland here. He's doing okay," Dr. LePeyre said.

"He's okay?" she was finally able to say.

"He's hydrated. No more vomiting. No diarrhea. Drinking a little water and keeping it down. My guess is he got hold of some kind of poison. But he never made a peep. Not one. He's good to go," Leland said.

"Oh my gosh. Thank you. Thank you so much. I thought . . . Oh thank you so much," Lang said, sliding down the side of the kitchen island, relief making her limp.

She was at the vet's before they opened.

"Oh!" Leland said, unlocking the door.

"I'm so sorry," she said. "I thought you meant to come now."

"No, no, it's fine. Sorry about the lights. I need to leave them off," he said. "If people see lights on, they think we're open and start coming. Come on back."

She followed him back to Victoria, who stood up on his back legs, wagging his tail furiously and shimmying like a go-go dancer, the IV rattling against the wire cage.

"Don't think we need this anymore," Leland said as he held Victoria still against his stomach and eased the needle out.

Lang could see bruised puffs under Leland's eyes and a weariness to his face that hadn't been there yesterday. She knew he had been here all night, watching over the little dog she'd finally claimed.

THIRTY-SIX

....

The day after she brought Victoria home from the vet, Lang walked idly around the garden with Katie D., looking for signs of her emerging plants. Victoria ran around the yard showing no sign of ever being sick, but Lang kept her eye on him. This first garden inspection in early spring reminded her of an Easter egg hunt. She spotted the first baby buds of sedum pushing up between the hollow, brown stalks from last year and the blunt spears of green lilies clustered in tight bunches.

"Come on, Katie D. Let's look for the baby plants," Lang said, but Katie D. sat in a heap on the rock wall.

"I don't feel like doing anything," Katie D. said.

"Suit yourself," Lang said, but she walked over to her granddaughter and felt her forehead for fever.

Suddenly Victoria began to lunge from side to side, then charged abruptly toward the sidewalk.

"Victoria!" a voice boomed. Lang turned to see Dr. LePeyre walking slowly up her stone steps from the street.

"Leland! Hello!" Lang said. She put the clippers safely in her back pocket and reached out to shake his hand as she introduced Katie D. Katie D. hid her face in her hands.

"Well, my pleasure, my little brown-eyed girl," Leland said.

"They look like doo-doo. They said it at school today," Katie D. said, tilting her facedown. "Katie Doo-Doo, they called me."

"Who said that?" Lang asked.

"Oh, sweetie!" Leland said, dropping to his knees before Lang could speak. "Your eyes are the eyes of legends, the eyes that can launch a thousand ships and cause countries to go to war. They are so beautiful. Songs are written about these eyes of yours. *You, my brown-eyed girl*," he sang, unfazed by his off-key rendition. "Your eyes are warm and endless. You just want to fall into them. Look here." He gently raised her chin with his thumb and shined his penlight into her eyes. "Oh yes, these are the most beautiful and exquisite human eyes ever documented."

"You're a ophthalmologist?" Katie asked.

"Well, you're as precocious as you are beautiful," Leland said. "What do you know about ophthalmology?"

"My mommy takes me. To make sure my eyes work. They might be bad," Katie said.

"What? Why would she think that?" Lang asked.

"Sometimes little children can't see, and they can get sick," Katie said. "And die."

"Sweetie, that would never happen. You don't need to think about anything like that," Lang said. It certainly wasn't her place to say, but Lang didn't think Sarah necessarily needed to be so realistic as far as the little girl was concerned. She pulled the rubber band taut with her thumb and snapped it against her wrist. Leland looked away from her hands quickly.

"Well, believe me, your eyes are precious. And rare. And incredibly beautiful," Leland said, interrupting her.

"I like blue eyes. I want pretty eyes. Will I get them?" Katie D. asked.

"Oh, but you have pretty eyes already. My favorite color is brown. That color stands for wholesomeness and earthiness. And steadfastness and simplicity and friendliness and health. It's a very important color," Leland said. "UPS is brown. The big square delivery trucks? They're very dependable."

"Yours are *almost* brown," Katie D. said, shining the penlight in Leland's eyes.

"Almost. I would like them to look like rich espresso, like yours. But they let me see, so I'm glad for them. Even if they're not quite brown," Leland said.

"Okay," Katie D. said softly. "I'm very friendly."

"Who said that to you today?" Lang asked Katie D.

"No matter anymore. Well then, now that we've made the proper introductions, how is the patient? I was taking a walk and thought I'd check in on Victoria. He seems to be doing fine? Eating okay?" he asked. Victoria stood on his back legs, balancing like a tightrope walker.

"Yes! He was back to normal the day I picked him up. No sign of ever being so sick," Lang said. Victoria turned his head to watch Lang as she spoke, tottering sideways but never losing his balance.

"She likes ballet," Katie D. said, standing on tiptoe and dancing with the little dog.

"I wanted to write you a note. Or at least call. What you did . . .Well, I just really, really appreciate . . . I didn't know until . . . Sorry," Lang said, putting her index fingers on her temples for a moment.

She thought of the little dog's eyes fixed on hers and the almost imperceptible wag of his tail when he was so sick he couldn't lift his head.

"No problem at all. I'm just glad he's bounced back so quickly," he said.

"I know you spent the night there. That you were up with him all night," Lang said.

"Well," he said, "this was a very sick puppy." He looked down at Victoria and scratched the dog's ears with both hands.

"Can he have a snack with us?" Katie D. asked.

"Oh, honey, I'm sure he doesn't have time," Lang began.

"Sure!" Leland said before Lang finished her sentence. "I was just thinking how much I could use a snack. Low blood sugar."

"We've got chips! Can I fix them real nice since there's company?" Katie D. asked before running to the kitchen.

"Would you like something to drink? Iced tea? I think I've got some beers," Lang said.

"I'll take one. A beer," he said.

"Well, come have a seat and I'll grab one," Lang said to Leland. "After you, Leland." She made sure she brought up the rear. She opened Jack's mini fridge on the porch, and there were her glasses, folded neatly in front of a six-pack of Heineken.

"Cheers," Leland said as he clinked his bottle on hers. "Here! Here!"

Victoria immediately ran over to him and sat on his haunches, and they both laughed at Victoria thinking their toast was an invitation to come. Leland reached into his pocket and tossed a kibble into the air. Victoria sprang straight up and caught it in his teeth.

"Katie D.!" Lang called, suddenly anxious about being alone with Leland. She heard the clank of dishes in the kitchen.

"He's a natural," he said. "For agilities. You ever see those dogs that catch Frisbees? Well, they have a whole national competition."

"You're kidding!" Lang said, thinking how refreshing her chilled eyeglasses felt on the bridge of her nose and wondering what was taking Katie D. so long.

"No, I tried to work with my dog on it, but she just drops the Frisbee out of her mouth. Absolutely no interest. But Victoria has the true instinct. I bet he could be ready for competition in a week. Watch this," he said, pulling an old tennis ball out of his pocket and bouncing it hard on the porch. Victoria leaped up and grabbed the ball in his mouth at the peak of the first bounce.

"Come, Victoria!" he commanded.

Victoria dropped the ball and ran obediently over to the vet.

"Good job," he said, rubbing Victoria's neck. "We need to work on the retrieving part. I'm serious, though. Do you think I could work with him? I really do think he's a natural," Leland said, his face flushing.

Lang realized he was not comfortable asking this of her. She remembered him talking about Victoria's agility the first time they were at the vet. Had that been a hint?

"Well, sure," Lang said, not sure what else she could have said. She excused herself to go check on the chips.

THIRTY-SEVEN

....

Lang woke up early the morning of her sixty-fifth birthday. She'd been dreading it for weeks. She'd made several battle plans, all of them unbearable. She canceled her pedicure as soon as she got out of bed, realizing perfectly painted toenails would make her feel even more wretched.

She considered hiking the Sugar Springs Trail, the flat, wide trail Jack had always tried to get her to hike. He had talked about it so much she could picture the spring running over gigantic gray boulders that looked out of place among the smooth, brown river rock along the creek. An enormous tree had fallen over the spring, making a natural bridge, and he said they could picnic there. He had known he could lure her almost anywhere with food.

Jack had been an avid hiker—avid everything, really—and had hiked every trail within a day's drive. He would pick a national park and methodically hike every single trail in the system. He had kept notebooks on all of them, rating and commenting on each trail.

Had he kept a notebook on me? Plotting how he could deceive me?

She flipped through one of his notebooks. Chickamauga National Military Park had four stars and a note in his clear handwriting that said "great for riding bikes." Cumberland Gap National Historical Park and Frozen Head State Park each had three stars. The Sugar Spring Trail had five stars with a note that said "flat, easy, Lang."

Lang ate a bowl of cereal with slices of banana that should

have been composted. She flipped through the newspaper, not reading her birthday horoscope. She thought about going back to bed, sleeping this birthday away. Victoria sat at her feet, watching her intently.

"Okay. We are hiking. You and flat, easy Lang," she said out loud, flipping through Jack's trail book and seeing how far they had to drive to find a trail he hadn't commented on. She wanted an easy trail that she could discover on her own.

She decided on Paw-Paw Loop. It was described in the trail guide as an easy one-mile loop, and although it was an hour away, she thought she would just as soon drive as sit in the house today.

Victoria stood in the passenger's seat with his front paws on the top of the open window, the force of the wind ruffling his snout. When Lang stopped to pick up lunch, Victoria sat demurely in his seat, as if he'd been riding shotgun in cars all of his life. He eyed a piece of mayonnaisey tomato in her lap, salivating over the pale orange chunk on her pants, but not moving from the passenger seat.

She found the trailhead easily and was relieved not to see any other cars parked in the dirt parking slips. Victoria led the way down the sloping trail that would not have been wide enough for two people. Unused to walking off the leash, Victoria kept turning around, making sure Lang was still behind him.

The trail was lovely, bordered by enormous hemlocks on one side and a wide, rushing mountain stream on the other. Watercress grew in a lush mound in the water, a thick, inviting pillow of verdant green. Lang remembered Jack telling her watercress was good for something. A cure for bad breath? She couldn't remember. She exhaled into the palm of her hand, checking her breath.

She crossed over an old wooden bridge. A few of the boards had rotted out, so Lang carried Victoria over as he licked her jaw in gratitude. They walked along the stream for a while, masses of maidenhair ferns on either side of the trail, nary a weed among them. She'd never seen anything lovelier in any manicured garden she'd paid to see.

Victoria stopped abruptly when the tips of gigantic rhododendron met in an arch over the trail, making a canopy of flamboyant blossoms. As big as salad plates, the deep magenta blooms made a fairy-tale passageway. Even the little dog seemed to know this was magical and not to be obliviously trotted through.

Later, Lang sat on a boulder just off the trail to take it all in and to rest for a minute. Victoria leaped up on her lap and curled into a ball. She rubbed his fur absentmindedly and stretched out on the cool stone. The lichen stood stiff against her back, and the early spring sun played across her face. The warmth of the little dog on her belly made her feel grounded.

It was late afternoon by the time she got home. She saw the balloons fluttering on her mailbox and thought someone must have mistaken her address for someone else's.

It wasn't until she saw Teddy's car in the driveway that she realized the balloons were for her and that he had remembered her birthday. And to think he'd made time to buy pastel helium balloons.

Victoria ran ahead, looking back at Lang expectantly at the door, then leaping straight up when he reached Katie D. at the stove.

"Oooooh! Hey, girl! Grandie's home! Grandie! Happy birthday!" Katie D. shouted, throwing her spoon down on the counter and splattering thick red sauce.

"Hello!" Lang said.

"You came home!" Katie D. said, kissing Lang and wrapping

both her arms tight around Lang's head. Her grandchild smelled like garlic and baby sweat and fabric softener. Lang picked her up, and when they finally pulled their heads apart, Lang could tell that Katie D. had been crying.

"Do you love the balloons? Mommy said it would make you feel special. She tied them on real good," Katie D. said, sniffing.

"Oh, I love them!" Lang said, wondering where Sarah was.

"I didn't know where you were," Katie D. said, pressing her face into Lang's neck.

"We sure didn't," Teddy said, stirring a lobster pot brimming with a thick, crimson, bubbling sauce. "We had a bad feeling you were going to miss your own party," he said. He was not smiling, and this made Lang laugh out loud. "Hang on. I need to take this call from Hank. We need to talk after dinner. For real."

"They say you pay for your raising, when you—" She stopped speaking, forgetting how the quote went exactly.

"Raise your own," Lillian said, announcing her presence as she marched through the front door, spry and fashionable. Lang wished she had half of her energy and style.

Victoria leaped vertically, almost eye level with Lillian and inches from her Chanel suit.

"You go freshen up. Come here, Victoria," Lillian cooed, scooping the dog up in her arms.

"He's filthy! We've been out in the woods all day," Lang said, thinking how ironic it was her mother supplied the last part of the quote.

"*You're* filthy," Lillian said, squeezing the dog's face next to hers. "Run along and clean up. Disappear. Poof!" She flicked her fingers at Lang as if she were sprinkling her with water. "I'm sorry. I shouldn't have done that. I hated it when my mother did that to me. No one should have to disappear."

"It's not personal. It's just a little saying Fancy had," Lang said.

"How could telling someone to disappear not be personal?" Lillian asked.

Katie D. sniffled and put her sticky hands on Lang's cheeks, turning her face to the dining room. Pink crepe paper hung in uneven loops over the chandelier, and the table was set with the good china and Fancy's pale pink cut-crystal goblets. White linen dinner napkins were rolled and tied with enormous crepe paper bows that lay in limp mounds on the table. A bouquet from the Piggly Wiggly stood in a silver vase on the middle of the table. Baby's breath and red carnations hovered over the clear cellophane wrapper.

"Do you take that plastic stuff off?" Katie D. asked, furrowing her forehead.

"It's optional. Completely up to the designer. I think it adds interest," Lang said, and Katie D. looked relieved.

"Mommy said to make it special. She said real flowers on the table. And she made the sauce not from the jar."

"Is that what smells so delicious?" Lang asked. "Where is she? I can't believe she went to all this trouble and didn't get to come. Oh, I could just dive in right now."

"Yoo-hoo! I saw balloons, and my curiosity got the better of me," A. J. said as she opened the front door without knocking. "Is it Katie D.'s birthday?"

"Come in!" Lang said.

"Surely you don't think you can have a party and not invite me—oh god, joke's on me," A. J. said when she saw the table, immediately stepping back out of the front door to leave. "I am mor-tee-fied! It really is a party. Is it your birthday, Lang?"

Katie D. pulled on Lang's hand to pull her down, cupped her hands around Lang's ear, and asked with garlic-tinged breath if A. J. could stay at the party.

"I would love to have her at the party," Lang said.

"And him?" Katie D. asked, pointing toward the road. "He looks left out."

Lang turned and saw Leland at the bottom of the stone steps, holding a loose leash.

"Hello!" he called, waving. "We were just out taking a walk."

"Who the hell is that?" Teddy asked.

Lang raised her hand in a weak wave.

Katie D. hurried down the crumbling rock steps. Lang watched Leland lean down toward her, then look up at Lang and boom out, "I accept with pleasure! A birthday dinner!"

He and Katie D. walked up the steps, and an elderly German shepherd trailed behind them.

"Well, if it isn't a gentleman caller, and Lang, you are still not presentable," Lillian said, extending her hand to him, palm down.

Leland bowed as he took her hand and kissed it with a flourish. "Your daughter looks lovely, as do you," he said.

"No! Bad girl! Be nice!" Katie D. shouted. Lang wasn't sure who she was talking to, but she hoped it was her mother.

Victoria sprang at the old dog's head, silently leaping up and attacking his ears. The older dog lay down with his paws over his head while Victoria leaped over him, again and again.

"The rope-a-dope! That's right, Rommel, use the old rope-a-dope for protection," Leland said, laughing. Katie D. squealed and tried to grab Victoria.

"He's okay. They're both playing. See how Rommel's tail is wagging? And Victoria's ears are flopping and no one's growling? Their backs are flat. No fur is standing up in ridges. Look! Rommel hasn't acted like this in ages," Leland said. They all watched Rommel lay on his back with all four legs up in the air and roll from side to side, apparently in ecstasy, while Victoria attacked his ankles and throat and jowls.

"Dinner is served!" Katie D. said, gesturing toward the

steaming plates full of heaped spaghetti, now on the table.

They burst out in applause, and Leland put his fingers over his mouth and made an ear-piercing wolf whistle. They all looked at him, but he just shrugged and said, "It's been a long time since I've been to a formal dinner party. Never one worth whistling over."

"Well, he's not exactly refined, but that's adorable," Lillian said, winking at him.

"This spaghetti is delicious!" Leland exclaimed after they had all sat down and started eating.

"Is it Bolognese? I can tell she roasted the tomatoes. Nothing canned, which is impressive. I've spent a great deal of time in Italy. Not too much in Bologna," Lillian said to Leland.

"So, you've been here before?" Teddy asked Leland.

"Yes. I came to check on Victoria after he was so sick. But this is Rommel's first time. Hope not his last. He hasn't had this much fun in years." He smiled at Lang, and his dimples made him look so adorable she had to look away.

Rommel turned in a slow circle as Victoria ran around him, faster and tighter so that the little dog looked like a whir.

"And you're divorced?" Teddy said.

"Teddy!" Lang said sharply.

"No. My wife died. I'm a widower," Leland said.

"What happened? Heart attack? Cancer?"

Lang sat still as Teddy behaved rudely. She remembered sitting in the bleachers when he cheated at that city tournament, silent.

"She was killed by a drunk driver. A boy not even old enough to drive," Leland said. "Poor thing."

Something about the way he said it made Lang think he was referring to the boy as much as to his wife. Surely not.

"This spaghetti really is divine!" A. J. exclaimed, and Lang looked at her gratefully. "I've got to have the recipe. I'm going to try it. Does your mom really roast fresh tomatoes?"

Katie D. looked at Teddy, but he shrugged his shoulders. "I don't know how Sarah makes it. It's one of her secrets. One of many apparently."

Leland went back for seconds of spaghetti, giving Katie D. two thumbs-up on his way to the stove.

"He's a very good eater," Katie D. said solemnly.

"Yes, he is," Lang said.

"He's trying way too hard," Teddy said, louder than Lang thought necessary.

"Probably half starved for a homemade meal. Doesn't even care he's the only one making a piggy of himself. The spaghetti sauce is that good," A. J. said.

They all sat silently at the table, having covered the food topic as much as possible.

"Are those real?" Katie D. blurted out, pointing at A. J.'s chest.

A. J. looked alarmed and crossed her forearms over her breasts.

"The pearls!" Lang said quickly. "The pearls, she means."

"Oh, these!" A. J. said, grasping the heavy, pale strand of pearls on her chest. "Oh, yes. They're Mikimoto pearls. Walker bought me these when we were in Japan."

"Mine are black Tahitian pearls. Very rare. I have a piece of jewelry from every country I've been to," Lillian said.

"Look here," A. J. said, unclasping the necklace. "Feel of 'em with your teeth. See how they feel? Like there's a dustin' of corn meal on them? Fake ones feel silky smooth. Like plastic. You need to learn the difference. Never too early," she said.

"No settling in my family," Lillian said. "Only the real-live, genuine article. As far as jewelry, anyway. People are in a different category, of course." She looked at Teddy, but he was focused on Leland.

"There's cake!" Katie D. blurted out. "It's hoe-made."

"Literally," Teddy said under his breath.

Lang squinted at him, wondering about his comments.

Katie D. brought the birthday cake out by herself, dozens of candles softly illuminating her face as if she were the subject of a chiaroscuro painting.

"What a beautiful child. Look at her! She looks like a Caravaggio," Lillian said. "She has Elizabeth's mouth."

"I think she looks more Caucasian," A. J. said.

Lillian was chewing, and Lang was surprised she didn't start in on A. J. with her mouth full. But she never said anything about the painter, even after she swallowed.

Lang looked at Katie D.'s full rosebud mouth and thought of her own thinning lips. Clearly her mother was trying to ingratiate herself to her. Finally.

"This cake is incredible! Where did you get it?" Leland asked.

"I made it myself! Mommy helped. You have to beat the clear egg part until it turns into white icicles," Katie D. said.

"Where is your mom? She should have joined us," A. J. said.

"I wanted her to. But she said it was just for family," Katie D. said.

"She's not family?" Lang asked pointedly, looking at Teddy. "I'm calling her right now. Pound cake is my all-time favorite." Leland handed her his cell phone, and Lang squinted at the numbers as she dialed.

"God. That is a to-do! I've never even separated an egg successfully. I'm learning in my Bake Your Way into His Heart class, but the yolk always splits and spills into the white," A. J. said.

"No, if even a tiny bit of yellow gets in, it ruins it," Katie D. said.

"A homemade pound cake. Now that is an act of love," Lang

said into the answering machine.
Sarah never picked up the phone.

THIRTY-EIGHT

··

Katie D. held the pink rhinestone leash, and Victoria trotted right beside her, heeling like a show dog as they walked to the vet's for heartworm pills. Lang was grateful every time Victoria stopped to sniff at shrubs and patches of grass; she still needed time to catch her breath, but she seemed to be catching it quicker.

"Do they look like hearts? Do they curl into the shape of one?" Katie D. asked Lang, brushing the hair out of her eyes with the back of her hand. A vinyl magenta pocketbook swung from the crook of her elbow.

"I think they are some kind of something with beautiful dark eyes like melted Hershey's Kisses and curly thickets of shiny golden hair, and the second they are born, they worm themselves into their grandmothers' hearts," Lang said, trailing her fingers through Katie D.'s hair. She imagined the chocolate kiss melting on her tongue and swallowed.

Katie D. tilted her face up and chortled. "You are a silly worm," she said.

Lang leaned down, kissed Katie D.'s forehead, and said, "Heartworms are actually more serious."

Katie D. guffawed and said she got it.

Lang fumbled over her comment, wondering what there was to get, what joke she'd made unintentionally. Her brain seemed to be skipping. Missing beats. "They're not *silly* worms. They're *serious* worms," Katie D. said, reading her mind.

"Right, they infect the heart. The organ," Lang said finally, although she didn't know for certain that they did not wiggle around in heart-shaped patterns. "I just know it's very bad if a dog gets heartworms, and that mosquitoes carry the disease, and we're getting close to mosquito season. So," Lang said. She reminded herself she didn't need to finish her sentence with a coordinating conjunction. Not that she was judging. She rolled the rubber band with her thumb but did not flick it.

When Lang, Katie D., and Victoria got there, they stood at the counter while the receptionist held up her index finger to indicate she would be a minute. Then she continued her phone conversation, which was not about animals.

Dr. LePeyre walked by the doorway behind the receptionist, passing before Lang could raise her hand to wave.

"Lang!" he said, backtracking and walking in front of the receptionist, who managed to immediately end her conversation.

"They don't have an appointment!" the receptionist said.

"Oh, we just need to get heartworm pills," Lang said, heat rising in her cheeks.

"Don't be crabby. We *want* business, remember? That's why you have a job," Leland said. "Victoria! I see you have your competent young trainer on the other end of your leash!"

"Down, girl!" Katie D. commanded the already seated dog, beaming at her new title.

"May I give Victoria a treat? Perfect name, by the way. Don't think I ever told you that," he said, handing Victoria a biscuit when Katie D. nodded. Victoria held the treat in his front paws and nibbled on it. "Would you like a treat as well?" he asked Katie D., holding up another dog biscuit. "Just kidding. I've got Oreos and cheddar Goldfish. They're better together than you might think. Come on back."

They followed him back to his office. Lang refused the chocolate cookie; she didn't like to eat in front of people, especially strangers. But she could hear Leland and Katie D. crunching the crisp wafers in their mouths, and her mouth watered. She swallowed and took a single Oreo. Lang carefully twisted her Oreo apart and scraped a wad of stiff, white icing into her mouth with her front teeth, holding it on her tongue until it dissolved into thick, sugary cream. She tried to savor every bite of her food; she had read that made you eat less.

"Grandie smashes these up to make dirt pudding," Katie D. said.

"We make it together," Lang said quickly, mortified that he might think she ate Oreos alone.

He laughed and offered her another cookie. His eyes twinkled when he smiled, and she took another Oreo.

"Is that lady on the phone going to die?" Katie D. asked.

"One day, but not for a long, long time. Why?"

"Because she's crabby," Katie D. said. "That's very serious."

"I agree. But it won't kill you. And some days that's unfortunate," Leland said, rolling his eyes. "Kidding, of course."

"It can. Mommy told me about it," Katie D. said as she offered her chocolate wafer to Victoria.

"No! Chocolate's not good for dogs," Lang said, wondering why in the world Sarah would teach Katie D. being grouchy could kill you.

"Katie D., may I try something with Victoria?" Dr. LePeyre asked.

"By all means," Katie D. said, bowing.

He held a biscuit over Victoria's nose and said, "Up!" He raised the biscuit as the dog stood on his hind legs. He held it still for well over a minute, then said, "Good dog, Victoria," and gave the dog the cookie.

"That's the best performance yet, Victoria. Impressing someone, perhaps?" he said, arching his eyebrows at Katie D. "You've got a regular circus dog, Miss D. I bet the next time I see her, you will have taught him to serve cocktails on a silver tray!"

Lang smiled at the idea of her male dog in a French maid outfit, balancing martinis on a tray. She immediately realized no one had mentioned any outfit.

By the time they left with a package of heartworm pills, Katie D. had invited Dr. LePeyre to dinner.

"I accept with pleasure," he said, bowing deeply to Katie D., who bowed back.

Lang felt her face flush and said, "I haven't been cooking much lately. It might be that Dr. LePeyre would rather take a rain check for dinner." She tried to give him an out, give them both an out, but he interrupted her and said, "I eat anything," and held up a dog biscuit.

The receptionist, back on the telephone, printed out the receipt for the heartworm pills and looked Lang up and down.

"You can get these cheaper on the Internet," she said in a voice that was not one you would use to give someone a helpful hint.

THIRTY-NINE

····································

Lang wrapped her hands around the obscene, oversize coffee mug and thought about the dream she just had. How could she be having sex dreams about Leland LePeyre? At her age?

A nuthatch hung upside down from the feeder, and three black-capped chickadees took shifts snatching sunflower seeds and vanishing into the woods. A handful of goldfinches, still drab-feathered and plain, lighted sporadically on the feeder.

"Looks to have gender identification issues," Leland had said about Victoria. She didn't realize she was smiling until the rose-breasted grosbeak swooped down to the feeder, scattering the lesser birds.

They'd watched these particular birds for years, she and Jack. She felt her face deflate as the bird fed, its carnation pink breast vivid against its black feathers.

She set her coffee down on the table, rubbed her hands together absentmindedly, and then opened her grandmother's bird encyclopedia to the very back page. There was a record of bird sightings, dating from March 2, 1929, in Fancy's handwriting: "Flock of cedar waxwings in Winterberry, nest of screech owls in hemlock by swing."

Lang skimmed over the entries, noticing her grandmother's handwriting change from a neat, clear script to an unsteady, jagged scrawl. She wondered if hers looked just as uneven now as she wrote: "Two rose-breasted grosbeak. March 11, 2013. (Believe they are the same two documented since 2001.)"

It was too much, the birds coming back this year, making it

so clear her life was a void now. Empty. Too big a part of it was missing, and she was too old to start over with a new one. She walked to her bedroom and climbed in the bed she had just made.

"Come!" she commanded Victoria, patting the mattress. But Victoria sat on his haunches on the floor, looking at her.

"Come! Don't make me feel guilty for getting in bed," Lang said. Victoria sprang up on the bed, licked Lang's cheek, and then prodded Lang under her jaw with his nose before leaping down and resuming his position on the floor. Lang rolled over, burying her head under Jack's pillow and breathing in what remained of his scent as she closed her eyes and sank into sleep. *He just hadn't wanted to worry me.*

Suddenly there was a flash of shrill noise. She jerked up suddenly from her dream, but there was only the dog sitting beside the bed, watching her.

"Fine," she groaned and forced herself out of the bed. She walked through the house, checking for a defective smoke alarm, but she was sure the sound had come from her room. She looked at Victoria, who seemed to be inspecting the house as well. He nodded up at her quickly. *Wassup.*

She was up now and decided she may as well stay up. She called Sarah to invite them to come dye Easter eggs. Then she invited A. J. and Leland to hunt eggs in the morning.

She put a few dozen eggs on to boil, prepared the bowls of food coloring, then she panicked.

"Can you stay and help me?" she asked Sarah and Teddy when they delivered Katie D. "I've bitten off a little more than I can chew."

"Mom, you should have told me on the phone," Teddy said.

"No more fighting," Katie D. said.

"No one's fighting, Katie D. We're having a discussion. A grown-up discussion," Teddy said.

"What color is your egg?" Sarah asked, peeping over her daughter's shoulder.

"I'm making brown. I soak him in red then I soak him in green. Makes him brown," Katie D. said.

"A brown Easter egg?" Teddy asked.

"What about leaving him red?" Sarah asked. "Such a pretty soft red!"

"I like brown. It stands for friendly. And it's healthy. Like me," Katie D. said. "So you don't have to worry, Mommy."

"That's right! What's better than a friendly, healthy girl!" Lang exclaimed. "With an egg to match the color of her eyes?"

Teddy glared at Sarah, pursing his lips. "What color were they?" he asked.

"What? What color was what?" Lang asked.

"No, no more fighting! You promised," Katie D. said.

"Here, give me a job. Let me help," Sarah said quickly.

"I'm going then," Teddy said.

"Daddy? Don't go. Stay and make some pretty eggs with me," Katie D. said.

Teddy walked over to Katie D. and kissed the top of her head. "You don't need me, sweetie. You are doing just fine by yourself."

"Teddy! No, don't say that. Please stay," Sarah said.

"But Daddy and me will hide them in the morning, right, Daddy?"

"You bet. I'll pick you up at dark thirty, and we'll give the ole bunny a run for his money," Teddy said.

"Pick me up?" Katie D. asked.

"Yes, sweetie. Daddy has a big meeting out of town, but I won't miss our egg hunt," he said.

"Teddy, please. Can I talk to you for a minute outside?" Sarah said.

"It's okay," Lang said. "We can finish them between us. Go

on, Teddy. Do what you need to do, then we'll surprise you with them."

Teddy tightly squeezed up his face and turned away from them.

"Really, we can do it. I promise," Lang said. "What?"

"Nothing," Sarah said as Teddy left. But her blue eyes looked strained, and Lang thought she looked pale. Frazzled.

"This is violet and rose and yellow. The longer you leave them in, the darker they'll get. Sorry. I'm sure you knew that," Lang said.

"No, I've never dyed eggs. Katie D. has always done it over here, and my mother never . . . Well, anyway, this is a first."

"Okay, if you want a stencil, do it like this," Lang said as she carefully taped the silhouette of a chicken onto an egg. "Duct tape. I thought I'd do some of these for that job I've got next week. I've hollowed them out, and I'll wire them in so the arrangement will have these bejeweled eggs popping around it. What do you think? Too much?"

Sarah stared at Katie D. like she'd never seen her before.

"Look. It's solid chocolate." Katie D. held the dark brown egg up and smiled, and the edges of her eyes tilted up just like Jack's.

"Sarah? Is everything okay?" Lang asked. "Katie D., you look exactly like your grandfather!"

"Yes. I think they will be perfect in the arrangement! Very pretty. How do you know all this? How do you think it all up? You really have such a way," Sarah said, and Lang had the distinct feeling she was changing the subject.

Later, Lang hid 120 exquisitely decorated Easter eggs in the yard, perching them on ancient dogwood crotches and on the edges of bird feeders and wedging them in the old stone wall at the edge of the woods.

Making Arrangements

A. J. arrived early the next morning with a bag of cheap plastic eggs.

"They're filled with M&M's and jelly beans," she said, rattling a bright pink plastic egg.

They hid forty-eight more. The entire side garden was punctuated with small, colored ovals of all shades. "I'll leave them for you to use in your arrangements for the Barrington Women's Club. Kidding. I doubt you use plastic eggs."

"I don't use anything for them anymore. They fired me. If it weren't for my grandmother starting the club, I'm sure they'd dismiss me as a member entirely," Lang said.

"What? Why?"

"I don't think Emmeline likes her father associating with Lillian. Not that I blame her," Lang said.

"You should petition them. Call that Laura Jean. Bypass Emmeline. Wait, how are you going to get me in if they're mad at you?" A. J. asked.

"That's my main problem. My financial problems are secondary to your membership in the Barrington Women's Club," Lang said.

"You don't have to be so crabby. They won't dismiss you," A. J. said. "They can't."

"I don't really care if they do," Lang said, wondering again why Katie D. thought crabbiness was life threatening. "I have other accounts, but that's my largest one."

When Sarah arrived a few minutes later, she had a scalloped watermelon rind filled with melon balls, blueberries, and strawberries. "I saw it in a magazine. It had instructions, but I don't know. It didn't turn out right," she said sheepishly.

"It had a handle for a basket, but it broke when I tried to pick it up," Katie D. said.

"Where's your daddy?" Lang asked. "I thought he was coming."

"It holds the fruit salad just fine," Sarah said quickly, setting the watermelon down on the table. "The handle was just a bonus."

"Okay then, you all have a good hunt and don't eat too much candy," Sarah said. "See you around three?"

"Where are you going?" Lang asked.

"Oh, I've got a few errands. Calls to make," Sarah said.

"On Easter Sunday?" A. J. asked. "I am by no means a CEO, but I don't think you're supposed to work on Easter. So."

"Your calls can wait, Sarah. You've got to stay for the egg hunt. I insist," Lang said.

Sarah looked at Lang. She reminded Lang of the dog, when it first cowered on the front porch. "It will be fine," Lang said. "Come on, honey."

"Where's Victoria?" Katie D. shrieked, apparently already well into the Easter candy.

"Oh, he knows where all the eggs are hidden, so I had to keep him inside," Lang said.

"Well, it's time for the hunt," A. J. said. "Let him out!"

Lang looked at her blankly.

"I'd just about pay to see an Easter egg-hunting circus dog," A. J. said.

Victoria bolted out of the front door, leaping up and licking melted chocolate off Katie D.'s nose before charging through the yard and racing in circles, each one tighter and faster than the last.

"Has everybody been into the chocolate bunnies but me?" A. J. asked.

Sarah walked over to the magnolia tree, its branches splayed out and heavy. She peered up at a jewel-pink egg balanced on a limb. A. J. snatched it, then poured the contents into her mouth, struggling to keep her mouth closed as she chewed.

"God almighty, that's incredible," A. J. said. "How long since I had a mouth full of chocolate?"

"From the looks of you, never," Lang said, walking over to the stone wall. Suddenly she didn't think her legs would hold her up for another second. She sat down, and Victoria trotted over to her holding a whole egg in his mouth. He plopped it down at her feet, then rolled it closer with his nose. She was exhausted. The pace of the flower-arranging business was wearing her out, but she needed every single order to make the house payment. And she hadn't even begun to pay A. J. back for her loan. Or think about the balloon payment coming up.

"You want me to peel it? Fine," she said, handing the slippery egg to the dog. Victoria carried it daintily over to the sidewalk and ate it, holding it steady between his paws while he nibbled it, as if he knew it was a seasonal delicacy to be savored.

The bright green leaf flickered, and Lang realized a praying mantis was on the shrub next to her; its wings blended in perfectly with the new growth on the laurel, and if it hadn't moved, she never would have noticed it. The tiny triangular head swiveled, and it clutched its arms up to its chin, not unlike her when she ate. It shoveled its food in, intent on every bite. The insect was long and thin with no heaviness to it at all.

She remembered something about the female cannibalizing her mate after mating. She wouldn't mind being a praying mantis. A long green wisp, eating everything voraciously, tearing her mate apart bit by bit.

Stop it!

She hooked her index finger and pulled the rubber band so taut she felt it cut into the inside of her wrist. Just when she was about to release it, the band snapped, hurtling through the air. Lang rubbed her wrist, feeling the rubber band's impression. She would get a new one as soon as the hunt was over.

Katie D. raced through the front yard, spilling eggs from her straw basket as she ran. Victoria, finished with his egg, took off after her, leaping head high as soon as he caught up with her.

Sarah stood awkwardly in the front yard, shielding her eyes from the sun.

"What can I do?" she asked Lang. "Please, let me help you."

"Oh, you are wonderful. Help me up, and we'll get started serving lunch," Lang said. She shouldn't have sat on the low wall; Sarah had to grab her wrists and lean away as Lang shifted all her weight forward. Even then, she barely made it up. She followed Sarah up the steps to the kitchen.

"Time for lunch!" Lang said from the kitchen, pouring sweet tea into glasses of crushed ice and sticking a mint sprig in each one.

Lang heard her mother's loud voice before she saw her, dressed in a pale pink linen suit with a soft ruffle at the hem. She wore a wide-brimmed hat with a cluster of cut roses in the ribbon, rivaling A. J. in her garden party apparel.

"Well, I can see I'm late for a party," Lillian said. "Martin couldn't come because his daughter is suddenly demanding his presence at every holiday function."

"Oh, let me get a picture. All of you," Sarah said. "Katie D., you stand by Grandie and Lily. Three generations, all together at the house you grew up in."

"No! Wait! I don't want any pictures of myself unless I'm ready," Lang said, but Lillian's hand was already around her, clutching her ample waist.

"Let me get one with you, Sarah. Make it four generations," A. J. said, reaching for the camera.

Sarah quickly snapped the picture and tucked the camera in her pocket. "I'll send you copies."

"Well, it would have been really special with you in it. All of us together as long as I had to be in it," Lang said. Was it her imagination or did Sarah look pained?

"Well, lunch is served!" Lang said, waving her guests toward the table.

"Needs salt," Lillian said. "Elizabeth! Bring some salt if you please. I love this—just white meat, mayonnaise, and celery. Call me a purist."

"Why do you call her Elizabeth?" Katie D. asked. "Her name's the same as mine."

"That's what I named her, and that's what I call her," Lillian said.

"Now then, Sarah," Lillian began, and Sarah nodded, her mouth full. "Where's her father? Or Teddy rather?"

Sarah's face flamed a feverish pink as she frantically tried to chew up her chicken salad so she could speak. She finally swallowed and said, "I think maybe there was a mix-up? I think—"

"He forgot me," Katie D. said. "I got ready early. Mommy gave me the flashlight because it was too dark. I waited and waited in the window. It got too long, and Mommy said that was enough waiting. So we went to McDonald's, and I got to have anything on the menu. We left him a note on the door in case, but it was still there when we got home."

Everyone sat in a stunned silence, watching the dark-eyed little girl with golden ringlets matter-of-factly explain why her father wasn't attending the Easter egg hunt.

"Why that little no-count bastard. He ought to be hung up and switched," Lillian said.

"No shit," A. J. said under her breath.

"Let's clear the table for Grandie," Sarah said to Katie D., standing up.

"Too much cussing at the table?" Katie D. asked, following her mother to the kitchen.

"Not enough," A. J. muttered.

"I don't know what's going on anymore. I feel like they're not telling me something. Like they're having serious problems with their relationship," Lang said. "And if something happens to Katie D.'s little family . . . well, I can't think of anything worse. It would break my heart."

A. J. briskly stirred sugar into a glass of water.

"Someone's heart is going to be broken," Lillian said cheerfully. "That's for sure!"

FORTY

....

few days after Easter, A. J. came by after breakfast, dressed in a stylish tennis outfit. There was an oval cutout between her breasts and a little flouncy ruffle at the hem of her pink skirt. Her sweater hung casually around her back, like she had draped it there as an afterthought. But it matched the ruffle perfectly.

"Get ready, Lang. We've got a court at ten. It's a weekday, so it won't be crowded. Probably be just our court," A. J. said. "You won't have to chat with anyone." A. J. stretched from side to side in her fitted skirt, a limber windmill. Her legs were already evenly tanned, and there was barely any jiggle on the back of her arms.

Lang hadn't played tennis since her diagnosis. She thought it would tax her body. For all she knew, laying off tennis for a year was the sole reason she wasn't dead.

"I don't think so. Maybe when it gets warmer," Lang said.

"You're kidding, right? It's sixty degrees out there. Gorgeous weather. I am by no means a meteorologist, but I don't think we'll see another day like this for a while. It's what I call a bonus day. The only nice day we've had for a good two months of cold and fog. Before you know it, we'll be in the middle of a heat wave. Today's a freebie, so," A. J. said.

Lang stared at her. Her head was upside down, dangling between her ankles.

"Let's go. Peggy's the fourth, and you know how crabby she gets when anyone's late," A. J. said.

"I'm sorry. I'm not sure I'm up to it. Not yet," Lang said. She wondered if there was some disease where a foul sense of humor was a symptom. Katie D.'s comment about Leland's crabby assistant stumped her.

"Lang, honey. What are you waiting on?"

"Well," Lang said.

Victoria sat on his haunches, looking up at her. His tilted his head to one side like he was waiting on an answer. "You don't have the luxury of waiting time out. Waiting for a better moment. None of us do. Go. Go! Get changed please."

"Fine. I'll change." Victoria snapped his head up at her in a quick nod of approval. *Thas wassup!*

A few minutes later, Lang walked out to A. J.'s car self-consciously, aware of her rear end in her short skirt.

A. J. studied her outfit closely, then offered to bring by some of the tennis clothes she was weeding out. As if Lang could fit in anything of A. J.'s.

"I can't do it!" Lang blurted out suddenly as soon as they drove through the gates by the tennis courts. "I can't play."

"Lang, it's fine. You'll see. Just like riding a bike."

"No! I forgot my tennis panties," Lang said, enunciating each word loudly as she realized she was wearing her ratty underwear under her short tennis skirt. *What is the matter with me? I can't even dress myself anymore.*

"We'll buy some in the shop. Only take a second. They're waiting for us on the court," A. J. said. "Sarah will find some in a flash." Lang followed A. J. up the wide steps leading to the Manker Patten Tennis Center, tugging her skirt down as far as possible and grateful no one was behind her.

"Oh, no, we don't have them anymore. Everyone wears those built-in bike shorts now, so we quit carrying them," Sarah said.

A. J. looked at Lang pointedly, like Lang brought this on herself by wearing outdated tennis clothes.

"I'm so sorry," Lang said. "Everyone's waiting on the court to play."

"Take these," Sarah said. She went behind the counter and pulled off her black leggings.

"What in the world? I'm not taking your leotards. You'll freeze! Plus, I couldn't get these over my left ankle."

"They stretch, she's fine, and they're all waiting. Put them on!" A. J. said. "Not that they need to stretch."

"Yes, I'm fine. Go on," Sarah said, tugging at the hem of her skirt, which looked short, but not obscene.

"I'm glad you're out here, Lang," Peggy said, rushing toward Lang when they finally made it to the tennis court.

"Sorry we're late. It's my fault," Lang said.

"You get a bye," Peggy said, kissing the air six inches in front of Lang's nose after Lang reflexively took a step back. "But don't be late next week," she said, wagging her finger at Lang's face.

Peggy hit a hard shot down Lang's alley, winning the point. But that was the first shot of the match, before Lang was used to the feel of the racket in her hand, before she'd found her balance at the net.

After the first few games, Lang couldn't tell she'd missed a single week of tennis, and her net game grew more aggressive with each set. She stayed perched right on the net, not backing up for lobs but reaching a little farther for each ball. Her stitches didn't pull at all, but she was winded.

She loosened her hand and changed her grip slightly before walking to the other side of the court. She apologized for having to sit down for a minute, but Peggy acted like she wanted to rest, too.

"Have you gone over the list of new member prospects for the women's club?" Peggy asked.

"What? No. I'll call you about it tonight," Lang said, getting up before she was quite ready.

A. J. tossed the ball high and stretched up long in the air, slamming an ace into Peggy's court. Lang reached out to smack A. J.'s palm in a brisk high-five, but A. J. ignored her.

"I need you to guard the alley. I'll get everything else," A. J. said tersely. "I have no idea what you're doing up there at the net. You're all over the place, and I don't know where to go."

"I thought you wanted me to play the net?" Lang said.

"Not hog every single ball! Did it never not occur to you I might want to hit a ball, too?" A. J. snapped. "Everything's not always all about you!"

Lang froze between the two lines that differentiated between the singles and doubles court, holding her racket perfectly still and willing herself not to cry. It was her very first day back on the court after her husband had died and after she'd been diagnosed with cancer. And A. J. was mad at her for going for balls.

A. J. was a rigid, self-important bitch, and Lang was suddenly furious at herself for getting close to her. She was done with that materialistic, narcissistic, meddling busybody. She didn't need this in her life. At all.

"Are you serious? Playing tennis?" Teddy asked incredulously when Lang told her where she'd been.

"Yes, I played in my old Monday game," Lang said on the phone. "But I don't think I'll be playing anymore with them."

"Well, I should think not. At least you still have *some* sense," Teddy said.

"Not because of how I played. I played fine and felt fine," Lang said defiantly.

"I'm sure you did. Just don't try it again," he said.

Lang bit her lip, aware of the burning ache in her knees. It felt like her cartilage was molten lava.

"I might play again. Just with different people."

"Mother! I don't think that's wise. I don't think you should be running around like that. Stressing your body. Plus, you could fall. And who do you think would take care of you?"

She imagined not him.

"I've got it all on go for the sale. Finally. All this legal stuff takes longer than it should. You just need to sign and get ready for the easy life," he said. "It will be fine, I promise. No more worrying about that old roof leaking and the pipes freezing. I think you'll feel relieved to be out from under it."

"Well," Lang said, looking up at the discolored patch on the ceiling.

"I'll hit with you if you're bound and determined," he said in a softer voice. "You've done it enough for me. Remember how you'd give me a piece of bubble gum if I could hit twenty balls in a row?" She knew he was smiling. Could hear it in his voice.

"Dad's instructions," Lang said.

"You've been through a lot—physically and also emotionally. I just don't want anything else to happen. Like a broken hip on top of everything else," Teddy said.

"Well, I'm not going to just sit here. I don't have that luxury," Lang said.

"That's my point! You *will* have that luxury if you sell the place! You can spend the rest of your life on your ass if you want," he said.

"I don't want to!" Lang said, irritated about him mentioning her rear end.

"I know that. You can make as many flower arrangements as you want. Bake cakes all day long. That's a good activity for you, plus you're good at it. I'm just saying that people hurt themselves on the tennis court who don't have cancer and who haven't been compromised with radiation. It's not like your heart hasn't had a toll taken on it. It burns the good with the bad, the radiation. You need to take care of yourself! It's like you are just asking for trouble!" Teddy said sharply.

"By playing a game of tennis?" Lang asked. His mood turned violent so easily lately. She should have just agreed not to play.

"Yes, Mother," Teddy snapped. "By running around and trying to keep up with the others and setting yourself up for an injury. Remember when you pulled your back and couldn't move at all? Dad had to do everything. He took care of you. He had to put your socks on and tie your shoes. And he's not here anymore. A pulled back would be the least of it," he said.

It was only after they'd hung up that Lang realized her hand was cramping. She spread out her fingers slowly and realized she'd been squeezing the phone with all her might, trying to stop his words.

FORTY-ONE

....

Lang was glad there weren't many people at the aquarium. She hated it when throngs of people were there, all trying to press their noses against the thick glass to see the bottom of the Tennessee River up close.

She and Katie D. watched the gigantic catfish swim back and forth on the bottom of the tank. His mouth was pulled in a wide line, like someone had stretched the corners from gill to gill with their index fingers, and his long whisker-like tentacles wavered in slow motion through the water. He was twelve-feet long and weighed over four hundred pounds. The sign said he was sixty-five years old—exactly Lang's age.

Katie D. loved the river otters. They stood at the Plexiglas wall, hoping the playful animals would show themselves. It always cheered Lang when she spotted them, exuberantly chasing one another down the little waterfall in the exhibit, sleek and graceful, a dark current themselves, hurtling through the water. She remembered the kayakers on the way to A. J.'s mountain home, then pictured the flounce of red lace on the stark white sheets.

"What's your favorite fish?" Lang asked Katie D.

"Those blue striped ones. Do you think my eyes might change colors? Babies' eyes do, teacher said."

"I hope not." Lang traced her finger over Katie D.'s eyebrow. "You, my brown-eyed girl," she sang. Her voice was rough and uneven, and she tried to remember the last time she sang a song out loud.

"That's the song Lele sang me," Katie D. said.

"I remember. Your eyes are warm and real and comforting. If I could, I'd change my eyes to yours," Lang said. "Friendly!" she added enthusiastically, victoriously remembering the word she had been searching for.

Lang insisted on buying her a souvenir, and after much deliberation, Katie D. chose a plastic back scratcher in the shape of an alligator.

The heat of the afternoon blasted them like a furnace as they left the air-conditioned gift shop. Sarah stood by the entrance, fanning herself with a plastic cup. Her blonde hair looked dark, and clung in wet clumps to her neck.

"Oh, I didn't realize what time it was. Have you been waiting long?" Lang asked, looking at her watch.

"Oh, it's fine," Sarah said.

"You should have come inside," Lang said. "We were shopping, and I would have bought you a back scratcher. The catfish one."

"Oh, I was early. It's fine, really," she said.

"God, it's hot!" Lang said, holding her hair up off her neck. "The air is like pudding. It's not natural—no rain all spring and then this dry steam. If that's such a thing. I don't know what's happening with the weather."

"We can stick our piggies in the water! And it's shady over there," Katie D. said, pointing to a cherry tree with outstretched branches. "Please, can we stay?"

"Sweetie, we've got to get going. Remember, we have to go to the grocery store," Sarah said.

"Please, Mommy? I'll play real nice."

"I wouldn't mind sitting down for a minute," Lang said.

"Just for a minute. Then we have to go," Sarah said.

Katie D. squealed as she sloshed off downstream, skimming the surface of the water with the plastic alligator.

Making Arrangements

The man-made creek outside the aquarium curved along the path of the Tennessee River. It was the perfect depth and width for wading and splashing and toe soaking.

Lang took her sandals off and plopped down on the smooth concrete riverbank in the shade. "Sit," she said, patting the concrete. "It feels heavenly on my feet. I didn't think you'd wait outside. It's so hot!" Lang leaned down and dipped her bare wrists in the water to cool herself.

Sarah looked back at Katie D., then slowly followed Lang to the shade.

"It's supposed to rain," Sarah said.

"I wish it *would* rain! Pour torrents. It's so dry," Lang said as she looked up at the sky. "This weather. Nothing would surprise me."

"Yes," Sarah said. "It's all out of whack."

"Are you worried about her sight?" Lang asked.

"What? No! Did something happen? Did you notice something?" Sarah asked sharply.

"No, not at all. Everything's fine. She just mentioned an ophthalmologist a while back, and I wondered why she'd seen one. That's all."

"Oh, I just want to make sure everything's fine with her eyes," Sarah said. "That's all."

They both watched Katie splashing in the water.

"We used to bring her here. Jack and me. We'd get frozen Cokes and sip them while she played in the water. You want one? My treat since I didn't buy you a back scratcher. And because I made you wait out in the heat."

"No, I'm fine. Thanks," Sarah said quickly. She turned away to watch her daughter, but Lang could see her mouth stretched thin and tight.

"I don't know. There are always rough spots in relationships," Lang said haltingly. "But I feel it's important to have a committed relationship. For Katie D. He still wants to marry you." She tried to choose her words carefully; she hadn't meant to blurt out anything about marriage. She wanted to make Sarah feel safe confiding in her, but she didn't want to come across as prying. She thought if she opened up a little herself, Sarah might feel safer. "One thing is, I've discovered, a live man is easier to communicate with than a dead man."

Sarah stood up immediately and grabbed her shoes. "We need to go," she said.

"I just mean, Teddy's here, and every relationship has troubles, but they can be worked out. Jack isn't here, and so the problems left are just with me. To deal with. I can't even talk to him about it."

Sarah lurched through the water toward Katie D., her giant steps almost comical. Lang watched Katie D.'s face change from delight at seeing her mother in the water to puzzlement as Sarah picked her up and walked away.

"Bye, Grandie!" Katie D. called over Sarah's shoulder. Lang waved. The wake behind Sarah was rough and uneven. Lang rubbed her thumb over her wrist, feeling for the rubber band she hadn't replaced.

FORTY-TWO

....

Lang shouldn't have been shocked at his invitation. Still.

She froze on the phone, her mouth agape, the receiver pressing on her ear, until Leland said, "Hello? Lang?" Then she collected herself enough to somehow blurt out an agreement to dinner.

She was sixty-five years old and sick. She knew she was going to get sicker. What was she thinking agreeing to go to dinner with a man, any man, but especially one who talked to animals like he was Dr. Dolittle? She should warn him now and let him off the hook.

She called Leland back the next morning to cancel the dinner date, and his receptionist answered the phone.

"Is this Mrs. Eldridge again?" the receptionist asked. Lang detected a sneer in her voice and felt like some pathetic stalker.

"Oh! I just figured it out. Once a m-m-month. I didn't know how often to give the heartworm pills," Lang said, not waiting to speak to Leland.

Fine.

She would go on the miserable dinner date. They would both be so ill at ease their stomachs would roil up after the first bite, and neither of them would ever put themselves through something like that again.

"Ode-a-lay-he-who!" A. J. sang out as she clattered her manicured fingernails lightly on the glass pane.

She was acting like nothing had happened on the tennis

court the other day, like she was breezily popping in for no good reason.

"Oh. Hello," Lang said icily.

"What's the matter? Are you okay?"

"Yes. I'm fine."

"Lang? What? What is it?"

"Nothing!"

Lang focused on the potting soil she had been sterilizing in the microwave. She squeezed her face up tight.

"Is it Teddy? What did he do now?"

"It's not Teddy. It's you!" Lang blurted out.

"Me? What did I do?"

Lang turned her back to A. J. and kneaded the warm soil.

"What? You have to tell me!" A. J. grabbed the big plastic bowl and shook it as she spoke. Dirt spewed over the counter.

"You told me to stay in the alley. Not to take any balls," Lang said accusingly. "You don't think I'm any good."

A. J. stared at Lang, her face fixed.

"I don't even know why you asked me to play," Lang said.

A. J. set the bowl down and whirled around to face Lang.

"I've been begging you for months to get me in that fucking club, and you act like your hands are tied!" A. J. shouted, waving her hands in the air. "Fine. So be it. But then you two discuss the list of new members right in front of me. Just to rub it in!"

"You're on the list," Lang said. "You're one of the new members we'll be discussing. So I guess you don't need me anymore. I guess you can just latch on to Emmeline and Peggy and see what rung they can get you to on the social ladder."

"You got me in?" A. J. asked. "Why didn't you tell me?"

"They'll tell you. They do some surprise invitation with all sorts of hoopla that I didn't want to spoil for you. A. J., to tell you the truth, the Barrington Women's Club is the last thing on my mind. But congratulations. You made it in, whatever that's worth."

"They voted me in? It was unanimous?" A. J. asked in disbelief.

"A. J., I haven't been to a meeting in years. I have no idea," Lang snapped.

"Oh, honey. I'm so sorry! I had no idea! I never would've meant to hurt you. I mean it!"

Lang turned her back to A. J.

"Look, you're going to have to look at me." A. J. squeezed herself between Lang and the counter and held Lang's face in her hands. "You are my friend. I have people I know and socialize with. But you are my only friend. Do you hear me? I'm so sorry I hurt you. But we are going to have to work this out," A. J. said.

"You just stuck me in the alley and left me. Like you wanted me off the court," Lang said. "Like I was dead weight."

"Oh, sweetie. I'm so sorry. I'm not nothing but a aggressive sleazebag, tennis court or not. You know that by now. You're better than all four of us put together. You control the entire game from a six-foot circle," A. J. said, and she put her arms around Lang and held her. "Please? You can't not forgive me. You do."

Lang didn't know which was harder: forgiving or not being able to forgive.

FORTY-THREE

....

L ang! When's the last time you had your hair cut?" A. J. asked when Lang told her about the dinner date at the Café on the Corner with Leland. She swished her fingers back and forth, snipping the air.

"My hair cut? I just got my hair *back*! There has to be enough hair there to cut before I go to the beauty shop," Lang said.

"I'll see if Cyndi can work you in. She does mine," A. J. said, already dialing on the phone and holding her index finger up at Lang like Dr. LePeyre's receptionist did. "No, that's okay. I knew it was a long shot." She hung up and turned to Lang. "Looks like I'm the stylist today. Don't worry. I cut my hair until I could afford not to. So," A. J. said, fluffing her own hair in the mirror.

"Hey," Sarah called from the foyer. "I've been trying to fax this to you, but it won't go through. It's another order, and they put a short deadline on it, so I wanted to bring it over."

"We just had ESPN. Lang's got a hot date. I summoned you telepathetically. Hair! Makeup! Wardrobe! Work with me, people," A. J. said, clapping her hands.

"You got the *pathetic* part right," Lang said. "It's *telepathically*, not *telepathetically*."

"Pick, pick, pick," A. J. said, undeterred by the correction. "You know what I mean."

"Well, that's great. I'll just leave this on the counter," Sarah said, heading back out the door.

"No, you need to help me decide what to wear, or I swear I'm not going," Lang said.

"Don't be ridiculous. Sarah, go grab that white wrap out of her closet. No stay here. I'll do it," A. J. said as she walked into Lang's bedroom.

Lang slowly shook her head at Sarah. "What am I thinking?"

"I need to head out. I'm sure it will be fine," Sarah said.

"I can't do it. It's too soon," Lang said.

"Sarah! Set down here and help me! Quit acting like you have a plane to catch and tell her what to wear! I'll trim her hair. Lang, be still!"

They both sat down docilely, and Lang wondered if she should have screamed commands at Sarah from the very beginning.

A. J. made Lang try on several blouses and two dresses and a long skirt before deciding on a pair of linen pants and a relatively unstretched black boatneck T-shirt. Sarah took off her turquoise linen patterned scarf and offered it to Lang. "This will be so pretty on you. Your eyes," she said shyly.

"Oh, no. I couldn't," Lang began.

A. J. snatched the scarf and held it up to Lang's face. "Take it. She's right."

A. J. ran her wet hands through Lang's hair, then quickly snipped it, tousled it, and scrutinized it before snipping it again. Then she ordered Lang to close her eyes while she made up her face.

"I don't know why you didn't petition the board over your flower orders. Emmeline Harrison doesn't own that club," A. J. said. "It's just not right. I bet they don't even know. No one should have stood for that, you being widowed and all."

"I used up all my clout getting you in," Lang said.

A. J. stopped clipping, and they stared at each other in the mirror.

"I'm kidding," Lang said. "That was a joke, and not a good one."

"It's true, isn't it? You had to throw your weight around and use your grandmother's name to get me in," A. J. said.

"A. J., they're lucky to have you. If you're willing to be in that club, the Women's Club of Barrington will be much better off, I can promise you that. They need a breath of fresh air. So," Lang said.

"I'm going to sign up for the decorating committee and order all the flowers from you. Lots of them," A. J. said as she began snipping with a vengeance.

"Stop!" Lang said suddenly and stood up. "I can't go. This is ridiculous!"

"It's just for dinner. You're making too much out of it," A. J. said.

"I don't look right," Lang said when she saw her features emphasized with eye shadow and blush.

"You look elegant," A. J. told her. "But don't get the mussels. They're so messy you'll spill on your blouse."

"No, *you're* making too much of it! I feel like you're trying to make me different than I am. Better," Lang said.

"No, honey," A. J. said. "This is a good thing. A really nice thing. We're happy for you. You know, like your mother made you over on prom day or for your first date. Getting you all ready for something special."

Lang snorted.

"My mother mixed baby oil and iodine and put me in the backyard with a record album covered in aluminum foil. She said a little color was worth a whole counter of fancy foundations," A. J. said. "What? It made you tan faster."

"Mine gave me a DIY manicure," Sarah said.

"What about you? I bet Lillian knew every trick for shiny

hair and a peaches-and-cream complexion," A. J. said.

"Well, she wasn't really around much," Lang said finally. In truth, she hadn't laid eyes on her mother from the time she was three until the day Fancy had died.

FORTY-FOUR

....

Lang could see the top of Leland's head, a smooth, shiny pink, as he walked back and forth on the road, checking his watch. He was early for the date, and she realized Leland LePeyre was as nervous as she was.

Lang relaxed a little. They were both out of their comfort zone, not just her. What was she thinking, putting them both in this awkward, humiliating, thank-god-that's-over, I-swear-I-learned-my-lesson situation? She couldn't stand watching his sparsely haired head a second longer. He looked almost as pathetic as she had earlier, submitting to A. J. styling her hair and picking out her clothes.

She looked in the mirror, almost expecting to see a dewy, unlined face, innocent and expectant, the way A. J. had said she would make her over. But there was only an old woman with a ridiculous amount of jewelry on, the skin under her chin sagging.

Lang had wiped a dry rag over her cheeks and eyelids, making the white rag splotchy from her concealer.

"Leland," she called, waving. "I'm ready! I'll be right there."

She went to her bedroom to grab her purse, then was startled to see Leland at the door. His navy golf shirt was buttoned all the way up to the top, and she did a double take at his macramé belt. She felt sorry for him for a minute, then realized she was in no position to judge. She looked like some Medicare Malibu Barbie doll with her orange skin and heavy makeup. She rubbed the inside of her wrist.

"Okay!" she said too brightly. "Let's get this over with so we can each go back to our lives." She was certain she said that out loud, but Leland looked completely unfazed.

"All righty then," Leland said, and Lang noted this was already the second time he'd used this silly phrase, which did not bode well for the dinner date. She bent down to give Victoria a treat and heard a click. Leland stared at his phone, obviously perplexed. "I'm not sure if I took a picture or not."

"Well, I hope not," she said. "I don't like pictures of myself if I'm not prepared. Even if I am prepared usually."

"What? You should! Wait, it worked," he said, and he held the phone out to her. "I'll get it printed out at the drugstore." She squinted at the picture of Victoria and herself.

"Is Café on the Corner still okay with you? I think the food is the best, and it's right down the street, and hopefully it won't be packed this early," he said.

Lang wondered if he didn't want to be seen with her, but he pointed to his ear and said, "I can't hear anything if there's background noise."

"Huh?" she said, cupping her hand to her ear. They both laughed quickly, eager to dissipate some of the tension they felt.

"Now, I know you have a little dog and an adorable granddaughter, but that's about all I know. Tell me about yourself, Lang Eldridge," he said after they were seated at a linen-covered table under a tall window. "Besides the fact that we both have names that start with the letter *L*. I read somewhere the letter *L* is symbolic of living life to the fullest, so that's my criteria for dating. So far it's between you and Lisa. Kidding. Sorry, I guess I'm babbling on. I'm a little nervous."

"Oh. Well. Me, too." Lang placed her hands on the round green vase holding a white spider chrysanthemum splayed out against three fuchsia snapdragons. She felt the coolness of the glass against her palms. She plucked a brown withered pod off the snapdragon and rolled it between her fingertips. There was a loud click, and Leland looked at his phone in bewilderment.

"Sorry. My daughters gave me this phone and showed me how to take pictures with it, but I haven't quite figured it out. You look so pretty there with the flowers," he said. "I was trying to take a picture, but not of this!"

Lang focused on the flowers, studying them like she'd never seen a bloom. She didn't know what to say.

"Where did you get that belt?" Lang asked.

"Oh. I made it. My wife was in a nursing home for a few weeks before she died, and they had activities. Macramé was one, and I liked having something to do with my hands while I sat with her. She couldn't do it, but I thought maybe if she saw, or heard me, something would click, and she'd come back. She couldn't see anything. She was in a coma, so anyway. Sorry. I should have just said I ordered it from a catalog," Leland said.

"I wouldn't have believed it," Lang said. "No, seriously, I'm so sorry. I shouldn't have made a joke under the circumstances." What was she doing cracking jokes about his pathetic macramé belt? And making him talk about his wife? She didn't even know him!

"No apology necessary. So let me see if I can find the picture I took." He squinted at his phone for a minute, then said, "Nope, I can't. Tell me about you."

"Well, recently widowed, as you know," she began, blushing. She brushed over that detail as if she were cheating on Jack by being here. She stared at the petals spilling over her fingers.

"That Katie D. is a bright spot, isn't she?"

"She is," Lang said, motioning for another glass of wine. "I love my son, of course." She felt slightly guilty that it was her grandchild, not her child, who made her feel effervescent on the inside. "Teddy is a sweetheart. Just has a ways to go it seems. I don't think he knows what he wants to do. He was a really good tennis player when he was younger, but nothing since then has panned out. Except for Katie D.—" Lang paused and thought of the first time she held Katie D., the tiny thing staring straight into her eyes, focused and unblinking as she hungrily gulped the bottle Lang fed her. Her gaze had been intent and serious, as if she were sizing Lang up, calculating whether this would be a relationship worth pursuing.

"They're not married, Teddy and her mother. Not because of Teddy. He wanted to. He begged her! It was Sarah. Katie D.'s mother. Can you imagine?" Lang said, practically clucking her disapproval as she rubbed her wrist. The months with the rubber band hadn't done a thing. "I wish they would. For every reason. One, so that Katie D.'s not illegitimate. I swear I can't stand it! Katie D. uses Teddy's last name, but they're not married. I don't even know if that's legal. I think Sarah is playing it like they were briefly married and now are divorced."

"Playing it?" Leland asked.

"You know, making it seem like," she said with exaggerated enunciation, leaning closer over the table. "I get this from Teddy. Do you know that 'hooking up' insinuates having sex?" She quickly told herself to shut up.

"Anyway, Teddy brings Katie D. to dinner at our house regularly. My house, I guess. Not as much recently, I guess. I don't know. Lately he's been playing a lot of tennis again. They gave him a free membership at the tennis club just to have him around. Makes them look good, I guess, having such an accomplished tennis player around."

"Sounds like he's doing well," Leland said.

"He thinks I should go to a nursing home. Make macramé myself," Lang said, already regretting bringing up the macramé again. She shouldn't drink at all.

"He's wrong. You would be terrible at it," Leland said. It took her a minute to realize he was trying to make a little joke. "You have to be ready, and I can tell you right now, you aren't close to being ready for that."

"How do you know?" Lang asked. He didn't know anything about her. He had no idea that her cancer was beckoning again, that Teddy's family life was questionable at best, and that she was on the verge of bankruptcy. She never should have let him take her to dinner.

"You're much too much alive," he said. When he smiled at her, his eyes crinkled at the corners, and his dimple undid her.

She took another sip of red wine, then spun around her wineglass as the wine sloshed perilously close to the rim. "I really think if they'd gotten married, if he'd had them as a real family, he would have bucked up. Gotten a job. Hanging around the tennis club all day wouldn't be an option. I don't get it. It seems to me if you are into someone enough to have sex with them, you need to be into them enough to marry them. Really, unless you are willing to marry whoever you're in the bed with, you have no business hooking up," she said.

"It's a different world," Leland said. "I was definitely born sixty years too early."

Lang laughed out loud and ordered the mussels.

She didn't notice the oily stain she'd left on Sarah's scarf until she took it off that night.

FORTY-FIVE

....

L ang and Victoria drove out to Brow Lake to walk the easy loop around the lake. She thought she might have better luck on flat ground than she did walking up her hilly street.

Victoria leaped in the water aggressively, as if he were on a mission to save someone. He kept his head above water as he jumped in and swam the length of the lake. His eyes were on her as she slowly walked alongside him on the road, his little back legs bowlegged as they sturdily churned the water.

Several dogs joined them, making a play date for Victoria with no arranging or responsibilities. When Lang caught herself thinking about "play dates" for the dog she hadn't wanted, she thought maybe Teddy had been right. It was time for her to be sent to the retirement home, if not committed.

She rested on a wooden bench. The little lake rippled in the breeze. Banks of mist hovered in cloudlike drifts above the water. A pair of red-winged blackbirds flew out of the reeds nearby, a flicker of scarlet vivid against their dark feathers, and she thought of Jack. If he hadn't died, she wouldn't even know he'd mortgaged the house. *He* would be the one fretting and panicking about how he would keep everything together. Not her. She would be able to look at the blackbirds and enjoy them for what they were. The pair of birds disappeared over the tree line, and she wondered what else he'd lied about.

Lang walked into her house just as the answering machine clicked and Teddy's voice filled the room. She reached for the receiver then stopped.

"I heard you were out with some man last night. Seriously, someone said that. As if that could happen. I know you were probably meeting with the priest or the florist supply guy, but I just wanted to let you know people are getting the wrong idea. Small town and all. Kind of creeps me out just thinking about it, and I'm sure it does you, too," Teddy said. "Whatever. We need to talk about Shepherd's Arms. There's an opening. But we need to move on it now. As in *right* now!"

Lang turned the answering machine off. Victoria followed her out on the front porch and curled up beside her in the old wicker chair. Jack's lifeless body appeared in her head, the stubble dark against his pale, waxy cheek. She tried to see Jack napping on the porch swing, his book splayed out on his chest. She stared at the empty swing and saw him forging her name. Marking off the days on his calendar until she died.

She wondered if Teddy was right, if the very idea of a relationship with another man was ridiculous. What was the point?

Mrs. Eubanks nodded up at her as she slowly trundled past, her torso bent to the right. She waited on the road until Lang reached her arm up to wave. Then she nodded and slowly continued on. Then three blonde strollers came by, waving at the same time.

She knew if she weren't sitting out here on the porch, if she dropped dead in the kitchen, they would walk right on by, not even slowing their pace.

FORTY-SIX

....

Leland and Lang had been seeing each other regularly in the weeks since their first dinner date. Each morning Lang filled the coffeepot to level six, making two oversize cups. Leland usually stopped by on his way to work, graciously accepting coffee as he reviewed Victoria's tricks.

This morning Victoria played dead in Leland's arms, draping his limp body across Leland's forearm and dangling his head near his paws.

"Release!" Leland commanded, and Victoria whipped his head up and snapped up his treat.

Victoria hadn't quite mastered this trick. The dog kept popping up for his treat, then collapsing into apparent unconsciousness when he realized it wasn't quite time.

Leland stopped by often after dinner now as well, bringing his old dog, Rommel. They would walk the two dogs together, Boone hobbling stiff-legged behind Victoria, falling with a thud every time Victoria stopped to sniff anything.

This evening, he handed her a plastic grocery bag of homegrown tomatoes, still warm from the sun. Lang held one up to her nose, marveling at the deep, uneven color as she inhaled the tangy, earthy ripeness.

"You cannot buy this. It's one of the top ten best smells on earth in my book. A homegrown tomato," Lang said. "You can tell how it's going to taste just by breathing in the skin."

"Yep. Hard to beat. It's up there with fresh-cut grass. I want to be buried in it. Just cut the grass and dump it in my coffin.

Has to be cut that day, though," Leland said.

"Peonies. Fill mine with peonies then. All colors," Lang said.

"I want to be completely covered up, so it's just grass that's visible," Leland said. Lang began to laugh at the idea of it, green grass mounded up in a casket. Then she thought of Jack's pale, still body in the casket, and her face fell abruptly.

"I want to invite you and Katie D. to my daughter's picnic," Leland said quickly, as if he'd been saving the invitation for a gloomy look on her face. "They live out in the country with a donkey and a horse, and you would love her garden. Lots of kids for Katie D. You could meet all my family at once. Get it over with. Worst-case scenario: you come back with the best sweet corn you've ever tasted."

Lang was so shocked at the idea of meeting his family that instead of asking if he was out of his mind, she mumbled, "Oh, sweet corn is up there with the homegrown tomatoes."

"You are acting like a twelve-year-old girl. Of course you're going!" A. J. said when Lang told her about the invitation she was planning to refuse. "The daughter invited you. Obviously. Or he wouldn't have mentioned it. Plus, how can you deprive Katie D. of a pony ride and a gazillion kids on a farm and probably homemade ice cream?"

"She would never want to go. Katie D. won't know a soul, and I'm not going to put her through that."

"How many more days?" Katie D. asked her daily.

When it was finally time, Katie D. arrived with her pink polka-dot backpack bulging with a swimsuit, a change of clothes, a sweatshirt in case she got cold, webbed sandals, silver high-heeled mules, and hiking boots.

"And a nightgown in case they ask me to spend the night,"

she added, showing Lang each item.

"Sorry," Sarah said. "I told her all she needed was a swimsuit."

"No, you were right, Katie D.," Leland said. "Better safe than sorry. Sarah? You up for going? Best Boston butt this side of the Mississippi, and each of my daughters tries to impress the others with their side dishes, so the eatin' is top-notch."

"Oh, no. I can't, but thank you for asking," Sarah said.

"Oh, please come!" Lang said. "I insist. As a matter of fact, if you don't come, then I'm not going."

"Mommy! You must come!"

"You simply must," Leland said.

"Well, I don't think I can—" Sarah began.

"You're going," Lang ordered flatly.

"Let's go," Leland said cheerfully, shooing them all toward the car.

The long gravel driveway curved up through the woods, finally opening up to a pasture of horses grazing behind a primitive wood fence and a field of sunflowers. A large, rustic farmhouse with a wrap-around porch loomed at the top of the hill. A band of small children came running toward their car.

Shouts of "Granddaddy!" chorused through the air, and Lang counted thirteen children ranging from toddlers to teens, all racing to welcome Leland. She watched him squat down in the field to embrace them.

"Oh, that's too bad," Katie D. said. "That little boy is going to die, isn't he, Mommy?"

"What? Why would you say that, Katie D.?" Lang asked.

"He's going to be blind soon. Look. He has glasses," Katie D. said.

"Just because a child wears glasses doesn't mean he's going to die!" Lang said. "Sarah?"

"That's right. Remember, sweetie? What we talked about?" Sarah said.

"Some babies get real bad diseases?"

"Yes," Sarah said, and her voice broke.

Lang wanted to turn around and see if she was crying, but she didn't want to embarrass her.

"Goodness, there are a lot of them!" Lang said. "Almost too many to count. Can you count them, Katie D.?"

"One, two, three, four, five, twelve . . ."

More people were on the porch, shading their eyes from the sun, but beginning to move toward them as well. Lang's first instinct was to flee.

"Yes, they seem to be multiplying to me, too. Look at them moving toward him in a pack. These children look like miniature Amish guerillas. Except for that one." Lang studied the young black man hanging behind, towering over the group. "Who is that?"

"I'm counting fourteen with the baby," Sarah said, sniffling. "Maybe he takes care of the farm?"

Lang took the opportunity to whip her head around and inspect Sarah. Her face was blotchy, and she wiped at her nose. Lang wondered why she was crying but knew better than to ask.

"Maybe he's adopted, but it seems like Leland would have mentioned that," Lang said. "I don't know. Maybe not."

Leland swooped down and picked up two children as the others surrounded him.

"Do you remember *Gulliver's Travels*," Lang asked, trying cheer Sarah up. "All the Lilliputians tied up the humans? I'm sensing a very sinister ending to this picnic. Don't fall asleep!"

Leland opened Lang's door and introduced them. Monty Brown was the young black man, but no explanation was given about why he was there. No "He's our neighbor" or "our care-

256

taker" or "my grandson."

"Well, pleased to meet ya!" a little girl said as she curtsied.

"Dorrie, good god! You are not Eliza Doolittle! Stop making an ass of yourself," a larger girl said.

"I'm telling you cussed," Dorrie said.

"My grandmother's friends cuss," Katie D. said.

"She's in *My Fair Lady* at school. I'm Francine," the first girl said, sticking out her hand.

Benjamin, Wardie, Patsy Ann, Charlotte, Charlie, Elena—the introductions seemed endless.

Lang was overwhelmed by the tribe of friendly, well-mannered munchkins who couldn't have been nicer, though it was clear their main interest was Katie D. and Victoria. Victoria rose to the occasion, walking on his hind legs as the children cooed and clapped and fed him chunks of barbecue.

"Sorry. I didn't tell you there was a whole nation of them. Didn't want to scare you off," Leland said.

"Well, they're lovely. Really," Lang said, watching Katie D. walk into a path in the sunflower field, surrounded by Eliza Doolittle and the others.

"*Children of the Corn*," Sarah whispered, and Lang laughed. She tried to remember if Sarah had ever made a joke before.

"Hey, Daddy!" a grown woman shouted, hurrying toward them. "You must be Lang. I'm Rhetta. I'm so glad you came," she said, reaching both arms toward Lang.

Lang felt herself stiffen before the woman even touched her. She tried to relax her shoulders and breathe as Rhetta threw her arms around Lang's torso. Suddenly she knew how Sarah felt.

"Come on up, and I'll get you all a cold drink. Frozen margarita? Beer? Wine? Oh, we have iced tea, too," Rhetta said after she hugged Sarah as well. "Lang, give me a hand? We'll be back with drinks."

Lang followed Rhetta reluctantly, looking back at Sarah, Katie D., and Leland. He snapped a picture of her with his phone and gave her a thumbs-up sign.

"I've heard all about Victoria. She seems to be quite a hit. He, I mean," Rhetta said.

"I think he loves the attention," Lang said.

Lang looked out at the children all clustered around an enormous bonfire. Katie D. held Victoria, who alternated between bolting back to life for a chicken leg then collapsing over Katie D.'s forearm.

"So you all get together a lot?" Lang asked.

Rhetta laughed. "Overwhelmed? There are a lot of us. We do get together a lot, I guess. My husband would say constantly. But we do. I've got three sisters and two brothers, all as close as we can possibly be in age. So, we are all pretty enmeshed. When Mom died, I guess we got together more regularly. All of us come here on Sunday afternoons, and we take turns having Daddy for dinner during the week."

"So who's Monty?"

Rhetta looked shocked. "You don't know?"

Oh, Lord. Another surprise. Leland had an illegitimate child.

Rhetta snapped a chocolate rectangle off a Hershey's bar. "He killed my mother." She held the candy bar out to Lang.

"No! What?"

"Not on purpose. He was drunk. Hit her with a stolen SUV. It's been eight years this fall. Anyway, Monty was in the foster system, and for whatever reason, Daddy felt called to take him on," Rhetta said. "I know what reason actually. Not that it's the easiest thing. Mom's motto was something Gandhi said. 'The weak can never forgive. Forgiveness is an attribute of the strong.' She instilled that in us from day one. And so when she was killed, what else could we do? We had to forgive the little asshole." She rolled her eyes heavenward when she said *asshole* and shrugged her shoulders.

"So he's a part of your family? After what he did?"

"Pretty much," Rhetta said. Really, what choice did we have?"

"Wait. I don't understand. Monty killed your mother, then took her place? I'm sorry. I shouldn't have said it that way."

"No, you could say that. You nailed it actually. It's crazy. So consider yourself warned," Rhetta said. "It's strange. I don't even think of him as the person who took her from us anymore. I never would have believed that could happen. I hated him so much when it happened."

"I'm so sorry. I don't think I could forgive someone like that."

"Well, you'd be surprised at what you can do for love. I love my dad. I love my kids. And if I let that hate stay in my heart, it would spoil everything I have. Anyway, you are the first guest he's brought around. Ever." She settled her eyes on Lang. "So that says a lot for you. Oh, and one thing. I don't know anything about your relationship. I have all the details on the dog and the grandchild. You and my dad may be purely platonic. Not my business," Rhetta said, waving her hands in refusal. "But I want you to know we are so glad he has someone he is interested in. Someone he likes to be around." Her hazel eyes turned slick with moisture. "So you can just relax and know that we're glad you're here. No matter what."

Lang braced herself as Rhetta leaned toward her and squeezed her arm. But instead of feeling pressure, Lang just felt warmth from her hand.

She never should have let Rhetta leave without asking her where the bathroom was. Lang felt the chocolate bar hit her stomach and turn her bowels cold and slick. She felt the familiar clench of her insides—a fist of pain so hard and tight it rippled through her whole body. She panicked as she opened a closet door, a pantry door, and the door to the basement, frantically searching for a bathroom. She keeled over as her stomach convulsed.

"Are you okay?" Sarah asked, appearing suddenly in the hallway. "Come on, let's sit down."

"I'm sick," Lang said, pressing her back against the wall.

How Sarah knew how to get her to the closest bathroom, Lang never knew. Only that somehow Sarah led her through a narrow hall lined with closed doors, through a bedroom, and finally into a bathroom. Sarah raised the toilet seat and held her hair back as Lang vomited, smoothing Lang's forehead with a cool washrag and speaking softly.

It was back.

FORTY-SEVEN

·······························

What are you thinking?" Teddy asked. "Please tell me I heard wrong, that it's someone's idea of a joke. Please tell me you're not dating at age seventy!"

"I'm not seventy," Lang said weakly. "I just turned sixty-five."

"Mother! You can't be serious! Daddy hasn't been gone a year, and you have some kind of boyfriend?"

"He's not my boyfriend!" Lang said. "Why would you say that?"

"I've heard you're together constantly. You walk around the neighborhood with your dogs? I'm cringing at the very idea!" Teddy said accusingly.

"Did Sarah tell you?"

"Sarah? What does Sarah know about it?" Teddy asked, agitated.

"Nothing. I mean there's nothing to know! He's the vet, and I had to take Victoria. I still have to take him, so we've gotten to know each other a little."

Lang was at a loss. Were people making fun of them? Did they roll their eyes as they drove past, like they were pathetic or cutesy?

"Don't you remember that couple down the street who got married at age eighty or something. He died, and his kids were left with—hello—nothing?"

"Oh, Teddy. That's what you're worried about? Your inheritance?"

"You are sitting on a gold mine with this property, and you know it. What do you think is going on here? Do you have any idea how valuable this land is? Do you know what could happen if you married him without a prenup? I'm just saying this is not a good idea. At all. Isn't he younger than you? And how much further away from dad could you get? This guy looks like a Weeble."

Lang had no idea how old Leland was. *Is he younger?*

"I think you would spare yourself a lot of trouble if you just nipped it in the bud. And sooner rather than later. You are in no position to get involved with anyone. In fact, I insist on it."

"Teddy. You know I'm sixty-five years old. Fully grown. I'll consider your advice as advice. Unsolicited. That's all." The words seemed to come out of her mouth on their own, but once they did, she was glad.

Lang stumbled over her feet and seemed to fall down on the tennis court in slow motion. She lunged toward a ball, reached out her racket, and then was suspended in the air. She knew she was going to fall down hard. She felt a flash of fear, not because of the pain, but for a potential injury. She saw the uneven scallop of the tree line against the soft blue-gray sky, then a blur of bright tennis dresses on the court beside them just before the coarse grains of rubico from the court's surface exploded into her knees. She lay still on the court, assessing her pain. Her knees were on fire, but it was the burning sting of scraped skin, not broken bones.

"Oh my gosh! Is she okay? Is anything broken? Don't move her? Call nine-one-one! Should we call nine-one-one?" All the voices mixed together, a cacophony of high-pitched panic.

There were a dozen people surrounding her, and Lang wondered if her panties were showing. She'd rather have a broken bone than her enormous rear end exposed. She frantically tried to pull at the back of her skirt, but it hurt too much to reach.

"It's okay. I'm okay," Lang said weakly.

"Oh god, look at her face," someone said loudly, as if Lang couldn't hear. Lang touched her throbbing cheek and felt what seemed to be warm quicksand.

"Okay, she's okay. Thanks, hon. Come on, Lang," A. J. said, shooing everyone back to their courts.

"You wanna get up?" Sarah asked, tugging Lang's skirt down with both hands. Where had she come from? "Here, hang on to me. We're going to go real slow."

Lang sat up slowly and looked at the mess on her knees. The mixture of blood and dark grains of rubico looked like the dirt sundaes she and Katie D. made with crushed Oreos and red velvet pudding.

"Is this stuff on my face?" Lang asked, feeling the same warm gritty mixture on her cheek.

"Let's get you up and home. Okay? But if anything hurts really bad, we'll get an ambulance," A. J. said. "So."

"Should we call Teddy?" Sarah asked.

"No!" Lang said emphatically. She felt like a disobedient child who was about to be grounded. The difference was the confinement would be to a nursing home, not her room.

The next day, Lang felt like she'd been run over by a life-size version of Katie D.'s road paver. The side of her face throbbed so hard it felt like woofers were vibrating inside her skull. Parts of her that hadn't even touched the tennis court felt emulsified, and the parts that had slid across the court felt like they had been skinned alive. She thought the main ingredient in rubico had to be ground glass.

"Mother! That's it. Look at you. What were you thinking," Teddy said when he saw her.

"I know. I was wrong. I have no business playing tennis anymore," Lang said. She couldn't imagine even getting out of the bed, much less playing tennis.

"Well, I'm sorry you hurt yourself. I told you this would happen. I hate to say it, Mom," Teddy said, obviously pleased. "There's a time and a place for everything. You taught me that. 'To everything, there is a season, turn, turn, turn.'" He sang the words softly, and she looked away from him.

"I know. You can say it out right. Go ahead and say I told you so," she said.

"I don't mean it like that. I'm sorry. I just don't know what else to do. Really. I actually have someone interested in hiring me. As a tennis pro. But where does that leave you? I don't want to think about it if you got sick again and I was far away," he said.

"I know. I think you're right. I'm ready. I need to go on and move. There. This is all too much for me, with everything and the trial. So if you wouldn't mind, just get it in order."

"Okay, Mom. I think that's for the best. It's going to be just fine. I'll help you with everything and get you all settled in," he said. He smoothed the sheets down and tucked them around her feet. He kissed the top of her head before he left and said he'd be back later with the paperwork.

"Oh my god! They need to put you on one of those meth billboards," A. J. said later when she eased quietly into the house. 'This Is What Meth Looks Like.' It's a compliment really," she said when Lang glared at her. "You look nothing like what you look like right now. In real life you don't look at all like this. So."

"Hers wasn't elective," Lillian said, looking pointedly at A. J. When had her mother slipped in?

"I'm getting more ice," A. J. said huffily, and walked out of

Lang's bedroom.

"How'd you know she had work done?" Lang asked.

Lillian shrugged her shoulders. "You can just tell, really," she said, placing her fingertips on her own forehead. "You were smart not to. Of course you don't need to. Your skin is so beautiful. Youthful, actually."

"No, it's not," Lang said

Her mother stared at her, and Lang tried to adjust herself in the bed. She was more uncomfortable because of her mother's gaze than because of her stiff, aching body.

"Was he good to you? Your husband? Were you happy?" Lillian asked.

"Why would you even ask that? Of course!" Lang snapped. She gingerly scooted her hips back, thinking of Jack creeping around behind her back and giving her papers to initial last year.

"Why wouldn't I? Methinks thou dost protest too much. Here, let me help you," Lillian said as she plumped the pillow and smoothed down the sheets. "I can stay if you want me to. I could take care of you. Do things. If you wanted me to."

Lang couldn't think of anything worse and knew the horror was clear on her face.

"Or not," Lillian said.

Late the next afternoon, Lang drove herself to Shepherd's Arms. Before, she'd been so against the idea she hadn't even really seen the place.

It hurt to turn her head, so she just stayed in the right-hand lane, puttering along behind a line of tractor-trailer trucks.

Teddy was right. She should go ahead and get settled in a place like this so that if she got really sick, she wouldn't be as much of an inconvenience. On paper selling the house was a win-win-win. 1. She'd guarantee Katie D. would stay in Barrington (or at least not move to Oregon anytime soon). 2. She'd have money to ensure she'd be taken care of physically. 3. She'd be in Teddy's good graces.

But still. She couldn't imagine living in a place like this.

She walked right through the lobby, not stopping to tell the receptionist she was visiting. She didn't want a tour. She wanted to take it in on her own and get a feel for what it would be like to live here.

"Today's not a good day. Come back another day," the woman bleated from her wheelchair.

"Hello, Mrs. Webster," Lang said. Both of them looked surprised she called the woman by name, and Lang wondered how she could remember such a random piece of information but never know where her glasses were.

"Just this once, honey," Mrs. Webster said, motioning Lang in like she was directing traffic. "Move along."

Lang made her way to the elevators, turning her face away from the metal cart carrying trays of cafeteria food. She wanted to cover her nose to keep from smelling the scent of ammonia mixed with canned gravy. She tapped at Mrs. Ball's door before walking in.

"Hello, Mrs. Ball. I was just here with your daughter," Lang said.

"Looks like you got run over by a truck," Mrs. Ball said.

"Yes, your daughter already pointed that out," Lang said. She ran her fingers over her temple, wincing as she noticed how clear Mrs. Ball's skin looked. Lang thought she would probably fit in better at Shepherd's Arms than Mrs. Ball did.

FORTY-EIGHT

···

Lang had assumed Lillian's doctor's appointment was just a regular checkup the way she had casually mentioned it. But Lang was concerned when her mother asked if she could stay with Lang for a few days.

"I have to have a touch of surgery, a little bowel obstruction. But I need to tell you something first," Lillian had said cryptically. But then Emmeline's father called and by the time Lang remembered to bring up the big secret, Lillian had changed her mind about revealing it.

Lang moved slowly through her house, readying Katie D.'s room for Lillian. No surgery was minor at Lillian's age. She was finally coming home. A lifetime too late.

How many times had Lang done this? As a little girl, she'd kept roses in a vase in the guest room all summer. Even if there had been no reason to believe her mother was coming home on that particular day, it had comforted Lang to know she could and that the house would be ready for her.

She stripped the bed and washed all the bedding, even though the sheets were clean. She wanted it to be perfectly fresh. The last time she had changed Katie D.'s sheets, she had to rest before taking off the pillowcases. Now she zipped through the task, whipping sheets out flat and pulling them taut. Ironic that the cancer was back. Or *iconic*, as A. J. would say.

Lang unwrapped the little round specialty soaps she'd been saving and put them by the bathroom sink. She debated using them for her mother but decided no one would appreciate them as much as Lillian would. Plus, if she saved them much longer, they'd lose their scent.

She was vacuuming the rug by the bed when someone forcefully grabbed her elbow.

She jumped and yelled, "Teddy! You scared me! I didn't hear you come in."

He held Sarah's paisley scarf in a wad.

"Sorry. I've been yelling for you. What planet are you on? What are you doing with this?"

"Oh, I need to get it back to her. I spilled something on it, and I need to take it to the cleaners out by the mall. I've had it out so I'll remember, but I never go out that way anymore."

"Well, I hope they can clean it. It's the only thing she has from her dad. He brought it to her from India or something." He paused. "Okay, I've got the papers together. We need to get the property listed on the market before the winter. Get this mother sold! Get some money!"

"Oh. Teddy, Lillian's having surgery. I need to wait until she recuperates. She's coming here, so I can't be showing the house with her in bed. Can we wait a few weeks?" She should have soaked the scarf days ago.

"Are you kidding me? Isn't that like the blind leading the blind? Can you even take care of yourself? Why don't you both go check in at Shepherd's Arms? Maybe you could share a room."

Lang thought he was teasing, but his eyes were a flat, hard blue. Nothing merry about them.

"No, I'll take care of her here. She has an obstruction in her bowel, and abdominal surgery can be tricky." Not that he had even asked. "Excuse me. I need to go down and get the walker out of the basement."

Lang needed to get away from him, collect herself, and take

a full breath of air. She eased her way down the narrow basement stairs, holding on to the rail with both hands. She could
not afford to fall again.

Victoria scampered ahead of her, sniffing the dark, forgotten corners of the old furnace room. Jack had lined the win-
dowless room with crude shelving, adding a wine rack and a
vegetable bin along the walls. She breathed in the earthy tang
of coal and remembered how terrified she'd been of this room
as a child. Dark and dangerous, the tiny room burned all winter.

She heard Teddy yelling upstairs and quickly closed the
door and made her way up the steps. The walker thumped
loudly behind her as she dragged it.

"It's something every time. Do you have any idea how much
is involved in this paperwork? You just act like, 'Oh, maybe
later, it doesn't suit me to an exact T at this particular second.'"

"I'm so sorry, Teddy. I appreciate you doing everything, and
I know that's what I need to do. I do. Just give me a little time
is all. She'll be up and at 'em in no time if I know Lillian, and I
promise we'll list it as soon as she's on her feet."

"Okay, Mom. That's fine. But that's it. No more. You don't
seem to understand what's involved here. If you don't sell this
place, well, I don't know what's going to happen to you. You
really don't have any options." He snapped his briefcase closed
with a quick click of finality, just as Leland tapped on the door.
"What are you going to do about the balloon payment?"

"Oh. Come in," Lang said stiffly as Leland let himself in.

"What the hell is he doing here?" Teddy said.

"Teddy. How are you?" Leland said cordially, reaching out
his hand. "Glad to see you, too."

"We walk the dogs," Lang mumbled, looking down at the
feet.

"Mom! I thought I made myself clear on this. You are not

getting involved with him. And not just you," he said to Leland. "Anyone. You are in no position!"

"We just walk the dogs around the neighborhood," Lang said.

"No, it's not just walking the dogs. We enjoy each other. Immensely," Leland said. "And I'm not sure how much business it is of yours."

Teddy's eyes flashed like cobalt-blue daggers. His chiseled jaw was set.

"Pick," he said coldly to Lang.

"What?" Lang asked, stunned.

"Me or him."

"Teddy! You're my son! Don't ask me something like that. You know I love you. I could never pick someone over you. Please don't be this way." Lang put her hands on Teddy's shoulders and tried to make him look her in the eye.

"Lang," Leland began. "You have every right to your own life."

"Leland! Please!" Lang said sharply. "This is between Teddy and me!"

Leland turned quickly and walked down the steps to the road. He took them two at a time, and she worried that he was going to fall.

FORTY-NINE

here's Victoria? Lang walked around the house, calling for him. The little dog had been missing for hours.

He was nowhere to be found. She called Teddy to see if he remembered seeing him when he was here. Had the vacuum cleaner scared him? She tried to remember the last time she'd seen him.

Teddy showed up at her door within the hour, clutching a handful of chopped hot dogs to lure the little dog. "We'll find him, Mom. Have you searched the whole house?"

"Yes. He must have followed someone. There are runners and walkers all over the place. You don't think anyone took him, do you?"

"No," he said gently. "He's just lost and probably finding his way back right now. I'm going to check outside, around the house. You stay here in case he comes home."

Lang eased herself down in the wicker chair on the porch and watched the back of Teddy's head as he descended the stone steps. She felt relieved to be back in his good graces, but she still felt torn. She had just discarded Leland. Without even thinking it through, she had chosen Teddy with no question.

She walked through the house again, opening every single hinged thing—closet doors, cabinet doors. *Where is he?*

She called Leland's office and asked the receptionist if anyone had found Victoria, but she made sure the woman didn't disturb Leland.

Then Lang posted herself on the top step and asked everyone who came by to be on the lookout for a little pale, fluffy dog that was perfectly silent. Always.

"Any luck?" Leland called out from the road.

"Oh! L-l-l-leland!" she stammered. "You came? For Victoria?"

"Any sign of him?" Leland asked.

"None," Lang said, shocked to see him. She knew she needed to thank him for coming to help and apologize for her behavior. She knew he should be at work, but all she could say was, "Where could he be?"

"He had his collar on, didn't he?" Teddy called out from the side yard.

"Yes. I'm sure he did," Lang said. *Did I put it back on after I bathed him? What if Victoria was lost with no identification at all?*

She started to go inside and check the laundry room but didn't want to leave Leland alone with Teddy.

"What are you doing here?" Teddy asked Leland when he rounded the corner.

"I came to help find Victoria," Leland said evenly.

"We've got it. You don't need to stay," Teddy said.

"It's okay. I can cover our walking route. See if maybe he wandered off on a walk by himself," Leland said as he headed down the steps to the road.

"*Our* walking route?" Teddy glared at Lang.

Leland came to the edge of a smile, his dimples barely indenting. "You don't need to concern yourself with our walking route, or for that matter, with our relationship," he told Teddy. "You won."

Lang was as silent as the dog.

FIFTY

....

That night Lang left the porch light on and a bowl of Teddy's chopped hot dogs at the door. She couldn't sleep between worrying about Teddy's ultimatum, Leland's apparent disgust, and Victoria's absence. She sat in the willow-back chair by the front door and watched the bowl of hot dogs through the sidelight. Oh, yes, and she was worried about Lillian's impending arrival. The vacuum cleaner still stood upright by the side of her bed, and Lang couldn't remember if she'd cleaned the toilet.

Instead of finishing Lillian's room, Lang made a poster with Victoria's picture on it and printed "LOST!" in bold letters across the bottom. She used the picture Leland had taken of Victoria and herself. She tried to crop herself out, but since her hand was holding one of Victoria's paws, it looked like she was the one who was lost.

She hoped someone had Victoria. She couldn't bear to think of him hit by a car and killed, or curled up under a tree somewhere, suffering alone.

"We'll find him, Grandie. I promise we will. I know it," Katie D. said when she arrived the next morning. They trudged through the neighborhoods, nailing the posters she'd made on telephone poles. "My mommy's looking, too. On the computer. She knows some ways to find lost dogs online," Katie D. said.

When Lang finally sat down on a park bench, she noticed

her hands were quivering, like a mild electric current was running down her arms.

When she got home, she made another sign for the front door announcing her temporary absence and thanking whomever might be reading it for finding Victoria.

She was late picking up her mother at the hospital, and she still hadn't had time to go to the grocery store or do anything except change the sheets.

She sat in Lillian's hospital room, wondering why they had called her if they were nowhere near ready to release her. Her mother looked wonderful; she was rested, and her hair was perfectly styled. She did not look like she had been lying in the hospital for four days.

"Well, you're a sweetie to come get me. Martin Vandergriff is no help. Did you know he had a little stroke? Not bad enough that he's paralyzed or anything, but still, not exactly an improvement. They told me to eat lots of protein to help heal quickly, but of course I don't eat meat. Greek yogurt. Not the store brand, and I like it plain. If you don't mind," Lillian chirped. "It will be good for your bones, too. The calcium. That's why I'm not hobbled over. That and stretching. Do you stretch?"

"I'll have to go to the store after we get back." Lang glanced at her watch. It was almost five o'clock. She wondered whom she could call about Victoria. Leland was miffed, and Teddy was mad at her.

"Oh, I'm having my things delivered to your house. UPS," Lillian said.

She called Sarah at work, apologizing profusely for bothering her. She had no idea how she was going to store Lillian's things. "I just wondered if you could go by my house after work and wait. It's getting dark, and we are still at the hospital, and I'm just sick about him being lost," Lang said. "I wouldn't ask you if I weren't desperate." To her credit, Sarah acted like it was no imposition at all.

Lang watched the clock. She forced a tight smile when yet another nurse came in to check her mother's blood pressure. Then another one came to check her mother's temperature, and yet another one came to change her dressing.

"Is she coming home today?" Lang finally asked.

"We're working on it," a nurse said testily.

By the time Lang pulled into her driveway, it was almost eight o'clock. She was too tired to go back to the store for Greek yogurt and knew it would take a monumental effort to get her mother unloaded and into the house. What was she thinking? They should both go to the nursing home. Ask for a two-for-one discount.

"Thank you, Elizabeth," her mother said softly in her ear as Lang reached across Lillian's lap to help her with the seat belt. Lillian leaned her head toward Lang's, resting her forehead against Lang's temple.

"You're welcome," Lang said, jerking her head back at the same instant the seat belt released. "Can you walk up the steps?"

"By myself? Can you help me? Get that man, Leland. Or Teddy," Lillian said. "I feel like my stomach will split open if I move. I don't feel too well actually. I almost wonder if we should go back to the hospital."

Lang knew the feeling. She rested her fingertips on her stomach and remembered how the smallest movement seemed to pull the stitches apart.

"It just feels like that for a while," Lang said. "They put two layers of stitches in. They'll hold."

She wondered if it would be easier just to drive her mother

right back to the hospital and try again tomorrow. She was so exhausted after the long day she didn't know if she could get herself up the stairs, much less help her mother up.

"Thank you for bringing me here. I know it's hard," Lillian said. "Having me here after all these years."

"It's fine. Okay, let's just rest a minute," Lang said after she swiveled both Lillian's legs out of the car door. She imagined both of them stranded at the foot of the steps on the road, huddled together in the dark.

"I don't know what would happen to me if you weren't here to take care of me," Lillian said. "I thought there'd be money from the last two husbands, but their children got it. They sued me."

Lang staggered away from the car and leaned against the rock wall. She could barely care for her mother while she healed from surgery, but for the rest of her life? They would both need to go to the nursing home soon, in all seriousness, and how much would that cost? How much money could she possibly get for this property?

Suddenly the porch light came on, and they were bathed in a soft glow. Sarah walked out on the porch, then down the steps toward them.

"Here, let me give you a hand. There we go," she said as she hoisted Lillian out of the car and helped her up the steps. "Come on now. Let's get something to eat. I made dinner."

Lang slowly followed Sarah up to her house, pulling herself up with the rail. She never could have gotten her mother up these steps.

Lang looked at the sign on her front door: *Thank you for finding my dog!*

She thought about taking it down, but instead pressed the paper flat against the wood, smoothing the edges down. She left the porch light on, just in case.

Making Arrangements

Once inside, she stood in the foyer and smelled the mouthwatering aroma of roasted chicken wafting from the kitchen. If her knees weren't so arthritic, she would have fallen on them.

"Sarah, I don't know how to even begin! You have no idea. I am famished and exhausted. And heartbroken. We can't find him anywhere," Lang said.

"It's no trouble, and I'm so sorry about Victoria. Maybe he'll turn up?"

"I hope so. It's been over twenty-four hours. I can't imagine what's happened. I can't think about it."

"I'm starving!" Lillian called. "Can we eat?"

"Here, I'll get your plates," Sarah said.

"No, I will. Go get wine from the basement. If you don't mind," Lang said, getting three plates from the cabinet.

"Oh, no. Don't serve me. I can't stay."

"Sarah," Lang said sharply. "Go get a bottle of wine. Now! I'm sorry. I can't argue with you."

"Better get two," Lillian said.

Lang laid the plates in a row and began to cut into the chicken. She wanted to wrangle off a leg and eat it over the kitchen sink before Sarah came back.

Suddenly there was a piercing scream from underneath the floor.

"Oh my god. She fell! Are you okay?" Lang yelled as she ran to the cellar and scrambled down the steps in the dark, not minding her balance.

There was a familiar jangle, and Lang froze, straining to hear it again. It sounded like the tags on Victoria's collar.

"Lang! It's Victoria! Oh my gosh! It's Victoria!" Sarah yelled.

Victoria sprang up into Lang's arms, and she caught him on

277

a single high bound. He licked her face frantically and tried to burrow up under her armpit. She sat down on the bottom step and leaned backward and forward with the wriggling dog and felt a smooth edge of her shattered life slip back into place.

"He was in the coal room with the wine. Not making a peep. I know he heard me walking around, but he didn't whimper. I thought I heard something in there, a tiny mouse scratching maybe. He was just sitting. Waiting," Sarah said.

"Thank you," Lang murmured as Victoria burrowed up underneath her sweater. "I owe you."

"No. You don't," Sarah said plainly, and walked up the basement stairs in the dark.

By the time Lang finally made it up the stairs, Sarah was gone.

FIFTY-ONE

....

L ang clipped a deep violet hydrangea the size of a cantaloupe for her mother's bedside table. What had she done to offend Sarah? Why had she bolted out of the house before eating dinner last night? Later, she had left a message on Teddy's phone agreeing to sell the house and all the property.

She was surprised to see A. J. walking up the sidewalk and shushed her with two fingers over her lips. A. J. was in her jogging outfit—a pair of Lycra shorts and a tiny elastic shirt that looked like a bathing suit top.

"What are you doing here? You need to go change! You can't wear that to a club meeting!" Lang hissed. Of all times for A. J. to dress down, the Barrington Women's Club meeting was not one of them. "You need to wear a suit and your pearls. No cleavage."

"Oh, you're going to kill me, but I refused my membership invitation," A. J. said.

"What? Why?" Lang asked, stunned, wondering if that had ever been done before.

"Lang, they're going to ask you to resign. I overheard someone talking about it," A. J. blurted.

"That's why you refused them?" Lang asked as she burst out laughing. "You hounded me for almost a year, and you refuse their invitation?"

"What? Why are you laughing? They mean it!"

"Oh, A. J. I'm sure they do. But if you want to be in it, you have my blessing. Whether I'm in it or not. I promise," Lang said. "Go! Go change for the meeting! You don't want to be late!"

A. J. broke into a quick jog back home just as some brakes squealed and a door slammed on a brown delivery truck.

The UPS man walked up the sidewalk, carrying a large shoebox wrapped in brown paper. *Dependability,* Lang thought as she looked at the brown uniform.

"Delivery for Lillian Whitmire?"

Lang repeated the name to herself, wondering what kind of man Mr. Whitmire had been before accepting the package.

"That's all? This one package?" Lang asked.

"You should be glad," Lillian said as she clumped her way to the porch on her walker. "What if I had furniture and china and rugs for you to deal with?"

"Well, here, let me open it up," Lillian said, ripping into the package. "There are some things in here for you."

Lillian held up a strand of dark pearls that seemed to glow from within. "These. I want you to have them," she said. She reached for Lang's hand and laid the pearls in her palm, then closed Lang's fingers around them. "They're valuable. Very valuable. So if you sell them, don't take less than fifteen."

"These are worth fifteen hundred dollars?" Lang asked incredulously. "Not that I would ever sell them. I'll keep them in the family. Pass them down to Katie D."

"Fifteen thousand. And you do with them what you want. If they can help you out one day, sell them. But get what they're worth. Same with these. Four husbands. Four diamond rings."

"I can't take these things. They're too valuable."

Lillian looked up at Lang and slowly began to smile at her.

"What else would I do with them? You do anything you want with them. They're yours," Lillian said.

Lang reached into the box for a stack of letters. There were dozens of them, thick blocks of letters, each neatly tied with string. She sat heavily in the wicker chair and flipped through the letters, recognizing her own handwriting. She knew what they said without opening them.

"These are mine. I wrote them to you," she said.

"Why do you think I kept them? Toted them with me all over the world?" Lillian asked. "Here. This is the first batch. I keep them in order."

Carefully opened and resealed, the letters were in chronological order. The addresses changed from a tentative scrawl at first to a decent cursive by the last few in the second stack.

Her mother was eighty-six years old and had just had surgery. Lang should let it go. It had been too long. What was the point?

"You saved my letters," Lang whispered. "All the letters I wrote you. I thought you never got them because you never wrote me back."

"You got three of them, didn't you?"

"How could you only write me three letters? In all that time? Three postcards over a lifetime. That was all," Lang said. Her voice trembled with fury and heartbreak, but she willed herself not to cry.

Lillian pulled out another block of bound letters from the box. Then another. And another until they lined the table, stacked one on top of the other. Every one was addressed to Elizabeth Langford Deakins at 525 Summertown Road and stamped Address Unknown in red ink.

"Here they are. One letter for every day. I knew you wouldn't get them. But you got three. Three didn't come back to me. That's more than I hoped for," Lillian said.

"You wrote to me? You sent me all these letters? Why didn't I get them?" Lang said. "I don't understand."

"What a beautiful hydrangea! I can't believe you have anything still blooming. You have such a green thumb, Elizabeth!"

Lillian said. "And you're just getting started with it. I'm proud of you, you know. Making a business for yourself. Taking care of yourself like that. I hope you go all the way. Use the money from my jewelry to convert that little carriage house to your first shop, then open a flower shop in every state. Elizabeth's Lilies. How's that for a name?"

"No. Don't change the subject."

"Because of your smarts. Your resourcefulness. You don't have to latch onto someone to be taken care of. You can take care of yourself," Lillian said.

Lang laughed at the thought. Her life was a disaster. She was about to lose her house. Her cancer was lurking just over her shoulder, threading its way into her belly.

"Why didn't Fancy give me your letters?" Lang demanded.

"Oh, Lang." Lillian gingerly eased herself down on the other wicker chair. "I've wanted to tell you the truth for sixty-three years. Since it happened. But I promised not to. And I figured after everything that happened to you, after everything that was taken from you, the least I could do was keep that promise. Increase your chances of being happy."

"What? Tell me what?"

"I'm going to tell you now. It's time. A lifetime is long enough," Lillian said. "I promised your grandmother I'd carry it to my grave. And I almost have. I almost told you before the surgery. I decided if I came through the operation, I'd tell you the truth, and if I didn't, you weren't meant to know."

"What is it? Just tell me!"

"When your father died, your grandmother blamed me."

"Fancy? Blamed you for what?"

"I was having an affair with a married man. I know it was wrong. Don't say anything," Lillian said, waving her hand toward Lang. "Your father found out and told her. Told your grandmother. I don't know. When he killed himself, she told me I might as well have held the gun."

"Killed himself?" Lang whispered. "What?"

"You didn't know."

Lang held her face still. She made herself suck air into her lungs. This was all too much.

"What?"

"I'm sorry. I don't know what she told you and what she didn't. But she told me she'd raise you and educate you and give you everything you needed. If I left."

"He committed suicide?" Lang asked.

"He did. He was always that way. Had that in him. Moping and gloomy. Not that I don't blame myself. Just not entirely," Lillian said.

"How?"

"Shot himself. It was awful," Lillian said, looking away from Lang. "You can imagine. Really, I hope you can't imagine. That was the whole point, to spare you. I had no place to go. Everyone knew. Everyone in Barrington. When she told me she'd take care of you if I just *poof, disappeared*, I refused. I told her no. And I took you to a boarding house downtown. Not in the best neighborhood, but it was all I could afford. And then you got sick. I took you to a doctor, but he didn't find anything wrong. You got thinner and thinner. And then you started coughing. I took you back to the doctor, but I hadn't paid. We rode the bus over to Murphy, but they wouldn't see me. She'd called already. Called every doctor in seven counties. And that's when I took you back to her. To Fancy."

"You gave me up," Lang said.

Lillian looked at Lang with a despair that was unbearable to Lang. Lang hoisted herself up and walked over to the edge of the porch. The china-blue hydrangeas blended with the green of the laurel. She blinked her eyes hard to clear them and wiped her eyelids with her fingertips.

"You had pneumonia," Lillian said softly. "You were so sick by then you almost died. I heard they said you would have been dead by that night if you hadn't gotten the antibiotics. So yes, I would have given you to the devil himself if he promised he could save you."

Lang looked out at the garden, turning away from her mother.

"I remember a metal crib. Cold bars," Lang said.

"You were in the hospital for two weeks," Lillian said. "In a coma for thirteen hours. Fancy sent me to Europe, as far away from you as possible. That was part of the stipulation; not only was I not allowed to see you, I wasn't to be in the same country. Much less the same state."

"Just like that. You gave me up to her?"

"No. Not just like that. And don't think it hasn't tormented me every single day. Think about it for a minute. What if it was Teddy? No, Katie D. If it were Katie D. and you couldn't take care of her and she was deathly ill. Would you want to hold her dead, still body or give her to someone who could cure her? If you knew you could save her, give her a good life, would you sacrifice yourself or her?"

"I would keep her with me! I would never do that!" Lang said.

"Well, you're more sure of yourself than I was. I don't know if I would do it differently even now when you get right down to it."

"That's not what you do when you love someone," Lang said.

"Isn't it?" Lillian said.

Lang suddenly reached forward and put both hands on her knees. She dropped her head lower than her heart and felt the inside of her skull whirl like the whole world was shaking back and forth, flinging oceans against opposing shores.

FIFTY-TWO

L ang drove slowly across town to the mall with Sarah's scarf in her pocket. She had a few days between flower orders, a rarity these days, and she wanted to check this chore off her list. There was a shop that supposedly worked magic on any stain, and Lang had high hopes for the printed silk scarf.

She knew she shouldn't be driving with all the storm warnings out. They'd been issued all summer long in big block letters scrolling across the bottom of the television set, advising people to stay indoors. But there was nary a drop of rain—just all the drama of a storm—lightning, thunder, and wind. Plus, she'd always heard the rubber tires would protect you from lightning, so she was probably safe on the road.

She needed to get out of the house and away from her mother. Lillian was perfectly fine now, clicking around the house in high heels and smoking cigars in the garden just a few weeks after surgery. She was forcing Lang to keep the windows closed during her favorite season and depriving her of the sweet, heavy scent of gardenias and peonies. Also, the patterns of the tile on the fireplace seemed cold and calculated now, and she couldn't run her hand over the heart pine banister her great-grandfather had carved without seeing Fancy tell her mother to "Poof. Disappear."

She got to the mall as the first raindrops fell and barely made it through the automatic doors before the heavens finally caved in and released a season's worth of rain, like a dam bursting open. Lang watched water rush down in deafening sheets and flow against the curb, widening rapidly. She hoped it would be over quickly, before the roads flooded.

Lightning struck in the parking lot, and Lang jumped away from the doors. She passed through the food court and inhaled the smell of freshly baked cinnamon buns mingled with sizzling hibachi steak. She looked around for someone serving samples, but everyone behind the counters seemed glued to the TV.

There was some weather alert. Something about a tornado warning. Like a tornado could ever hit near a mountain range. She stood at the register to buy a sweet roll, but no one waited on her. Probably for the best.

"BIG SALE!" was plastered in the Victoria's Secret window. She tried to remember the last time she'd bought new underwear, picturing her sagging, discolored panties. She finally decided not being able to remember was an indication it was time for more, and she walked in the store.

Nothing in the store was sensible. Lots of "butt floss"—what Teddy called thongs.

"Need some help?" an older woman asked. If she'd been younger, Lang might have been embarrassed, but this woman had reading glasses perched below her eyes, and she did not look like she would wear any of the underwear she was selling.

Lang looked at the bras, trying to decipher the terms "enhancement" and "half-demi."

"Not sure which to try," Lang said. "Surely that's not thunder?" There was a deep rumble that sounded like they were blasting underground, maybe for a tunnel.

"It's thunder," the saleslady said as she whipped out a measuring tape and wrapped it around Lang's bust, then snatched a handful of bras and showed Lang to a pink-wallpapered dressing room. She was all business, except that she kept looking out toward the entrance nervously.

"I'll be right outside to check the fit," the woman said. "They say this weather is going to be pretty bad. It's all over the news."

"I know. We need the rain, though," Lang said.

Lang tried the first bra on and could not believe her cleavage. She was the sort of person who looked better with her chest covered; low-cut things only revealed her bony chest. If she could only take a large clump of her massive lower half and distribute it in her bra cup, she'd be in business. She needed to even her body out, not be skinny above her belt then absolutely enormous below it.

But this particular bra, or whatever it was, seemed to shove all her body fat up high on her chest, so her breasts looked like somebody's from the Elizabethan period, spilling up against gravity.

She turned sideways and looked at herself in the mirror, then leaned forward and admired her plump spillage.

"Ready?" the woman asked outside the door.

Lang stared at herself in the mirror. The skin on her chest was clear and relatively smooth. But the skin on her neck seemed to have lost its grip on her throat, and her middle plopped out like a girdle had literally snapped, releasing pounds in a tired whoosh.

She counted back to the last time she and Jack had had sex. "Let's wait," she'd said, like she had all the mornings in the world.

She turned away from the mirror, unhooked the bra, and quickly put her old beige bra with the spent elastic back on.

"No, that's okay. This is not going to work," Lang said as the lights flickered. "I don't know what I was thinking."

She left and walked through the food court just as lightning struck the enormous skylight, illuminating the mall with a dramatic flash that seemed to last for minutes. Thunder shook the building within seconds. Suddenly there was a loud crack, and the skylight shattered. People screamed and ran pell-mell and crawled under the tables as rain pelted them with a force she'd never seen. She wasn't sure if it was the rain or the pellets of glass from the skylight.

She crouched under a table and tried not to panic. It was pitch-black, but the flashes of lightning were even more terrifying, illuminating people scrambling in terror and lurching through the food court. She listened to their wails and screeches; an otherworldly dimness lit up the mall as the emergency lights gradually came on.

A little boy near her held his hand out to her and looked right at her, bewildered. Blood covered his hand and ran down his arm. Lang looked around for his mother, for the police, for anyone to help.

"Come on, sweetie. Let's find your mother," Lang said to the boy as she wrapped his hand in Sarah's scarf. Blood immediately seeped through the paisley pattern, disguising the oil stain from the mussels. She scanned the food court for anyone frantically looking for a child, but it was bedlam. Women screamed, children were crying, and men were running.

She took him into Victoria's Secret where the saleslady was frantically dialing on the phone. "I can't get through to the plant! My husband!" She grabbed her keys and ran out toward the mall.

"No! You stay! I need help!" Lang grabbed the saleslady's arm and spoke in a slow, calm voice she'd never used before. "Come with me. We need to wait here, just for a few minutes." Lang led them to the back wall, right to the pink dressing room where she had just been topless. *Weren't you supposed to be near a support wall?*

The tiny curtained room was dark; apparently the emergency code didn't consider lighting necessary for anyone trying on clothes. She held the boy on her lap, lifting his arm up above his heart and wondering if she should have tied the scarf into a tourniquet. The little boy's sobs slowed to deep shudders, and she felt around on his arm, trying to find the source of blood.

Flashes of lightning illuminated the shop like paparazzi flashbulbs, one brilliant shocking strobe flash after another, and the thunder was deafening. There was a terrible crash near them, and Lang pushed the little boy and the saleslady under the little bench in the dressing room. She lay on top of them, facedown, and wondered how long a tornado could last. She thought of Katie D. and Lillian and hoped they were safe.

She made the little boy and the clerk wait until the lightning was a weak flicker and the thunder sounded far away before they crawled out from under the bench. There was not that much blood on him, so she was glad she hadn't tied her scarf around his bicep, risking the amputation of his arm.

They wandered out into the obliterated food court. The counter of the hibachi grill lay on its end against a pillar; its cheap underpinnings of plywood and boards were splintered like matchsticks. Cinnamon buns, amazingly intact, dotted the carnage, making the whole thing look like an edgy advertisement for decadent pastries.

Rain fell through the broken skylight, plastering her hair to her scalp and pooling on the undersides of overturned tables. The three of them staggered around the devastation, shocked.

"Do you see your mommy? What was she wearing?" Lang asked the little boy.

"Matthew!" a woman screamed and rushed toward them.

"His arm is hurt. He needs to go to the doctor. It was bleeding, so," Lang said.

The woman fell to her knees and hugged her son, weeping and patting him as if to make sure he wasn't broken. Then she stood and wrapped her arms around Lang.

"You are an angel," she said, sobbing. "I prayed God would send me an angel. Send Matthew an angel. That he would be protected. And He did."

"No, I'm no angel. I didn't do anything," Lang said.

The woman placed both hands on Lang's face and looked her in the eyes. Lang could feel her fingers trembling as they pressed on her face.

"I asked God to send us an angel. And He did," she said. And the woman bowed her head, still holding Lang's face, and began to pray. "The God who equipped me with strength and made my way blameless. He made my feet like the feet of a deer and set me secure on the heights. He trains my hands for war, so that my arms can bend a bow of bronze."

"Is that the Psalms, Mommy?" Matthew asked.

"It is. And this is our warrior angel. Standing right before us," the woman said.

Matthew reached up and put his hand in Lang's.

"She's right, you know," the saleslady said. "You saved me, too. I probably would have been killed if I'd rushed out in the thick of that storm."

The food court was suddenly swarming with police and firemen and TV reporters. Lang stepped away from the bright light of a TV camera and was grateful to take an EMT's arm as she stepped carefully over shattered planters and uprooted plants and shattered glass.

By the time she finally made it home, Lang was numb. She sat in the driveway in amazement, looking at the trees standing untouched and the pea gravel clean as a whistle. There was not a leaf out of place. She walked inside her house.

"Teddy!" He had come to check on her! No matter what, he wanted to make sure she was all right. Or maybe Lillian had called him. "I'm okay, sweetie. It was so scary, but no one was hurt. How did you know I was out at the mall? Is Lillian okay?"

"Mom, what are you talking about? Of course she's okay. Here. I brought the papers. I got your message." He held the stack of white sheets out. "Here and here," he said.

She looked at her name typed clearly. Katherine Langford Deakins Eldridge. It was highlighted in yellow, not to be missed.

"There was a tornado. Out by the mall," she said, putting the papers on table. "Lightning struck it. Did they say anything about it on the news?" She clicked on the TV. Newscasters were on every channel, donned in rain gear and talking about the tornado that had just touched down.

"It's all over the news!" Lillian said. "We lost power for a little while, but I didn't know where it hit. Martin's whole house was destroyed, but he's fine. I was so worried about you!"

"Right here." Teddy tapped the pen on a yellow mark. "They say it was an actual tornado?"

"How could you not know about it?" Lillian asked.

"Nothing more than a little rain where I was. And a great interview on NPR," Teddy said.

"There was a little boy. Lost from his mother. And a saleslady who was trying to leave in the middle of it. And all this noise. Explosions," Lang said.

"The best thing to do is stay away from windows," Lillian said. "He wants to go on a trip while they repair his house, so we're going to a little inn down in Georgia. I don't know how long I'll be gone."

"Mom. Just sign it."

"I was the one who helped them. I think I kept them safe."

"You kept them safe?" Lillian asked.

"That's great. I'm sure you did. Nice work. Here." He placed the pen in her hand.

"Oh my gosh!" Lang yelled, pointing at the television set.

"There he is! That's his mother!"

The woman's face peered into the camera as she told everyone about her angel, about the woman who had saved her little boy's life and kept him safe during the storm.

"She's talking about me, Teddy. Look! That's the little boy I helped," Lang said.

"Okay, so you did your good deed for the day. Here you go," he said. He pressed her fingers around the ink pen. "I'm sorry. That's really great. Really, Mom. I'm proud of you. But we need to get going on this or we'll miss our opportunity. We need to list it before winter. Nothing sells in winter, and your balloon payment is coming up soon."

"Teddy, I can't do this. I know you want me to. But I don't want to go there."

"What are you talking about? You can't *not* go there! You don't have the money! All you have to do is revoke the fucking trust, sell off the land, and pay back the bank. You're going to lose the house! Is that your genius plan?"

"I'm making the payments on the loan. I'm on schedule."

Teddy dropped his head down in his hands.

"Okay, let's just say somehow you make the balloon payment. Don't ask me how, but what about the cancer trial? You can't be in it if you don't have a caregiver. That's the deal," he said smugly. She thought he looked glad that she had cancer. It was his ace in the hole.

"Your mother is a great deal more resourceful than you realize. Than any of us realize," Lillian said.

"Teddy, all I know is, I'm not ready. Not yet and not like this. This house has been in my family for over one hundred years. I was a baby here. I know it inside and out. Where my great-grandfather carved the mantel by hand and the spindles on the stairs. My grandmother's handprint is in the sidewalk, her tiny baby hand. And you don't even care about it. You just want to plow it down. Raze it all and build twenty prefab houses on teeny-tiny patches of land."

"No, it will be way more than twenty. We've already got it drawn up. We can get thirty-five lots and a clubhouse, and even a little common property. We'll make a killing! Enough for you to go wherever you want."

"Doesn't sound like she wants to go anywhere," Lillian said.

"Please! This doesn't have anything to do with you, so if you don't mind, keep out of it. Mom, if you don't want to go to the nursing home, you can buy another house somewhere. Maybe not up here in Barrington, but anywhere else! Hell, you'd even have enough left to hire someone to take care of you. So you could do the trial and have the money. Just sign it," he pleaded.

"Teddy, I'm not. I'm sorry to disappoint you, but I'm not selling it. Not now. Not like this."

She watched Teddy's face turn a waxy beige and thought of Jack lying dead in the hospital.

"I do not have time for your sentimental antics. You do not have time for your sentimental antics. Literally." He rubbed his lips together, clenching them in a long, thin line. "If you don't sell this property, I will be forced to leave."

"Now, Teddy. That's not true. Don't do that," Lang said.

"No! You don't do this. It's your decision. Do you want me and Katie D. to stay here? Do you want to be a part of her life? Or are you going to make us move to the other side of the country?"

"Teddy, it's not an either-or."

"Sign the goddamn papers!" he screamed. The color had come back in his face. It was swollen and mottled.

"Let's just talk about this when you're calm. Calmer."

"Okay. Fine. Don't sign. Keep your motherfucking house that all your dead relatives hover around in. You are choosing this house over your family. You are choosing those precious boards and this roof and those old tiles over your own living relatives. We may as well be dead, too, if you do this. I mean it. Consider us dead. Because to you, we will be."

Lang watched him storm down the steps to the road.

"What a hothead," Lillian said. "He sure didn't get that from you."

Lang didn't see the mutilated magnolia strewn all over the yard until she looked out the kitchen window. The garden was a war zone—branches as thick as tree trunks seemed to have been hurled from the sky onto the hemlocks and hydrangeas. The ancient magnolia was split down the middle.

"Did you hear the tree fall?" she asked Lillian.

But her mother was already in the other room, preparing to leave.

FIFTY-THREE

···

G randie, can I come spend the night? And can Mommy come, too?" Katie D. asked on the phone.

"I can't think of anything nicer! Did you all get any rain?" Lang said. But the truth was, she was exhausted. Lillian, apparently completely recovered, had just left with Martin Vandergriff, and Lang was planning on getting in her pajamas and going straight to bed after a hot bath.

"I'm scared. I don't like it here. I have a haunted tree branch in my room. I don't want Mommy to be here alone," Katie D. said, crying. "It's a danger."

"Sweetie, I'm on my way. You pack your things and tell your mommy to pack up, too." What had Teddy done? He left in such a rage she wondered if he'd snapped completely. These kinds of things were in the newspaper headlines all the time.

Lang locked her doors at the stoplight near Sarah's apartment and looked straight ahead. They really shouldn't be living in such a seedy neighborhood. She was uneasy, expecting looting and vandalism at any moment.

The thick, dark roots of the gigantic oak sprawled out in the air, reaching almost to the power lines. The immense trunk lay in the street, blocking both lanes of traffic, and the branches covered buildings on both sides of the road. The unsettling mass of dirt and rock and roots looked like a gigantic Medusa's head, its roots snaking out wildly against the concrete block apartment building.

Surely not.

Lang looked up and down the street. There were no cars, only Sarah's little compact station wagon. Lang looked up at the streetlights, then up at the buildings, looking for light, a glow. Nothing. Everything was dark.

Lang fumbled with her keys. She didn't seem to have any feeling in her fingers. She put the keys securely in her pocketbook, then checked them to be sure they were there.

She walked into the little apartment. Yellow, green, red, and brown confetti was plastered to everything—the walls, ceiling, floor, furniture. Sarah stood on a chair with a beach towel and wiped the walls, starting with the ceiling. It took Lang a minute to realize she was cleaning up leaves.

"Oh my god!" Lang exclaimed. Branches from the oak tree lay in the living room and in Katie D.'s bedroom, and there was a gaping hole in the wall of the apartment. "I can't believe this!"

"She was in my bed with me, thank goodness. We're lucky," Sarah said. "It would have killed her." She trembled as she spoke.

"Why didn't you call me? Where's Teddy?" Lang asked.

"He's not here. He wasn't here. He doesn't know yet," Sarah said.

"Sarah, get your things together. Oh my god, this is a mess."

"Oh, no, I'm getting it cleaned up. Thanks, though," Sarah said.

"No. It's not safe. There is a tree through the whole wall, and the apartment is wide open. Katie D. is not safe, and you're coming with me. Now."

"Please, Mommy? It's our rain check. You promised at Christmas," Katie said, crying. "And it's rained everywhere. My bed is wet. And my jammies."

"Well, just for tonight. They'll be fixing it soon," Sarah said.

Lang knew no one was coming to get that tree. She expected it would stay in the middle of their apartment for weeks.

"You'd better get anything you can't live without. I've got dry clothes for you both, if you don't mind muumuus.," Lang said. "And call Teddy and tell him to come home. We can figure all the rest of it out later, but he needs to come home."

"I already tried. The phones are out," Sarah said. "I don't know where he is. If he's even okay."

"He's fine," Lang said. She didn't want to say he had no idea of the danger his family had been in.

Lang looked around the ruined apartment. Dishes and books and kitchen chairs lay strewn against the interior wall, like a fire hose had blasted them.

"What about Billie? Is she okay?" Lang asked.

"Her son came and took her home with him right after Christmas," Sarah said.

Lang jerked her head around, knowing she should be glad for the old woman. But she remembered Teddy covering his face and looking away when she'd vomited in front of him.

"Is that his briefcase?" Lang asked. "Leave him a note. Tell him I've got the papers. He'll come."

Sarah gathered up Teddy's briefcase and the blue satin bunny and followed Lang and Katie D.

FIFTY-FOUR

....

L ang started the spaghetti, chopping the onion and celery and garlic while Sarah and Katie D. changed clothes.

"Lang?" Leland called out from the foyer.

"Leland! Are you okay? Was the storm bad at your house?" she asked.

"I'm fine. A few branches went down, but I wanted to check on you. I came by earlier, but you weren't here. I just wanted to be sure you were safe," Leland said.

"We're okay. Everyone's okay," Lang said.

"I worried when you weren't here. It said on the news a tornado hit out in Westwood, and I thought that's where your family lived. Are they okay? Have you talked to them? I had a horrible feeling you were with them and that something happened," Leland said.

"Grandie! Lele! Daddy's coming! Mommy said!" Katie D. yelled as she leaped up into Leland's arms. "We're having a rain check! You sit by me."

"Oh, I'm not sure I can stay for dinner," Leland said after he twirled her around the room a couple of times. "I need to go. Get on back to the ranch, as the saying goes."

"You can stay," Lang said as Teddy walked up the steps. "This is my ranch. And I want you to stay."

Dinner was tense. Teddy ate the homemade spaghetti quickly, scraping his fork across the pools of sauce left on his plate. Sarah twirled the noodles in a perfect coil around her fork, then put it down, untouched.

Lang noticed a slight tremor right above Teddy's jaw. A twitch she'd never seen before.

"Eat up, Mommy! It's good!" Katie D. said.

"It's so delicious!" Sarah said, raising the fork to her mouth. She looked like she was swallowing live slugs as she slowly chewed the pasta.

"Your tummy still hurts?" Katie D. asked Sarah.

"It's okay. You eat, sweetie," Sarah said.

"I can fix you something else," Lang offered. "You have an upset stomach?" Lang was doing everything she could to make the dinner enjoyable. She didn't bring up the storm or Sarah's apartment, but she could tell Sarah was extremely anxious.

"No! It's fine! I'm sorry. I don't feel well. Excuse me," Sarah said and went to the bathroom.

"Well, you seemed to have weathered the storm all right," Teddy said to Leland. "I bet you make a habit of it, landing on your feet. Taking advantage when it behooves you."

"Teddy," Lang chided gently.

"No, the storm didn't do anything to me. Not much. But I'm heading home. Thank you for a delicious dinner, Lang," Leland said.

"Come by for leftovers tomorrow?" Lang said, scooting her chair back from the table. "I'll plan on you for lunch then?"

He looked at her, not speaking for a few seconds. Then he tilted his head and smiled. "I don't think so. But thank you," Leland said, nodding his head at Teddy.

"He has a ranch," Katie D. said after Leland closed the door.

"I'll bet he thinks he does. Or thinks he will soon. Okay, you lured me here with the papers. What's it going to be? Are you going to sign them or are you just still playing whatever little manipulative game you've been playing with me? You should have left them in that hovel of an apartment for all the good they're doing anyone," Teddy said. "Let the storm chop them up and swirl them down to Miami."

Lang quickly flipped through the papers, signing her full name on every highlighted yellow line. She concentrated on writing her name correctly, trying not to think about the significance of her signature.

"You better, Mommy?" Katie asked when Sarah came back into the room.

"Yes, sweetie. I'm fine."

"Katie D., would you like to sleep with me tonight? I'll run you a tubby," Lang said quickly, leading her to the bathroom. Sarah and Teddy needed some privacy. All of them under one roof would be difficult under any circumstance, but Teddy was like a taut wire on the verge of snapping. She could at least make sure he and Sarah had time alone and get out of his line of fire herself.

Lang held a capful of pink bubble bath under the spigot, then flipped her hand around quickly under the water. Katie D. cooed as the bubbles churned up from the surface of the water, thick and airy and white.

"You soak, and I'm going to get your nightgown ready," Lang told her. "You want the white one, right?"

In her bedroom, she could hear them so clearly they may as well have been on the other side of the bed. They were arguing about something. Testing? Was Teddy doing career testing? *About time.*

"Who *is* the father then?" Teddy said loudly.

"Teddy, don't."

"Sarah. The tests came back clearly. Don't fuck around with me."

"Teddy, you *are* her father. Look at Katie D. in the eyes and tell her you're not her father."

"Her eyes? That's how I know I'm *not* the father! Two blue-eyed parents can't have a brown-eyed child. How long did you think you could play me?"

"That's a myth!"

They were silent.

"A myth? What does that mean? You've checked? That's all I need to know then," Teddy said.

"Teddy, don't do this."

"I've been the laughing stock for six years now. Everybody knows it apparently. I'm surprised they didn't run it on the news wire all over the country. Joke's on me," he said.

"Teddy, think about her. About Katie D. She loves you. Try telling her you're not her father. She would never believe you, and that's what matters."

"You knew. You knew the first time she opened her eyes, and they were brown. Who was it? That other pro at the club? Somebody taking lessons? Who? Why didn't you tell me?"

"You have raised her—*are* raising her," Sarah said evenly.

Lang stood by the side of the bed, holding the white nightgown to her chest. What difference could that make now? Katie D. was already his. What choice did he have?

"Goddamn it, Sarah! Who is it? They asked at the lab if I had a brother. They said that there was some kind of overlap or something, some common genes, but that I was definitely not her father."

Lang could hear the stillness heavy in the room next to her. She knew they were completely silent and not whispering. Not moving. The void of sound hung like a thick layer of lead.

She imagined Sarah's face, stricken and horrified, frozen in that moment of truth and unable to soften. The bed gave silently as she fell on it with a thud, still clutching the nightgown.

"No. Not him. No," Teddy said. His voice was high and soft, like a pleading girl knowing her begging was futile even as she whimpered the words.

"I'm so sorry."

"Grandie, I'm done!" Katie D. called from the bathroom. The child stood in the doorway wrapped in the white ribbed towel Lang reserved for guests. Her hair was slicked back, still dripping with water. Her shoulders were a soft alabaster color. And she looked up at Lang with the big melted chocolate eyes that were clearly Jack's.

FIFTY-FIVE

··

The house was quiet when Lang finally got out of bed. She didn't know if it was empty or not; she hadn't heard any sounds of life all morning.

She looked at Victoria still curled up in the bed. He opened his top eye and looked at her warily. The sheets were pulled back invitingly, and her eyes were prickly from lack of sleep.

"Up you go," she said to the dog. She pulled the sheet taut and folded it down neatly at the top before fluffing the pillows.

Her kitchen was spotless. The pot of dried spaghetti she'd left soaking in the sink was scrubbed clean, and the place mats were stacked neatly, all the fringed edges lined up, with the cloth napkins in a heap on top of them. She peered at the faded blue fabric on top of the trash and realized it was Jack's Auburn sweatshirt she'd given Teddy.

The letter sat squarely on top of the stack of signed papers.

Dear Mom,

I am so sorry I didn't get to tell you good-bye, but I just got word the job starts in the morning! I think it will be a good move for me.

It's probably for the best, all in all. Your property will only increase in value, so you can't go wrong by holding on to it. Call the bank and refinance the loan. You're in good enough shape to do it now, and that should allow you to keep the house.

And for the record, I'm proud of you for pulling yourself together, up by your bootstraps, as it were.

You're a trooper, Mom. Just so you know.

I love you.

Teddy

Lang folded the letter carefully and ran her fingers down the seam. Teddy thought he'd spared her. That she didn't know about Jack and Sarah. *Oh my god.*

The phone rang six times before the answering machine picked up. The nurse gushed the news over the telephone. She'd been accepted to the trial! They needed her to come in this afternoon and go over the details, do final testing, and "*blah blah blah.*" Except the nurse said it enthusiastically. "*Blah! Blah! Blah!*"

Even if she had someone to take care of her, she wouldn't do the trial now. Why would she? What was the point? She thought about how easily she could slip between the sheets of her freshly made bed and close her eyes for a little while.

She hurried to the toilet and began gagging before she had time to collapse down over the bowl. She was sick, her insides roiling up again before she could empty her mouth.

She wasn't sure if it was the cancer or the fact that her husband had fathered her granddaughter. She vomited again at the idea.

If she had sold her house as soon as Jack had died, would she have spared herself this? Spared all of them? Would Teddy ever have questioned his paternity? He would have been too busy to do anything but clear trees and count money. Had this house cost Lang her family?

Lang's bowels convulsed, over and over. She flushed the toilet after every heave, until finally the tank couldn't fill enough to keep up with her. She didn't want to open her eyes and see the remnants of her insides in the bowl.

But there was nothing to see anyway. She was completely emptied. Of everything.

FIFTY-SIX

....

A t first she thought it was Teddy. He'd come back! But the steps were light. Tentative.

"Hello?" Lang called from the bathroom.

"Oh! I'm sorry. I knocked, then came on in. I thought you might be resting and didn't want to wake you. I just needed to get my things," Sarah said. "I had to get Katie D. to school this morning, and we were running late. Are you okay?"

Lang nodded her head and waved Sarah on with her hand. *Go on.* She held her head over the toilet bowl and heaved. Nothing.

She heard Sarah upstairs in the bedroom, clicking over the floor in her heels—back and forth, around the bed, to the bathroom, down the stairs.

"Here, I brought you a warm washrag. Let me help you into bed," Sarah said, holding the cloth out to Lang.

"No," Lang said, and pushed herself up from the floor.

Sarah reached for her arm, and Lang stumbled backward.

"Do you want me to call the doctor?" Sarah asked.

"Where are you going? Your apartment is not inhabitable," Lang said, ignoring the rag. Sarah's face was an unnatural pink, like she'd been standing over boiling water.

"Oh, Teddy got the job in Oregon, so we are meeting him out there. I'm going to pick Katie D. up early from school as soon as I get us packed and head out."

Lang slowly eased herself toward the sink. She avoided the mirror as she washed her hands.

"I know," Lang said.

"That we're moving?" Sarah asked.

"That you're not." Lang reached for the lid, and it slammed down on the toilet. "He said not till the end of school."

"What?"

"I know about Jack. And you. I heard last night," Lang said, slowly lowering herself down on the toilet seat. Her legs felt quivery and not strong enough to hold her like cooked noodles. Victoria immediately jumped up on her and curled into a ball. She felt the dog's weight sink heavily onto her lap, and she buried both her hands into the dog's fur, relieved she had a place for them.

"Oh. Oh. I'm so sorry. Please know I'm so sorry. I'll go." Sarah's face seemed to crumple in slow motion.

"No. You tell me what happened," Lang said.

Sarah stood still at the door, shaking her head. She wiped her nose on her sleeve.

"It wasn't like that. I didn't . . .," Sarah said.

"Tell me," Lang said. Her voice was jagged. Broken.

Sarah wound the hem of her sweater into a thick rope, twisting it tight as she looked furtively around the tiny bathroom. Trapped.

"I had a baby boy. Samuel, Sammy, I called him," she said haltingly. "He had Krabbe disease. It's rare. Usually fatal. Affects the myelin sheath. I was married. Sammy was fine when he was first born. Normal, except with the swallowing. Then we found out he was blind. That's when my husband left. When we knew he would never see. But that was nothing. In hindsight." Sarah looked away from Lang as she spoke.

"I was at the hospital a lot with him. They tried the bone marrow transplant, but it didn't work. Then, especially at the end, he was in intensive care, and I just stayed there. The same people were there in that little waiting room all the time.

Morning, noon, and night. It was the same time you were having chemo. Almost seven years ago." She looked at Lang and
put her face in her hands. "So Jack was there waiting. For you.
We got to know each other, all of us waiting on the people we
loved. He loved you."

"Don't," Lang warned.

"He couldn't breathe at the end. Sammy couldn't. Pneumonia. I knew it was bad. I slept there, in the waiting room, for
two nights. They let me in to see him every four hours. He was
so sick. He couldn't see me. I knew he couldn't. But he turned
his head toward me before I even spoke, and I know I comforted him. So I sang to him. Told him stories. I got so tired of the
ones I knew I just repeated lyrics of songs. Every song I knew.
The Rolling Stones. Aretha Franklin. He didn't care." Sarah
sniffed and turned to look at Lang, then she quickly looked
away. "I put pieces of ice in my mouth to ease my throat. But I
kept singing to him. All day. Through the night. I knew it
would happen any day, at any hour, but then when he died,
when he was gone, it was like I'd had no warning at all."

Lang watched her, pressing her lips together in a thin, tight
line.

"I went down the stairwell to get to my car, but I didn't
make it down one flight. I just sat down on the bottom step
and curled up against the wall. I didn't look up when the door
opened. I couldn't. I thought whoever it was would go on past.
But it was him. Jack."

Sarah looked up at Lang, shaking her head.

"I didn't even know his last name. He just hugged me.
That's all. That's all he meant it to be. I don't know. It happened. It was my fault."

"In the stairwell?" Lang asked, trying not to picture Jack
slamming her passionately against the concrete wall. They
hadn't had sex for months while she had chemotherapy. She

hadn't known it was a problem.

"I'm so sorry. I was sorry then, but not as much as he was. He was mortified. We couldn't get out of there fast enough. Each of us."

Lang tried to filter the details, only digesting what she needed. She put her hand on her stomach.

"It was the one time? That long ago?"

"Yes, it was so clear he loved you."

"Sarah, stop it. D-d-d-don't you ever—" Lang took a deep breath of air.

Sarah doubled over suddenly, clutching her stomach, then apologized as she sat up.

"What about Teddy? How could you do that to him? To all of us?"

"I didn't know! Not that it matters as far as what I did, but I knew Teddy from work. We were friends. Teddy was easy. Funny. And light. I was in a bad place. So dark. I thought about going to sleep and just never waking up. The days hurt so much. By the time I realized I was pregnant again, it didn't even enter my mind it might be—might not be Teddy's baby. And then I met you all. But I didn't think it could be. I counted back, and it didn't make sense. Then she was born. I'm sorry. You don't want to hear this."

"Go on," Lang said. She remembered Katie D. when she was just a few days old, her face inflamed and squeezed tight, her tiny sea creature fingers that were almost translucent.

"She was perfect. Her face was strong, and she had a little barrel chest, and she nursed voraciously. My heart soared, and I promised her, promised God, that I would give her the best life I could.

"Teddy was crazy over her. He swaddled her like a little pink football and acted like he was running plays when he carried her. I remember the day I knew she could see. I tested her the minute she was born, moving in front of her from side to side. Seeing if her eyes followed me. She followed my fingers with her eyes. Tracked them. I was so thankful she wasn't blind that their color never entered my mind. And by the time I knew it was a possibility, we were a family. Teddy and me, and Katie D.

"There was nothing I could do that would make any sense by then. No matter what, the pain it would cause, is causing now, was catastrophic. *Is* catastrophic. And I am so, so sorry. But every day, Katie D. loved you more and more and loved Teddy more and more . . ." She looked at Lang, pain twisting on her face. "So I did nothing. I just tried to spare him by not letting him marry me. Which makes no sense."

Lang stared at the deserted bird feeder out the kitchen window.

"I am so sorry. It doesn't matter, I know. But I am so, so sorry. If you want, I'll send you news as she grows up. No, I'm sorry. Of course not," Sarah said.

Lang watched the slope of Sarah's slender shoulders as she carried her three heavy bags. She didn't know where they could be going. It was clear they weren't going to meet Teddy. She just knew that they couldn't be here.

FIFTY-SEVEN

....

The next days were like the long days she holed up in the house after Jack died. Leland pounded at the front door for a ridiculous amount of time, then walked around the house, trying every other opening. She watched his shadowy outline as he crunched on the leaves and tried to peer through the windows.

Lang made up her bed every afternoon when she finally got out of it, centering the brown toile pillow shams over the heavy cream matelassé pillows. She studied the perfectly made bed, her sole accomplishment each day.

She watched the light change through the transoms, dreading the harsh glare of the overhead sun. Midday was the worst time; she didn't know why. She ate cereal sporadically over the sink when she realized she was hungry and opened the front door for Victoria when he waited silently in the foyer. *Foy-yay.*

She heard voices echoing through the house on the answering machine. A. J. called constantly. After a few calls, she would just leave one-sided conversations on Lang's machine. She aced someone at tennis. The museum offered her a paid position as event coordinator. She turned down the women's club invitation after all. She asked Walker for a divorce.

Finally she threatened to call the police if she didn't see any sign of life. Lang turned the porch lights on to placate her.

Leland left messages about the spaghetti they were supposed to have for lunch or about walking the dogs, and he would just call to check in. She deleted them.

Then Katie D. called to tell her that Sarah was sick. Her

voice was muffled, secretive. Lang turned back the bed, put her head under the pillow, and closed her eyes. She hoped Sarah was miserably sick.

Was there a support group for something like this? Surely those people on some of those sordid talk shows had meetings or support groups to get through their various seamy traumas. She didn't even have the wherewithal to find out.

A. J. called about a floral job. Lang knew Sarah must have told her to call. Had she explained why she couldn't tell her herself?

What day was it? She had a payment coming up next week.

Let them take the house, she thought. *Let them bulldoze it down with me in it.*

She put the pillow tightly over her ears when the phone rang again.

"Grandie? Mommy is in the hospital. They won't let me in to see her. I want you," Katie D. said in a tiny, quaking voice.

Lang jerked her covers off and hurried to the phone.

"Katie D.? What's wrong? Where are you, sweetie?"

"The ambulance brung Mommy to the hospital. I'm so cold. Grandie, is Mommy going to be okay?"

"Katie D., you sit tight. I'm on my way," Lang said, grabbing the old quilt on the way out the door. She rolled through every red light she could, not heeding their warning. She didn't know what was going on with Sarah, but if something happened to her, what would happen to Katie D.? Sarah had no relatives. Would she go into foster care?

Lang vaguely recognized the froglike woman at the hospital's front desk. Her neck was swollen as wide as her jaw, and her eyes bulged.

"I need to find Katie D. Eldridge. She's here. In the hospital. I don't know where," Lang said. The woman peered at her computer, in no hurry. Lang resisted the urge to shake her.

"No patient by that name is here," the woman said.

"I'm sorry. Sarah. Sarah is the patient," Lang said.

"Last name?" the woman asked, taking a sip of a diet drink.

What the hell was Sarah's last name? Damn her. Lang couldn't think of it. It had vanished without a trace in the recesses of her brain.

"I'm here for her daughter. She's six. They brought her mother in, and she called me from here, and she's scared, and I need to find her," Lang said.

"Are you a relative?"

"Yes. No. Yes," Lang said.

The woman peered over her glasses at Lang and looked at her suspiciously. "You don't know her last name, but she's a relative?"

"Grandie?" Katie D. said in a small voice. Lang turned to see the child shivering on the blue vinyl chair in the corner of the waiting room, clutching her blue bunny.

"Sweetie, are you cold? Here," Lang said, wrapping the quilt around her.

"I'm very cold," Katie D. said. "And very scared. Where's Lele?"

"I don't know," Lang said. She wouldn't mind him being here herself, but she'd already blown it with him.

"Will you sing me the song about the girl with brown eyes? Like mine?" Katie D. asked.

She held Katie D. close and rocked her slowly. "I'll try," she finally whispered.

She sang softly about finding her way, and how Katie D had grown, well aware of both the truth and irony of her words.

She sang the lyrics to the song until Katie D. fell asleep, draping herself across Lang's lap. She stared at the large plastic clock until the doctor finally appeared and told her Sarah's appendix had ruptured, spewing infection all through her body. He told her matter-of-factly that Sarah's organs were shutting down, and he might have to put her into a coma.

The doctor looked down at his clipboard and told her that the next twelve hours were critical and advised her to see Sarah at the next visiting hour. Lang wondered if that might be the last time Katie D. would see her mother alive.

Lang sat still, not disturbing Katie D. She wanted the child to sleep peacefully while she could and delay the terrible truth.

The enormous clock on the wall moved in slow motion. The minutes felt like hours—days even.

Lang closed her eyes for a minute and felt the child's weight, warm and heavy against her belly. Katie D.'s breath was slow and deep. She gathered Katie D.'s fingers and held them carefully in her hand. Tiny perfect pink knuckles, not much bigger than a baby's.

She watched the people in the waiting room, little huddles of families. All ages of connected people staked out camps in various sections of the plastic chair-lined room, waiting on news about beloved family members. They looked worn and haggard. Worried and frail. They acknowledged her with occasional nods, looking at her through dark, sunken eyes. She looked back with the same.

"Sweetie, it's time. You can go see your mommy," Lang said softly when they announced visiting hours.

"Can we bring her home?" Katie D. asked.

"Not yet, but you can go see her. She's sick, but they are taking good care of her. Go with the nurse," Lang said, motioning to the nurse standing at the door.

"Are you coming? To check on her?" Katie D. asked.

"No, just one at a time. You go. She'll be happy to see you," Lang said.

Katie D. reached in her pocket and pulled out a sticky red

glob—the stolen candies from Valentine's. "I'll tell her you brung them for her."

Lang sat alone in the chair in the nearly deserted waiting room.

"Coffee?" an older woman asked her. "It's free. Down the hall."

"Oh, thank you. Yes, please," Lang said.

The woman returned with two small white Styrofoam cups of coffee and a handful of sugar packets.

"Is it your daughter in there?" she asked.

"My daughter? No, no. I don't have a daughter," Lang said. The woman looked at her expectantly. "I'm sorry. I'm going through a bad time here." She couldn't speak.

"Aren't we all, honey. Aren't we all," the woman said, squeezing Lang's shoulder before she returned to her seat.

Lang watched the double doors open automatically, then close again. Where was Katie D.? She looked at the people coming back to wait and could tell how their patient was doing by their faces. They were either more creased and dropped or brighter, like they had gone back through the automatic doors for a facial.

Katie D. finally danced through the double doors, skipping toward Lang.

"Is she better?" Lang asked.

"She's resting. I told her you sent the candies, and she loves them very much."

"She ate them?"

"I just know," Katie D. said, curling up on Lang's lap. "The nurse gave me this doll baby. She said I could play with it, but I have to leave it here and let somebody else play with it if their mommy gets sick. They only have the one."

Lang watched the newscasters mouth the weather and the news. She occasionally squinted to read the typed headlines running below, but nothing held her interest. Was Sarah going to die? Would the state take custody of Katie D. if she did? Would she even have a chance of getting custody?

"It was on accident!" Katie D. said, making her voice into a squeak and tossing the doll on the floor.

"You," Katie D. said in a deep voice. She raised the bunny above the baby doll, hovering it in a threatening way. "You drinked. And drived. And killed my mommy!"

"I'm so sorry. I'm just a little baby. A bad little baby. Please don't hurt me," Katie D. squeaked.

"You are very bad. A very bad baby," Katie D. growled.

"Sweetie, babies aren't bad," Lang said. "Her mommy will take care of her even if the baby does bad things."

"It's a boy. He knowed better," Katie D. said.

"He *knew* better," Lang said.

"Yes. He did," Katie D. said.

"Yes. He did," Lang whispered.

Lang put her arms around Katie D. and stroked the bunny's silky blue ears.

"His mommy has to forgive him," Lang said. "When her baby is bad." Lang tried to remember the quote by Gandhi, the one about forgiveness being an attribute of the strong, something the weak were unable to do.

"She can't."

"She can. She has to. She has to be strong. People have to forgive each other, Katie D.," Lang said softly. "Or they lose too much."

Katie D. rested her head against Lang's chest. Lang wondered if she'd fallen asleep again.

"Grandie? Will Mommy wake up in morning time?"

"I hope so, sweetie." Lang didn't know what would happen if she didn't.

FIFTY-EIGHT

....

L ang didn't want to spend the entire night in the brightly lit hospital waiting room. But she would have. It was only after Katie D. asked if they could go rest in Lang's bed that Lang loaded her up and headed home.

She tried to carry Katie D. into the house but couldn't even pick her up. The little girl seemed to weigh five hundred pounds. Lang scooted one arm under her knees and the other one behind the child's back and heaved her toward the car door again.

Panting from the exertion, Lang sat on the edge of the car seat and wondered if she could have carried her if she weighed only ten pounds. She felt herself getting weaker every day. Under the streetlight, she looked at the curve of Katie D.'s cheek, the full pucker of her perfect little mouth, and how her upper lip dipped in at the center just like Lang's did.

If Sarah died, she would *have* to do the trial. What choice did she have?

Lang woke Katie up, and slowly they trudged up to the house and fell into bed.

The rich smell of freshly brewed coffee roused Lang from a deep sleep, and it took her a minute to realize Lillian must be back. Lang groaned and rolled over.

The smell of bacon sizzling in the skillet lured her into the kitchen, and she tore off half a bacon slice. It was cooked perfectly—not too crisp and still a little chewy.

Making Arrangements

Lillian twisted oranges over the squeezer, moving her wrist back and forth.

God was a prankster. Jack, obnoxiously fit, dropped dead. Sarah, the dewy epitome of youth, was in a coma at death's door. Her mother, who couldn't be bothered when Lang was a child, now bustled domestically around her kitchen with three times the energy of Lang.

"Breakfast fit for a queen. I wanted to serve it to you in bed. Are you hungry?" Lillian asked.

"I don't like breakfast in bed. But thanks. How was your trip?" Lang asked, taking the other half of bacon.

"Fine as far as trips go. He needs a nurse. Not a wife."

"Are they not one and the same?" Lang asked.

"Not for you, they're not. You don't have to settle like that. I like that Leland, and it looks like he can take care of you, but you have a business. Your own business that is consistently booming. I don't know why you don't turn that little carriage house into a shop. It's right on the road back there and is charming as can be. Perfect location for street traffic."

"Thanks for the vote of confidence, but I'm trying to get into a cancer trial just now. And I can't unless I move to a nursing home or hire a caregiver, which means selling this whole thing. So there won't be any carriage house," Lang said. "They'll bulldoze it down first."

"Sarah."

"What?"

"Ask Sarah to help. She needs a place to live. You need someone to live with you. I would do it if you want, but I don't think you want me to. Not that I blame you."

Lang snorted and looked away.

Katie D. padded in. Lang's white nightgown trailed behind her like the train of a wedding dress. Or a christening gown.

"I'm taking my blue bunny to the hospital for the children

317

to have there," Katie D. said. "I'm leaving him for them."

"Leaving him there for good?" Lang asked.

"Yes. I have to. They don't have anything. He'll be loved," Katie D. said. Her eyes welled up with tears as she stroked his dangling ears.

"Wait. I have something," Lang said. The only thing she could see clearly right now was the fact that she was not about to let Katie D. lose that blue bunny. Not with everything else the child stood to lose. Lang opened the chest full of dolls. "Do you think these would be good?"

"They would be! And Blue Bunny could stay with me?"

"Yes, drink your juice, and we'll head back to check on your mother," Lang said as the phone rang.

Lang walked as fast as she could to the phone, but the answering machine picked up before she reached it.

"Mrs. Eldridge, we need to get in touch with you! We're saving a spot in the cancer trial for you, but we need to know if you're committed. We've left you several messages already. It's not fair to hold a place for you if you aren't going to participate," the nurse said tersely.

"Is she mad at you, Grandie?" Katie D. asked.

"Maybe."

"How come?"

"I need to let them know I'm not going to be in the trial."

"You're not? I thought you wanted it."

"I know I did, but I changed my mind. I think," Lang said.

"Why come?"

"Well, I'm not sure I can be in it. The medicine they want me to take will make me so, so sick. Too sick to take care of myself. And anyway, we don't need to worry about that now. Let's go check on your mommy."

"She'll be in that trial," Lillian told Katie D. "She loves you too much not to."

They got to the hospital in time for the 8:00 a.m. visitation, but Sarah's bed was empty. The sheets were pulled off already and lay in a heap on the floor.

The hospital should have called her. She had gone to the trouble to leave her number with three different people last night and explained they were leaving for the night. How could they let this child walk in and find her mother gone? Dead?

"Where's Mommy?" Katie D. asked.

Lang dropped to her knees and held Katie D.'s face in her hands. "Oh, sweetie. Oh, Katie D. Your mommy loved you more than anything in the whole wide world."

"Where is she?"

"She's in a good place. A better place," Lang said carefully.

"She's in room three twenty-two," a crisp voice said behind her. "We moved her last night."

"It's better there?" Katie D. asked. "Room three twenty-two is good?"

"Let's go see," Lang said in a stunned voice.

Sarah was sitting up in bed poking around at her tray of liquids.

"Oh, come here! Bless your heart! They told me Grandie came to get you." *Thank you*, Sarah mouthed silently.

Hate you, Lang mouthed back.

"Can Mommy have the quilt?" Katie D. asked. She pulled it out of Lang's arms and tried unsuccessfully to cover Sarah with it.

"Excuse me," Lang said, and then went in the bathroom. She ran the water and tried to breathe deeply. The toilet roared like an engine when she flushed it, and she had to compose herself all over again.

"Mommy, is that your own bathroom?" Katie D. asked when Lang came out.

319

"Yes, isn't that nice?"

"Can I use it?" Katie D. closed the door, then opened it to make sure it didn't lock. Then she closed it with finality.

Sarah and Lang looked around the little hospital room awkwardly, both anxious for Katie D. to be done in the bathroom.

"Thank you for coming. For getting Katie D., I mean. I know that's not, well, not what you would want to do."

"It's okay. It's fine. And you're doing okay, I guess?" Lang said quickly.

"Yes, thanks. They did a good job. Lucky really. I shouldn't have waited so long to get to the hospital, but I'll know next time," Sarah said, laughing weakly. "Not that it can happen twice."

"How long are they keeping you?"

"Till tomorrow or the day after. Then Katie D. and I are headed out to Oregon. With Teddy."

"With Teddy?"

"Well, he doesn't know. But I think it's the best thing. We'll figure it out. I hope we will. Besides me, he's her only family." Sarah's face flushed a mottled crimson, and she turned away from Lang.

Lang walked over to the window and looked down at the parking lot. An ambulance flashed its red light, but there was no sound of the siren. She watched the doctors in white coats rush around somebody on a stretcher and wondered what had happened. It could have been anything. Something routine. Something ridiculous. She heard the industrial whoosh as Katie D. flushed the toilet.

"He's not her only family," Lang finally said.

"What?"

"I can't lose her," Lang said quietly. "I can't bear it. So." She rubbed her fingers on the blue bunny's ears. They felt soft, worn, and easy on her fingertips. She was thankful for that.

"You will never lose her," Sarah said.

"I don't know how much time I have, but I know I want to spend it with her," Lang said.

"Oh, don't say that. Not about Katie D., but about how much time you have left. She told me you were accepted into the trial, so I think that's great news. I just have a good feeling about it, for what it's worth."

Lang pulled her face into a tight smile. "I'm not doing it."

"What? Why not? What happened? I thought you were in!"

"I am. But I don't meet all the requirements anymore." Lang looked at the pressed board cabinets by the hospital bed. She couldn't say his name, couldn't tell her Jack should be here while they poisoned her again. She didn't want him in her brain, poisoning it.

"What do you mean? Does not meeting the requirements mean the cancer's in remission? So that's good, right?"

"It means I don't have anyone to take care of me. I don't have any support. That's what it means," Lang snapped. Sarah's skin was smooth and full, even after near death. It wasn't fair.

"I'm sorry," Sarah said, looking miserably at her. She looked like someone had rubbed their dirty thumbs under her eyes, leaving dark smudges.

"No, it's okay. I could sell the house and go to a nursing home and probably be in the trial. But I just can't. I know it's crazy, but I can't do it. Probably if I'd done it a year ago, he never would have had a heart attack. The stress of money probably caused it in the first place. And Teddy would have been busy chopping the land up into tiny squares and not had time to delve into whatever in god's name made him start all this in the first place. And I would still be Katie D.'s grandmother. And not know anything different," Lang said.

"No. You can blame anyone but yourself. Don't ever do

that," Sarah said. "And you will always be her grandmother. As much as you want to be. I've wondered how to tell her anyway. She'd be devastated not to have you. She loves you!"

There were two sharp knocks on the door, and it swung open immediately despite neither of them signaling an okay. A nurse wheeled a tray of machinery and needles in front of her and told Lang she needed Sarah for a few minutes.

Lang knocked on the bathroom door, wiping at her eyes.

"Did you fall in?"

Katie D. stepped out with plastic gloves on her hands.

"They have these in there," she said.

The nurse announced Sarah needed to rest and that it was time for them to leave.

"We need to rest up for our trip, Katie D," Sarah said.

"Our trip?" Katie D. asked.

"Yes, our trip, remember? We're going on a big adventure, across the whole country. To Oregon."

"I don't want to go away, Mommy. I'll be real good," Katie. D. said.

"You are real good, sweetie. You are the best thing," Sarah said.

Lang watched Sarah kiss the top of Katie D.'s head and envelop her in her thin arms. She needed some meat on her bones.

FIFTY-NINE

....

Lang finally ate the perfect soft-boiled egg she'd made for her mother before it congealed. She'd been waiting all morning for Lillian to wake up. Really, as far as the trial was concerned, all she needed was someone to drive her home from the treatments when it got right down to it. Lang could prepare meals beforehand so she wouldn't have to ask Lillian to cook. It's not like Jack had been that helpful when she was throwing up. And there was nothing her mother liked better than inching around in her town car, driving jerkily all over town.

In a way, Lang was relieved her mother would be here for a while. She could finally delve in and find the answers she'd waited her whole life to know.

She spooned blackberry preserves into a tiny cut-glass bowl, angling a demitasse spoon beside it. At eleven she boiled another egg, cut the crusts off two pieces of salt-rising toast, put a pale lavender spider chrysanthemum in the silver bud vase, then called softly outside her mother's bedroom door.

"Are you awake in there?"

She turned the clear glass doorknob silently and slowly pushed the door open. Lillian lay face up in the bed, perfectly still against the pillow. Her head was tipped back, and her mouth was agape. Lang let go of the breakfast tray and never noticed the sound of china exploding on the wooden floor. Suddenly she heard a deep strangled gasp from her mother's chest, but it wasn't followed by another.

Lang pulled her mother down to the floor, called 911, and

began pumping Lillian's chest rhythmically. Her mother spoke, Lang was sure of it. Her words were raspy, almost incoherent, but Lang thought she heard her mother tell her she loved her.

"Mama?" Lang looked at her mother, placing the palms of her hands on her mother's cheeks and turning her face toward her. "Mama, what is it? What, Mama? I'm sorry!"

Lang began the chest compressions again, watching her mother's face for a sign of consciousness or a struggle for words. For anything.

Lang hovered her cheek just over her mother's mouth, listening for the sound of breath, then she pumped her arms on her mother's sternum, keeping time, keeping the rhythm of her heart. Lang watched the yellow egg yolk slowly ooze onto the braided wool rug as she checked for the hint of a breath, straining to feel a puff of air against her cheek. Then she straightened her elbows and tried to ignore the catch in her belly as she pushed and pushed on her mother's heart, forcing it to beat.

The chrysanthemum blossom lay still on the floor like a pale, spiky sea creature, plucked out of the water.

The EMTs loaded Lillian on a stretcher and immediately took over the CPR, placing an oxygen mask over her mother's face and starting an IV line in her arm. Surely they wouldn't do that if she were going to die.

"Is she okay? She was trying to tell me something," Lang said desperately. "I think there was something she needed to say."

One of the EMTs looked at her, his elbows locked as he rapidly compressed her mother's chest.

"You did good. You did everything right," he said finally, as they hoisted her gurney into the ambulance and closed the doors. Lang watched the red penetrating light on the ambu-

lance throb as it drove down the hill until the sound of the
siren was gone.

There were only six people at her mother's funeral—A. J.,
Leland, Katie D., and herself, and Martin Vandergriff, who
came in a wheelchair pushed by a nurse.

The priest had never met Lillian, so he stuck to the burial
rites, reading straight from the prayer book. The entire service
took less than fifteen minutes.

Her mother would have been mortified by the pitiful service. No important pallbearers, no tributes, no church packed
to the gills with sniffling mourners dressed in black. Her
mother's funeral was another one of Lang's failures.

She shouldn't have had the funeral here in Barrington. She
should have buried her mother in Paris. Or Greece. Or any of
the places she loved more than her daughter.

SIXTY

······················

The sun hung low at the bottom of the sky by the time she and Katie D. got to her house. The light was weak, but pure, illuminating every autumn leaf so that they shone like jewels. Amber, topaz, ruby.

Lang took Katie D. outside and told her to pick the prettiest things she saw in the garden.

"We're going to make an arrangement."

"For Mommy?" Katie D. asked. Lang ran her hands over the child's hair, noticing the sunlight glistening off it.

"Are you sad about Lily?" Katie D. asked, leading Lang to the split magnolia tree.

"I am," Lang said, thinking of her mother and that whatever could have been could be no longer. "I'm so sad." She peered up at the old initials, their edges darkened and burled. *L. M. + A. D.* She imagined her parents in the garden, young and in love, and quickly turned away from the magnolia.

The afternoon sun warmed her face, and she tipped it up, not used to sunlight in this spot of the garden. The fallen magnolia branches had left a gap, an opening in the thicket of greenery that had made her garden so private. She could see clear over the brow now, the view of the blue-gray mountains framed perfectly by the magnolia leaves.

Lang showed Katie D. how to cut the branches at an angle, just above the next set of leaves. Some of them were just buds, embryonic nubs of green. Katie D. busily filled her shallow basket with deep purple hydrangea and scarlet maple leaves, cutting the stems into sharp tips.

Making Arrangements

"What are you doing, Grandie? Why aren't you clipping?" Katie D. asked.

"Oh. I'm just wondering," Lang said, looking over the garden at the carriage house. "What do you think about making that into a little shop that sells cakes and flower arrangements?"

"I've always wanted a cake shop," Katie D. said.

"Me, too," Lang said, picturing Elizabeth's Lilies and Bou-Cakes painted above the wall of casement windows facing the road.

"No! Bad girl!" Katie D. said to Victoria who peed near a stand of forsythia. The long strands were swollen and alert.

Suddenly it occurred to Lang they might be able to force some of the forsythia to bloom. It was too early in the season but worth a try. She explained the basics of photosynthesis to Katie D., wondering if she had it exactly right herself, as she clipped an armful of branches and put them in a bucket of warm water.

Lang showed Katie D. how to anchor the arrangement by putting in the longest stems first, then fill it out by cutting a few shorter stems. She asked Katie D. if she liked the colors all mixed together or in separate clumps, then showed her how to make it work.

When it was done, Lang let Katie D. chose a grosgrain ribbon to tie around the vase. Lang cut the ends of a chocolate-brown gingham ribbon.

"Mommy is so sorry," Katie D. said.

"What?" Lang asked, shocked. Surely the child didn't know!

"She's so sorry we have to move. She told me no matter what that you loved me. Always," Katie D. said.

"Oh, sweetie."

"I know, Grandie. I told her she was a big silly. I just want one more red flower. It needs a red."

Lang studied the arrangement and saw immediately Katie D. was right. It needed a flash of red to finish it out.

"You have the eyes of an artist. Now let's pick the perfect red," Lang said.

Lang set Katie D.'s bouquet down on Sarah's hospital table and put the forsythia branches in the bathroom. Torn cotton balls seemed to have exploded over her bed.

"I'm so sorry about your mother," Sarah said. Lang pulled her mouth in a wide, tight line and studied the flowers.

"This is from Katie D.," Lang said, turning the best side of the arrangement toward Sarah. "She arranged them herself." The wad of material under Sarah's arm was Fancy's quilt—or what remained of it. Lang turned her attention to the arrangement and moved a piece of greenery.

"I'm so sorry about the quilt!" Sarah said. "The nurse pulled it off during the night, and it ripped. I should have told her to be careful with it. I'll fix it for you as soon as I'm out of here."

Lang wanted to gather it up and spread it out so she could ascertain the damage. So little of the original fabric remained it could hardly be called "Fancy's quilt" anymore.

Lang picked up a flower print square and rubbed her thumb over a greasy spot.

"That reminds me of your scarf. I was taking it to be cleaned when the tornado came. I used it for a bandage for a little boy, and now it's gone," Lang said. "I know it was special, that it was a gift from your father."

"It's okay," Sarah said. "I never really wore it. I'm glad some good came out of it."

They both looked out the window. Morning light streamed in the room, illuminating the tufts of cotton.

"It's broke!" Katie said, pointing at the torn pieces of fabric. "That's bad, Mommy."

"It was too old. It was time for it to be replaced. I want something new and fresh," Lang said.

"But Fancy made it herself!" Sarah said.

"Katie made this arrangement herself," Lang said. "Cut the stems and picked the colors."

"Grandie's looks like switches, but it will be pretty in a little while. Grandie says so," Katie D. said doubtfully.

"It's forsythia. Yellow blooms, if it works," Lang said, realizing she had indeed arranged a big bucket of switches.

"Oh! I've heard about that. Forcing it or something," Sarah said.

"Wh-w-w-w-would," Lang stuttered, then stopped speaking. The question she wanted to ask Sarah was too important and she couldn't make the words go past the back of her tongue. She excused herself to collect herself in the restroom.

"Wear some gloves when you wipe," Katie D. called out. "They help with germs."

Lang looked at herself in the little square mirror. How had she gotten so old? She squeezed her hands together as she scrubbed them over the sink and asked herself what she had to lose. She smiled broadly in the mirror and breathed evenly, trying to imagine smooth, even words. She squinted at her reflection, glad she couldn't make out the lines around her mouth.

"I'm next," Katie D. said as she closed the bathroom door. *Alligator food*, she mouthed at Lang. "I love you, Katherine Deakins," Lang said.

She flexed her hands, spreading her fingers wide, then pulled them into tight fists. She felt the tips of her fingernails cutting into her palm.

"Sarah, would you be my caretaker for the trial," Lang asked plainly, releasing the words in a whoosh. "You and Katie D. could live in the house with me, and I could qualify for the trial."

Sarah scrunched up her face and stared at Lang. Rows of thin creases lined her forehead.

"I-i-i-it would be hard on you, I know. I completely understand if you don't want to commit."

"No! Yes! What I mean is yes. If you're sure. We would. Yes!" Sarah said.

"I'll pay you, of course," Lang said. "Maybe not until down the road, though."

"No," Sarah said. She reached her hand out to Lang. Lang clasped Sarah's cool, thin hand in hers, careful of the IV taped around her wrist. "Thank you."

Three days later, Sarah was wheeled out of the hospital, hidden by the flower arrangement on her lap. The leaves had faded to a dull brown, but vivid yellow blossoms burst like rays of sunshine out of Sarah's hands.

SIXTY-ONE

....

After she had her blood drawn for the last time and signed the paperwork admitting her to the trial, Lang called her lawyer.

The next day Lang waited in the reception area that could pass for a medieval barrister's chamber. Dark, carved walnut bookcases, tiger oak tables, and heavy Queen Anne chairs lined the walls of the perfectly proportioned room. Except for a subdued buzzing of the telephones, hushed whispers were the only sounds.

When the receptionist murmured he was ready for her, Lang had to clear her throat to answer in a regular tone of voice.

Terrified she would stutter, she bared her teeth in a wide grin and exchanged pleasantries with her lawyer once she was inside his office. He told her not to worry, that he would take care of everything before she even told him what she wanted. She assumed immediately he'd heard about the whole sordid thing by the way he vacillated between patting at her forearm and shaking his head sympathetically. Or maybe he was just sorry about Jack's death, and she was being paranoid.

He sat down at his desk and rapidly seesawed his pencil between his fingers, tapping the eraser and soft lead tip on a pale yellow legal pad. He squinted at her, and she couldn't tell if he was thoughtful or amused.

Lang thought about Katie D. She closed her eyes and placed her index fingers on her temples and tried to breathe. The pain she felt made her nauseous.

"Are you all right?" he asked.

"Yes. No. I'm fine," Lang said. "I need to change my will."

"I understand. Yes, of course, and it's probably wise to go ahead and take care of that immediately. You never know what—" He stopped talking and looked at Lang, obviously realizing she was familiar with the unexpected by this point. "I'm so sorry."

"The will is only read after my death?" she asked.

"Correct. It will be probated after your death," he said, flipping through the pages in her file until he reached the one he wanted.

He looked across the table at her.

"Just initial here and here, where it's highlighted. We'll remove Katherine Deakins Eldridge from the beneficiaries," he said.

At least she wasn't being paranoid—he clearly knew every dirty detail.

"Remove her?" Lang asked. "That's not what I'm changing. I'm taking the land out of the trust altogether. I'm not leaving the house or the land to Teddy."

"So sorry," he said, flipping through more pages. "I just assumed."

"He'll ruin it. He'll go through it and end up with nothing," she said.

"All right. The new beneficiary of the house at 525 Summertown Road is going to be . . .," he said slowly, looking up at her.

"Sarah Anne Wingfield," Lang said plainly.

"What relationship is she to you?" he asked.

"She's the mother of my granddaughter," Lang said. "Katie D.'s mother."

"Lang, she's no relation to you. Are you sure you don't want to leave the house to Teddy? Just keep the stipulations?" he asked.

"Yes. My life insurance goes to Teddy. And Sarah will do right by him."

He looked up from the document and stared at Lang. "Am I to assume the stipulations remain the same for Sarah? The property is not to be divided and the exterior of the house can't be changed in any way."

Lang stared back at him, unsmiling, and said plainly, "No. No stipulations at all. She can divide it up into high-rise condominiums if that's what she wants. Or lease the land as a trailer park. It will belong to her. Free and clear. In every sense."

SIXTY-TWO

....

Lang squinted at the compost heap, wondering what she'd done with her glasses until she pressed her hands to her chest and felt them around her neck. Leland had made her a macramé glasses holder out of some kind of silky yarn, and she rubbed it between her thumb and index finger. It was soft, cool to the touch, and easy on her skin.

She stopped at the magnolia tree at the edge of the garden and traced the new set of initials with her finger. L. L. + L. L. Lang LePeyre + Leland LePeyre. He said he would make the second L into an E if she said no and refused his marriage proposal. But she told him it wasn't necessary just yet and to leave the L for now.

Something green was growing profusely over the top of the pile, but she knew she hadn't planted anything in the compost heap. She wondered if Leland had thrown out the bunch of spinach that was beginning to liquefy in the refrigerator. She walked toward the compost and saw the thick, glossy leaves of the Lenten rose spilling over the sides. She hadn't noticed them all summer, all fall even, when the plant was camouflaged in the woods by all shapes and textures and hues of green. Now, at the end of November, with the foliage gone on trees and shrubs and underbrush, the Lenten rose looked like life itself. It sprang verdant and bright green among dry, lifeless leaves, all the color of dirt.

The plant had spread during the year and grown more substantial.

She remembered the sliced roots, pale and vulnerable. Leaking. Forgotten when her husband died. Jerked up out of its place and left for dead.

A flash of red swooped toward the feeder, then flew off abruptly. Lang instinctively looked for the female cardinal but couldn't find her anywhere. Her gaze lit on two mourning doves sitting placidly by the birdbath, almost like they were sunbathing. Both of them bottom heavy and drab, they adjusted themselves every so often, ruffling their feathers and looking at each other expectantly. One of them flicked its tail, and she noticed the elegant fan of feathers. Each one had a perfect white tip with a detailed black swirl separating the white and gray. Their feathers looked like they would be soft like down. Comforting.

She'd never thought of doves as beautiful. Doves were drab-feathered, lackluster, and as boring as they were bottom heavy.

But she watched them now, sitting side by side, attentively preening each other and moving closer as they puffed out their chests into pillows, then back to a smooth, sleek softness. This pair of birds was so much alike, not like the brilliant male cardinal and his frumpy wife. *Both* of these birds were frumpy.

She should move the Lenten rose to a better spot—at the top of the steps or in front of the bench Leland had repaired. She shouldn't let the plant be wasted here in the compost pile. But she wasn't about to bother it. The plant she'd left for dead a year ago was not just alive, but ridiculously so. It was thriving in the pile of refuse and getting ready to bloom.

Her cancer trial began the Monday after Thanksgiving, and she hoped to have the same luck as the Lenten rose.

There was one letter left, but she didn't want to open it. Not because that was all she had left of him, but because she didn't want to go backward. Not now.

She slowly opened the letter.

Dear Jack,

The hardest part of all this is not knowing when exactly I am going to die.

You know me. I want it to run like clockwork. I'd go ahead and order the flowers now if I could. That's right. Order. I always thought I'd have flowers from my yard at my funeral, but who would arrange them? My shrubs would be mutilated by churchwomen hacking at boughs of hydrangea or forsythia or bittersweet.

Oh, I hope it was in the spring! It's hard to be that sorrowful about anything when dormant branches are suddenly bursting with new green, and tight buds are itching to unfurl. Such hope!

I'm sorry I left you. I'm so sorry we didn't get to sit on the porch in the rocking chairs, our walkers by our sides, and grow old together. I'm sorry not to be there with you when you teach Katie D. to waltz before her first dance. Or expose her to Ayn Rand. Or comfort her when her heart is broken.

I can't bear to think about that child's heart being broken. Any more than I can stand to think of yours being heavy.

Promise me you'll heal. That you'll go on from here.

I love you,

Lang

She folded it up, creasing the seams with her fingers until the paper was a small perfect square. She held it in her hand, pressing the four sides. The irony of the letter was not lost on her. If she were near Jack with a walker, she'd whack him with it. Hard.

Lang set the dining room table with china from three lifetimes, Fancy's, Lillian's, and her own. She'd gone through all of it, keeping what she could use and discarding the rest. Fancy's Columbia pattern mixed with the durable, plain pattern she'd chosen for herself over forty years ago. There was a smattering of rich, deep eggplant on all three patterns, making the different designs look intentionally combined.

Teddy's postcard was on the refrigerator: *Happy Thanksgiving, Katie D. I'm sorry I can't be there with you. The snow here is deep and fluffy. Powder. Perfect for skiing. Take care of Grandie.*

Lang was glad he didn't say he wished Katie D. were with him out there. She hoped Katie D. didn't wonder if he did.

"Oh! I brung brought purple turkeys, and they match these plates," Katie D. said as she carefully set pinecone turkey place cards for A. J., Leland, and Sarah. "You're by me," she told Lang. Katie turned two turkeys toward each other and made them kiss before setting them in the center of the plates.

"I'm glad. I wouldn't want to be anywhere else," Lang said.

In the kitchen, Lang stirred the pale yellow custard until her hand ached, then handed the spoon to Katie D.

"Don't stop stirring!" Lang said as she rinsed some of the dirty dishes and checked on the sweet potatoes Sarah was peeling.

Katie D. grimaced as she concentrated on scraping the sides of the pot, keeping the mixture moving as instructed. A slow current of boiled custard.

"Here," Lang said, cupping her hand over Katie D.'s and pulling up the spoon. "Let's turn this down a little. You don't want it too hot."

"Burled custard," Katie D. said.

"*Boiled* custard. My grandmother showed me how to make this when I was just a little older than you. And her mother showed her. And her mother before that," Lang said, wondering if it was bad luck to pass on anything from her mess of a family. She remembered Fancy throwing out the batch of custard that had curdled when Lang added the eggs too soon.

Katie D. stopped stirring, and Lang took the spoon. "You

have to keep it moving. Don't stop, or it will burn," Lang said, stirring up flecks of black from the bottom of the pot.

"I ruined it?" Katie D. asked. "I'm sorry. You can forgive me?"

"Well, I can. I sure can forgive you," Lang said. "But it's not all your fault. I had the heat too hot."

Lang ran her finger over the back of the wooden spoon and tasted the custard. She spit the burned liquid out in the sink.

"Oh no! What are we going to do! It's for Thanksgiving!" Katie D. wailed.

"One little mistake can make a big mess if you let it," Lang said. "The trick is not to let it."

"But it's our burled!" Katie D. said.

"Okay, let's think here for a minute," Lang said. "We need something sweet for dessert. And at this point, easy."

"Well, this is not in the same league as boiled custard, but it's sweet. And easy," Sarah said. "S'mores?" She held up a bag of marshmallows and a Hershey's bar.

"That's not special, Mommy," Katie D. said. "It's not a family recipe!"

"Well, it can be," Lang said. "It can be our family recipe. From now on. Show me, Katie D. Show me how to make them in the microwave."

Katie D. hid her face against Lang's chest, and Lang looked at Sarah as she breathed in the smell of her granddaughter's hair.

"Oh, Grandie, you have pearls!" Katie D. said as she reached for them. Lang felt the child's warm, fragrant fingertips pull against the loose skin on her throat.

"They were my mother's. One day they'll be yours, one way or another," Lang said, thinking of the little stone carriage house. Her mother had left her enough money to keep the property and renovate the little stone structure. "Do you like necklaces better or cake shops?"

"Cake shops! Are they real? They don't look like A. J.'s," she said. "They're dark and shiny, but they have rainbow colors."

"I think they're real. But I've never checked. Do you want to see? Test them with your teeth?" Lang asked, reaching for the clasp. "Remember, A. J. showed you?"

"No. I don't need to. I believe they're real," Katie D. said, resting her fingers on Lang's cheek. Lang closed her eyes and inhaled vanilla and pencil shavings from her hands.

"Everything you can imagine is real," Sarah said softly. "Someone famous said that. I believe it's true."

Lang reached out to Katie D.'s mother and pulled her toward them. "It makes sense to me," Lang said. Lang felt the warmth from the two of them as they leaned into her, and felt Sarah rest her head on her shoulder for a second.

"I don't never believe I've seen such a sight as y'all!" A. J. said as she walked into the kitchen. "Sorry I'm late, but Leland's later."

Lang felt the tightening in the bridge of her nose and blinked back tears as she smiled at A. J. "Alligator food," Lang mouthed silently to A.J.

"I love you, too, Lang," A.J. said, her eyes glistening.

"Lang! Katie D.! Sarah! What smells so good?" Leland called from the foyer. "Oh! You all are truly a sight for sore eyes. Wait! I'm going to take a picture of you. Hold on, I want it to be perfect. Look here at me! Lang, stop looking at Katie D. and look at me. Wait. Hold on. Wait one more second—"

"No, I'm not waiting. On anything. I'm not. I'm not waiting anymore," Lang said, and squeezed her family to her. "Take me now! Take me!" she exclaimed, beaming as the shutter snapped.

~THE END~

Acknowledgments

Of all the people I want to thank for making this book a reality, I will start with Alice Smith, who said, "Of all the things you've written, I like *Making Arrangements* the best." So I took it out of the drawer where it had been for three years, rewrote much of it, and put it out there.

Meg Aiken encouraged my endeavor every week, urging me on and inspiring me by her example to "Do the work!"

So many folks spread the word, especially Katie Stout, Vivienne Nichols, Janie Dempsey Watts, Clare Gruber, Sherry Peardon, Mems Bicking, Chris Simon, Melanie Young, Carolyn Cary, Nini Davenport, Priscilla McLaughlin, Valorie King Bowen, Lynda Minks Hood, Laura Cameron Craddock, Sue Duffy, Janie Kelley, and Betsy Hardegree Smith, among so many others. Lots of friends sent e-mails, blabbed on my behalf incessantly, and shared my posts on social media, but the aforementioned were almost as persistent (though not as obnoxious) as I was.

My brood—Alex Nation, Robby and Julianna Robinson, and Mikey Robinson—went to bat on their cell phones, texting the Kindle Scout link to my book like crazy, as did a slew of my wonderful nieces and nephews.

My father, the late Paul Kelly, would have lent his aid any way he could have, as always. And my mother, Mary Ferris Kelly, painted the "Woman in the Garden" on the cover of the book, as well as encouraged me to write from the time I could hold a pencil. My brother, Buzz Kelly, and sister, Woo Kelley, are the most supportive siblings anyone could ask for. Ever.

And my husband, Dan Robinson, listened to me drone on about this novel for five years, suggested changes when asked, and cheered me on incessantly.

Thank you!

Thank you for reading *Making Arrangements*. If you would take the time to write an honest review on Amazon, it would be most appreciated! I'd love to connect with you on Facebook, where there are a few videos of the characters in *Making Arrangements*. My twitter handle is @fkrobinson. I am ferrisrobinson on Instagram, and my website is www.ferrisrobinson.com.

Lang would love to share her recipe for her fabulous caramel cake! Find it at ferrisrobinson.com.

Made in the USA
Middletown, DE
27 April 2017